## Also by Janice Maynard

*The Runaway Bride of Blossom Branch*
*One Sweet Southern Summer*

For additional books by Janice Maynard,
visit her website, janicemaynard.com.

JANICE MAYNARD

# THE
# Southern
# Charmer

CANARY STREET PRESS

CANARY
STREET
PRESS™

Recycling programs
for this product may
not exist in your area.

ISBN-13: 978-1-335-52310-5

The Southern Charmer

Never Let Me Go

This is a work of fiction. Names, characters, places and incidents are either
the product of the author's imagination or are used fictitiously. Any resemblance
to actual persons, living or dead, businesses, companies, events or locales is
entirely coincidental.

For questions and comments about the quality of this book, please contact us
at CustomerService@Harlequin.com.

TM is a trademark of Harlequin Enterprises ULC.

Canary Street Press
22 Adelaide St. West, 41st Floor
Toronto, Ontario M5H 4E3, Canada
CanaryStPress.com

Printed in U.S.A.

# CONTENTS

To Charles—

This is a big year for us.
Thanks for always being my cheerleader—for the writing
and in life. All the books are true because of you. Love always…

# THE SOUTHERN CHARMER

# Chapter 1

Gabby Nolan seldom left her office for an official lunch break, but with the holidays in view—even at a distance—she couldn't resist the pull of the local coffee shop just minutes away from her desk. The aroma of cinnamon, nutmeg, and gingerbread—plus beautiful decorations overhead and in the windows—made the small family-owned business a popular destination, even with its large corporate rival only two blocks away.

She loved this time of year. Despite the lack of snow, a December Monday in Atlanta was festive. With daytime temps in the low fifties and nights that seldom hit freezing, many people had already gone all out with colorful exterior lighting, attractive garland-wrapped columns, and everything else that went along with decking the halls.

The city was ablaze with symbols of love, peace, and joy.

Unfortunately, all of life's problems still existed, even if momentarily obscured by warm, fuzzy feelings.

She ordered her usual black coffee with a shot of cream, waited for her steaming cup, and grabbed her favorite table in the back corner. The fat book in her leather tote was a new treat, compliments of the library. She'd been on the waiting list for it at least six weeks and was looking forward to cracking it open.

Her cozy spot was a comfortable distance from the drafty front door, and with her back to the wall, she had security. Like the hero in a cowboy movie.

Nothing could surprise her.

Until someone did.

"Gabby?"

The low voice was instantly familiar. The blood froze in her veins. Her entire body tensed. When she looked up from her book, her stomach pitched and tightened painfully.

"Jason?"

He nodded, his smile guarded as he ran one hand through his wind-rumpled blond hair. "May I join you?"

He looked older, less upbeat perhaps. There was absolutely no acceptable response to that query except a muttered, "Yes, of course."

Jason Brightman removed his leather jacket, hung it on the back of his chair, laid his phone on the table, and took a sip of what appeared to be a caramel-laced hot herbal tea. "Thanks," he said. "I'm glad to see you, Gabriella. It's been a long time."

They both knew *how* long. Eighteen months. Tomorrow would be exactly a year and a half since that infamous June 7. The day Jason had stood at the altar and changed his mind about marrying Gabby's best friend, Cate Penland.

For the first time in their acquaintance, Gabby challenged him. "Why do you call me that?" she asked, the words barely concealing her confusion and impatience.

He lifted his chin, his blue-eyed gaze sharp. "It's your name, isn't it?"

She huffed, her finger tapping the page of the book. "On paper, yes. But you know very well everyone calls me Gabby."

"That's just it." He sipped his drink, apparently finding it cool enough to swallow. "You're the least gabby person I've ever met. You're quiet and intense and watchful. Much more a Gabriella than a Gabby."

"I prefer Gabby," she said firmly, ignoring the way her heart skipped when she heard him say the longer version of her name.

He smiled at her. "I'll try. But don't shoot me if I slip up sometimes."

This line of conversation was not going to end well. It was far too personal, for one thing. She didn't want Jason peering into her soul. He had a gift for noticing details and seeing beauty in the unremarkable. That skill served him well in his photography. But she couldn't have it focused on her. She wouldn't.

After taking a slow breath, she exhaled. "How are things with you?" she asked. "Did you pick up the tea habit in London?" She knew he'd been there recently. Leah had mentioned it. Leah, who was her and Cate's other best friend.

"No." His expression turned moody as he drained half his cup. "After everything that happened last year, I developed a bad case of insomnia. The doctor took me off caffeine entirely. It's been a bitch, to tell you the truth. But at least I'm sleeping at night."

"Things are settled now, aren't they? Couldn't you ease back into the coffee habit? It's the only thing that gets me through the day."

"Settled? Why would you say that?"

She sputtered. "Well, you've gotten the life you wanted."

He stared at her. Her comment had come out sharp and accusatory. Even she heard the note of heat. And regretted it. But she couldn't take the words back, though a nicer person might want to unsay them.

Jason rubbed his forehead with the heel of his hand. In his posture she saw exhaustion and grief. *She* had resurrected those emotions. Regret tightened her throat.

Despite his turbulent mood, he was as handsome as ever.

Tall, lanky, powerful. His sleekly muscled body had the build of either a baseball player or a football quarterback. In truth, he played both sports and played them well, in high school *and* in college. Jason had always been the consummate "great" guy. Men loved hanging out with him. Women flocked to him. Though to be fair, Jason hadn't dated indiscriminately at the University of Georgia. That was where Gabby had first come to know him.

Though they both hailed from the small town of Blossom Branch, Georgia, their worlds never collided as kids. Jason's family had been wealthy and privileged. Gabby's had been... well...neither of those.

His pain made her feel petty and small. "I'm sorry," she said stiffly. "I didn't mean to sound so judgmental."

He stared at her. "You're angry with me."

She grimaced. "I shouldn't be. Cate is deliriously happy with Harry. And they're married."

"But I hurt her badly." His gaze was opaque now, his feelings hidden.

"Yes, you did," Gabby said. "You waited far too long to call off the wedding. It was a terrible day."

His expression was bleak. "You think I don't know that? I'll have to live with those memories the rest of my life. I suppose I owe *you* an apology?"

She shifted restlessly in her chair, glancing at her watch. "Of course not. You didn't do anything to me."

"I'm sorry anyway. You love Cate."

His attempt at understanding her feelings only made her feel worse about her personal guilt. After quickly stuffing the unread library book in her tote and slipping her arms into a lightweight hip-length jacket, she jumped to her feet. "I have to get back to work," she said. Then—swallowing inwardly to prep the lie—she managed to look at him with a cool glance. "It was nice to see you."

He stood as well. "Liar."

The word held no heat, but her face got hot. "That's mean and rude."

"You didn't even finish your coffee."

She glanced at the table. He was right. Her cup was still two thirds full. The proprietors were big on saving the planet, so they offered heavy earthenware mugs to anyone who wanted to drink on-site. She'd barely touched hers. Jason's cup was not empty either.

"Work," she muttered.

He stared at her. His lips finally lifted in a semblance of a smile. "Cate told me a long time ago that you'd had four promotions in five years. I doubt you're in any danger of a reprimand." His gaze softened. "Sit back down. Please. It's the season of forgiveness. Will you give me another chance?"

She gaped, startled by the oddly personal nature of his request. "Another chance to do what?"

He shrugged. "To be a decent human being. To reenter polite society. My friends abandoned me en masse when I did the unthinkable. No one wanted to be accused of taking my side against Cate."

"Everyone loves her," Gabby said.

"I know that. I love her, too, but I'm not *in love* with her. That's what I realized months before the wedding, though I was afraid to call it off. The whole thing was a giant tsunami. Beyond my control. Her parents had spent a ridiculous amount of money. Over a thousand people had RSVP'd. I was a coward, Gabby. To be honest, I don't know if I'll ever get over what I did."

She couldn't think of a response.

He grimaced. "Sit down. Please."

The look of vulnerability did her in. She had never seen Jason vulnerable. Guys like him always seemed impervious to the emotions that plagued lesser humans.

Against her better judgment, she sat.

Picking up her coffee mug occupied her hands and gave her a reason not to look into his eyes. She was afraid of what he might see in hers.

One minute ticked by. Then two.

Finally, Gabby sighed. "I know Cate forgave you a long time ago. There's no reason for me to hold a grudge."

"But it seems like you do," he said quietly.

There was no way to express her feelings about the wedding that never happened, so she decided to lighten the mood. "When I was a kid," she said, "one of my favorite books Mom read to me was all about goofing up. The reason I liked hearing it over and over was because Big Bird insisted everyone makes mistakes. I'm neither judge nor jury, Jason. I think you've probably punished yourself enough."

He tapped his spoon on the table, his hand restless. "So will you forgive me?"

"I don't think it's necessary, but sure."

"I appreciate that." He sighed and leaned back in his chair, causing two of its legs to leave the ground. "Thank you, Gabby."

It was incredible to her that he seemed genuinely moved by her words. It wasn't her place to forgive him. Only Cate could do that. And she had.

Gabby was in a far different relationship with the unwilling groom. They were friends...barely. Their interactions with each other over the years had most always been in the presence of other friends, with one memorable exception. Her people appeared in the Venn diagram of his people. She and Jason moved along the same plane...in the same universe. But most of their lives were separate.

Because he was so clearly lonely, though, something inside her cracked and softened. She knew what it felt like to be on the outside looking in. Her smile this time was more genuine. "How have you been these last months?" she asked. "What have you done with yourself? I know you went on the Machu Picchu honeymoon because Cate said she didn't want to bump into you here in Atlanta."

He winced. "Yeah. She insisted."

"And how was it?"

His smile was brilliant. "Peru is amazing. If I hadn't been so low, I'm sure it would have been even better. But I took pictures like mad. Some of them turned out far more beautiful than I expected. I've sold several. And I've spent a good part of the last year and a half traveling the globe."

"That's awesome."

"My parents are disgusted. They still want me to do the doctor or lawyer thing. Like their friends' sons. They won't let it go."

"Parents can be difficult."

"Yep."

She glanced at her watch. "I really do have to get back to the office, Jason. But I'm glad we had a chance to clear the air. I wish you all the best."

As he had been before, Jason was on his feet in seconds, his innate manners part of his upbringing. "Have dinner with me," he said. "Soon."

Her hesitation was visceral. "Why?"

The bald question didn't faze him. He cocked his head, shoving his hands in his back pockets. "Why not?"

"Cate was the only thing you and I had in common. That connection is broken."

He frowned. "We've been friends since I first met you at UGA. You were quiet and serious, but I always enjoyed talking to you."

"Don't do this. Please." Inside, she was a bundle of nerves. Her own secrets threatened to choke her.

"Is having dinner with an old friend such a burden? It's the holidays, Gabby. I would enjoy spending time with you. No agenda, I swear."

She wanted so badly to say yes. The strength of that wanting gave her pause. "I work fifty- and sixty-hour weeks sometimes," she said, the words flat. "You have a much more lenient schedule."

He chuckled softly. "That sounded a lot like an insult. My mother would like you."

"No insult. Just the facts."

"Give me your phone. Unlock it."

Like a sheep on her way to a bad outcome, she handed it over. Jason added his info in her contacts. Then he used her phone to text himself. "There," he said. "I'll keep in touch with you. When you have a free evening, let me know."

All her evenings were free. Except for laundry and meal prep. But she wasn't about to tell him that. "We'll see."

"Ouch," he said. "You're tough." Then he studied her face more carefully. "But maybe you've had to be. Don't you work with a lot of men?"

She nodded slowly. "When I started, only six percent of the staff was female. We're up to ten percent now, but it's still a good ole boy network for the most part."

"Do you like your job?"

"Does it matter?" She laughed softly. "Poor deluded rich boy. That's not a valid question. Most people in the world work to earn money to live. Food. Shelter. Wi-Fi. I have a solid job with good pay and good benefits. I need to support my mother. Grimes & Hancock makes all that possible. So, do I like my job? Depends on the day. But I don't want to lose it, so I'll say goodbye now. End of story. Take care, Jason."

Before she could do more than suck in a startled breath, he leaned forward and hugged her briefly. "Goodbye, Gabby."

The clean, masculine smell of him scrambled her brain. He was big and warm and impossible to dismiss.

She eased past him and fled.

Through the window, Jason watched as Gabby scooted across the street and hurried down the block. She was slender and tall, at least five-ten. Beneath that black winter trench coat, her ivory silk blouse and gray pencil skirt were professional and sexy at the same time. At the table, he had seen the way her top clung to her breasts.

He had forgotten that her eyes were gray. With her finely drawn features and the silky, raven-black hair that curved at her jawline, Gabby could have been a model. He had a hunch, though, that being subjected to personal scrutiny in the fashion world would have been a nightmare for her.

The prestigious accounting firm where she worked was just out of sight around the corner. It had an extensive history in Atlanta as well as an enviable client base. People like NFL stars, film legends, and even Elton John, who owned a posh condo nearby.

Jason wasn't at all surprised that Grimes & Hancock recognized Gabby's worth. She was more than smart. She was brilliant. He remembered being slightly intimidated by her in college. Though she wasn't shy, her innate reserve and phenomenal intellect kept people at a distance.

Did she realize that? Most of what he knew about her had come via Cate. The two women, along with Leah Marks, were close friends.

When she was gone at last, he ordered another drink and sat down again at the small table. As he had done time and again in the past few months, he tapped the note function on his phone and pondered his next steps. Once upon a time, he and his ex-fiancée, Cate, had planned to establish a combination gift shop and art gallery here in Buckhead—a melding of their two skill sets. Now Cate had married Harry. She had also opened a cute gift shop in Blossom Branch a year ago.

From what Jason heard, Just Peachy took off immediately. Cate's sister was working as manager. Both locals and tourists flocked there, drawn by the prime location on the town quad and the wide assortment of curated merchandise.

He was happy for Cate. And relieved. Despite the fact they had cautiously mended fences, he didn't feel comfortable accepting the occasional polite invitations that came his way from the newlyweds. Harry Harrington was his distant cousin. Though Harry was a decade older, he and Jason had been the closest of friends for many years. Harry had mentored him in all sorts of ways, both business and personal. Their tenuous family connection was less important than the relationship they had built.

Now Jason had lost *both* of his best friends, at least in the way they had once related. Would the time ever come when things would be comfortable between the three of them? He hoped so, but he had his doubts.

As he eventually walked to his car, he thought about Gabby. In fact, he had never really *stopped* thinking about her since he saw her sitting and reading. The unexpected encounter had jolted him.

Even in a crowded public shop, there was a stillness about her—an air of peace and tranquility. God, he envied that. When he sat with her, he felt an almost physical pull. Surely his response was a combination of factors.

One thing was embarrassingly clear. He needed to get laid. He was in his late twenties, healthy and physically active. But the feel of a woman's body had become a distant memory. In the last year and a half, he'd had opportunities for any number of one-night stands in countries around the world. He'd given in once. Early on. In Peru. To see if connecting sexually with another woman would take his mind off his and Cate's dreadful wedding day.

It hadn't worked. The momentary release left him feeling even more guilty than before. After that miserable night, he had consciously chosen to stay away from the female sex. Celibacy never killed anybody. Besides, military men down through the ages had faced months or sometimes years of involuntary abstinence.

Jason could do the same.

But today... Gabby... Damn, she was tempting.

He ran through his list of errands, battling the traffic across town. As he loaded up his car with various items for his in-progress remodel, he wondered if Gabby would ever call him. Likely not. So he had a decision to make. Leave her alone? Or see if the small thread of friendship between them could be strengthened?

He liked her. Always had. The idea of spending time with her was tantalizing.

His life had survived the disaster of his aborted wedding. Cate had forgiven him. Her world was rolling along in positive ways. Perhaps now it was time for Jason to get serious about reinventing his future. Perhaps that new day could include Gabby Nolan. Probably not, but perhaps.

Time would tell...

Gabby was familiar with regret. She'd experienced dozens of missed opportunities over the years. And tasted at least as many bitter regrets in the aftermath.

Why had she treated Jason with such indifference?

The whole time he sat across the small table from her in the coffee shop, she had felt her heart knocking against her ribs. Turns out, her old crush on him was dormant, not dead. Seeing Jason in the flesh had thawed all those inappropriate feelings and fantasies.

Was she scared? Did she even know what she wanted? Jason

had made a simple overture. Nothing alarming or out of line. He had invited her to dinner.

But Gabby had panicked. A year and a half ago, this man had been on the verge of marrying her best friend. And to be clear, Cate was a literal beauty queen. Multiple crowns, to be exact. Classically enchanting looks. Stunning, really. A strong woman with a beautiful heart and a warm personality.

Gabby was none of that. She was guarded. Didn't trust easily. Kept to herself at work. No one would ever describe her as charming.

She'd tried socializing over the years but wasn't a fan of strange men groping her boobs on a first date. She lived a simple lifestyle. Though her salary was increasingly generous, she didn't come close to the financial resources of Jason Brightman.

They had nothing in common.

Even as she told herself that, she realized it wasn't exactly fair or true. Jason had suffered. He had been the butt of gossip. Perhaps even scorn. He'd become a pariah, at least temporarily.

Now he had reached out to an old friend. An old acquaintance, at the very least. Didn't she owe it to him to offer kindness? It was the holiday season. A time when the Scrooges of the world were supposed to find love in their hearts.

She didn't want to love Jason.

But maybe she could be nice to him.

Maybe…

The hours passed slowly after Gabby's impromptu coffee date with Jason. Work was heavy. Not as bad as tax season, but still laden with end-of-the-year chores. Tuesday and Wednesday came and went. Every night at home, she pulled up Jason's contact info and wondered if she had the guts to call him.

At the end of the day Thursday, she shut down her computer and stretched her arms toward the ceiling. Her usual chosen mode of exercise was to jog around the neighborhood after work. Running made her feel strong and free. But now that it was December, dark fell early. Gabby wasn't a fan of being out alone at night. Her apartment was in a nice location, but bad things happened everywhere.

Maybe she should join a gym for the winter. It seemed like an extravagant use of her hard-earned money. Still, she needed the exercise. Without it, she was wound too tightly. Her body and her mind needed endorphins to stay on an even keel.

Because she had come into the office extra early that morning, she planned to leave at five on the dot. Not that her boss would care. He knew how hard she worked.

There was only one ladies' restroom on this floor. Down the hall and around the corner. Gabby made her way there and back in fifteen minutes. Looking in the mirror had been a mistake. The dark circles under her eyes were the result of sleepless nights. She'd spent far too much time thinking about Jason.

When she came in sight of her office, her steps faltered. A tall, familiar man stood in her doorway with one hip propped against the frame.

It was as if her imaginings had conjured him up out of thin air.

"Jason? What are you doing here?"

# Chapter 2

He shrugged. Beneath his smile, she thought she detected a note of strain. "I was in the neighborhood. Thought I'd stop by and see if I could talk you into having dinner with me tomorrow night."

Her heart leapt and sank in almost the same second. She *wanted* to have dinner with him. Thankfully, though, she had a good excuse to keep her from doing something self-destructive.

She was weak when it came to this one man.

"I really appreciate it," she said. "But I can't this weekend. I'll be driving to Blossom Branch. I promised my mother I'd take her to pick out a Christmas tree and then set it up at home. I'll have to get into the attic for the ornaments."

Jason ran a hand through his sun-kissed hair, pushing it back from his forehead. He was probably overdue for a haircut. "I could help," he said. "I can haul heavy things, and I'm good with the older generation. Besides, I haven't been to Blossom Branch in ages. Are you staying over? I'll get a room at one of the B and Bs."

One phrase jumped out at her. *The older generation?* "Jason..."
She gnawed her lip. Maybe no one had ever told him her history. Or maybe he'd forgotten.

His gaze narrowed. "What did I say wrong?" he asked.

"Nothing wrong. I thought you knew. My mother had me
when she was sixteen. She's in her forties."

He blinked. "Oh. I'm sorry. I didn't know."

It seemed rude to tell him he couldn't go with her. But the
thought of sophisticated and wealthy Jason Brightman peeking into her mother's life made her squirm. "Why would you
want to go to Blossom Branch? Don't you have things to do
this weekend?"

"I've been working nonstop on this house I bought. It's a
fixer-upper. I'm enjoying the challenge, but a break sounds
appealing. Besides, I..." He trailed off. His cheeks flushed.
"I've never put up a Christmas tree. Never decorated one. My
mother always hired a professional designer to come in and do
our whole house. I wasn't allowed to touch anything."

His words might be a deliberate manipulation of her feelings, but the poignant image of a sweet little boy wanting to
help squeezed her heart. Then she frowned. "You and Cate
were together in your apartment one Christmas."

"True. But we were both crazy busy. The building where
we lived didn't allow anything but artificial trees because of the
fire hazard. It seemed like a lot of trouble to buy a fake one we
didn't really want. Besides, we spent time at her family's house
and mine. And we traveled some. So, no tree."

"I see."

He cocked his head, studying her face. "Do you think my
being there might bother your mother or make her uncomfortable?"

It would have been a good time to dissemble, but Gabby had
never been a proficient liar. She shook her head slowly. "No.
She loves meeting new people."

"Then it must be me who's the problem." It was his turn to frown. "If you don't want to spend time with me, it's okay to say so, Gabby. I don't want to pressure you. I understand when no means no."

Gabby stood at the edge of a terrifying precipice. To back away from danger would be terribly anticlimactic. And she would undoubtedly be left with regret for a missed opportunity. One she had thought about for years.

But if she went forward… Her stomach twisted with anxiety.

Jason seemed to be interested. Maybe it was nothing more than friendship he wanted. Either way, he had sought her out. Even in the face of her reticence, he was making an effort to break through her habitual walls.

"I'd like to spend time with you," she said quietly. "But isn't this a little sudden?"

"We've known each other for years. It's not like we're strangers who met in a bar last night."

"True." She couldn't tell him the truth. That she didn't want to get involved and have her heart broken.

Yet this wouldn't be anything serious. Could she enjoy his company and let that be it? Was temporary fun worth a long-term cost?

"I guess it would be okay," she said. "If you're sure. I'll give you my mother's address, and we can meet there."

He shook his head slowly, grinning. "You're tough on a man's ego, Gabby. Why don't you let me drive us both? There's lots of room in the back of my SUV for a live tree. Or if the tree is too big, we can even tie it on top."

She wrapped her arms around her waist. "I think you're used to getting your own way, aren't you?"

The smile faded. "Not always. But I like you. And I hope the feeling is mutual."

Oh, it was mutual. And then some.

"Fine," she said. "I'm taking off half a day tomorrow so I

won't be rushed. Can you pick me up at three? I don't want to get tangled up in Friday afternoon traffic."

He pulled out his smartphone and tapped the navigation icon. "Tell me your address," he said.

She rattled it off and watched him calculate the distance from his place to hers. His eyebrows shot up. "Good grief."

"What?" she asked, mildly alarmed.

He smiled. "I live barely a mile from your apartment. I can be there in ten minutes, no problem."

Gabby was confused. She had been to Jason and Cate's apartment half a dozen times. It was at least half an hour from where she lived.

When she said as much, Jason shook his head. For a moment, he looked grim. "I moved out of there when the lease was up. That's why I've bought a place of my own."

"Oh. I thought when you mentioned a remodel you were flipping a property."

"Nope. Just creating a nest for myself. The house was pretty much a mess when I bought it, but I'm making slow progress."

"Where are you living in the meantime?" She knew colleagues who had done renovations. Apparently it could be a nightmare.

Jason shrugged. "I'm there for the duration. I've got a mattress on the floor and a minifridge. Plenty of restaurants nearby. Hopefully I'll be done by spring."

"Good grief, Jason. That sounds dismal."

"I may crack one day—install cable and internet. But this is my version of a hair shirt. The stripped-down existence is good for me." He grinned ruefully.

"If you say so." She was flustered now. Easing past him into her office, she grabbed her coat and purse. "If you change your mind, text me."

He sat on the corner of her desk, watching her flutter around the small space. "I won't change my mind."

When she headed for the door, he touched her arm. Lightly. His big fingers wrapped around her wrist gently. He didn't move until she looked at him. "I'm looking forward to this weekend, Gabby. I have you to thank for that. I appreciate your hospitality."

His deep blue eyes mesmerized her. The gratitude in his words bothered her somehow. She wrinkled her nose. "Don't speak too soon. You may be sorry."

"I'll take my chances."

They were so close she could see the stubble on his jaw. He had probably shaved early that morning. More than anything in the world, she wanted to lean forward and kiss him right on the mouth. The urge was so shocking her knees trembled.

Years ago, she'd had a terrible crush on Jason. Even at the time she had known there was nowhere for it to go. He was a fierce lion, the master of his pride. Gabby was a field mouse.

Then, when Cate and Jason got serious—and later became engaged—Gabby excised that silly crush with all the exactitude of a surgeon's knife. Jason had been nothing more to her than her best friend's life partner.

On the day of the wedding, Gabby had struggled, found peace, and ultimately dealt with horrifying guilt. All those emotions had taken a toll. Since that awful day, she'd barely spent any time with Cate. They had seen each other, of course. But usually in the company of Leah, and never for very long.

She knew Cate wondered about her. Heck, Gabby wondered about herself. Everyone thought Gabby was so focused and smart and *together*. She'd heard it a hundred times. The truth was, she appeared to be making admirable strides in her professional life, but as a woman, she was a babe in the woods—little more than a neophyte when it came to men and love and happy-ever-after.

The silence in her office mounted. The door was pushed to,

not quite closed. Out in the hallway, she could hear chatter as people left the building.

Jason still held her arm. She could smell his aftershave. Or maybe it was the scent of his shower gel. Though he was three or four inches taller, with her standing and him perched on the desk, their eyes met.

"I'll enjoy your company," she muttered quietly, the words stiff and formal. "Goodbye, Jason."

The man didn't pick up on verbal cues. "Let me walk you to your car," he said.

Outside, dark was fast approaching. The sun set around five thirty, but tall buildings all along the block cast long shadows. She always used the garage across the street from Grimes & Hancock. Its monthly rates were reasonable, and the six-level structure was well-lit.

Truthfully, it was nice to have an escort. Sometimes being a woman and always on guard could be exhausting. With Jason at her side, she felt safe.

When they were standing beside her navy-blue Kia, he watched her unlock the car door. "Are you still a runner?" he asked, seemingly out of nowhere. "I remember you were very dedicated on campus."

She jingled her keys in her hand, wondering why he was still with her. "Three seasons a year. Right now, not so much."

"Because?"

"A woman. Jogging alone after dark. You do the math."

"Well, that sucks," he said, the words indignant.

"It is what it is." She didn't spend a lot of time worrying about whether life was fair or unfair. Growing up the way she did had meant learning to be resilient and resourceful. It was far easier not to rail against things that weren't likely to change anytime soon.

"What if I ran with you?" he asked.

Gabby's heart did a funny little bump. "You run?" She stared at him skeptically. Not because he looked out of shape. His body was ripped. But Jason was exactly the kind of man who would have an expensive gym membership somewhere that offered kale smoothies and Egyptian cotton towels in the locker room.

He rocked back on his heels, giving her a challenging gaze. "I don't *not* run," he said. "I think I can keep up with you."

"Because I'm a girl?"

"Nope. Because I like a challenge. You've always been good at everything. I assume your fitness approach is no different."

"What about your dinner? Or mine?" She was stalling, trying to decide if she could play Jason's games and not get hurt.

"Are you starving?" he asked.

"Not really."

"Then let's run first. We can grab a burger later."

There was no legitimate reason to turn him down. She liked Jason. A lot. And she had missed running. A lot.

She exhaled. "Okay. There's a fountain in front of my building. I'll meet you there in forty-five minutes."


Jason experienced a jolt of jubilation that was way out of proportion to what was about to happen. He and a female friend were going to jog around her neighborhood and try to stay warm—hardly a romantic movie script.

Besides, Gabby still didn't trust him. Would she ever? Hard to say. She claimed he didn't owe her an apology. Truthfully, though, she might never be able to get past what he had done to her best friend.

At his place, he stripped down and changed into athletic pants and a long-sleeve T. With his favorite toboggan and an insulated jacket, he was good to go.

Gabby's sprawling apartment complex was easy to find. Peachtree Court dated back to the late 1970s. Unlike some unfortunate spots in the city, this area had been preserved and improved over the decades. The landscaping was up-to-date, the paint fresh, and the parking lots nicely paved.

He'd spared a moment to google the place while he was changing clothes. According to the city's website, Peachtree Court was home to a wide range of ethnic and socioeconomic groups. Everything from retired couples to young families and single professional adults, as well. The neighborhood wasn't fancy, but it was solidly middle class.

Gabby certainly had the financial resources to live somewhere more upscale. Clearly, she had her reasons for being here. Maybe she liked not living alone. As far as he could tell—even on a cold winter night—Peachtree Court was a hopping place.

About half of the apartments were decorated. Strands of multicolored lights outlined rooflines. Christmas trees stood in living room windows. Teenagers hung out on the lawn, a few of them smoking. The smell of dinner cooking filled the air.

He found a visitor spot and parked. Gabby waited for him at the fountain.

She waved at him in the gloom. "Over here."

As he joined her, she propped a foot on the fountain edge and stretched. He tried not to notice the way black spandex showcased her legs. The North Face jacket she wore was a twin of his, though hers was deep red and his dark green.

He chuckled as he joined in the stretching, feeling the pull of tight muscles. "We look like Mr. and Mrs. Claus."

Gabby raised both eyebrows as she adjusted her ear warmers. "I certainly hope not. We haven't even gained the holiday fifteen yet."

"I thought that was a college thing."

"Holidays, too," she said.

He changed the subject. "I like your neighborhood, Gabby. It's strikes me as cozy and fun."

She switched legs on the fountain. "It is. I've tried and tried to get my mother to move up here so I can keep an eye on her. It would make my life a lot easier, but she adores Blossom Branch."

Something about that statement confused him. "If she's so young, why do you need to keep an eye on her?"

Gabby finished her warm-up and straightened. She stared at him with a rueful expression. "I can fill you in later. It will make more sense when you've had a chance to meet her. C'mon," she said. "Let's go."

She took off, and he followed.

For the first two miles, Gabby ran like she had stolen a priceless painting and the cops were after her. Jason kept up, barely, but he was sure as hell glad he had long legs. Eventually she moderated the pace.

He'd anticipated more of a jog, but Gabby was serious about her running. They weren't even able to talk. Maybe that was a conscious choice on her part.

He had opened a workout function on his smartwatch before they started. After five miles, he wondered how far his running mate had in mind. Fortunately for him, she rounded a traffic circle and returned toward Peachtree Court.

By the time they made it back, Jason knew he would be sore tomorrow. It had been some time since he pushed himself this hard. But he liked it. His limbs were loose, and his head was clear. Even the cold air felt good in his lungs.

They walked the last half mile, cooling down. When the fountain came in sight, his partner smiled brightly and gave him an odd wave. "I guess I'll see you tomorrow. Thanks for running with me."

He tugged her stubby ponytail. "What about the burger?"

"You go on without me," she said, not quite meeting his gaze. "I may throw together a salad since it's late."

He put his hands on her shoulders. "It's not even eight, sweet Gabby. Don't make me eat alone." Beneath his hands, her bones felt fragile. It was odd. Nothing about her suggested anything but strength. Yet when he touched her like this, he realized how small she was. Tall, but small. It was a conundrum.

"I'm all sweaty."

"So am I. We'll hit up a diner I know."

"Red meat is bad for you," she said, the words prim.

He brushed a stray hair from her forehead. "Let's live a little."

When she looked up at him, she didn't have to look far. Beneath the artificial glare of the nearest streetlights, her smoky eyes looked dark and mysterious. "I think you're a dangerous man," she said slowly, the words almost contemplative. "And I don't know what to do with you."

"I'm harmless," he swore. "Eat a burger with me. I'll bring you home before nine thirty. Easy-peasy."

When her stomach growled audibly, he chuckled.

Gabby rested her forehead against his chest, though she didn't touch him anywhere else. Her arms hung at her sides. "Fine," she grumbled. "But this isn't a date. I'm paying for my own meal."

Her stubborn resistance irritated him enough that he stepped back, releasing her. "Never mind," he said curtly. "I'll see you tomorrow." He turned on his heel to walk away. He'd never had to pressure a woman for a social evening. He wouldn't start now.

A combination of anger and embarrassment made his mood surly. He strode toward his car, regretting that he'd ever come here tonight.

"Wait, wait."

Behind him, an urgent female voice carried on the chilled, misty air.

He stopped, took a deep breath, and faced her. "What?"

She gnawed her bottom lip. "I'm sorry."

"You don't sound sorry."

"Well, I am," she insisted. "I was being bitchy."

"Because?"

Gabby's body language was tense, her arms wrapped tightly around her waist. She was either cold or unsure of herself, or both.

He saw her swallow. "Jason…"

Hearing her say his name softly made him itchy with *something*. "What?"

"I'm not very good with men," she said.

He stared at her, confused by her words. That statement could be interpreted a dozen ways. "Have there been many?" he asked. Perhaps it was too personal a question, but she'd brought it up.

She pursed her lips. Her eyes might have flashed with annoyance, but it was hard to tell in this light. "A few," she said. "Nothing serious."

"Um…"

She read his mind. "No. I'm not a twenty-seven-year-old virgin."

His neck got hot. "I didn't think you were." He groaned inwardly. "Why are we having this incredibly awkward conversation?"

"Because men like you expect things."

"Men like me?" He knew he should probably be insulted, but he was caught in a morass of weeds and trying to find his way out.

Gabby paced in a small circle. "You're handsome and charming and rich. I doubt I could list the women you've been with on two hands. You're asking me to be *social* with you, but I worry that it's code for something else."

His temper flared again, but he didn't move. "It's a hamburger, Gabby. Not a hookup."

"And the trip to Blossom Branch?"

"I need a distraction. It's my home, too. Or it was in the past. I like spending time with you because I don't have to pretend. You've seen me at my worst. And to be perfectly clear, I could list my sexual partners on one hand with one extra finger. I played a lot of sports in high school and college. My parents expected good grades. If you think I was the stereotypical frat boy banging everything that moved, you're dead wrong."

"Oh."

"Yeah," he muttered. "Oh."

"I'm sorry," she said. "Sorry I offended you."

He rolled his shoulders and shoved his icy hands into his pockets. "I don't need sex from you. Not to say it wouldn't be great, but right now, I need a friend. I was hoping that could be you."

Gabby sucked in a sharp breath. He heard it and wondered again what she was thinking. "I'm nothing at all like Cate," she said bluntly. "Not in charm and personality, and certainly not in looks."

For a moment, he was tempted to walk away. To bail on something that had barely begun. He'd never expected the re-kindling of a low-key relationship to be so difficult. But despite her prickly reactions, he found himself oddly drawn to Gabby Nolan.

"Cate and I broke up," he said. "In case you forgot."

"Why?" she asked. The single word was barely audible.

Ah. So that was it. She didn't understand. Maybe Cate hadn't explained. Maybe Cate had found it too uncomfortable to talk about.

"Cate and I were the best of friends," he said. "And yes, we were friends with benefits. But during our engagement, I began to realize we weren't caught up in a grand love affair, a grand romantic passion. We were playing the part of a bride and groom, but beneath the cake tastings and the venue tours, there was something missing."

"Did Cate have that same feeling?"

He rubbed the back of his neck. It wasn't fun to relive this topic. "I think so. At some level. But she was the bride. Even more than me, she couldn't imagine calling a halt. The fact that she and Harry fell head over heels so quickly after the almost-wedding would seem to indicate that she knew what I knew. We weren't right for each other. If either of us had been brave enough to talk about it, we could have avoided a lot of heartache."

Gabby nodded slowly, coming to stand at his side. "Thank you for sharing that with me, Jason. Let's go eat. I'm starving."

# Chapter 3

Jason woke up Friday morning, pumped for the day to come. He had slept like a rock the night before. Though his mind wandered as the day passed, he forced himself to check off a few items demanding his attention.

Over the last several months, he'd found enormous satisfaction in using a sledgehammer to knock down walls and demolish Sheetrock. Goggles and masks had become his friends. The work was hard and dirty and sometimes painful, but he carried a vision of himself living in this house. That image kept him going.

Gabby had softened over their late-night burger dinner. She even laughed at a few of his lame jokes and forgot to be on her guard with him. He loved seeing her genuine smile. Maybe his honesty about the wedding had bridged an unseen gap between them.

In a booth at the diner, they had found themselves surrounded by off-duty cops and hospital personnel who were getting a bite to eat when their shifts ended. No one batted an eye at his and Gabby's running attire. By the time he eventually took her home, he felt as if they had crossed the first hurdle.

Today, he knew he had to stay on his toes.

Even with a pep talk, he almost screwed up. He was so in the zone with his projects, he worked right through until two o'clock. Then he was forced to scramble as he showered and shaved. After that, he changed into khakis and a navy cotton sweater with a soft button-down underneath. He packed an overnight bag, tossed in his toiletry kit, and loaded the car. The sky was blue as could be. Not a cloud in sight.

He didn't need a coat at the moment, but he threw one in the back seat just in case, along with a scarf.

When he parked at Gabby's apartment, he texted her.

The response was immediate. Running late. Come on up.

The casual invitation pleased him. He wanted to see her home, her nest. Maybe it was revealing.

When she opened the door at his knock, her bright smile cut him off at the knees. Until now, he hadn't known she could look like that. Open. Happy. Friendly. "Come on in, Jason," she said.

"Hey," he replied, feeling weird and excited all at once. "Take your time. I'll just hang out and play something on my phone."

She nodded. "I'm almost packed. My last appointment ran late—of course. The one day I was trying to get away early."

"It figures. If you're going to be a few minutes, could I grab peanut butter from your pantry? To make a sandwich? I forgot to eat lunch."

She blinked and froze. "Um…"

"Um what?"

"I don't have peanut butter."

"You're out?"

"No," she said carefully. "I don't have it."

"Are you allergic?"

"No."

He frowned. "Nearly everybody in the country has peanut butter in their pantry. It's an American staple."

"Sorry. Not me. You're welcome to rummage in the fridge and cabinets. Help yourself to anything that looks appealing. I'll be ready to go in twenty minutes."

He'd done it again. Stepped on some invisible land mine. Who knew this woman had so many hidden layers?

Because he felt a strange vibe, he didn't press the peanut butter issue. It wasn't important. Odd, but not important.

Gabby stopped in the doorway, just shy of the hall. Her back was toward him. Then she turned around. "Jason," she said. "You might as well know the truth."

"I don't understand," he said. And he didn't. But he'd done something to ruffle her feathers. Again.

She tucked her hair behind her ears and sat down in one of the chairs at her small kitchen table. He didn't know whether to join her or not until she waved a hand at him. When he sat as well, she sighed. "I want to get on the road, but it's silly not to let you see who I am. I don't mean to be mysterious. Cate and Leah have always known most everything about me. I assumed you might have also. But apparently not."

He stretched out his legs under the table. "Cate never told me anything *personal* or private about you. She's always been incredibly discreet. It's one of her gifts, I think."

"Ah." Gabby played with a saltshaker shaped like an ear of corn, her gaze downcast. "I grew up dirt-poor," she said bluntly, shooting him a wary glance. "Or maybe whatever is lower than dirt. I told you that my mom had me when she was very young. There was no support anywhere. I never knew my grandparents. I don't know if they kicked her out for getting pregnant. I just don't know. But somehow, she got by. When I was old enough, I found a part-time job to help out. As a little kid, though, things were bleak."

He reached across the table and squeezed her hand. "You don't have to tell me these things, Gabby. They're in your past. None of it matters."

"But it does," she said quietly. "If we're going to be friends, we have to understand each other."

He managed a smile. "That sounds like a tall order."

She lifted her chin. "But doable."

"Okay." He waited, sensing she had more to say.

At last, she glanced at her watch and muttered something under her breath. "I'll cut to the chase," she said crisply. "I don't keep peanut butter on hand because it represents painful memories."

"Got it."

"Oh, hush," she said, giving him an exasperated smile. "I'm trying to get this off my chest. Be quiet and listen."

He mimed zipping his lips.

She stood and paced the confines of the small kitchen. "My mother took me to an evangelical church when I was little. Some people called us *holy rollers*. But Mom loved it. She liked the energy and the excitement and the feeling of family, I suppose. Especially since she had none. We went every Sunday."

Jason was mesmerized. He could almost see little Gabby in a pew, her legs swinging. Questions hovered on his tongue. He stayed quiet, though. He couldn't decide if these memories were painful. Her expression wasn't bleak. But she had stepped into the past.

Her tale continued. "The pastor was a large, jovial man. Very *country*. But kind and compassionate. Each week he called kids up front for a children's time. He would teach us a single Bible verse and then hand out *treats*. Most every Sunday, it was packs of peanut butter crackers. He always gave me an extra, and the other kids pretended not to notice. As soon as we were dismissed, everybody ran back to their seats. You could hear the crackling of the wrappers and then lots of chewing."

So far, Jason hadn't a clue how this connected to Gabby's peanut butter–free cabinets, but he was determined to listen and learn.

She shook her head slowly. "I was always hungry, and I *always* wanted to open my crackers like the other kids."

"But?" He couldn't help himself now.

"But Mama slipped both packs of crackers into her purse. When I went to school Monday through Friday, I qualified for free lunch and breakfast. But the weekends were sparse. My mother and I had those peanut butter crackers for Sunday night dinner and washed them down with milk."

"Gabriella…" His heart felt like a jagged piece of glass inside his chest. "Couldn't the church do more?"

"They were all poor. Just not as poor as us. At Christmas and Easter and a few other times, we'd receive a food basket. Plus, we were able to choose things from the Clothes Closet several times a year. We got by." She stopped and wrinkled her nose when she gazed at him. "But I confess, I've detested the taste and smell of peanut butter ever since."

He stood up and took a step in her direction, perhaps intending to hug her or comfort her. He honestly didn't know.

Gabby shook her head slowly, her eyes bright. With tears? "Don't feel sorry for me, Jason Brightman. Those experiences gave me the drive and determination to succeed in school and in life. I learned that failure wasn't an option for me. I had to look after my mother and make her proud. That's all I cared about." She stood abruptly. "We need to go. Let me finish getting my things together." And then she disappeared.

Was she embarrassed about saying those things to him? He hoped not.

His hunger had disappeared. It was entirely possible he might never eat peanut butter again. He hurt for that innocent child and her resilient mother. The world could be a cold and harsh place. He'd had the extreme good fortune to grow up never knowing any of those experiences. Somehow, that shamed him.

When Gabby returned fifteen minutes later, he took her larger bag. "I've got this," he said. "You lock up."

In the car, an awkward silence lengthened. For half an hour, he was able to use traffic as a legitimate reason not to talk to his passenger. Once they were out of town and on the way to Blossom Branch, he cleared his throat. "Will we get the tree this evening? And may I take you and your mom to dinner?"

"That would be lovely. Thank you. She loves eating at the Peach Crumble. I know it isn't fancy, but—"

He cut her off. "But the food is amazing. I remember. Sounds great."

The little town where he and Cate and Leah and Gabby had grown up was only eighty miles northeast of Atlanta. In no time at all, it seemed, he was steering the car along familiar byways, though like any place, changes were evident all around.

His favorite spot was the town square, or to be more exact, the quad. Many years ago, city managers with keen foresight had earmarked two square blocks of the community for a park. Not only had they preserved the grassy spaces, but a beautiful gazebo had been erected right in the center. Seeing the heart of Blossom Branch again brought a ton of good memories. Jason remembered hearing bluegrass music there. Kissing his first girlfriend beneath an oak tree. Eating ice cream.

As he steered carefully between cars parked at the curb, he saw that one beloved tradition was still in vogue. To the left of the gazebo, an enormous blue spruce had been erected. It was covered with decorations that caught the afternoon light, despite the fact dusk was fast approaching. On the other side of the gazebo, a plywood Santa with eight reindeer—plus Rudolph and a fancy sleigh—were poised to lunge into the sky.

When he glanced sideways, he caught Gabby smiling, the delighted, uncomplicated smile of a child. Only Gabby was no child. She was a fascinating, beautiful, sexy woman. The more time he spent with her, the more he felt the pull of something that was both alarming and undeniable.

"Look," she said softly. "It's beautiful."

"It is," he agreed.

"They don't cut it anymore," she said. "Underneath all that magic, the root ball is wrapped in burlap and watered for the entire month. On New Year's Eve, the town will raffle off the tree. One lucky farmer will take it home and replant it."

"I like that idea, but digging it up must have been a bear of a job."

"I'm sure…"

Earlier, when they reached the outskirts of town, Gabby had begun giving him directions. Now, after passing the heart of the charming community, they headed out the other way. Eventually, the houses they passed were older and not as upscale.

When Gabby told him to turn one last time, they pulled up in front of a tiny place that was maybe eight hundred square feet, judging from the outside. It was a white-frame, one-story structure with a leaning chimney and a gravel driveway.

"Did you tell her I was coming with you?" he asked.

"Sort of…" Gabby made a face as she got out. "We'll wing it."

He grabbed her two bags from the trunk and followed her to the tiny concrete porch. She must have had a key, surely… but she rang the bell. Jason saw the curtains twitch. Moments later, the door swung wide.

"Gabby, my baby!"

The woman grabbed her daughter in a tight hug. Her eyes closed, and a look of absolute joy brightened her narrow face. She was shorter than her daughter, but with the same build. Her dark hair brushed her shoulders. A few strands of gray aged her, but mostly, she and her only child could be mistaken for siblings in this light.

Gabby stepped back. "Mama, this is who I told you about.

Jason Brightman. He's going to help us get a tree tonight after we eat dinner. Jason, this is my mother."

He held out his hand. "Hello, Ms. Nolan. It's nice to meet you." The older woman's grip was strong, but her fingers were cold.

She smiled up at him, her expression mischievous. "Are you my daughter's young man? I've been waiting for her to bring someone home. Call me Dahlia."

Gabby made a sound that amused him, but he didn't acknowledge it. Instead, he concentrated on her mother. "I am her friend. But that's all so far. Let's leave it at that. Dahlia is a beautiful name."

"Thank you," she said. "Come inside before we all freeze."

It was a chilly night as December nights went in Georgia, but the little house was cozy. And almost *too* warm. A real fire burned in the fireplace. Jason took it all in as Gabby disappeared down the hall, presumably to her old room. It occurred to him he'd forgotten to make a hotel reservation, but if he couldn't snag a B and B in town, there were always rooms at the chain motels out by the interstate.

Dahlia fluttered around the room. That was the best way he could describe it. She sat and stood and sat again. Was his presence making her nervous?

He cleared his throat. "I told Gabby I'd like to take you two ladies to dinner. She suggested we eat at the Peach Crumble. Is that okay with you?"

Gabby's mother brightened again. "Oh, yes. I'm not much of a cook. It's always nice to have someone else do it." She smoothed a nonexistent wrinkle from her pants. They were black denim. Her shoes were plain black sneakers, and her top was a simple red cotton button-up. She had fastened a gaudy Santa Claus pin at her shoulder.

"You did a great job with your daughter," he said quietly. "She's very smart. I'm sure her boss is happy to have her there."

Dahlia nodded slowly. "Yes. I know she has a good job. But

I'm most proud of the way she cares for her friends. She cooks for the old woman in 3C. Twice a week. And there's a single mom who gets one night to herself each time my Gabby baby-sits the three-year-old twins. I adore her for doing that. Raising kids alone is hard."

"I'm sure that's true," he said, his mind racing. "I didn't know Gabby was so involved with her neighbors."

"Oh, yes. She has a huge heart. I know she wants me to move to Atlanta, but I can't imagine living anywhere but Blossom Branch."

He wanted to ask if she was born here, but it seemed too personal a question.

Fortunately, Gabby entered the room before he bobbled the conversation. She had changed out of her office clothes and was wearing black stretchy pants with a soft pink pullover that looked as if it might be cashmere.

Her cheeks were flushed. "Sorry, Mama. I know you must be starving. I got away from work later than I meant to. And there's always traffic."

Dahlia beamed. "No worries, baby girl. I had a snack to hold me over. But I'm ready to head out anytime you two are. I've put the screen in front of the fireplace and separated the coals."

Jason nodded. "I'm hungry, too. Let's go."

He wasn't surprised when Gabby took the back seat so her mother could ride up front. Dahlia oohed and aahed over Jason's car. It was a midrange vehicle. Not a Porsche, but not a tiny Kia either. The leather upholstery and seat warmers impressed Dahlia. She snuggled deeper into her spot. "I could get used to this."

Gabby met Jason's amused gaze in the rearview mirror and shrugged. He wondered how many times she had tried to buy her mother a new car. Probably half a dozen at least. He knew her that well.

The restaurant was crowded, but after a short wait, they were lucky enough to get a booth by the window.

"I love people-watching," Gabby said.

"Me, too," said Dahlia. "I can always tell who grew up here and who's a transplant. But I don't mind the rich folk moving to Blossom Branch or buying vacation houses. Their money has kept this sweet little village alive."

"You're right about the newcomers," Jason said. "There are a lot of small towns in Georgia that got bypassed by the interstate and slowly dwindled to wide spots in the road. I love the fact that Blossom Branch is scrappy and intriguing and so very welcoming to strangers. It has heart, I think. That's what's so attractive." In fact, he could say the same about Gabby.

Gabby sat quietly as her mother and Jason enjoyed a lively conversation. Dahlia was often shy around strangers, even though she enjoyed the company. But Jason set her at ease right away.

Dahlia had urged Gabby and Jason to sit beside each other. Now she faced them as she ate her pot roast and mashed potatoes and green beans. It bothered Gabby that her mother seemed so hungry. Was she not eating enough breakfast and lunch?

Jason took a sip of his tea and smiled. "So, what do you do for fun, Dahlia?"

Gabby's mother blanched. Her entire demeanor changed. "I see a friend over there," she muttered. "I'll be back in a moment. You two children finish your meals."

Jason shot Gabby a startled look. "What did I say?"

She rubbed his arm briefly to comfort him. "Not a thing. It's hard to explain." She lowered her voice. "My mother struggles with several mental health issues. Her boyfriend, my dad, was killed in a motorcycle accident three weeks before I was born. The grief, combined with postpartum depression, broke her, and she never fully recovered. It's understandable, but I feel guilty that I haven't been able to help."

He frowned. "And no one back then got counseling for her?"

"Apparently not. She's never been able to manage a full-time job, but she works twenty hours a week at a local nursing home. She's happy there...and loves caring for the patients. Nothing medical, of course. She reads books aloud and sings to them and helps write letters to faraway family members if they want. I hope she'll always have that outlet."

"I'm sorry I said anything," he muttered.

"Don't be, Jason. It's hard to know what will set her off. Even I make things uncomfortable at times. Mostly she lives firmly in the present. But it's as if she *slips* sometimes. I never can tell if she's seeing the past, or if she simply withdraws when she's not able to handle a situation."

"You're a good daughter," he said quietly.

She poked at the remains of her chicken and dumplings. "Doesn't seem like it sometimes. I've always felt this crushing responsibility to make things up to her. My being born changed her life forever."

"Isn't that true of all kids?"

"This is different. You know what I mean."

The waitress brought the check. When Jason insisted on taking it, Gabby glared at him. "I have money," she said. "Give it to me."

He shook his head, his gaze taunting. "Nope. A gentleman takes care of the ladies in his party."

"We're *not* a party."

"I don't need gratitude," he said. "But you're not paying for dinner. End of story."

Gabby grimaced. "I'm used to paying my own way."

"Too bad. I'm here, and I'm paying."

"Well, don't try this at the Christmas tree lot."

"Your threats are meaningless, Gabriella Nolan."

Dahlia appeared at his shoulder. "Why are you arguing with my daughter?" she asked, her voice calm.

Gabby grinned. "Busted."

Her mother raised an eyebrow. "And why do you call her Gabriella?"

Jason took his credit card from his wallet. He looked at Dahlia. "I try to call her Gabby most of the time. But you gave your baby girl a beautiful name. I happen to like it."

Dahlia beamed. "Her father picked it, but he—" Her face paled, and she began to wring her hands. "I want a Christmas tree," she said. "Can we please go now?"

Outside the restaurant, the walk to the car was strained.

Gabby put an arm around her mother's narrow waist. "Does Mr. Dave still have the big tree lot out on Highway 16? Or is there somewhere better?"

"I only want a Dave tree," her mom said. "His are the best."

Gabby slid into the back seat again. She leaned forward and showed Jason her phone. "We're only five miles away. Here's the map."

Now that they were all three closed up in the car, the silence was more noticeable. Jason punched in a Christmas channel on the satellite radio. Soon, holiday music was a welcome diversion.

They didn't need a diversion for long. The locally famous Christmas tree farm was easy to find. When they turned onto a well-marked side road, a string of vehicles said they were in the right place.

Jason eased forward. "I'll let you two ladies out and find a place to park."

Dahlia punched his arm. "I'm neither old nor feeble. I think my daughter and I can walk a quarter mile." She pointed. "Take that spot there."

Jason shot a glance over his shoulder at Gabby. "Yes, ma'am."

When they climbed out, they were instantly surrounded by the scent of fresh-cut evergreens. As they walked toward the trees that rested against roped walkways, the smell deepened. Gabby inhaled sharply. Christmas had never been a particularly wonderful time for her. Even when she found a job that paid well, her mother wasn't impressed with expensive gifts. Dahlia did like decorating the house, but only to a point.

Once, when Gabby was fourteen or fifteen, her mother told her that Christmas sometimes made her sad, because she had always wanted a big family, and it was just the two of them. The statement hurt, though she knew Dahlia hadn't meant to wound her.

All Gabby's life, she had tried to make her mother's life happy and fulfilling. But there were many things beyond Gabby's control.

The crowds made it tricky to assess the available offerings. Jason lifted first one tree and then the next, letting Dahlia examine them. Her house was modest in size. The nine-foot trees were out. But she insisted that the six-footers were too small. In the end, they finally found a seven-foot contender that was full and nicely shaped.

Jason hoisted it up, and they made their way to the small wooden booth to pay. Gabby had cash in her hand before Jason could reach for his wallet.

The gray-haired man running the credit card machine and making change looked familiar even with his head bent. He wore denim overalls and a crisp white dress shirt. When he straightened and spotted Gabby's mother, he smiled broadly. "Dahlia Nolan. I haven't seen you in so long."

# Chapter 4

The Christmas tree lot was well-lit. Gabby saw her mom blush noticeably. "Maybe if you ever came to church," Dahlia said, "we might have run into each other."

He grinned at the tartly worded retort. Then he held out his hand to Jason. "I'm Dave Langford. Thanks for helping these two lovely ladies find a tree."

Jason rested the tree trunk on the ground and returned the handshake. "Happy to do it. You have a good selection. And a nice setup."

Gabby held out the cash. "Seventy-five dollars for the seven-foot ones, right?"

Dave nodded. "Yep. And ten dollars from every tree is going to the town benevolence fund to pay for food baskets."

Dahlia glanced at her daughter with a tremulous smile. Then she looked back at the man who seemed to be flirting with her. "That's a lovely thing to do, Dave. No one should have to go hungry, especially not at the holidays."

Gabby stepped closer to her mother, concerned. She was

startled when Jason made the same instinctive move. Now they flanked the delicate woman, who was visibly shaken.

Jason touched Dahlia's arm. "Are you ready to go?"

"Yes."

Dave picked up on the odd moment. "Can I give you folks a hand? Will you be tying it on the top of your vehicle?"

Gabby shook her head. "Thanks, Mr. Dave. But you have a lot of customers. Jason's SUV has a split back seat. We can fold down one side and slide the tree in from the rear. It won't be a problem at all."

"Okay." He stepped out of the booth and stood in front of Dahlia. "Would you like to have dinner with me sometime this month?"

Perhaps he was extending this invitation in front of an audience on purpose.

Dahlia's hands fluttered at her waist, fingers twisting. "I don't go out much," she said. "But thank you."

He touched her arm lightly. "Just about anybody in this town can vouch for me. I'm harmless as a kitty cat. Think about it, Dahlia. Please."

Another family came up to pay for a tree, and the connection was broken. Jason hoisted the tree onto his shoulder and followed the two women back to the car. The Fraser fir barely fit, but Jason was able to close the rear door.

Once again, the ride home was buffered by cheery carols.

At the house where Gabby had spent much of her formative years, they all piled inside. Fortunately, Dahlia relaxed. She chatted with Jason as he and Gabby wrestled the tree into a cast-iron stand with a water reservoir at the base.

The tree had fluffed out in the process. "You picked well, Mama," Gabby said. "I like this one."

Jason looked from Dahlia to her daughter and back again. "Do I need to get boxes down from the attic?"

Gabby assessed her mother's mood. "It's late," she said, smiling. "We'll wait until tomorrow to put all the ornaments on the tree. Thank you so much, Jason. I'll call you around lunchtime maybe."

Dahlia's eyes widened, hearing the dismissal in her daughter's voice. "Jason is staying here, isn't he?"

Gabby held on to her smile. "We only have the two bedrooms. He'll be more comfortable at a hotel."

"My sofa is a gold-medal napping sofa." Dahlia's mischievous smile returned. She went to Jason and clasped his hands in hers. "I'd be honored to have you spend the night. Assuming you can cancel your reservation, of course."

Jason hesitated. He looked at Gabby with a questioning glance.

She didn't know what to say. This weekend was far too cozy already. If Jason walked out the door, she would have a chance to regroup. To remind herself of all the reasons she needed to keep a distance between them.

But Dahlia was having none of it. "Stay," she urged him. "We can play a board game or watch TV."

Gabby winced inwardly. Jason hardly seemed like the kind of man to play a board game on a Friday night. "I'd hate for you to lose your deposit," she said. "Most places in town charge a one-night cancellation fee."

Jason smiled at her in a way that made her knees wobbly. His sun-kissed hair gleamed. His blue eyes seduced her. "Honestly, I never got around to making a reservation." He looked at Dahlia. "If you're sure, Ms. Nolan, I'd love to stay here."

Gabby started to panic. The prospect of a seminaked Jason Brightman sleeping a few feet away from her bed twisted her stomach with all sorts of feelings. None of them were negative.

Her mother was aglow with enthusiasm. "Perfect. You're welcome to get the fire going again."

"Mama." Gabby exhaled. "We can do that later. And I don't

think Jason will want to sleep with the fire. Most people like a cool room at night."

"Oh." Dahlia nodded. "Of course." She smiled at her visitor, the one who wasn't related to her. "Do you enjoy Monopoly? Or gin rummy? I have Cokes and Moon Pies."

Gabby groaned inwardly. Jason had the tough, toned body of an athlete. It was a good bet his usual diet didn't include a lot of sugar and carbs. Even so, she saw him smile gently at her mother.

"Rummy and Moon Pies? It doesn't get much better than that. Count me in."

"Oh, goody." Dahlia beamed and hurried away to the kitchen, presumably to get the table ready.

"You should go," Gabby said. "This will be neither sophisticated nor healthy. And the sofa is lumpy. Why don't you save yourself?"

He frowned slightly. "Are you a reverse snob, Gabby? For your information, I've slept on grass mats and sleeping bags out under the stars in the last eighteen months. I've eaten meals I couldn't identify, and I've made it through not one but two bouts of food poisoning. Nothing about this evening with your mother is a problem. You're the one who doesn't seem to be having fun. Why is that, do you think?"

Before she could find a suitable retort, he paused just long enough and then took her face in his hands and kissed her right on the mouth. It was a tender kiss. One that wouldn't be too embarrassing if Dahlia returned. But oh, the heat.

His lips moved on hers with confidence. She responded automatically, her lips clinging to his, her arms lifting to encircle his strong, warm neck.

Over the years, she had fantasized about kissing Jason Brightman. The reality was far better than anything she had imagined. He muttered her name under his breath and put one arm around her waist to drag her closer.

Now they were pressed together from shoulders to knees. She felt his unmistakable erection. She also noted the rapid beat of his heart. Though it might have been hers. Hard to tell. It was impossible to catch a breath.

A sound from the kitchen jerked them apart.

Jason was pale. "I didn't know I was going to do that. I'm sorry."

She stared at him. "Sorry for the kiss?"

"No," he said. His laser gaze made her want to run far and fast. It had the heat and focus of a predator. "But I'm sorry I didn't ask first."

Gabby reached for every shred of nonchalance she could summon. "No apology necessary. It was nice."

"Nice?" He glared at her now.

She made herself pat his impressive chest. "You're a good kisser," she said. "Besides, we can blame the mistletoe."

He seemed confused until she pointed over their heads. Last Christmas, Dahlia had taped a sprig of plastic mistletoe to her living room light fixture. No one had ever removed it. The red velvet ribbon was a bit on the dilapidated side now.

"Ah." Jason scraped both hands through his hair and removed his sweater. His shirt rode up for a moment, exposing a strip of his flat, tanned belly. He tucked the tail in quickly. "Your mother will be waiting for us. Let's go play rummy. But I warn you, I'm good."

The way he said those last two words made the uncomfortable heat in her midsection increase. Her thighs tightened automatically. It was impossible not to hear what he said with a sexual connotation. Had he been throwing out sexual innuendo? Or was he simply talking about a card game?

"I'm sure you are," she muttered.

In the kitchen, Dahlia had been surprisingly efficient. Three places were set at her table. The small, rectangular piece of furniture was made of a light wood. Though it had a few scratches and dents, Gabby had always loved the beautiful antique.

Paper plates held the promised Moon Pies, and plain glass tumblers had been filled with ice and Coca-Cola. In the center of the table, a single deck of cards lay beside a note pad and pencil.

Dahlia sat down. "Come on, you two. I'm ready to play."

Jason and Gabby joined her. After they took a few moments to sample the goodies, serious play began. Gabby liked playing games to keep her mother amused. It was soon apparent that Jason was a shark. He drew and discarded and in no time fanned his cards on the table. "I'm out," he said.

Gabby stared at him. "You can't even let my mother win?"

Jason smiled at the woman in question. "I'm sure Dahlia would take offense at that. Serious rummy players are very competitive."

Dahlia nodded. "He's right. The women at my church can get a little nasty, truth be told. But there's nothing wrong with playing your best."

In forty-five minutes, the game was over. Jason beat Gabby's mom by fifty-five points. Gabby came in a distant third.

"That was so much fun," Dahlia said, beaming. "We can play again tomorrow, but I'm off to bed." She kissed Gabby's cheek. "Good night, love."

Jason heard Dahlia's door close somewhere down the hall. He knew Gabby was feeling edgy after their kiss. Hell, he was too. Instead of flirting with her the way he wanted to, he kept his voice even. "If you'll point me to the bedding, I'll make up the sofa."

"I'll get it," she said.

In only a moment, she met him in the living room carrying a stack that included a light blanket, two flat sheets, and a pillow already in a case.

"Here you are," she said. "Feel free to use the hall bathroom if you want a shower. I'll be out of there in fifteen minutes."

And then she was gone.

The evening suddenly felt flat. Jason wondered why he had gotten himself involved in Gabby's personal life. Ever since she told him the peanut butter story, she'd been on her guard with him. On the other hand, he genuinely liked her mother. And because he had done nothing but work on his fixer-upper for the last month, it was nice to have a change of pace.

It was impossible not to hear water running in the hall bathroom. It made him uncomfortable in more ways than one as he imagined Gabby—wet and naked—just steps away from him. His body responded to that image, and there was nothing he could do about it. He was wildly attracted to one of Cate's best friends. If that wasn't a recipe for disaster, he didn't know what was.

When he heard Gabby's bedroom door open and close, he took his own turn in the shower. The hot water was plentiful, but the bathroom was cramped and dated. One end of the shower rod was dangerously loose. Maybe he could repay Dahlia's hospitality by fixing a few things around the property.

By the time he made it back to the living room, the well-worn sofa looked more appealing. Though he was physically tired, his mind wandered. He added a small log to the fireplace and lit a couple of matches. The room was plenty warm, but he had forgotten how nice it was to have a real fire.

He arranged the sheets and blankets and settled onto the cushions. Not bad. Unfortunately, he often slept naked in his own bed. His current attire—T-shirt and sleep pants—was too warm. But he couldn't very well strip down in a communal room where anyone might wander in.

Finally he dozed off. It wasn't a restful sleep. The old house creaked and popped, much like his fixer-upper. When his eyes opened for the third time, he decided he might as well not fight it. With his hands tucked behind his head, he stared at the ceiling and thought about Gabby.

What was he doing? Did he have a plan, or was he acting on impulse alone?

All he knew for sure was that he liked spending time with her. And he *wanted* her. That admission was disturbing, even if he was the only one who knew the truth.

He and Cate and Harry had some mending to do if their relationship was to survive for the long haul. Gabby had witnessed Jason's worst moment. Even if she professed to forgive him for hurting her friend, she most probably had unresolved feelings toward him, and not the good kind.

Why was he inserting himself into her life?

Without warning, the object of his thoughts appeared. She wore a gray sweater over a white cotton nightie. Her feet were bare. She stood on the opposite side of the coffee table and faced him, her arms crossed over her chest. "I could hear you moving around. You aren't asleep," she said.

He sat up and yawned. "Nope."

"You should have gone to a hotel. That sofa is a mess."

"No," he said. "It's not bad. Do I make you uncomfortable? Why did you try so hard to kick me out?"

Gabby stared at him, looking vulnerable and beautiful and wary. He ached with lust that disturbed him.

When she didn't answer, he repeated his question. "Why did you want me to go to a motel?"

Her chest rose and fell as she took a deep breath and then exhaled. "Because I didn't want to do this." She sat down beside him, took his face in her hands, and kissed him.

His brain struggled to catch up. But his body was faster. She smelled like lavender and sunshine. Her skin was incredibly soft. He tried to take charge of the kiss, but Gabby was a woman on a mission.

She slid a hand under his T-shirt and found the plane of his chest. "You are a beautiful man," she whispered.

He cupped one of her bare breasts, caressing it through a thin layer of cloth. "Should we be doing this?" he groaned. He was hard already, so hard. And he was ninety percent sure there would be no second act.

Gabby whimpered when he rubbed her nipple.

With everything he had, he wanted to strip her naked and mount her on this dreadful sofa. The driving urge nearly pushed him over the edge.

At the last moment, though, his shredded self-control reminded him that if he wanted Gabby, he had to play the long game. This relationship was already complicated because of the past. If he botched the present, there would be no future.

He put his hands on her waist and eased her away from him. "I can't screw you on your mother's couch," he said bluntly.

She blinked at him. Her hair was mussed, and her cheeks were red. It could have been heat from the fire, but he had a hunch she felt the same burning need that threatened to turn him into a selfish monster.

"I have a bedroom…"

The words came out as a soft whisper, but he could see on her face that she didn't really mean them as a serious invitation. The little house had thin walls. They had already taken a dangerous chance. Neither of them was ready to explain this insanity to Dahlia. He knew that much without asking.

He brushed a thumb across her cheekbone. "All evidence to the contrary," he said gruffly, "I do respect both you and your mother. I would never do anything to cause problems. As much as I want you, Gabby, I can wait."

"Wait for what?" The confusion and yearning on her face nearly did him in.

He cleared his throat. It was dry and sandpapery. "I suppose I lied to you when I said I wanted friendship."

"You did?" She frowned.

"Yes. Though not intentionally. At first, I thought you and I could hang out platonically. But now..."

"But now what?"

He shifted sideways so he could better see her face. Plus, it extended the no-go zone between them. "May I ask you a question?"

"Of course," she said. But she looked suspicious.

"Do you remember that I asked you out one time—soon after we all arrived at UGA? Cate and I weren't dating yet. You were my lab partner in an entry-level chemistry class. I thought you were fascinating. And incredibly smart. But you turned me down." He grimaced. "I know this may sound like conceited-jock-speak, but I was shocked and a little hurt. So I never asked again. Though I've always wondered why you didn't say yes. Given what just happened on this sofa, I'm even more curious. Why did you say no all those years ago?"

Gabby stared at him, her face even redder now. Her expression was mortified and aghast. "I didn't know you remembered that day," she muttered.

"I remember," he said firmly.

She got to her feet and paced the confines of the living room. Her steps couldn't take her far. "At that point in my life, Jason, I had never even been *out* on a date. *Not one.* So I was scared to death when you asked me. Even as young as you were, you already had a reputation on campus at UGA. You were one of the popular kids."

He bristled. "That's bullshit."

"No," she said carefully. "You know it's true. Cate went out of her way to get me into Zeta Zeta Pi and make sure I was a part of things. But inside, I was still the bashful, dirt-poor kid from the wrong side of the tracks in Blossom Branch. You were a shiny meteor streaking across the sky. I thought you'd made a bet probably. With some of your friends. To see if you could date the weird kid. I had no self-esteem at all. Well, in academics, a little. But none when it came to my femininity."

He shook his head slowly. "I had no idea. I'm sorry, Gabby. I should have asked again. When you'd had a chance to spread your wings."

Her shoulders lifted and fell. "At eighteen, I was so backward emotionally. Maybe you didn't know this—Cate and Leah and I weren't really friends in elementary school. Our lives were too different. But when we all three ended up at UGA, we bonded during freshman orientation over our Blossom Branch connection. I had all my issues, and Leah was so dreadfully shy. Cate saved us. Literally. We never would have been so happy in college if she hadn't taken us under her wing."

"She's an incredible person," Jason said quietly. Once again, he felt the lash of regret. Even knowing that everything had turned out for the best, the burden of guilt was heavy.

"We should get some sleep," Gabby said.

He stood as well. "Where does this leave us?"

"I have no idea. I haven't had much experience with healthy adult relationships. I always assumed I'd be single and happy."

"With a cat?" He grinned despite their heavy discussion.

"A dog," she said firmly. "Maybe a basset hound. I love their morose disdain for life. A pet like that wouldn't expect much from me."

"Ah." He rolled his shoulders. "For what it's worth, I don't have much depth in the relationship department either. My parents have been unhappily wed for decades, and you know how my one engagement turned out."

"So you'll travel the globe, footloose and fancy-free?"

"Traveling the globe palls with no place to come home to… or no one," he said. "I've discovered that already. Besides, I've been rethinking the nomadic lifestyle. It may not be what I want after all."

"I see…"

He took three steps and pulled her into his arms, the top of her head tucked beneath his chin. "We could use each other for practice," he said.

She chuckled against his chest. "That's depressing as hell. You're assuming we'll crash and burn, and you're not wrong."

"Or something extraordinary might happen." He stroked her hair, inhaling the scent of her shampoo. "We might beat the odds."

"I told Cate and Leah years ago that a woman should look out for herself and not depend on a man to save her."

"What if we save each other?" he asked, deadly serious and hovering on a knife-edge between hope and despair.

She tugged free of his embrace so she could see his face. "Could we keep it a secret? Seeing each other, I mean. That way, if it fizzles out, no one will feel sorry for us."

He saw from her eyes that she was making a serious suggestion. But he wasn't willing to hide. He'd done enough of that in the last eighteen months, metaphorically at least. "I don't think so, Gabby," he said. "We're two grown-ass adults. It's the holiday season. If ever there was a time for hope and new beginnings, this is it."

She studied his face. "Can I think about it?" she asked. "I'm not being coy. I've always been the kind of person to make lists of pros and cons. To mull things over. This is important to me."

"It's important to me, too."

"I'll be your friend, no matter what," she said.

Jason shook his head slowly. "I don't think I can do that. When I saw you in that coffee shop, something happened to me. I *thought* we could be friends. I wanted that at the very least. But now I don't think it would work. Apparently this is going to be all or nothing."

She rolled her lips inward, staring at him with a look that was equal parts hope and resignation. "No pressure," she said. "Are you sure about that?"

He locked his hands behind his neck, stretching his back and spine to relieve the tension. "I nearly took you right there on the sofa. It was a close call, Gabby. And you feel it, too, or you would never have left your bedroom."

She smiled at him faintly. "Fair point."

"Go," he said starkly. "Get out of here."

"One more kiss?" she whispered.

The naked yearning on her face echoed in his gut. "One kiss." He would have given her anything, but perhaps it was best she didn't know that. Not yet.

When he dropped his arms, she curled her fingers in his and leaned in to meet him halfway. Their lips met, and the world stood still. Jason could hear his heart beating in his ears. The scent of woodsmoke and evergreens was a powerful aphrodisiac. Maybe the evocative smells reminded him of a boy's excitement on Christmas Eve.

Was he so desperate for her because of his long dry spell? Or did Gabby give him something no one else ever had?

She broke the kiss first and stepped back. "Good night, Jason."

And then she was gone.

# Chapter 5

Noises from the kitchen woke him when it was barely light outside. He pulled the pillow over his head and groaned. A huge yawn popped his jaw.

He felt like he'd been awake all night, but he must have dozed off sometime. His head pounded.

Soon, the smell of coffee and cooking bacon told him he might make it through the day if he could drag himself upright and find acetaminophen in his overnight bag. Easier said than done. But he powered through.

When he peeked into the hallway, the bathroom door was open. He took care of business and freshened up, throwing water on his hair to keep it down. The man in the mirror had the beginnings of a beard and dark shadows under his eyes.

He leaned both hands on the sink and bowed his head. He honestly didn't know what the hell to do in this situation. Should he drive back to Atlanta and return to pick up Gabby tomorrow?

That might be the smartest course, but he couldn't. He

wouldn't. He wanted to be with her. Period. Here in Blossom Branch. Or in Atlanta. He was winging it, and he couldn't find it in himself to regret that. Maybe in some ways, all the uncertainty made this new part of his life more exciting.

When he entered the kitchen, only Dahlia was there.

"Good morning," he said.

Using tongs, she scooped up the three crispy strips of bacon frying in a pan and laid them carefully on a paper towel. "Good morning." She waved a hand toward the sink. "Coffee is ready. Help yourself. Mugs are in that cabinet. Breakfast will be done in five minutes."

"Can I help?"

"Heavens, no. If I can't throw together toast and bacon and eggs, they might as well put me out to pasture. Sit down and drink."

Her laughter made him smile. "Yes, ma'am."

He wanted to ask about Gabby, but he didn't. For the first time in months, he decided to indulge in caffeine. The coffee was good, very good. Hot and strong. Just the way he liked it. He sipped the life-giving liquid and cradled his aching head in one hand.

When Gabby finally showed up, she was perfectly groomed, but her smile was shaky. The sweater today was pale yellow. It clung to her breasts subtly.

"Coffee?" he asked.

"Oh, yes." She sat down carefully. "Good morning, Mama. Thanks for making breakfast."

"Happy to do it. You kids eat plenty."

The three of them dug in. Silence reigned for the first few minutes. Then Dahlia dropped an unwitting bomb. "How did the two of you meet?" she asked. "I don't think Gabby has mentioned you, Jason."

He saw Gabby's eyes go wide. What little color there was in her face faded.

"Um…" His brain raced, but there was only one possible thing to do. He exhaled. "Gabby and I met in college at UGA, Ms. Nolan. More recently, I was engaged to Cate Penland."

Dahlia's eyes widened. She might be emotionally fragile, but she was no dummy. She knew Gabby's best friends were Leah and Cate. Her gaze went from Jason to her silent daughter and back again. "You must have been through a lot this last year, Jason. I hope you're on the mend."

"It was my fault," he said bluntly. "While it's true that Cate and I were not a good match, I waited too long to call things off. I kept telling myself everything would be okay. The wedding was a huge, embarrassing mess."

She reached across the table and patted his hand. "My poor boy. Life kicks us in the teeth at times, doesn't it? Most of us have a few terrible mistakes in our pasts. People gossip about our failings. Point fingers. The best thing we can do is keep on living. One foot in front of the other and all that. Eventually, the days are not as dark. I hope my daughter has brought some light into yours."

Jason nodded his head, stunned. His eyes burned. This resilient woman was sharing her hard-won wisdom with him. Gabby was visibly shocked. Perhaps her mother never talked about the past.

"Thank you, Dahlia," he said hoarsely. "That means a lot. As I told Gabby, I don't know if I'll ever be able to forgive myself."

"Then you're a fool," she said sharply. "This might have been your first huge misstep, but it won't be your last. We grow from those broken places. I'm not the same person I was when Gabby was born."

"It must have been hard raising her on your own," he said quietly.

Dahlia nodded. "Incredibly so. But she was mine. And I adored her. Still do," she said, squeezing her daughter's hand.

"I love you, too, Mama." Gabby squeezed her mother's hand in return.

Jason didn't know what to say now, but help came unexpectedly.

Gabby rubbed her thumb over the back of her mother's narrow wrist. "You should know, Mama, that Cate is very happy now. She married Harry Harrington. Turns out, he's had a thing for her for a long time. When she ran out of the church, he was the only one who moved fast enough to follow her."

"That sounds romantic," Dahlia said.

"Well, not at first." Gabby winced. "Cate was a mess, as you can imagine. She told Jason to go on the honeymoon without her so she wouldn't have to bump into him around town. Harry offered her a place to hide out…so she wouldn't have to go home and deal with well-meaning friends and family. That gave her time to work through her feelings."

"So, who is this Harry person?" Dahlia asked.

Jason exhaled, realizing he still had a few unsettled feelings about a lot of things. "Harry is a distant cousin of mine… ten years older than me. Once upon a time, when my parents wanted to travel to some exotic location without their annoying son, they asked Harry to keep me while they were gone. He was only sixteen, but he came to my house, and honestly—it was one of the best weeks of my life. After that, we were tight. As I grew up, he became a mentor. I had no idea he'd ever had romantic feelings for my ex-fiancée, so their marriage surprised me, to say the least."

Dahlia frowned. "Were you jealous?"

Gabby stared at him as though she might have wanted to ask the same question but hadn't.

He mentally sifted through the months since he had heard the news about Cate's relationship with Harry. From the beginning, he had asked Harry to look out for Cate…to make sure she was okay after the wedding debacle. That certainly hadn't included putting the moves on her.

"No," he said. "Not jealous at all. But I worried that Cate might have rushed into something."

Gabby smiled at him. "Pot. Kettle."

He knew exactly what she meant. "This is different," he insisted. "I've been a single man for a year and a half. No rushing for me."

She didn't press the issue, but he knew what she was thinking. Since that day at the coffee shop, he had wasted no time inserting himself into her life.

Not that she seemed to mind.

Jason snitched the last piece of toast. "Shall we decorate the tree?" he asked, hoping to shift the conversation to something less personal.

Dahlia shook her head. "That's more fun when it's dark outside. We'll do that tonight. Gabby, has Jason seen Cate's store?"

Gabby looked at him inquiringly. "I have no idea."

"No," he said. "Cate wanted to get married in Blossom Branch, but her parents insisted on the big Atlanta affair. This is the first time I've been back here in almost two years." He and Cate had visited Cate's grandparents in February before the wedding. The older couple's Blossom Branch home was a beautiful example of past architecture. After the *almost* wedding, Cate and Harry had spent some time there.

Gabby stood and began clearing the table. "I don't think either Jason or I want to run into Cate today. But we can drive around town so he can see what's changed."

Dahlia began loading the dishwasher. "You know Cate's sister is managing the store. I doubt there would be any awkward encounters. Unless Becca spooks you."

Jason chuckled. "Becca is great. But I imagine this would be a very busy time for her. The Saturdays in December are prime shopping opportunities. I *would* like to explore, though. Are you up for that, Gabby? You're welcome to join us, Ms. Nolan."

"Stick with *Dahlia*," she said. "*Ms. Nolan* makes me sound ancient. And thanks for the invitation, but no. My friend next door is teaching me how to knit. We're making small blankets for the pets at the animal shelter. Even if my pieces turn out crooked, it doesn't matter. The dogs and cats don't mind."

He laughed. "Does that mean you're a pet lover?" He hadn't seen signs of an animal in the house.

"No," she said. "I could never afford one while Gabby was growing up. I hate that she didn't get to have those experiences, but for a family in financial distress, pets are not an essential item. I know my girl missed out on so many things..." Her voice trailed off. A look of deep sadness came over her face like a cloud.

Gabby shook her head firmly. "Don't be silly, Mama. I had everything that mattered. Besides, you know I'm allergic to cats." She shot Jason a wry look. "We found that out one weekend when I went to a birthday party in the neighborhood. I came home with my eyes swollen almost shut. As you can imagine, that didn't help my reputation as the odd kid in the class."

Dahlia bristled. "You were never odd. But children are remarkably cruel."

Jason tried to steer the conversation in a more positive direction. "Well, Gabby...are you up for showing me everything I've missed recently?"

She dried her hands on a blue-and-white dish towel. The kitchen was spotless again. "Sounds good to me."

Soon, they were in the car and driving around town.

Blossom Branch was famous for many things, but peaches especially. Over the decades, acres of large orchards had provided a source of income for locals and even now served as a draw for tourists. The merchants in town long ago bought into the peach theme. Like the Peach Crumble, other businesses had gone with "peach" names.

Peach-aria for pizza. Peaches to Go if you needed catering. The Peach Pit had been the popular bar and restaurant hangout for decades. The list went on and on. Peaches and Cream served his favorite ice cream.

He took note of the busy streets and the bustle of holiday shoppers. The town had been quieter when he was a kid.

When he said as much, Gabby nodded. "You're right. Some townspeople didn't like the attempts to draw in outsiders. But honestly, a community like this would have died if it hadn't continued to reinvent itself."

"Did you and your mom ever live anywhere else?" he asked.

Gabby stared out the front windshield, her profile all he could see of her face. "No. Only here. When I went to college, my mother grieved, and I was terrified. But we both adjusted. I think she knew I had to spread my wings if I was going to make our lives different. More secure." She sighed. "I'm not jealous of your money, Jason. Not even a little bit. But I've never been out of the state of Georgia, so I envy you that. Maybe one day when Mama doesn't need me as much, I'll travel, too."

Jason thought about everywhere he had been in the world. The things he had seen and learned. Travel had made his life immeasurably richer. But in the end, it was relationships that kept a man warm at night.

"You're a good daughter," he said. He wondered if Dahlia needed Gabby as much as Gabby thought she did. Maybe Gabby's caretaker relationship was ingrained now. From where he was sitting, Dahlia seemed self-sufficient. Then again, he hadn't been around long enough to know for sure.

As he stopped at a red light, Gabby half turned in her seat. "I have an idea. Would you like to have lunch with Leah and her fiancé? If they're available?"

His stomach clenched. He hadn't seen Leah since the wedding. She was probably as pissed at him as Gabby had been. "Fiancé?" he asked, stalling.

"Yes. Lucas swept her off her feet. Literally, in the beginning. He's the fire chief here in Blossom Branch. They met when there was a blaze out at Leah's camp. Fortunately, everything was okay. One of the buildings needed repairs, but no one was hurt."

He put his foot on the gas when the light turned green, turning onto a street they had missed. "Do you think Leah *wants* to see me? I'm guessing her opinion is about the same as yours."

Gabby pulled her phone from her purse. "She's so ridiculously happy right now, I doubt she'll hold a grudge about the wedding. Besides, when I talked to her day before yesterday and told her I had bumped into you, she asked a lot of questions. To be honest, she's curious. Do you care if I call her?"

Jason gripped the wheel until his fingers ached. "Not at all."

Then he sent up an urgent prayer to the Almighty. *Please let Leah Marks be otherwise occupied.*

Gabby could tell Jason was nervous. It sounded as if he had been hiding out from family and friends for the last year and a half. If that was true, then a moment like today would be painful. It was clear he still carried a heavy load of guilt.

At first, she had thought he deserved his misery. Now she wasn't so sure.

Leah jumped at the chance to have a meal together. She said Lucas was off today, so that was good. When Gabby suggested meeting at a restaurant in town, Leah insisted on inviting them to lunch at her house. Apparently, Lucas had smoked a beef brisket overnight, so they had plenty of food.

When Jason pulled up in front of the large brick bungalow with the white columns and trim, Gabby sighed. "I love this place. Wait until you see the inside. Most of the windows and hardwood are original."

Jason got out and locked the car. "I like it from the street side, too."

Leah's classic Blossom Branch house was two stories tall with an attic on top. The steeply pitched roof lines and dormer windows looked like something out of a fairy tale. Gabby tried not to covet, but it was hard.

At this time of year, hanging baskets were missing from the wraparound porch. Even so, the house was perfect.

Leah greeted them at the front door with a hug for Gabby and a hesitant smile for Jason. "It's nice to see you again, Jason," she said softly. Then she held out her arms. "I think we need a hug, too, don't we?"

Gabby watched Jason's face as her friend embraced him. Jason's body language was rigid, but he made it through the sweet moment. Leah exhaled as if she had done something hard but rewarding.

At that moment, a tall, gorgeous man walked down the hall. He grinned at Gabby and Jason. "I can't leave this woman alone for a minute. Here she is hugging a strange man behind my back."

Leah giggled. "He isn't strange. Jason, this is my fiancé, Lucas. Lucas, Jason." She slid her arm around Lucas's waist. "Gabby and Cate and Jason and I were at UGA together. You remember me telling you that."

The two men shook hands. Lucas nodded. "I remember." He smiled at Jason. "Gabby and Cate have been great supporters of Leah as she's been getting her camp off the ground. It was a huge undertaking. I'm very proud of her."

When he kissed his fiancée's cheek, she blushed. "Lucas is biased," she said.

Gabby shook her head. "No, he's right. You've done something amazing. Offering at-risk kids two weeks in the great outdoors, with what? Four different sessions? It's a huge undertaking. You're saving the world, and people like me do nothing but play with spreadsheets."

Jason shook his head, frowning at her. "Don't sell yourself short, Gabby. Everyone has a place. You're smart, and you understand numbers. Lots of people can't do that. So you make a difference, too."

Gabby let that one slide. It was nice of him to say, but she didn't believe a word of it. Not compared to what Leah had done and was doing.

As they walked down the narrow hall to the dining room, she smiled to herself to see Leah so bubbly and happy. Her friend was half a foot shorter than Gabby and more rounded. Because she had grown up in the shadow of three overachieving brothers, she struggled with self-confidence. Starting her camp and having the super-hottie fire chief fall for her had brought her out of her shell.

Lunch was fun after a few stilted minutes at the beginning. Lucas obviously knew about the aborted wedding, but because he hadn't known any of the involved parties until he met Leah and Cate, the wedding that never happened wasn't as huge a deal to him.

Leah took her duties as hostess seriously. During a lull in the conversation, she addressed Gabby. "How's your mom doing? I saw her at the grocery store last week. We chatted for a minute. She seemed…"

Gabby smiled wryly. "Normal?"

"I wasn't going to say that." Leah's words were indignant.

"It's okay. I knew what you meant. Truthfully, my mother is doing well right now. She's knitting blankets for rescue dogs at the shelter, and she still loves her job at the nursing home. Unlike me, she's a social butterfly."

"You work too hard," Leah said.

Jason nodded. "I've been telling her that."

"Don't gang up on me," Gabby said. "For your information,

I took part of yesterday off so Jason and I could drive here and help Mom get her Christmas tree. We bought it last night, and decorations are next."

Leah nodded. "I haven't done anything to deck the halls yet. Maybe Sunday afternoon. The days go by so fast this time of year."

Lucas grinned. "And the nights aren't long enough." Gabby and Jason laughed, but Leah turned bright red. Even so, her beaming smile said she didn't mind her lover's teasing comments about their time together.

"So, have you made any wedding arrangements yet?" Gabby asked.

Leah shook her head. "It's too nice right now. Once we start making plans, my mother will drive us crazy. So we're taking the time to enjoy being engaged. That's plenty for the moment. And this is our first Christmas together, of course. I love having Lucas to myself when he's not working."

Jason smiled. "I assume the camp is closed for the holidays?"

"More than that," Leah said. "None of our buildings are winterized. My dream is to have winter retreats eventually. The Georgia climate in January and February is typically mild, as you know. I'm not sure if I'll put up all new buildings or simply retrofit our current facilities with central heat and fireplaces. But it's exciting to think about."

"How did you start all this?" he asked.

"My great aunt died about the time I graduated from college. I think she wanted to give me a jump start to keep up with my brothers. She had no children, so she left me this house, a dilapidated camp from the seventies, and a chunk of money. That cash along with various grants was enough to get things up and running. It was a slow process. But finally, our very first campers arrived at the beginning of June."

"That's quite an accomplishment," Jason said. "I'd love to see the camp when you guys are free to give me a tour."

Lucas nodded. "Next time I have a day off, Leah and I would be happy to take you out there. It's only fifteen or twenty minutes from town."

Jason looked at Gabby. "And you've seen it all?"

"Oh, yes. It's very impressive." She probably should have visited more often, but during the summer, her visits to Blossom Branch were usually prompted by her mother's needs. It was hard to be two places at once.

Leah tilted her head toward Jason and shot Gabby a questioning glance when the men were engrossed in conversation. Gabby pretended not to see. She hadn't dated much over the years, and when she did, she certainly hadn't introduced her dates to Leah and Cate. She was always too self-conscious.

Gabby hadn't told Leah everything about Jason and the coffee shop and their growing attraction. It seemed too far-fetched. But she *had* shared the fact that she and Jason were reviving a version of their friendship. As the afternoon passed, Leah studied them none too subtly, as if trying to understand a weird phenomenon.

Fortunately, Lucas had no connection to the University of Georgia. He was essentially an outsider. Today, that was a good thing.

The brisket was delicious, along with twice-baked potatoes and a green salad with everything on it. Jason and Lucas ate impressive shares. Gabby and Leah did their parts. By the time they were all groaning with full stomachs, Lucas brought out a coffeepot.

"Who wants some?"

Gabby watched him pour, loving the way he kissed the top of Leah's head as he passed by her chair. He had grown up in foster care…lived a hard life. But none of that had soured him. He was a great fire chief, and he treated Leah like a princess.

In truth, Gabby realized that Lucas might have been a better match for Gabby than Jason. Lucas understood what it was like to feel insecure. To wade through a world fraught with pitfalls.

That didn't matter, though. She had never once felt sexually drawn to Leah's partner. The heart wanted what the heart wanted, regardless of whether it made sense. For a very long time, Gabby had seen Jason as an unattainable fantasy. First, when she was so young, a teenager starting college—she'd had no idea how to talk to him. Later, when he was engaged to Cate, she'd told herself she didn't care about him anymore.

Now, a year and a half after the wedding that would have bound him irrevocably to Cate, Jason was free. Unencumbered. And as wild as it sounded, he was interested in Gabby. Each time he called her *Gabriella* in that deep rumbly voice, her heart melted. He was masculine and yet not arrogant. Tough enough to sleep on a mat in the jungle and yet tender enough to be kind to her mother.

She had no defense against him.

None.

But she was neither naive nor gullible. Jason might be delightfully entertaining in the short term. If she worked up her courage, they could have fun together. In bed. For a *very* short time. After that, she would live her life, and he would move on. Or she would *move* him on. The important thing was for her to be in control.

Amid Gabby's introspection, Leah stood. "I'll grab dessert," she said.

Jason rose to his feet immediately. "Let me help, please. I want to see this great kitchen Gabby has told me about."

# Chapter 6

Jason knew his ploy wasn't subtle. But he wanted a chance to be alone with Leah, even briefly. When they were behind closed doors, he spoke in a low voice. "I'm sorry about the wedding, Leah. More than you know. I needed to say that."

She leaned against the sink and cocked her head. "You don't owe me anything, Jason. Cate is fine. I'm fine. But I do have a few questions about Gabby."

He frowned. "What do you mean?"

"I don't think you should toy with her emotions. She's incredibly smart when it comes to numbers, but a guy like you could get inside her head. And her bed. She's my *friend*, Jason. She had a very hard life growing up."

He hunched his shoulders. "I understand that now. I didn't when we were in college. All I knew then was that she was very shy."

Leah shook her head. "I was the shy one. Gabby was something else again. If it hadn't been for Cate, Gabby would have lived in a hermit bubble at UGA. Cate made her get out and meet people. Cate pushed her, and because Cate was incredibly popular and well-loved, other students let Gabby slide into the flow of sometimes cruel college social life."

"But she's so confident now."

"Yes," Leah said. "On the outside. She's *had* to be at Grimes & Hancock. In a mostly male enclave, she's developed this cool, poised, don't-mess-with-me persona. It's effective at work. She's well-respected."

"Isn't that because she's so good at what she does?"

"Of course. But you know as well as I do that women in the business world have to battle sexism, pay inequality, and sometimes outright harassment. Gabby learned how to stand up to her colleagues. Considering where she came from, it's astonishing."

"Then why do you think she has anything to fear from me?" Jason truly wanted to know. He had hurt Cate terribly. The experience dented his confidence. Not for anything in the world would he risk a repeat.

Leah pulled a key lime pie out of the fridge and began cutting it. "Hand me those plates, please."

"Got it." When he stood beside her, she scooped slices one at a time and set them on the four china saucers.

After she grabbed the whipped cream from the fridge along with forks and napkins, Leah gave him a pointed look. "Here's the thing, Jason. You're probably lonely and still recovering from what happened to you. So, getting intimate with Gabby might bring you healing and peace… I don't know. But I do know that behind Gabby's poised, I-can-handle-anything image, there are remnants of that little Blossom Branch girl who sometimes went to bed hungry."

His heart dropped to his knees, though after the whole peanut butter story, he shouldn't have been surprised. "Seriously?" he asked, wincing.

Leah nodded. "Over the years she's told me little bits and

pieces of what it was like for her. If I let myself think about it, it breaks my heart. You and I and Cate and a hundred other kids went to Blossom Branch Elementary, but her world was so very different from yours and mine. We all enjoyed summer vacations and scout trips and Christmas morning with grandparents. Gabby had none of that."

"So what are you saying?" he asked, his fists clenched at his hips. "How am I supposed to know what to do in this situation?"

Leah picked up a duo of dessert plates. "Grab those two," she said. "You take your cues from Gabby. The first moment you know you can't see a future with her, be kind enough to cut her loose. Otherwise, you'll have the pain of two wonderful women on your conscience."

When Jason reclaimed his seat at the dining table, he felt Gabby's eyes on him. But he couldn't look at her. Not yet. Leah's words sobered him.

*Was* he ready to be serious with a woman again? How did anybody know this soon in a new relationship? He liked Gabby. Clearly he had been attracted to her when they were in college. And recently in an Atlanta coffee shop that smelled of holidays and second chances, it was as if something had slammed into his chest.

He could chalk simple lust up to the fact that he'd been celibate for a very long time, since Peru in fact. But if that were the reason, wouldn't he have been pursuing other women? Until Gabby, sex had been a physical need, but nothing more. Now, he couldn't think of anything but having her. Binding her to him. Creating an intimacy she couldn't deny.

She touched his knee under the table. When he glanced at her, startled, she lowered her voice. "You okay?" she asked. Lucas and Leah were squabbling over whether the pie was too tart or just right.

He swallowed. "I'm great."

They had lingered over lunch an entire two hours. For Jason, the meal had been both absolution and pleasure. He liked Leah's fiancé. Plus, having a chance to offer his apologies to Leah had loosened the knot in his chest.

Despite Leah's protests, the other three adults helped clear the table and clean up the lunch debris. Jason was impressed with the updates Leah had done to her great aunt's house. The kitchen was perfect. None of the classic lines had been erased. Leah had found appliances that functioned happily in the current footprint.

When everything was in good shape, Gabby hugged her friend. "This was so much fun. Thanks for inviting us." She went up on her tiptoes and kissed Lucas's cheek. "I know you're taking good care of her. She smiles all the time."

Lucas laughed. "I do what I can. Leah is the best thing that ever happened to me. I don't forget that."

Leah pulled Gabby aside for a moment as the men went into the living room to see the new TV Lucas had installed.

Leah lowered her voice. "Why are you being so weird with Cate? She says you've hardly seen each other in ages. Every time the two of you set up a lunch date, you cancel at the last minute. What's going on, Gabby? Is it because of Jason?"

"Of course not. He and I ran into each other only recently. No, it's my fault, I guess. Work stuff crops up at the worst possible time. But I did see Cate when her store opened. Remember?"

Leah nodded, though her expression was skeptical. "I remember. But that was all of five minutes a year ago...and the opening day chaos meant she barely had time to talk to us. I don't really think that counts. She's worried she did something to upset you. Is that true, Gabby? Has Cate offended or angered you somehow?"

Guilt knotted in Gabby's stomach. "Of course not. Don't be silly."

"Promise me you'll talk to her," Leah insisted. "Soon. Before she worries herself to death."

"I'll try," Gabby said weakly, feeling the little white lie stick in her throat. How could she call Cate when she had no idea what to say?

Fortunately, the men returned to the foyer, saving Gabby from more uncomfortable conversation.

Jason offered his thanks as Gabby had, and soon they were out the door and on the road. He waited until Gabby fastened her seat belt. "Back to your mom's now?"

She shook her head slowly. "Not yet. I want to show you something."

There was an odd note in her voice he couldn't decipher. "Sure," he said. "Just tell me where to go." She and Leah must have had a serious, though brief, conversation while Lucas showed him the massive new TV. Something about Gabby's mood had changed.

She sent him on a winding journey—outside of town, like the route to her mother's place, but in yet another direction. Finally they stopped at a small gravel parking lot. There were no buildings around.

"We'll get out on foot from here," she said.

Jason grabbed a coat and wool scarf. The sun had disappeared, making the brisk breeze icier and less friendly.

Gabby bundled up, too. "This way," she said.

They were walking down a two-lane road that hadn't been repaired in years by the look of it. Maybe it was no longer a maintained highway. On either side, barbed wire fencing bordered what looked to be empty fields.

Eventually they rounded a bend, and Gabby stopped. "This is it," she said. "That trailer is where I lived as a little kid."

If she was trying to shock him, it worked. The single-wide mobile home was overgrown with weeds and bushes. The front door stood open drunkenly. Much of the metal frame was rusted out.

He cleared his throat. "How long?" he asked. "How long before your mother moved to where she is now?"

Gabby shoved her hands in her pockets, her expression pensive. "I think I was in second or third grade. I know so little about the past when I was very young. She's never been willing to talk about it. My guess is that her parents threw her out when she got pregnant. She and my dad must have lived here until his motorcycle accident. I'm sure the trailer was in better shape two decades ago. It's been almost three now."

"And how did she have the resources to move to her current home?"

"From what I've pieced together, a lawyer helped her pro bono. There were psychiatric exams. The state almost took me away from her. But the attorney found a social worker who agreed that my mother was competent enough to care for me. Between the two of them, they got her qualified for a government benefit. Those small monthly checks were enough to buy food and slowly purchase the house she's in now. I suspect someone sold it to her below market value. The floors are uneven, and the Formica countertops in the kitchen are chipped. You've seen all that, I'm sure. It's her safe space."

"But you'd like her to be in Atlanta with you."

Gabby nodded. "It's selfish on my part. It would make my life much easier. I worry about her."

"It's possible you're too close to the situation," he said quietly. "You've been her guardian angel for so long. Maybe she has improved. Slowly. Slowly enough that it's hard to see."

His companion glared at him. "You spend one night at her house, and suddenly you're an authority?"

It was a fair point, but his perspective had value. "Easy,

Gabby. I'm not the enemy. I think it's admirable that you want to move her to Atlanta. But from what I've seen in this brief time, she's managing well. She's in her forties, not her eighties. Sometimes people get better."

Gabby rubbed her nose with a woolly glove. "It's freezing out here," she said. "Let's go home."

In the car, they stripped off their outerwear. Again, he saw the soft pale yellow sweater she wore. With her dark hair, it was a great color. She glowed.

"Tell me why you took me there," he said.

She chewed the edge of her thumb. Her legs were curled beneath her. "I need you to know how different you and I are."

"Why?"

She was quiet for so long, he thought she wasn't going to answer, but then she exhaled. "We both feel a pull between us. You've apparently been punishing yourself with celibacy for the last year and a half. I've never been good with men, so celibacy is my default, too. It's possible we may end up in bed together. Because we're horny. Or lonely. Or some combination of both."

His heart jumped. Other body parts twitched. "I see."

"I'm not sure you do, Jason. What I'm trying to tell you is that sex is one thing, but there's absolutely zero possibility I'll confuse physical intimacy with a long-term relationship. You don't have to worry about getting involved in a situation that you'll have to walk away from. If anything happens, it will be mutual and temporary."

"And that rusted-out trailer?"

"I wanted you to see the real me. If I get naked with you, I want to know you know me and choose me."

He pulled over in the center of town and slid into a parking spot near the gazebo. "That's ridiculous. You're not a rusted-out trailer. You're a sexy, talented, beautiful woman."

"You know what I mean."

He turned off the engine and turned sideways in his seat. "I don't think I do. I'll agree that we had very different child-hoods. What does that have to do with now?"

She huffed. "You're not even trying to understand."

"Maybe we should communicate another way." He slid his hands underneath the silky swing of her hair and cupped her slender neck in his hands. "I do want to know you, Gabriella. Starting right now."

When he took her mouth, he was aware at some level that he hadn't asked permission. Her lips carried the faint, sweet tang of limes and whipped cream when he kissed her and slid his tongue against hers. His sex pounded as Gabby's lips clung to his. Her arms went around his neck. Beneath his fingertips, her skin was soft, so soft.

"I want you," he said gruffly. "So much. But I need to know you want this, too."

She pulled back and stared at him as if he were not making sense. "Can't you tell?"

"Yes. But the words would be nice."

Gabby rubbed her thumb along his stubbly jaw. "I would like to have sex with you, Jason Brightman. Soon and often. Just thinking about it puts me in a festive mood. How would you feel about a red bow on your—"

He put his hand over her mouth briefly. "Brat." Resting his forehead against hers, he sighed. "I thought this was going to be another lonely, awful Christmas. Last year on the twenty-fifth, I was in a tiny mountain village in Switzerland. I swear everyone I met there was part of a couple, even the old people."

"Poor baby." She kissed him softly.

"You smell good," he muttered. His brain raced to calcu-late logistics. They couldn't make love in Dahlia's house. And it was too cold for outdoor frolicking.

Gabby read his mind. "We can wait," she said. "Anticipation is part of the fun, don't you think?"

"I do not think." He groaned. His body was one big ache. In fact, he couldn't remember feeling so desperate.

She scooted away from him. As much as the confines of the front seat would allow. "Turn on the engine, please," she said, giving him a wistful smile. "Let's go to Mom's. That's why we came this weekend. The other stuff can wait until later."

Gabby knew Jason was on edge. She was, too. Their conversation in the car might have clarified a few points, but it had also exposed and intensified the stinging need between them. Honestly, those feelings terrified her as much as they beckoned.

Fortunately, the mundane afternoon kept things on an even keel. She found herself frustrated, though, when her mother let Jason do chores that Gabby had been offering to take care of for months.

First he put new bulbs in the burned-out floodlights on the four corners of the house. Then he ran to the home improvement store, bought two pieces of lumber, and came back to replace rotten wood around one of the soffits.

Gabby stood inside with her mother and watched him work.

"Mama," Gabby said, trying not to reveal her impatience. "I've told you for months I can do jobs around the house. In fact, I could have already done any of this stuff Jason is doing for you today."

Dahlia smiled and patted her arm. "I didn't want you to, sweetheart. You're so little. I'd hate for you to get hurt."

"I'm five-foot-ten. Not little at all."

"I mean your body. Men are much more suited to this kind of work. Look how fast Jason gets things done. He's a lovely boy. So polite and helpful."

Gabby fell silent, knowing she had lost the battle. Her mother ascribed to a worldview where gender roles were clearly spelled out. Despite understanding that, it hurt Gabby to know her mother didn't trust her to tackle certain tasks. And to be honest, she was surprised her mother had warmed so quickly to Jason.

As a rule, Dahlia was guarded around new people. She didn't trust easily. With Jason, she acted as if he had been part of their lives forever.

By five thirty, it was too dark for Jason to do anything else outside. When he came in to warm up, Gabby whispered an apology. "I'm sorry," she said. "I only meant for you to help with the Christmas tree. I can't believe she asked you to do all that other stuff."

He rubbed his hands together as he stood in front of the fire. "I offered, Gabby. It's fine. In fact, I like the physical labor. That's part of the reason my fixer-upper house is so much fun. Hard work can be its own reward."

She rested her head briefly on his shoulder. He smelled of cold air and fresh lumber and a masculine scent that was uniquely his. "Thank you for helping her," she said.

He kissed her cheek, a quick, circumspect caress. "You're welcome."

This was not what either of them wanted. A chaperoned evening with no intimacy in sight. Even so, she offered him the truth. "I'm glad you're here this weekend."

"Me, too," he said.

Dahlia fixed spaghetti and meatballs for dinner along with store-bought rolls. Gabby threw a salad together in a nod to healthy eating.

Jason was visibly enthusiastic as he plowed through two enormous helpings. "This is fabulous, Dahlia," he said. "Really, really good."

She beamed. "I'm glad you like it. I rarely cook just for me. It's too much trouble. But feeding a man with a healthy appetite is fun."

He chuckled. "You can feed me anytime."

Gabby couldn't help rolling her eyes, though she doubted

either of her tablemates noticed. They were too involved in their mutual admiration society.

Jason grinned at Gabby's mother. "You know, Dahlia, someone else who I'm sure would enjoy a home-cooked meal is the guy I met at the Christmas tree lot. Dave Langford? You seemed unsure about going *out* with him. But why not invite him here? He can see his tree all decorated, and you can feed him."

Dahlia's face went pink, and her gaze brightened. "Oh, I don't think so," she said, her fingers fluttering as she moved the salt and pepper shakers first one way and then the other. "He's very sophisticated. Plus, I'm no good on the phone. My tongue gets tangled up, and I never know what to say."

Jason chuckled. "He was wearing overalls and a cotton shirt last night. Doesn't seem so sophisticated. Besides, from what I observed at his tree lot, everyone in town likes and respects him."

Gabby scowled. "Butt out, Jason. This isn't a subject that concerns you."

Her mother patted Jason's hand. "Don't mind my sweet daughter. She's always been a little prissy."

"Mama!" Gabby was torn between embarrassment and hurt. *Prissy?* Was that how other people saw her?

Jason shot her an apologetic smile but didn't put a stop to the conversation. "You're young and beautiful, Dahlia. It's natural for some man to notice and want to snap you up. Have you ever thought about dating again?"

Gabby stared at her mother as a stranger would and realized that Jason's words were true. Her mother *was* beautiful. A hard life had added extra years to her face, but Dahlia Nolan was attractive. Her air of vulnerability would appeal to many men. Dave was obviously one of those.

Still, Dahlia might not have the ability to interact confidently with a man.

Apparently her mother had the same thoughts.

Dahlia smiled wistfully at Jason. "I'm sure my daughter has told you about the past. To be honest, I've *never* dated. Gabby's father and I were children playing at being grown-ups. When he was ki—" She paused, took a deep breath, and continued. "When he died, that was it for me. My only focus was little Gabriella."

"But she's turned into a successful woman. You cared for her and nurtured her. Isn't it time for *you* to have a fulfilling life?"

"I don't know if I have the courage to call Dave."

Gabby inserted herself. "Do you want to, Mama?"

The small kitchen fell silent. It was startling when the ice maker made a loud clunking noise.

Her mother stared at her, then at Jason. "I think I do." She clapped both hands over her mouth. "I can't believe I said that."

Jason squeezed her hand, smiling. "Gabby and I could drive you out to the tree lot tomorrow. That way you can sleep on it—be sure it's what you want to do—and you'd be able extend your invitation in person, not on the phone."

Gabby was as nervous as her mother. This idea was nice in theory, but the ramifications could be huge. And possibly negative.

"Jason," she said.

Dahlia interrupted, her gaze on Jason's face. "You're a man." She wrinkled her nose and wrung her hands. "Be absolutely honest. This is the twenty-first century. Will he be expecting intercourse on a first date?"

Jason was obviously flustered and rattled. But to his credit, he answered gently. "Sex is a part of most adult relationships. But usually not on the first date, and not if you don't want that kind of intimacy so soon. I imagine Dave expects to enjoy your company. That's it. If the relationship continues after one date, you can decide if you want to talk about anything more personal. Communication is the key." He stopped, chagrinned. "Although I sure as hell didn't take my own advice with Cate."

He included Gabby in his gaze. "If I had communicated more honestly, we could have avoided the disaster that was our wedding."

"I know you're right," Dahlia said. "Dave is a nice man, and I've known him one way or another for at least a decade."

Gabby frowned. "He looks older than you. Has he ever been married?"

"I think so. A long time ago. Somebody told me his wife died. So maybe we have that in common."

It was a dark connection. Gabby sighed. "You don't have to rush into anything, Mama. But I'll support you in whatever you want to do."

Dahlia beamed. Her face was still flushed with excitement. "I'll think about it overnight. We'll see how it looks in the morning."

# Chapter 7

Jason was no longer a tree-decorating virgin!

After he hung the fourth or fifth ornament on the Fraser fir, his blood pumped with holiday cheer along with a hefty dose of longing for the woman at his side. Gabby took the task very seriously. Having her so close, bending and reaching and smelling wonderfully feminine, distracted him time and again.

Was she enjoying this as much as he was? Or was their quietly choreographed dance around the tree simply a chore...something to be checked off a list of things she did for her mom?

The dynamic between parent and child was complicated, but sweet. Perhaps neither of them realized it, but they each mothered the other. The love between them was tangible. They had weathered hard times over the years.

Now Gabby was making sure her mother reaped the rewards of surviving.

Earlier, Dahlia had unearthed an old boom box that played cassettes. Her *Time-Life Christmas Treasury* filled the room with classic tunes.

Jason hummed along, feeling lighter than he had in months.

Unlike the old days he had seen in movies, the tree lights weren't a problem at all. They were new and in good condition. Six or seven strands of small, multicolor LED bulbs were now woven deeply into the recesses of the tree and all along the branches.

The ornaments were the final challenge.

Dahlia had boxes of them. Lots of boxes. Some ornaments from Gabby's childhood. Some from yard sales and rummage sales. A few nicer ones from shops in town. Dahlia hovered more than she helped. She seemed to enjoy watching. In a mathematical ratio, she probably only hung a single ornament for every three her daughter placed.

No one seemed to mind.

The tree was tall. Gabby and her mother filled the lower half methodically with fatter ornaments at the bottom and medium-size ones on the way up.

Jason's job was to stand on the ladder and let them hand him all the small bits and pieces. Glass Santas. Tiny glitter-dusted balls in red and green and gold. Silver crescents that looked like winter moons.

Eventually his back ached from reaching over and around the top of the tree, but he wouldn't have changed a thing. He had grown up with every toy and game a kid could want. Yet nothing in his childhood holiday preparations had come close to the quiet satisfaction in this room.

When they were finally done, Dahlia excused herself to go make hot chocolate. Gabby stayed behind with him, walking around the tree time and again to move first one ornament and then another.

He snagged her wrist. "It's perfect, Gabby. You can stop now."

She looked at him, their gazes almost eye to eye. He could

see the length of her lashes and the shades of gray in her irises. The dewy perfection of her skin.

"I don't ever stop for long," she said, her words wry. "My whole adult life has been spent on a treadmill of earning money and looking out for my mom."

"And you've succeeded in both areas admirably." He rubbed her cheek with his thumb. "Maybe you can cut yourself some slack. Maybe Dahlia can take care of herself."

Gabby frowned. "Why are you pushing this so hard? What's it to you? She's not *your* mom."

"No," he said. "She's not. But think about it, Gabby. She will likely live another four decades. That's a long time to be alone."

Her eyes widened. "When you say it like that, it sounds awful."

"And what happens when you marry and have kids? Your attention to her will be divided by necessity."

"I doubt I'll get married," she said. Her gaze slid away from his, though they were still so close he could inhale her scent.

"Why not?" He lifted her chin so he could see the expression in her eyes.

Gabby shrugged. "Look at what happened to you and Cate. If you hadn't finally pulled the plug, you would both have been stuck in a marriage that wasn't right. I don't want to take the chance. The averages are against me. I'd rather depend on myself than rely on a man who might or might not live up to his promises."

When she walked away from him—to join her mother in the kitchen—he let her go. The words stung, even though he knew she was talking about marriage in general and not him specifically. The topic made him restless.

He missed Cate's friendship. They had been tight for a long time. But the farther the calendar moved away from that miserable June 7 of the year before, the more he realized Cate had been like a beloved sister to him.

Gabby, on the other hand, was an entirely different proposition. No sibling emotions there. She was prickly and reserved. Private and reticent. Her body was tall and slender. Her personality was like an iceberg, all the interesting and dangerous parts below the surface.

He craved her in every way. Physically, he wanted her in his bed. Mentally, he found her sharp intelligence challenging and fascinating. Emotionally, he understood her hesitation when it came to their fledgling relationship. Neither of them felt a hundred percent confident they should be together.

What did that mean in the big picture?

When the two women returned with snacks, he took his and sat in an armchair, content to listen to mother and daughter chatter.

When the cocoa mugs were drained and the popcorn bowls empty, he set his on the floor. "What's on the schedule for tomorrow?" he asked. "Aside from a possible visit to Dave's tree lot?"

Dahlia shot Gabby a look and raised both eyebrows.

Gabby sighed audibly. "Mama likes me to go to church with her, but it's not my favorite thing to do. Her friends fuss over me like I'm a new baby trotted out for photographs. It's embarrassing."

Her mother patted her arm. "Won't be as bad in the morning. They'll all be gaga over handsome Jason."

The tops of his ears went hot. "I'd just as soon not go to church," he said. "No offense, Dahlia. But I'm sure some of that crew will put two and two together and realize I'm the nasty groom who left the town's favorite Peach Blossom queen at the altar. I'd rather keep a low profile."

"Nonsense," Dahlia said, her tone brooking no opposition. "That was ages ago. Besides, church isn't about you or me or Gabby. We're there to worship the good Lord and give thanks for our blessings."

Jason was struck silent for a moment. Dahlia had led a life of heartache, deprivation, and hardship. But she was one of the most positive people he had ever met. Her outlook on life humbled him.

Before he could protest further, Gabby's mother yawned. "Thank you so much for getting the tree up. It looks incredible. I'll enjoy it all month."

"And you'll make sure to keep it watered?" Gabby said, her tone worried.

"Of course, baby girl. I may be scattered sometimes, but I don't have a death wish. Besides, I'll put reminders in my phone. Technology is a wonderful thing. Good night, you two. I'm going to get ready for bed and read the new Tom Clancy book I got from the library. It's a nail-biter. See you in the morning."

She kissed her daughter, gave Jason a little wave, and then disappeared down the hall.

Gabby exhaled. "I'm sorry, Jason. You do *not* have to go to church with us. I can't get out of it, but you're a free agent. I'm sure you can entertain yourself."

This entire evening made her wonder if he regretted inviting himself along for the weekend. The tree took forever. And now Dahlia was putting the screws on for church attendance.

He sprawled on the sofa, stretched out his legs, and exhaled. "It's not a big deal. Is this the same place with the peanut butter crackers?"

She winced inwardly. Why had she ever told him that story? "Same building. Partly the same congregation. New minister. In fact, I've only met Pastor Garvey once. I got the impression he thinks the big city of Atlanta is a cesspool of sin and corruption."

Jason laughed, his blue eyes gleaming with humor. "Well, he's not entirely wrong, now, is he?"

"Very funny." She sat down beside him but at a circumspect

distance. "The tree is beautiful," she said quietly. "Thanks for all you did to help."

She loved this time of the day. Dark outside. The tree sparkling with light. Maybe she would put one up in her own apartment this year.

Jason reached for her right hand and played with her fingers. "You have a heck of a lot of rules about romance, Ms. Nolan. But I've decided you're worth the wait."

She wanted to jerk her hand away, not because Jason made her uncomfortable, but because his touch turned her stomach wobbly and her breathing weird. It was a phenomenon that scared her.

Her adult life was defined by control. That word more than any other. Her days were filled with order and routine. *She* called the shots. She made things happen.

Because she was educated and self-aware, she knew that her chaotic and sometimes upsetting childhood had transformed her into the woman she was today. She seldom took chances. Her money was deposited safely in the bank, not tied up in the frighteningly volatile stock market.

Now she was faced with an almost impossible decision. She could end things with Jason tomorrow afternoon. Tell him she wasn't interested.

To say those words would be a bald-faced lie, but it was the safe choice and one that left her in control. There would be no surprises.

As much as she tried to take that road, she couldn't. After years of thinking about him, fantasizing about him, admiring him from afar, Jason was here now. Beside her. Warm and alive and *real*. Not someone else's fiancé.

"You can't know that for sure," she said quietly. She let her fingers twine with his, aghast that such a simple, chaste action stole her breath.

"Know what?" he asked.

"Know that I would be worth the wait. I have very little sexual experience. Even worse than that, I don't let people into my life easily. You would probably be frustrated with me. There are less complicated women out there."

He slid his arm behind her and cuddled her against his shoulder. "I'll take that chance, Gabby. Besides, you don't have to let me in. I've *already* been part of your life for almost a decade. On the periphery, true. But we share friends and experiences. UGA. Hot autumn afternoons on the quad. Raucous football games. Challenging classes."

"You're talking about kids in college. We've been out in the world for a long time now. I've barely seen you for the last six or seven years. You and Cate spent time in Paris. By the time you returned, I was already at Grimes & Hancock."

He played with her hair, sliding his fingers though the strands and stroking her ear. "We're dancing around the real issue," he said, the quiet words neither humorous nor light. "You don't feel like you know me. You wonder if I still have a thing for Cate. You aren't sure if you can trust me."

Gabby froze. Was he right?

She sucked in a shuddering breath. "I *want* to know you," she said, the words sticking in her throat. "I *want* to trust you."

"And Cate?"

Their bodies were pressed together, side to side. Her arm wrapped around his waist in front. Her face nestled against his broad chest. Anyone walking into the room would see a couple enjoying time together. Gabby wanted to throw caution to the wind and coax him to her bedroom. The clawing need in her belly was fierce.

Beneath her cheek, she could hear the steady beat of his heart. Though she had always been overly aware of her height, with Jason she felt secure and warm. He was a man, and though she would bristle if anyone suggested she was the weaker sex, she liked the feeling of being sheltered. Protected.

"Cate isn't part of this," she said flatly. "If you wanted her, you would have married her. Even though it's unsettling for me to be one of her best friends and to contemplate getting cozy with *you*—her ex—it is what it is. I don't think that's a problem."

She felt the deep sigh that lifted his chest.

"So it's the knowing and trusting we need to work on," he said.

"Yes. I need time, Jason. It's been only days since you walked into that coffee shop, not months. I want to be sure."

"Got it." The tone in his words was an odd mix of grumpy and resigned. "You'll have to tell me the boundaries. I don't want to screw this up."

She had a feeling he was making fun of her, but she let it slide. "Kissing is nice," she said.

"We're not sixteen. What if we go too far?"

Those last six words sent a thrill through her body. She sucked in a shuddery breath. "There's no danger right now. Mama is in the next room."

He half turned to face her. "Is that an invitation, Ms. Nolan?"

She stared at him, memorizing the masculine features, the golden hair falling over his brow. The eyes that were indigo in this light. "Kiss me, please," she said. "I've wanted you to all day."

His face darkened, and his jaw went tight. "All you had to do was ask."

When he dragged her close, the embrace was equal parts desperate and frustrating. She wanted to see his bare body, touch all that smooth tanned skin. Instead, she let him coax her into the deep end with only a kiss.

His lips were warm and firm. They moved on hers with exactly the right pressure. After so many years of no kisses or disappointing kisses, she was ravenous. Her arms tightened around his neck. Her breasts ached. Her sex throbbed with a need only Jason could satisfy.

She barely noticed when he eased her onto her back and moved on top of her.

They were fully clothed. With a chaperone in the house.

Nothing was going to happen.

But when Jason gave her his full weight, tears burned her eyes. One slipped down her cheek.

"What's wrong?" he asked, the words sharp. "Am I hurting you?" He levered himself up on one arm and stared at her. A muscle ticked in his jaw.

"No, no," she said. "It feels wonderful."

Their gazes clashed, his hot with hunger, hers silently begging him to understand. Maybe she was a fool to think they could control this.

Jason came down on her again and sank his teeth into the curve where her neck and collarbone met. She moaned, her body burning from the inside out. "I want you," she whispered. "It's killing me."

He ground his pelvis against hers, his arousal evident. "Join the club," he groaned. "I think I have to get out of this house."

When he lurched to his feet, she was shocked. "Don't go."

His expression softened. "It's the only way, Gabby. This is too much and not enough. I'll be back in the morning."

She straightened her sweater, sat up, and made a snap decision. "We can go for a drive," she said. "I'll leave a note so Mama won't worry."

Jason stared at her, frowning. "A drive?"

"I know places we could park where no one will bother us."

The frown deepened. "Or we could grab a room at one of those generic motels out by the interstate."

"That seems sleazy."

"And doing it in the back seat of my car on a cold winter night doesn't?" He ran his hands through his hair. "You told me you needed time. I won't be the one who breaks those promises we made."

"I don't think we made any promises," she said. "I said some stuff and you listened. I do trust you, Jason."

"And you know me?" The words were staccato sharp.

"Not as much as I want to…but I will."

He was still and quiet for so long she had no clue what he was thinking. The tree lights cast rainbow patterns on his face. At last he muttered something inaudible under his breath. "Fine," he said. "Get your coat and write the note."

Gabby escaped to her room, shaking with a combination of nerves and excitement. She and Jason were going to have sex. Now. Tonight. She wasn't going to worry herself about regrets. She would deal with those later.

Though it took an extra three minutes, she removed her bra and changed into a nicer pair of undies, then used the bathroom quickly and freshened up.

There was no light shining from beneath her mother's door. She must be asleep. Which meant that Gabby could take Jason to her childhood bedroom. But if Dahlia wandered through the living room in the middle of the night and saw Jason missing from the sofa, the jig would be up.

The car would have to do.

She found Jason still standing beside the Christmas tree, jingling the keys in his hand. Had he moved at all? She tried to smile at him, but her facial muscles wouldn't cooperate. "I'm ready," she said.

He took three strides and stopped in front of her. "We don't have to do this, Gabby. Time is infinite. I can wait."

The scared, wanting-to-be-in-control part of her almost agreed until a bolder, more selfish Gabby seized the reins. "Maybe we *can* wait, but I changed my mind. I don't want to wait." If she wasn't going to be in a long-term relationship with

Jason, did the timing really matter? She had no experience with a carpe diem version of life.

But she was about to learn.

Gabby grabbed Jason by the shirt collar and kissed him. "Let's go."

The silence in the car on the way should have intimidated her. Made things weird and uncomfortable. Instead, it was intimate. Breath-stealing. Exciting.

Even the holiday songs playing quietly on the radio added to the feeling of hushed expectation.

She directed Jason through town and out onto yet another rural country road. "One of the farmers has a corn maze in October and November," she said. "We can park behind the ticket shed. No one goes there this time of year."

As it turned out, she was right. They passed only a couple of cars on their way. When Jason turned into the gravel parking lot, there wasn't a vehicle in sight. A couple of torn signs flapped in the wind. The medium-size wooden building was not even weatherproof. But it had enough bulk to hide a car.

When Jason slid to a stop and set the brake, she shivered.

He rubbed two fingers in the center of his forehead. "Are we really going to do this?"

"I vote yes. I was a very unexciting teenager. This is new for me."

When Jason turned off the engine, the silence resonated with a thousand emotions. He drummed his fist on the steering wheel. "I wasn't a particularly innocent teenager," he said. "But I've never done this. Last chance. We can go home."

She reached over and traced the shell of his ear with her fingertip. "No going home. No going back."

He caught her hand and held it to his cheek. "I want to know you, too, Gabby. You fascinate me and challenge me and destroy me. You can't imagine how much I need you right now."

She tugged her hand free and rubbed his lower lip with her

thumb. "The feeling is mutual, Mr. Brightman. Why are we wasting time?"

His rough laugh made her smile.

"Okay," he said. "I can't believe we're doing this, but I'm all in. Back seat or back of the car?"

The question held heat. She debated her options. "If we're in the back seat, we don't have to open the doors and let cold air in…"

"We can climb over both seats."

"I don't want to waste all my energy."

"Good point. Back seat it is. I'll go first and help you over."

"Um…" She gulped inwardly. No way was this going to be a graceful look for her. Before she could protest, Jason had rolled over the seat and settled onto his back with his head behind the passenger seat.

"Come on, Gabriella."

On the street side of the rough building, a telephone pole supported a large security bulb and fixture. Even in the back where they were parked, a faint glow kept the car from being completely in the dark. She slipped out of her coat. Jason wasn't wearing his. She also kicked off her black leather ballet flats.

The logistics of this maneuver were more complicated than she anticipated. She was a runner, not a gymnast. Being nervous and scared and excited didn't help.

"Here goes," she muttered.

"I've got you, woman." His smile was wicked.

She put one leg over the seat, rolled, and lost her balance, landing on her partner with a thump.

# Chapter 8

Jason was caught between heaven and hell. Gabby's knee had come dangerously close to unmanning him. Most of the air whooshed out of his lungs when she landed on top of him. But with an armful of the woman he wanted, all he could feel was satisfaction and breathless anticipation.

His hands found her butt. "Hey, there, beautiful." The words were wheezier than he'd intended them to be.

She raised up and stared at him, her gaze worried. "Did I hurt you?"

"Not at all," he lied. "You feel good in my arms. Not good," he clarified. "Great, amazing, exciting."

Gabby smiled at him, making all the blood in his body rush south. "I don't need a thesaurus," she said, her tone droll.

"Then what *do* you need?" He let his hands roam under her sweater, caressing the plane of her back, tracing her delicate spine.

She moved restlessly. "I forgot to ask about protection," she muttered. "I told you I'm not good at this."

He patted his hip. "I've got what we need. Relax. Breathe."

He heard her sigh as she wiggled into a comfortable position. "This is nice," she said quietly. "Can we get started?"

Should he tell her he had been ready all day? "There's no rush," he said. "I like holding you."

"I left my bra at home."

"I noticed." The heat streaking through his body threatened to incinerate him. What could he do to slow things down?

"Why don't you turn on your right side?" she suggested. "That way we can look at each other."

What would she see in his eyes, he wondered? "Sure," he said gruffly. The seat was barely wide enough for that maneuver.

Gabby turned on her left side and faced him. She hooked one leg over his hip to keep from falling into the floor of the car. "I like looking at you," she said. "You're a beautiful man. You were handsome in college, but maturity suits you."

"Ouch." He winced theatrically. "I'm not *that* old, am I?"

She put one hand under his shirt and laughed softly. "You know what I mean. Is it okay if I undo your pants?"

The artless question sucked every molecule of oxygen from his lungs. He felt dizzy, and his whole body tensed, waiting for something incredible and just out of reach. "Be my guest," he croaked.

He'd left his belt back at the house. On purpose. The logistics of this were going to be tricky. No sense adding to the task.

Gabby unbuttoned his pants and lowered the zipper. His black knit boxers were ordinary. When she reached inside and held his sex, he closed his eyes and ground out a ragged curse. "Maybe we should pause this until after the main event."

Her eyes rounded. "Why?"

He tucked her hair behind her ear. "I think you know why. I want to be inside you when I come."

Something changed in her expression. He watched her process his words. Saw the way a tiny smile lifted the corners of her lips as if his confession delighted her. She leaned forward and kissed him. "I could use my hand the first time. It might be fun."

Her fingers closed around him. Firm. Eager.

"I'm sure it would be *fun*," he said, reminding himself to breathe. "But we'll save that for another day. Please."

She wrinkled her nose. "Fine. Let's be boring then."

He laughed at her attempt to rile him. "We're hiding out in the country in the back seat of my car on a cold December night," he said. "I don't think *boring* is the right adjective. Let me take off your pants."

That shut her up. It was hard to tell in this light, but he thought she blushed. She was wearing thick stretchy tights. Before he tried to lower them, he rubbed her center. "This is where I want to be, sweet Gabby."

Her moan made the hair on his arms stand up. Thick lashes fanned out on her cheeks. Her teeth dug into her bottom lip. "Yes."

He grinned, though she couldn't see his face. "You like that?" He increased the pressure, stroking her firmly, rhythmically.

Gabby's head lolled back. Her chest heaved. "Stop," she said.

He complied immediately. "Why?"

She opened one eye and glared at him. "Same reason as you. I'm on a hair trigger. I want us together when the fireworks go off."

"No pressure for me," he teased. "Okay then. Let's get the first one out of the way so we can play."

Both of her eyes flew open. She stared at him. "Play?"

"You don't think once is going to be enough, do you?"

Her openmouthed astonishment told him they were going to have a lot of fun.

"I'm all yours," she said.

The way she stared at him as he wrestled her pants and undies to her ankles and removed them increased his arousal a hundredfold. "How do you want to do this?" he asked, barely able to get the words past the lump in his throat.

"Um..." She stroked his belly, careful to avoid his pulsing arousal. "You on top is fine," she whispered. "I'd like that."

He swallowed hard. "Then top it is." He sat up awkwardly, trying to give her room to move. "On your back, my lady." He extracted protection from his pocket, rolled it on, and shimmied his pants to his hips. One of them had to stay mostly dressed in case they had to make a run for it.

With Gabby looking up at him as he settled between her thighs, he felt the huge weight of what was about to happen. She trusted him. Perhaps not in the long term, but for now. For tonight.

When he slipped two fingers inside her, he found her more than ready.

The whole situation was ludicrous. But he couldn't have walked away if someone had held a gun to his head. He leaned down and kissed her. "You okay?"

She nodded. Her hands gripped his upper arms as he lowered his body and entered her. She wrapped her legs around his waist. When she breathed his name, he almost came right then. Instead, he tried listing states and capitals in his head.

The way her body took his, squeezed his sex, welcomed him with a soft gasp, made him shudder. The hard jolt of pleasure was incandescent. He didn't remember ever feeling such a frantic mixture of raw sensuality and ragged need.

Gabby hadn't said a word. When he went deep the first time, she closed her eyes. They were closed even now. He didn't like that.

"Look at me," he demanded.

When she did as he asked, her expression was obscured by the shadows. And she was silent.

"Gabby. Is this what you want? Do I need to stop?" He

couldn't bear the thought that she already regretted their crazy coupling.

She put a hand on his cheek. "Don't *ever* stop," she said. "This is perfect."

After hearing validation that they both wanted the same thing, he lost his wits. His world narrowed to feeling and emotion. He thrust long and hard. Moving inside her was better than seeing Inca ruins at sunrise. In Peru he had felt exhilarated but deeply alone. With Gabby, he discovered a connection that defied logic.

When he first entered her, he worried he would be too close to the edge to please her. Now he found a deep vein of patience. He kissed her once…twice.

"Gabby," he groaned. "Your body is amazing. So soft. So warm."

The flash of her smile was sweet and teasing. "I can't feel my feet," she whispered. "But I don't even care."

He nuzzled her neck and nipped her earlobe with his teeth. "Should I cut to the finish? I'd hate for you to get hypothermia."

She put both hands in his hair, massaging his scalp. "You're very good at this. I don't want it to be over. But…"

When he slid his hands under her ass, even her goose bumps had goose bumps. "My poor, frozen sweetheart." He was torn between reaching for the precipice and never wanting the moment to end. He felt intoxicated, powerful…as if he could conquer the world. Yet in tandem with those embarrassingly macho urges, tenderness swamped him.

Even as his entire body quivered on the edge of bliss, he concentrated on pleasing her. With one hand, he shoved her sweater upward. Then he bent and found the sharp-nubbed tip of her breast. When he bit down, Gabby cried out. Her body convulsed around his, triggering his own almost violent release.

He came long and hard, his face buried in the curve of her neck. His lover's fingernails sank into his shoulders. They strained against each other greedily, wringing the last drop of satisfaction from the moment.

Breathing heavily, he slumped against her.

Eventually, it was silent—even the sound of their breathing no longer audible.

He felt Gabby shiver hard.

"Oh, damn," he said, feeling groggy. "We've got to get you home." He leaned over the front seat and retrieved a handful of napkins from the glove box. "Here," he said, offering them to his quiet partner. "Do you want me to help?"

"No," she said, the single word scandalized. "I can do it."

In the end, he *did* have to help with her leggings. There was no room to maneuver. Finally, they were both appropriately dressed. But her feet were bare.

"Where are your socks?" he asked, wondering if he had ripped them off and not remembered.

Gabby chuckled. "Nobody wears socks with ballet flats. You're such a *guy*."

He frowned. "Well, at least a *guy* knows to wear socks in December." When he took her feet in his lap and rubbed them, he was more than concerned. "I'll turn the heat on," he said. "Your toes are probably blue."

"I'm fine."

Her words weren't convincing. He climbed over to the front and then helped Gabby execute the same maneuver. "Put on your coat," he said. Then he started the engine and bumped the heat up several notches. "Better?"

Gabby nodded as she slid her feet into those impractical shoes. "I'm fine." She fastened her seat belt and huddled into her down jacket.

He doubted her words, but he nodded. "Then let's go."

Neither of them said a word during the relatively brief drive back to Dahlia's house. At one point, he reached for Gabby's hand and held it. Her fingers curled around his.

He felt oddly off-kilter. Almost as if this was a dream.

The very best kind of dream.

When they parked out front, he realized they had forgotten to turn off the Christmas tree. He'd made sure to dampen the fire, but apparently neither he nor Gabby had thought about the tree lights. Even the drapes were still open.

It was an appealing sight, but he was reluctant to go inside.

Gabby must have been on the same wavelength. She sighed. "Earlier you said once wasn't going to be enough."

"True. But I was wrong about that—given the circumstances," he said wryly. "Perhaps if we'd had a soft, warm bed…"

"Maybe there's a reason grown-ups don't do it in the back seats of cars."

"Indeed."

By every metric, making love to Gabby tonight should have satisfied him. Especially after his long, self-imposed period of abstinence. Instead, he wanted her so badly right now his heart raced, and his body trembled.

Gabby exhaled. "We should get out," she said. "It's late. Even if you skip going to church, I still need to be with her tomorrow."

"Of course."

Once they were inside the house, things got weird. Gabby would hardly look at him. "See you in the morning," she said, closing the curtains and scooting toward the door that exited into the hallway.

His bedding was still stacked neatly on a chair in the corner. He couldn't even use that as a ploy to delay her.

"Don't I get to kiss you good-night?" he asked.

Gabby gulped inwardly. This was why she didn't indulge in casual sex. She never knew how to act when it was over.

If she was honest with herself, though, there was nothing at all casual about tonight's shenanigans. She and Jason had done it in the back seat of his car. Was that romantic and sweet, or desperate and tawdry?

It was the third alternative that terrified her. Being with Jason tonight had been searingly intimate. Funny and entertaining, true. But the way he stroked her and held her and moved inside her had felt almost sacred.

Never had she imagined giving herself to him like that. They both had been undeniably greedy and starving for the other's touch. He had whispered words of praise and longing and need. She could still feel the imprint of his hands on her body.

But now they were standing ten feet apart.

She cleared her throat. "I'm not sure that's a good idea."

"Why not?"

His gentle smile weakened her knees. "Well," she said. "I don't have much faith in our self-control."

"Ah. Mine, or yours? Be honest."

"Both," she said bluntly. "If I kiss you right now, there's a good chance I'll drag you to my bed."

"And that's bad?"

"You know it is. I'm not ready for my mother to find out that you and I are sexual partners—which she *would* discover if the sofa was empty."

"Sexual partners?" He grimaced. "That sounds cold. How about lovers?"

Something squeezed inside her chest. Her heartbeat fluttered. "Lovers? Is that what we are?"

When he crossed the room, she stood frozen. He put a finger under her chin and lifted her face toward his. "I *want* to be your lover, Gabby. Tonight was only the beginning." His blue eyes reflected the deep cerulean of a dusky Mediterranean Sea as he stared, laser-focused. The husky, masculine tone of his voice mesmerized her.

She had always thought the image of drowning in someone's gaze was silly hyperbole...over-the-top. This was a heck of a time to find out it was definitely possible. "Oh," she said. Her throat was tight.

Jason smiled. He ran his hands up and down her arms. "I won't kiss you then, Gabby. But we're standing in *my* bedroom, so walk away now."

"I can't," she whispered. She slid her arms around his neck. "I need you to kiss me," she said. "I really, really do."

Every scrap of humor left his face. His eyes darkened. A muscle in his jaw ticked. "You're not being fair," he growled. "Mixed messages."

"I know." She leaned her cheek against his collarbone. "I know." She exhaled, feeling a rush of power that was as foreign as it was delightful. "Maybe you ought to spank me for being so unfair to you."

His entire body went rigid. The way his hands tightened on her arms told her he was nearing the edge. "Damn it, Gabby. This isn't funny." He dragged her closer, close enough for her to feel the press of his erection against her belly. "I'm trying to give you what you asked for."

She went up on her tiptoes. "Maybe I was wrong."

When her lips met his, she could swear a coal in the fire hissed. Heat consumed her from the inside out as Jason resisted, his mouth unresponsive.

He was strong and honorable. She knew that much. But the moment he broke was unmistakable. As he growled her name, his arm tightened around her waist, binding her to him. The way he took charge of the kiss was enough to make a woman swoon.

The man knew how to kiss. And honestly, his intensity was flattering. It was as if he had been marooned alone on a remote desert island, and she was the first woman he had seen in years.

Even as his mouth conquered hers, his hands were every-where. Cupping her ass. Tangling in her hair. When she tried to breathe, he held her chin and took the kiss deeper still. "You don't make things easy, do you, Gabby?"

She pulled back, wide-eyed. "What do you mean?"

His gaze was wry, his eyes hooded. "You try so hard to be the good girl and tell me what we *should* do, but..."

"But what?" She frowned.

He cupped her face in one hand. "But a wilder Gabby—maybe *Gabriella*—keeps trying to escape that airtight box you've kept her in. You're not a tight-ass, by-the-book woman. Not really. Every time I touch you, it's like letting a genie out of a bottle. A hot, out-of-control, explosive version of yourself."

The picture he painted threatened her composure. *Out of control?* That couldn't be right. Control was the fuel that kept her life chugging along the track.

"I'm not out of control," she said, the words almost sharp. "I'm merely reaching for what I want. I thought you'd be on board with that."

"I'm on board," he said. "But I'm wondering if you're going to jerk the rug out from under my feet."

"That's not very nice," she muttered.

"But fair. You talk about dragging me to your bed, yet in the same breath tell me I can't kiss you. What's a guy supposed to think?"

She realized he was right. Her words and actions were all over the map. For someone who had always been the smartest person in every class she took, tonight was a lesson in humility. "I'm sorry," she said. "It's possible I'm completely out of my depth. I'll say good-night." She was embarrassed and exhausted and confused. Wanting Jason Brightman had scrambled her brain.

He tunneled his hands in her hair and pulled her close, kissing the top of her head. "We'll figure this out. I promise. Being horny never killed anyone."

"I don't know if that's true," she muttered.

Jason chuckled. "Some guys might try to argue the point, but don't worry. It's true. Good night, Gabby. Sleep well and have sweet dreams. Things always look better in the morning." He leaned in to kiss her on the lips but jerked back at the last moment. "Go," he said, his eyes glittering. "Go."

She turned and fled.

In her room, fatigue rolled over her in a crashing wave. It was all she could do to strip down and climb under the covers. Feeling clean would have been nice, but if her mother woke up, Gabby had no convincing explanation for why she would be showering at two thirty in the morning.

When she finally got still and found a comfy position, the quiet in her room made it possible to hear other things. The crack and pop of the house as the temperature dropped outside. The creaking floorboards as Jason crisscrossed the living room. Shouldn't he be settled on the sofa by now?

Her body felt strange. Half of her hovered on the verge of sleep. The other half kept reminding her what it felt like to make love to Jason.

It was every bit as amazing as she'd always imagined.

Which meant she had made a big mistake. Now that she knew, it was going to be so very hard to be smart about this situation.

Men liked sex. Jason had gone without for a long time. Gabby was convenient. That didn't mean he was her soulmate. She didn't even believe in soulmates.

Sex was about body parts. And orgasms.

She repeated that lecture to herself three times before she gave up. It didn't matter how much she tried to be sensible. Her silly heart yearned.

Still, the truth was the truth. This was only physical. She and Jason were young and healthy and shared a biological attraction. It made sense that they had indulged tonight.

But what about the future?

She'd told herself over the years that she was happiest on her own. That if she let a man into her bed and her heart, he would try to change her or control her. Spending nights with a carton of ice cream and a Netflix subscription had seemed the smartest choice.

Maybe the truth was more embarrassing. Maybe no man had ever lived up to her fantasy image of Jason. It was easy to say no to guys who didn't make her body shiver with longing.

Things were different now. Now she *knew*. Jason was her physical match. Their bodies were in sync. Who cared about more lofty emotions? She didn't love Jason. No way would she let that happen. She wasn't stupid.

But intimacy with him? Oh, yeah. That's what she wanted for Christmas. If Santa was listening, every item on her list was the same:

*Sex with Jason*

*Sex with Jason*

*Sex with Jason*

How did she go forward from tonight? Did she invite him to a sleepover at her apartment? Was his place far enough along for visitors? Was she willing to go to some fancy hotel room and buy privacy?

This whole situation was way outside her comfort zone. And great sex with Jason wasn't comfortable at all. She touched her breast beneath the sheet and sighed.

Was Jason right? Did she truly become a different, out-of-control woman when they were intimate? If so, that was terrifying. She'd been wary of dropping her guard with him, and now look where they were. Even if his lovemaking turned her inside out, could she possibly find a way to control the uncontrollable?

She didn't know what was going to happen next, but for once, she was determined to live in the moment. Maybe even let him take the lead. It might be scary and unsettling, but Jason was worth it...

# Chapter 9

Sunday morning came way too early. When Gabby's alarm went off, she groaned and silenced it. A glance at her phone told her it was far past time to be up if she was taking her mom to church.

For a split second, she contemplated saying that Jason needed to get back to Atlanta. She was sure he would back her up. But the thought of her mother's disappointment stopped that idea in its tracks. If Gabby was going to spend weekends in Blossom Branch, it made sense to pack them with plenty of mother/daughter bonding.

After a quick shower, she decided a ponytail was the way to go. There was no time to wash her hair, and she wasn't in the mood to spend effort making it look good with a styling wand or anything else.

She had brought a specific outfit for Sunday morning. Dahlia didn't approve of her daughter wearing pants to church. Gabby knew her mom would never be critical of anyone else's clothing choices, but for the two of them, a dress code applied.

The skinny navy corduroy skirt she had packed was warm

and comfy. She paired it with a dark teal sweater and knee-high boots. By the time she made it to the kitchen, she was yawning, but presentable.

To her surprise, Jason sat at the table already. He was dressed nicely, too, in dark khaki pants and a forest green turtleneck. The shadows under his eyes only made him sexier and more masculine.

The waffle on his plate was half-eaten. His fork halted mid-air. "Good morning," he said gruffly. No smile. No discernable expression. Nothing to echo last night's madness.

"Hey," she muttered. She kissed her mother's cheek and sat down at the table. "Thank you for fixing breakfast, Mama."

Dahlia beamed. "I know how you like my waffles and bacon. Jason seems to be a fan, too. That's his second one."

Jason looked guilty. "I couldn't help myself. This meal is perfection."

Dahlia chuckled. "Well, if it wasn't December, I'd be serving these waffles with a fresh peach compote. All of us here in Blossom Branch know a hundred ways to enjoy our town mascot."

Gabby swallowed a bite and sighed. "I don't know how you do it, Mama, but these are better than any restaurant."

Jason nodded. "Agreed."

Dahlia joined them. "So tell me, Jason. What do you do for a living? I don't think I've asked you that, and my daughter hasn't mentioned it."

Gabby saw the stricken look on Jason's face and intervened quickly. "He's figuring things out right now, Mama. And renovating a house. Before the wedding was called off, he and Cate were going to open a fancy art gallery in Atlanta. Buckhead, probably. They had planned for Cate to use her art background curating their shop inventory, and they were also going to offer framed prints of Jason's beautiful photography."

Jason was stunned to hear Gabby jump to his defense. Not that he needed defending, but still. "I'm finding my way,

Dahlia," he said. "As Gabby told you, I've bought a fixer-upper house that I'm having fun with. The hard work gives me time to think."

Dahlia cocked her head and stared at him. "If you were Cate's fiancé, I'm assuming your family is well-to-do?"

"Mama!" Gabby flushed, her discomfort obvious.

He smiled. "It's okay, Gabby." He turned to her mother. "To answer your question, yes. The Brightman family has been very lucky down through the years. For several generations in fact. I can't take any credit for that, though."

"What did you study at the University of Georgia?" she asked.

"I did a combo degree in business and marketing."

She took a sip of her coffee. "You're lucky to have so many choices. I know you'll do the right thing." She patted his hand on the table. "Having money is nothing to be ashamed of... unless a person is greedy." She grinned. "My daughter is about to pass out because I'm asking impertinent questions."

Gabby pointed at the clock on the kitchen wall. "The service starts at ten. Shouldn't we be going, Mama? You don't like to be late to church."

Jason was all too aware of his lover's embarrassment. Gabby was bristly as hell when it came to the differences in their economic status. That more than anything was the hurdle he had to cross if he wanted her in his life.

It was funny, really. Ever since he turned fourteen or fifteen, girls had chased him with an eager appreciation for his parents' social status. Now, when he had his eye on a woman who might be important to him and his future, money stood in the way.

His wealth was a subject he and Gabby needed to hash out, but not anytime soon. Right now, it was enough to explore their mutual hunger. Unfortunately, thinking about last night was a mistake. When his body reacted predictably, he excused himself from the table and went into the living room to fold the sheets and blankets he had used on the sofa.

Making love to Gabby changed something in him. Since returning from Peru, his days had been stuck in a rut of regret and guilt. Now, suddenly, he was ready to face the future, whatever it had in store for him or however he shaped it.

Hearing the two women in the kitchen made him smile. Their conversation revealed the depth of their relationship, though they might not realize it. In the back-and-forth of everyday words, the women spoke in a cadence that had been fine-tuned for years.

He called down the hall. "I'm going to warm up the car. You two come out when you're ready."

When the car doors opened a few minutes later, Gabby spoke up. "You sit up front, Mama. I'll be fine in the back." His eyes met hers in the rearview mirror. He couldn't help his teasing smile. Gabby's blush made him want to laugh, but he contained himself.

The little church Dahlia attended was only about half-full as the service began. By the time he and Gabby ended up on either side of her mother in the pew, Dahlia had introduced them to half a dozen of her friends.

Not sitting beside Gabby was probably for the best. Jason didn't trust himself. All he could think about was how long it would be before he could coax her into bed.

The service was fine, though the sermon was a bit heavy on the fire and brimstone angle for his taste. After it was over, he and Gabby lingered in the pew while Dahlia greeted her friends and said hello to the young pastor.

Jason was caught off guard when Gabby took his hand.

"Thank you for coming with us today," she said. "I know this isn't what you expected for a weekend getaway in Blossom Branch, but it means a lot to my mother."

He rubbed the back of her hand with his thumb. "I'd say this weekend has been a home run all the way around. I wouldn't change a thing."

Gabby's cool gray eyes stared at him. Her lips, shiny with pink gloss, curved upward. "Even freezing your very fine ass off in the back seat last night?" She whispered the question, obviously aware of their audience.

His gut tightened as the memories flashed in his brain. "Not a thing," he swore. "You were amazingly flexible, Ms. Nolan. Very impressive."

She laughed softly. "We're in church. Let's change the subject. I'm afraid of getting struck down by a bolt of lightning."

He grinned. "Is that a possibility?"

"I don't want to chance it."

When they stood and turned to join Dahlia, many of the parishioners were gone—with one notable exception. A man chatted with Gabby's mother nearby. He wore a three-piece brown suit and had a shock of familiar gray hair.

"Is that…?" Jason raised both eyebrows.

Gabby nodded. "Dave Langford."

"Should we join them or give them privacy?" he asked.

"How do I know? But to be fair, they're right in the middle of the aisle."

"True."

"Let's go," she said. "My mother may need backup."

The older couple seemed startled when Jason and Gabby joined them, but Dahlia's face showed relief.

Dave greeted them. "I was offering to take Dahlia to lunch. And both of you, too," he said hastily.

Dahlia seemed to gain courage from her daughter's presence. "I thought I might bring Dave home with us," she said. "I'd planned on cooking anyway."

For the span of several seconds, no one said a word.

Jason felt like an intruder.

Gabby found her voice and a smile. "I think that's a great idea. What time do you have to be out at the tree lot, Mr. Langford?"

"Call me Dave," he said. "Someone is covering for me until four." He touched Dahlia's shoulder for the briefest of moments. "I would enjoy a home-cooked meal, Dahlia. Thank you. I'd be delighted to come."

Jason was surprised when Gabby took over the situation. "Could we say one o'clock, Dave? I'll help Mom get everything together, but it will take us a bit."

"Of course. I'll be there at one sharp."

Jason realized Gabby had saved him from entertaining the older man while the women were in the kitchen. In the car, he congratulated Dahlia. "You definitely have an admirer," he said. "And you handled inviting him beautifully."

Gabby spoke up from the back seat. "He's right, Mama. You were perfect. Once you and I have everything ready, Jason and I will sneak away and eat somewhere in town."

"Oh, no," Dahlia said firmly. "I don't want to be alone with Dave. Not yet. I need both of you with me as my wingmen."

Her daughter laughed. "Where did you hear that, Mama?"

"I watch TV. I'm not a hermit."

By the time they made it to the house, Dahlia was working up to a tizzy. She hopped out of the car. "I cooked the chicken breasts this morning, but they're not shredded."

Gabby put an arm around her. "Calm down. We have plenty of time."

Jason followed them up the steps. "What are you making, Dahlia?"

"I thought I'd do chicken enchiladas. I assemble them and bake them in the oven with a sauce on top."

Despite the waffles, his stomach growled. "Tell me what I can do to help."

★ ★ ★

Gabby felt her anxiety rise. She would do anything to keep her mother from getting hurt again. But she couldn't wrap her in cotton wool. Maybe Jason was right. Maybe her mother's interest in Dave Langford was a sign that she had come a long way.

Still, any romantic relationship was a crapshoot. Dave seemed like a nice man, but what if he wasn't? Her stomach knotted.

Jason cornered her as she straightened the living room. "I can do that," he said. "Are you okay, Gabby?"

She clutched a blanket to her chest. "I don't know. It's my job to take care of her. What if this is a bad idea?"

Jason wrapped his arms around her. "We can get a feel for that at lunch. We're both here. And we're both old enough to sniff out a rat. Don't worry."

He kissed her, momentarily interrupting the runaway train of what-ifs.

His lips were warm and firm. When his tongue brushed hers, she found herself embarrassingly weak in the knees. "How do you do that?" she complained. "We're in the middle of a family crisis, and now I want to jump your bones."

"Mission accomplished," he said smugly. Then he rubbed his thumb along her bottom lip, his beautiful eyes dark with what might be the same thing she was feeling. "Any chance we could enjoy each other when we get back to Atlanta tonight?"

She swallowed. "Enjoy?"

"You know what I mean." He kissed her a second time, this one right below her earlobe, making goose bumps break out on her arms.

"Stop that," she said, urgently. "You and I are not important right now. My mother needs our help. See what's going on in the kitchen. I'll be there in a sec."

Jason cupped her cheek in one hand, his expression rueful. "Yes, ma'am. Whatever you say, Boss."

When he was out of sight, she wanted to sit on the sofa and

gather her wits. But there was no time for that. She took the
sheets Jason had used last night to the washing machine and
returned the folded blankets to the hall closet.

After the living room was spotless, she joined the other
two in the kitchen. Dahlia had piled all sorts of things on the
counter. Jason was on his tiptoes, retrieving a casserole dish
from a high cabinet.

"What should I do, Mama?" Gabby asked.

"Start shredding the meat."

Moments later, Jason joined Gabby at the table and helped
her with the messy task. He lowered his voice. "She's freaking
out a little bit."

Gabby nodded, her eyes on the plate of chicken in front of
her. "I know. Should we call this off?"

"I have no idea."

Dahlia buzzed around the kitchen. After a few minutes, she
seemed to zero in on the recipe. She took the bowl from her
daughter and began mixing the tortilla filling. Jason stayed at
her elbow, grabbing whatever ingredients she asked for.

She fretted when she spilled tomato sauce on her church
blouse.

Gabby opened the freezer. "Should I put this pie in the
oven?" It was a packaged apple dessert with streusel topping.

Dahlia nodded.

Gabby had witnessed Jason studying the tortilla process. Now
he stepped in with a suggestion. "I've got this, Dahlia. Why
don't you go to your room and relax a few minutes? Change
your top. Powder your nose. You want to be ready when Dave
shows up. Gabby and I can take it from here, I promise."

Dahlia hugged him, her eyes overbright. "Thank you, sweet
boy." She wiped her fingers on a dish towel and put her hands on
her cheeks. "I'm a nervous wreck. Maybe this was a bad idea."

Gabby hugged her mom. "It will be fun. Don't you worry
about a thing except getting to know Mr. Dave better."

When Dahlia exited the kitchen, Gabby looked at Jason and sighed. "That was exactly the right thing to do. Thank you, Jason. I never would have thought to take over the task."

He shrugged, still making tortillas. "Because she's the mom, and you're the child. It was easier for me."

"Maybe."

While they worked in tandem, she studied him surreptitiously. Even doing something as mundane as assembling a simple meal, Jason looked confident and relaxed. Did it come to him naturally? Gabby felt as if she had lived her whole life striving for relaxation. So far, the concept in general escaped her. Sometimes she thought she had struggled too long to ever find peace...or to recognize it if it ever landed on her windowsill.

Jason shot her a sideways glance. "You okay over there?" His smile held enough heat to make her move restlessly in her chair.

"I'm good," she muttered. He didn't need to know that she envied him.

When they had assembled all the enchiladas, Gabby lined them up carefully in a casserole dish.

Jason wiped his hands. "What about the sauce? And the sides?"

"I know how to mix the sauce. You should be able to find lettuce and cheese in the fridge. I'll get the Mexican rice together and do some beans."

Dahlia returned before her worker bees were done. She had changed clothes and was visibly calmer. "Oh, you two are the best," she said, beaming. She bumped her hip against Gabby's at the stove. "I've got this now. Why don't you two set the table?"

As it turned out, even with three adults participating, the meal was barely ready when Dave Langford rang the doorbell at one sharp. Jason ushered him into the kitchen.

Dave lifted his chin and sniffed appreciatively. "Smells great, Dahlia. My stomach is growling."

Gabby's mother smiled. "I've got plenty."

Over lunch, the four adults conversed about everything from holiday shopping to movies and whether the almanac said they would see any rare Georgia snow this winter. They touched on personal topics, but only briefly.

Dave shared that his first wife had died of cancer when she was very young. Dahlia told him Gabby's father had been killed in a motorcycle accident. There was a good chance Dave had gleaned more of the details over the years. Blossom Branch was a gossipy small town. But he didn't let on.

Finally Gabby touched Jason's arm and smiled at her mom. "If you two will excuse us, Jason and I need to pack up our things. We'll need to get on the road soon."

In the living room, Jason stared at her and lowered his voice. "Well, what do you think? Do we like him? Do I need to break his kneecaps?"

Her lips twitched. "Would you enjoy that? It sounds gruesome."

"I probably don't have it in me. My specialty in high school was making bullies laugh. That always seemed safer than physical violence."

His words were self-deprecating, but she had no doubt he could handle himself in a brawl. Jason was the kind of man who was tough but didn't need to prove it. Something about him made her feel safe, which was completely bizarre, because he could hurt her badly if she let down her guard.

"What time do you want to get on the road?" she asked.

He shook his head slowly. "That's your call. Do we leave her alone with him?"

"I don't know. It's probably fine. Let me grab my things, and we'll make a plan." It didn't take long. She was neat by nature. In ten minutes, she had her suitcase and toiletry kit together.

When she rejoined Jason in the living room, he was ready as well. Before Gabby could say a word, her mother and Dave appeared from the kitchen. Dahlia's expression was radiant. Dave seemed happy, too.

He dipped his head to all three of them. "Thanks for the great lunch. It was a real treat for me." Then he smiled at Gabby's mother, giving her his full attention. "I'll call you this week, Dahlia."

Suddenly he was gone.

In the moment of silence after the front door closed, the three adults left behind stared at each other.

Jason smiled first. "Well, *that* man is smitten."

Dahlia swatted his arm. "Oh, hush. All we did was talk." Her cheeks were pink. She looked as happy as Gabby had ever seen her.

"Will you go out with him, Mama?"

"I think I will. He's a very nice man. We have a lot in common. Both of us grew up here. We've both known sadness and loss. I'm not saying this is going to be a grand love story, but it will be fun to spend time with Dave."

Gabby hugged her mother's neck. "I'm so glad. You deserve to be happy—more than anyone I know."

Jason nodded. "I like him, Dahlia. He obviously has good taste in women."

"Oh, pooh," she said, blushing.

Gabby wanted to wallow in her mother's wonderful mood. But it was after three already. Monday was a workday, and she had plenty of chores to take care of before the new week began. Plus Jason must surely be ready to head home.

They left an hour later, after helping clean up the kitchen. When the house was pristine, Gabby lingered, feeling guilty for no discernable reason. But the feeling was nothing new. Her mother would always be the one left behind when Gabby went back to Atlanta.

In the car, she was quiet. So much had happened in one short weekend. What would Jason expect from her now? What did she want from him?

When he finally spoke, his words had nothing to do with sex or romance or even Dave Langford's courtship of her mother.

Jason lowered the volume on the radio and shot her a glance before returning his attention to the road. "How old were you when you first started feeling responsible for your mother?"

The simple question was shocking. Jason Brightman saw more than she wanted him to see. "What do you mean?" she asked, stalling to come up with an answer.

"You know exactly what I mean. You feel responsible for Dahlia. And from what I can tell, that feeling goes way back. So I'll ask you again. How old were you when you started feeling responsible? Or maybe you don't even know," he said.

*She knew.* But talking about it brought back so many feelings. Hard, terrifying feelings. Feelings no child should have to face.

Jason gave her space and silence. He wouldn't demand anything. But after everything he had done for her mother this weekend, the question wasn't out of place.

"I was twelve," Gabby said. The words were flat. She could talk about this without emotion. Maybe. "Someone had given my mother a car. It had over 250,000 miles, but it ran. We only needed it to get around town. One afternoon, we were headed to the grocery store. It was storming that day, only I'm sure that had nothing to do with what happened. The engine made a loud thumping noise, smoke came out from under the hood, and the car stopped dead. Mama steered it onto the side of the road."

"Must have been scary."

"It was." She nodded slowly. "But that wasn't the problem. My mother simply shut down. Here we were, stranded. And she did nothing. She just buried her face in her hands and huddled against the door."

"Damn, Gabby." He reached out and squeezed her hand.

"We had one of those government-issued phones preloaded with a few minutes a month. I asked her if she was going to call for help. She didn't even answer me."

"What did you do?"

"I knew how to use the phone. I had watched her. And of course we'd had lessons about 9-1-1 at school. I probably could have gotten in trouble for dialing the emergency center—we weren't technically in trouble. But it was the only phone number I knew. So I asked them to come rescue us."

"And did they?"

"Not the police. It was an old guy who owned the wrecker service. He must have felt sorry for us. He hooked up the tow truck and let Mama and me scrunch into the front seat with him. When he dropped us off at the house, that was it. The car was beyond repair."

# Chapter 10

Jason wondered how many times Gabriella Nolan was going to break his heart. How had she survived? He understood Dahlia's making it through. Her courageous, gutsy little daughter had protected her.

But during all those years, the child who should have been able to run and play and have sleepovers with friends had been forced to grow up far too quickly. In some situations, that kind of existence turned a person mean or cynical.

Gabby was neither.

"I'm so sorry," he said. "She's lucky to have you."

His passenger made an odd, strangled noise that sounded almost like wry laughter. But surely not.

"What?" he said. "What did I say?"

"Maybe before this weekend you assumed I was in an unhealthy, codependent relationship where I liked being needed. That my mother really didn't require so much of my attention."

"If I did, I'm sorry again. It's clear she leans on you. But it's also clear that your presence in her life has made a huge difference."

"I only did what I did because she's my mother. When I was an infant and a toddler, she cared for me against all odds. She had breaks with reality, but she kept me safe. She loved me. I owe her more than I can ever repay."

"I understand," he said quietly. Maybe not all of it, but he was beginning to comprehend that Gabby was someone exceptional.

When they pulled up in front of her apartment, Gabby sighed audibly.

"Home again," she said. "Thank you for going with me this weekend."

He put the car in Park and half turned in his seat. "May I come in for a few minutes?" he asked. "Not to stay," he said hastily. "But I want to talk to you about a couple of things, and it's cold out here."

She nodded. "Sure."

He grabbed her bags out of the trunk and followed her up the stairs.

Inside, he set down the luggage as she turned on lights and bumped up the heat. He would have carried the bags to her bedroom but decided at the last second not to go anywhere near her bed. Too much temptation.

"I had a great time this weekend," he said.

"Me, too." Her gaze didn't meet his.

"How about dinner a couple of times this week?"

Her head lifted. Her eyes focused on his face. "That's what you wanted to talk about? What are we doing, Jason?"

He had asked himself the same question. "Having fun?"

Her smile thawed some of his doubts. "There *is* that," she said. "But maybe we should take time to breathe. We jumped into the back seat of your car without thinking this through. Some people would call us reckless."

"What about spontaneity and romance?"

"You said we were horny. And I agreed. Maybe we need to take a step back."

"How about a compromise?" he said, feeling her slipping away from him and facing sheer, icy panic at the thought. "What if we use the workweek to decide what we want? I know your job is very demanding. And my wretched house needs a lot of TLC. We could take the time apart to be sure."

A frown wrinkled the spot between her brows. "Sure of what?"

He put his hands on her shoulders and kissed her forehead. "Sure that this pull we feel is worth pursuing. I've always liked you, Gabby. Long before I ever dated Cate, I asked you out. Surely that means something."

She rested her cheek against his chest. "You know we're far too different to have any kind of permanent relationship. So what we're left with is sex."

"I don't know any such thing." He slid his fingertips up and down her spine. "Five days. And maybe a little sprinkle of Christmas magic. Give me a chance to prove myself."

She toyed with one of his shirt buttons. "You don't have to prove anything to me, Jason Brightman. I'm already in your corner." Suddenly she looked up at him. "You said you wanted to talk about *a couple of* things. What else is there?"

He tucked her hair behind her ear, marveling at the smooth perfection of her skin. "It's my parents," he muttered. "They're having a huge Christmas gala next Saturday night. Black-tie. My presence is not optional. Come with me. Please."

She stiffened in his embrace. "Oh, I don't think so. I'm a homebody. That's not my thing at all."

"It's not mine either, but I have to go."

"There must be a hundred women you could take."

"I don't want anyone but you." As he said the words, something settled in his chest. Certainty. Peace. He had messed up his life so badly, but now he had another chance. Gabby was right for him. How he knew that, he couldn't explain. But he knew.

The question was, could he be the right man for her?

He tunneled his fingers in her hair and kissed her softly, his thumbs brushing her earlobes.

"Jason…" The way she whispered his name in a husky voice sent a flame straight to his gut.

When her arms immediately encircled his neck, he dragged her closer. "You've bewitched me, Gabby."

The kiss went from tender and teasing to desperate and determined in a nanosecond. This was a hell of a way to start their time-out. He didn't want to think things over. What he wanted was her.

Even as his body hardened and his breath sawed in and out of his chest, he tried to be reasonable. He needed her to trust him. Was this moment going to hurt or help his cause? As difficult as it was, he made himself take a step back. Literally.

"Jason?" She stared at him, her expression bewildered.

He shoved his hands in his pockets. "I only came here to talk to you, I swear. I wasn't trying to start something."

Gabby's cute little chin lifted. She looked like a queen facing down a subject who had pissed her off and now faced the consequences. "What a shame," she drawled. There was nothing *contained* about her right now. Emotion flashed and sparked, turning her stunning gray eyes to storm clouds.

"I want to go to bed with you," he said, choosing his words carefully, "but we agreed to a time-out."

Her gaze narrowed, making him sweat. "During the workweek," she said. "Those were *your* words. By my calculations, it's still the weekend. We might as well enjoy one last mistake." Her naughty grin confused him. Was this a test?

He frowned. "That sounds like you've already made up your mind. I don't think I want one for the road. I'm serious about you, Gabby."

Her smile faded. "You shouldn't be. I can't be serious about you. Don't get me wrong, Jason. You're a wonderful man. But you need to find someone else like Cate. A woman who understands and embraces your world."

"Screw that," he said, taking her by the wrist and reeling her into his arms. "I'm pretty damn sure my world is going to be you."

When he kissed her, an uncomfortable blast of confusion and desperation and sheer, wild hunger coursed through his veins. Gabby met him every step of the way. He loved that she was tall. They were perfectly matched.

He scooped her into his arms. "Last chance to change your mind."

She laughed—a low, sexy sound that raised gooseflesh on his arms. "I know exactly what I want tonight. You're wasting time."

At some level, the word *tonight* bothered him, but he was long past picking apart her vocabulary. "Okay then," he muttered. "Tonight it is."

Her bedroom was tidy and serene, much like its owner. Light from the living room spilled through the door. He tumbled her onto the bed and came down beside her, lifting her sweater over her head. Her bra was black mesh. Taut nipples lifted against the semisheer fabric. He touched her breasts, loving the way Gabby squirmed.

"I want to be naked with you," she said.

The imperious demand made him smile. Their interlude in the back seat had been amazing, but it had its limitations. "We'll get to that," he promised.

When he licked her through the bra, her hips came off the bed. "Jason…"

"Jason what?"

She groaned when he bit down carefully on a sensitive nub. "You're too slow," she snapped.

He chuckled, loving the way her personality sharpened in bed. No reticence. No reserve. Only raw, feminine desire. "Slow can be good."

Earlier, before the trip home, Gabby had changed out of her church clothes. Her black leggings were soft and thin enough for him to pleasure her through the fabric. When he moved to the other nipple and at the same time stroked her center firmly, the first orgasm ripped through her like a flash fire.

"I've got you," he whispered, holding her close and tight as she shuddered in the aftermath.

When she finally opened her eyes, her expression was equal parts pleased and worried. "How do you do it?" she asked. "I've never been good at, um…"

"Climbing the mountain?" He grinned down at her.

"Something like that." She plucked at the cloth covering his shoulder. "And we're both still dressed."

"It sounds like you're fixated on the subject of nakedness," he said soberly. "Maybe you should talk to your mom's pastor about that."

"Bite me," she said.

"Already did."

His smug retort made her cheeks flush. "Jason, I…" She trailed off, her expression hard to read.

"What's wrong?" He was so hard, he ached, but he knew tonight was a turning point. If sex was the only connection she accepted for now, he was going to make it good. Perhaps she didn't understand how rare it was to be physically in sync so early in a relationship. Maybe he could show her.

She toyed with his belt buckle, making him shiver. "Nothing's wrong," she said. "That's the problem. I've never felt like this with anyone else. It's freaking me out. How do you know what I like?"

"You always tell me," he said simply.

Suspicion narrowed her brows. "No, I don't. I never said a word."

"Your face and your body are incredibly expressive. I can see what you like and when you like it."

She stared at him with a mix of confusion and alarm. "I'm not sure I'm comfortable with anyone knowing me that well."

"Why?"

"I've not let many people get close to me. Leah and Cate. My mom."

"So it's men you keep at a distance."

"I wasn't a virgin when I got in that back seat with you."

Her mulish retort nearly made him laugh, but he restrained himself. "So you keep telling me."

"It's the truth."

"How many, Gabby? How many men have disappointed you?"

"Is this where we do the number thing?" She rolled her eyes.

"No." He shrugged. "But you've gone out of your way to tell me I'm *not* the first. Now I'm curious. Ten? Fifteen?"

She scowled at him. "Don't be absurd."

"More?"

She punched his arm. Hard. "Two. There. Now you know."

"Two men? Only two?"

"One in grad school. It was unexceptional, but I was too old to be a virgin anymore. The other was my second year at Grimes & Hancock. I was lonely. He was friendly. I discovered later that he had made a bet with several of his buddies that he could *melt the ice queen*. When I found out, I shut him down. And I told my most gossipy colleague that the one-time lover had a small penis."

"Holy hell." Jason fell back on the bed and roared with laughter. He laughed until his chest hurt, and he gasped for breath. Every time he thought he had himself under control, another incredulous chuckle started.

Gabby scooted up against the headboard and wrapped her arms around her knees. Her expression was wary as if she didn't know what to make of his amusement.

Finally she sighed. "Are you done?"

He nodded sheepishly. "Yeah. Sorry. Remind me never to get on your bad side."

"I don't have a bad side," she insisted. "But I don't let people push me around. My mother taught me strength comes from inside a person, and that it's insulting to be called the weaker sex."

He rolled to face her and stroked her leg. "There's nothing weak about you, Gabby. I'm continually impressed by all you've accomplished."

She played with his hair, sending shivers down his spine, and filling his sex with renewed heat. "Is the talking part over?" she asked, smiling sweetly.

"Yes, ma'am," he said. "Come here, woman. Let's get naked together."

Shedding their clothes turned into an erotic dance, but one that included gasps and quiet laughter. When they were both completely nude, he had to remind himself to breathe. Gabby was tall and slender—that much was true—but she had subtle curves in all the right places. Her ass alone was enough to make a grown man weep.

"You're staring," she said, folding her arms across her chest to hide her breasts.

"I can't help it. You have a delightfully feminine body. Strong and lean and soft, so soft." He ran a hand from her knee to her ankle. "I hardly know where to start."

"I like looking at you, too," she said. "Your muscles make my girly parts quiver. I guess that makes me shallow, but what can I say? I'm desperately attracted to you." She touched his erection.

He held himself perfectly still and let her explore. She was intent, her expression equal parts curious and eager. The feel of her hands on his body threatened to make the top of his head explode.

But he clung to control with the last fiber of his being.

"Let me know when it's my turn," he croaked.

Her frown was instant. "I'd rather just get to the main event. I'll feel too self-conscious to let you touch me unless we're—you know—"

"Screwing?"

"Yes."

"Too bad," he said, sliding a hand between her thighs. "I'm a staunch believer in foreplay."

Gabby wrinkled her nose. "I hate that word."

"What would you like to call it?"

"How about *the preliminaries*? That's descriptive, right?"

He propped his head on his hand, his brain racing to keep up with hers. This close he could inhale a light scent. It was something simple and sweet. Now that he thought about it, her perfume, or her shampoo, or whatever it was didn't match the Gabby she showed to the world. That woman was tough and whip-smart and didn't suffer fools gladly. The way she smelled tonight was far more innocent.

He realized that his lover's entire body was braced. "Relax," he said. "This isn't a dental procedure."

"Very funny."

He hadn't touched her intimately. In fact, his hand wasn't even moving. But apparently, Gabby was nervous.

"Kiss me," he said. When he leaned over her and found her lips with his, all the awkwardness melted away. It had been like that from the beginning. Gabby might not be one hundred percent sure about having sex with him, but when they kissed, it was as if they had been kissing each other for days. Weeks. Months. Years.

Her body knew his and welcomed him. At least for the *preliminaries*.

She frowned when his lips curled upward. "Why are you smiling?" she asked.

Her suspicious question amused him. "Because I'm having fun?"

"Oh."

This time, when he stroked her leg, she closed her eyes. A ragged exhale said she was not opposed to letting him take things to the next level.

"I like having you naked," he said, pausing to kiss her cheek, her throat, her belly. "Car sex was fun, but this is better."

She shuddered when he slid two fingers inside her. "Oh, yes. Much better."

After that, he lost his focus. Having Gabby so clearly ready for him was more than he could resist. He grabbed the protection he had dropped on the bedside table and took care of things. Then he touched her cheek. "Open your eyes, Gabby."

"Okay." Her face was flushed. Her pupils had dilated until the gray of her irises was almost all black.

"Keep them open." He didn't know where that demand came from. Honestly, it was damned hard for him, too. But when Gabby's gaze locked with his as he entered her, he felt invincible.

He saw trust in her eyes.

Could he shoulder that burden? Did he want to?

When she wrapped her legs around his waist, he was lost. He thrust wildly, his body racing toward the finish. Gabby came a second time, her choked cry impossible to miss. Her pleasure triggered his. His heartbeat was somewhere in the stratosphere when he groaned her name and let the tide take him.

He might have fallen asleep. Hard to say. When he came to his senses, his face was buried in the curve of her neck. The room was quiet but for their breathing. In that moment, he was content never to move again.

Finally he yawned. "May I stay the night?"

Gabby moved away from him, tugging the sheet to cover herself. "No. Sorry. My neighbors all know me very well. I don't want to answer a million questions."

Something in that statement stabbed a little knife in his self-esteem. Still, he had to do what was right. "Okay," he said, rolling out of bed and onto his feet. "I know you have to work tomorrow, so I'll get out of your hair."

He was hard again. No way to disguise that. The way Gabby stared at him didn't help. His clothes and hers were a mess on the floor. He retrieved pants and shirt, boxers, socks, and shoes. By the time he was dressed, Gabby had exited the bed and stood facing him, the top sheet wrapped toga-style around her slender body.

"Did we decide on anything?" he asked.

"About?"

His jaw tightened. "About this week."

"Thinking is good," she said, her words and tone prim.

"And the party at my parents' house?"

Gabby shook her head slowly. "Thanks for the invitation, but I don't think so, Jason. I'd be very uncomfortable."

He could see from her face that she really believed that. Because he couldn't help himself, he crossed the room and wrapped her in his arms. There was a sheet between them. And his clothes. But feeling her against his body made his pulse stagger and race again.

He stared deeply into her silvery-gray eyes, noting the way her thick lashes lowered when she was feeling shy. "Please, Gabby. I'll never leave your side, I swear. The food will be spectacular. I can guarantee great music. Plus, you have to see my mom's holiday decorations to believe them. Santa himself is probably jealous."

She used her free hand, the one not clutching the sheet, to pat his cheek. "I'll think about it." Then she paused and ran her thumb along his chin. "I don't want to bring up a touchy subject, but isn't there a good chance your mom invited Cate and Harry?"

His jaw dropped, but he snapped it shut immediately. He felt blood rush to his face. How had he blocked that out? "Um, yes. I'm sure she has. But it's fine. We're all good."

Gabby cocked her head, her perceptive gaze sneaking past his defenses. "You say that, but I'm not sure it's true. You're still carrying a ton of guilt. If I can see it, I'm sure they can, too."

Anger tightened his throat, though he didn't know if it was aimed at her or himself or the impossible situation. "Stay in your own lane, Gabby. I'm dealing with things."

She saluted. "Yes, sir."

He exhaled, trying to salvage his self-respect. His lover was kicking him out. He had just invited that same lover to a Christmas party where his ex was sure to be in attendance. Not to mention Harry, the man he loved like a brother, who was now married to his ex. December wasn't shaping up to be quite so jolly after all.

"I know not to call you at work," he said, which meant what exactly? He sounded like a fool.

Gabby snuggled closer, her cheek over his heart. "Texting is good."

He didn't want to walk away. Gabby was a pro at putting up walls. Since that first moment in the coffee shop, he had been chipping away at them. But five days would give her far *too much* time to think. She might decide he was a bad risk. A guy who had left one woman at the altar was a marked man.

Then, even as he absorbed her warmth, her incredible sensuality, he had to ask himself the most difficult question of all. Was being with Gabby where he was supposed to be? Was this quick-start relationship genuine? Or had it been something of a rebound fling?

God help him. He didn't think so.

What he had done to Cate at the wedding made him doubt

his own judgment. There was no question he was sexually attracted to Gabby Nolan. And in truth, *attracted* was a mealy-mouthed way to describe what he felt for her. He craved her.

Perhaps *he* needed the five-day test even more than she did.

He found her lips with his and kissed her slowly, banking the animal inside him who wanted to seize control. "I'll be in touch," he said. "Don't forget about me."

Gabby's smile was pure and happy. "I wouldn't dream of it. Good luck with your mortar and pipes and guy stuff."

"If you have a tough day at the office, feel free to come use my sledgehammer on a wall or two. It does wonders for stress relief."

She walked with him to the front door. "I'll keep that in mind. Good night, Jason. Be careful going home."

"It's not far."

This time, *she* initiated the kiss, going up on her tiptoes to give him only a taste of what he wanted. Her lips were soft and warm. They clung to his despite her telling him he had to go. "Bye," she whispered.

He released her and put a hand on the doorknob. "Five days, Gabby."

Her eyes rounded. "That sounds ominous."

"Not ominous," he said. "It's December. Anything could happen. I'll be sending Santa my list tomorrow."

"That's for kids," she pointed out, her eyes laughing at him.

"Christmas is for everybody, my dear Gabriella. I look forward to making a few of your dreams come true."

# Chapter 11

On Monday morning, Gabby Nolan was late to work for the first time in her life.

Only twenty minutes, but still...

A million questions had whirled through her head for hours. When she finally fell into a deep sleep sometime around four, her alarm was set to wake her a bare two hours later. There wasn't enough coffee in the world to take care of this no-sleep hangover.

Her assistant, Jamie, was visibly worried when Gabby arrived.

"Are you okay, Ms. Nolan?" she asked. "There's a lot of flu going around. You're a little pale."

Gabby dredged up a smile. "I'm fine, I promise. Just a sleepless night. I had a lot on my mind."

Jamie, who was working as a paid intern during her senior year in college, followed Gabby into the larger office at the back. "I can grab you a coffee from that shop you like. Or I have a Starbucks coupon. It's closer, and the Christmas cups are super cute."

"Thanks, Jamie. But I'm fine. Have you typed up the notes from Friday's meeting? I need to look over them first thing."

"Yes, ma'am. They're done. I'll grab them in half a sec." She paused and lowered her voice, her tone conspiratorial. "My mother always gets stressed at the holidays. She says men don't appreciate how much work goes into wrapping and buying gifts. Plus, you have to *decide* what to get everybody to start with. I'm not surprised you had trouble sleeping. It's a busy time of year. And this place has a little too much testosterone, don't you think?" She clapped her hand over her mouth. "Yikes. That's one of those things I can't say out loud, right?"

Gabby didn't know whether to laugh or cry. Compared to this fresh-faced twenty-year-old, she felt ancient. "It's fine between you and me, but I wouldn't make a habit of it. The best thing you can learn here at Grimes & Hancock is the art of discretion."

Jamie nodded vigorously. "Message received."

When the younger woman walked away, presumably to get the requested notes document, Gabby sank into her desk chair. This office had become a haven over the last few years. Numbers were comforting to her. They never changed. Any hiccups could always be tracked down with patience and determination.

She was good at her job.

Even on the days when work was demanding and hectic, she knew she could handle things. That calm certainty was askew today, not because of any crisis at G&H, but because her full attention was not going to be on her work.

Jamie popped back in. "Here's the report," she said. "And this envelope was on my desk when I came in at eight forty-five. Your office was still locked."

"Thank you. Will you close my door on your way out? I need a quiet hour before my eleven o'clock meeting with Mrs. Grant."

Jamie shuddered dramatically. "That old lady scares me."

"I'll admit she's intimidating, but her bark is worse than her bite. I need to be completely prepared when she arrives."

"Got it."

"Thanks, Jamie."

When she was finally alone, Gabby rested her elbows on her desk and put her head in her hands. She felt muzzy and achy and irritable. All because of a gorgeous man with Aegean blue eyes and a wicked smile.

She picked up the small white envelope and opened it. Her name was scrawled in black ink on the front. The single sheet of paper inside was folded once.

Good morning, Gabby. I didn't think you would appreciate flowers at work, but I wanted you to know I was thinking about you. In lieu of a floral bouquet, this note is good for one free Christmas tree expedition. I'll help select, transport, erect, and decorate the lucky evergreen of your choice—filling your apartment with holiday cheer. Just say the word. Talk to you soon…
Jason

Her heart pounded as if he was standing in the room with her. *Gah*, this was impossible. She was so far out of her comfort zone, she couldn't even see level ground. The only way to survive was to focus on work and pretend that everything in her life was normal.

*Pretending* was exhausting. Or maybe it was her sleepless night. Either way, she was running on fumes by the time she finally left work and headed for home.

She didn't want to cook, but she had skipped lunch. Without going to the store, her only choices were spaghetti or frozen leftovers from Thanksgiving. She chose the unappealing turkey dinner. After a quick nuke in the microwave, it wasn't half bad.

Despite her no-sleep hangover, it was maybe a good thing

she had an obligation this evening. That way she wouldn't sit around thinking about Jason like some lovesick middle school girl. She had promised Tanya, who lived in the building next door, to put the twins to bed. Tanya was headed out to do her Christmas shopping.

When Gabby entered her friend's loud, cluttered, cheerful apartment, she had to smile. The boys, Bo and Benji, were three and a half. They ran to her, shrieking, and almost knocked her down.

Tanya winced. "Sorry about that. I've bathed and fed them. There's a movie in the Blu-ray player and a stack of books on the counter over there. Call me if anything is burning down, and I'll be back in a flash."

Gabby grinned. "We'll be fine. Enjoy the evening. Don't rush. I always have a blast with your babies."

"You're an angel," Tanya said fervently. "I'll be back by ten."

"No worries." Gabby waved her out the door.

The next two hours were intense, hilarious, and demanding. The twins went ninety miles an hour until they literally collapsed in their room at nine o'clock. The two single beds were shaped like NASCAR vehicles. When she tucked them in, their cherubic faces and relaxed bodies belied the whirlwind they had dragged her through.

She sat on the carpet between the two low beds and watched them sleep.

Nothing could be sweeter or more appealing than a small child at rest.

Her heart ached with love for them. She and Tanya had met each other when Bo and Benji were only six months old. Tanya's husband had decided fatherhood wasn't for him and had walked away, never to return.

Gabby couldn't understand leaving your own flesh and blood. Her own mother could have given Gabby up for adoption, but despite Dahlia's grief and turmoil and mental state, she had carried out her role as mother.

Would Gabby ever have a chance to create a family? It seemed like a far-fetched dream at best. Unless she went the sperm donor route, she would need a man in her life. A husband, to be exact. Other people were entitled to their choices, but Gabby didn't want a child without a spouse.

Unfortunately, Jason wasn't a candidate.

She needed to find a man who understood how hard it was to come from nothing and always feel the specter of failure at your back. She needed a partner who knew what it was like to struggle financially. To live paycheck to paycheck.

Thankfully, she was long past that now, but her childhood years had marked her. She was frugal, financially conservative, and always planning for future disasters. There wasn't an ounce of *go-with-the-flow* in her entire body.

When she was sure the boys weren't going to stir, she got up and wiggled her leg, which had fallen asleep. Before she left the room, she kissed their rosy cheeks. Tanya's life was hard, but she had something far more important than money.

In the living room, Gabby curled up on the sofa and turned on the TV. After muting the sound, she surfed channels until she found an old movie. Then she picked up her phone to glance at emails.

But it was the text icon that caught her eye. Jason had sent her three texts in the last hour. It was no wonder she hadn't seen them. Wrangling two toddlers was a full-time task.

Smiling, she opened the texts...

Hope you've had a good day. Are you "thinking" about things?

When she hadn't answered, Jason continued...

Hello? Anybody home? I miss you.

And finally...

You must be tied up. Maybe we can talk tomorrow. Good night, Gabby...

She glanced at the time. Still early. Calling Jason wouldn't be out of line. But what would she say? Part of her wanted to wallow in great sex until things cooled down or burned out. If she did that, though, Jason would expect her to be his date next Saturday night.

Almost subconsciously, her brain had been picking at a painful problem. If she went to the gala with Jason, she would undoubtedly see Cate. Her stomach tensed. For the last year and a half, she had made excuses not to see her friend. Because she was a coward. It was as simple as that.

She owed Cate an explanation. If Gabby was going to attend the gala with Jason—and she did want to attend, no matter what she'd told him—she had to see Cate this week. It was far past time. Not only did she have to come clean about her guilty secret, but it was wrong to keep her distance from the woman who had done so very much for Gabby.

But first, how to answer these texts?

After a few moments of mental wrangling, she tapped out a response...

Thanks for your note this morning. Sorry—crazy busy day. And I'm babysitting tonight. Maybe we can talk tomorrow. Sleep well...

She shoved her phone in her purse to escape temptation. If she called Jason and asked him to come over, she was ninety-nine percent sure he would show up at her door in a heartbeat. He would be fun and entertaining and great in bed, but they would be breaking the agreement to think about their relationship. Five days. Time apart. Deciding what they really wanted from each other.

Minutes later, the movie palled. She grabbed her phone again. Before she could chicken out, she sent a text to Cate...

Any chance you're free for lunch tomorrow? Work and life in general have been super busy, but I would love to spend some time with you.

She hit Send and felt lightheaded with a combination of relief and dread.

Cate's response was almost instant...

Of course!!! Just tell me where and when!!

By the time they settled on a place and time, Gabby heard Tanya's key in the door. The mother of two was loaded down with packages as she came in. Gabby hurried to help her. "Looks like Santa was successful."

Tanya yawned and nodded, collapsing into an armchair. "I did ninety percent of my shopping in two hours. Blitzkrieg. Effective, but exhausting. How were the boys?"

"Angels, as always."

Tanya chuckled. "Right." She smiled at Gabby. "You're a lifesaver. You know that, don't you?"

Gabby shook her head. "It's a treat for me, I promise. Can I help you with anything before I go?"

"Thanks, but no. I'm going to stuff all this in the guest room closet and worry about it later. Go home and get some sleep. You look as tired as I am."

"Yeah. My bed is calling. Good night." They hugged, and Gabby was out the door.

All around the complex, Christmas lights gleamed. She felt a little Scrooge-ish about her dark apartment. But when she came home every night—often late—there was little inclination to decorate. It was enough to enjoy her neighbors' efforts.

By the time she had showered and put on her pajamas, her eyes were heavy. At least last night's bout of insomnia meant she was going to crash hard.

As she snuggled under the covers, it was impossible not to remember Jason's presence in her bed Sunday evening. She shivered, telling herself his masculine scent hadn't lingered on the pillowcases.

When she closed her eyes, the next four days felt far too long.

Tuesday was not much better than Monday at the office. At this rate, she would lose her job if she didn't get her personal life under control.

Though she hadn't told Cate, Gabby was taking the afternoon off. Lunch would only last an hour and a half at the most. But today's conversation wouldn't be easy. Gabby wasn't sure she could handle going back to the office if she was an emotional wreck.

The restaurant she had chosen was off the beaten path. It was more homey than elegant. One selling point was the high-backed booths that offered a modicum of privacy. She could have invited Cate to her apartment, but that might have raised questions.

So the Downtown Diner it was.

Gabby deliberately arrived ten minutes early. Cate was always prompt.

When her blonde, blue-eyed friend walked through the door, she was as gorgeous as ever. Cate was that rare woman who didn't see her own exceptional beauty. She was compassionate, kind, and during college had literally changed Leah's and Gabby's lives.

Leah's debilitating shyness and Gabby's extremely impoverished upbringing had put them at a disadvantage. Cate drew

them into her social circle, made sure they were part of her so-
rority, and generally kept them under her wing until they found
the confidence to tackle college life on their own.

The fact that Cate was an actual beauty queen was only more
icing on the cake. As a teenager, she had been voted Miss Georgia Peach Blossom four years in a row. No other candidate had
matched that record before or since.

Now here she was, her smile broad and her arms outstretched.
"Gabby. Thank goodness you called. I thought you were mad
at me, but I didn't know why."

Cate's hug was almost uncomfortably tight. Gabby returned
the embrace with her eyes stinging. This mini-estrangement
was all on her. Poor Cate was oblivious.

"Let's sit down," Gabby said. "They've saved that back booth
for us."

The two of them ordered right away. The menu was familiar, and they both were hungry.

Then Cate leaned forward. "I'm so, so glad you're free today.
I know we've had three or four lunch dates scheduled, but
you've been so busy at work you had to cancel every time. I've
missed you, Gabby."

The guilt stabbed deeper.

Before she could respond, the server brought drinks and a
breadbasket. Finally they were alone. "I'm sorry," Gabby said.
"I haven't been a very good friend."

"Oh, pooh," Cate said. "That's not what I meant. I couldn't
love you any more if you were my own sister. I know you came
to my shop opening in Blossom Branch, but that was forever
ago. Are you doing okay, honey? How's your mom?"

"My mother is great. I'm good, too."

"But?"

Before Gabby could answer, their food arrived. Honestly,
looking at the plate made her stomach cramp. She wouldn't be

able to eat a bite until she said what she had to say. She set her fork down and took a sip of iced tea.

She stared at her friend. "I'm just going to say it. Get it off my chest."

Cate's expression reflected her confusion. "Okay."

Gabby sucked in a lungful of air, feeling dizzy and faint. "I didn't want to be a bridesmaid at your wedding."

Cate paled. "I see." She bit her lip. "I wondered if you resented how expensive the bridesmaid dresses were, and then it was all for nothing. I even mentioned it to Leah when you started acting strangely. I'm sorry. I should have been more sensitive."

Gabby shook her head. "It didn't have anything to do with money."

"Then what? Was it having to stand up in front of twelve hundred guests? I know that was kind of terrifying."

"It was daunting, but no."

Cate reached across the table and tried to take Gabby's hand, but Gabby moved back in her seat. Here was a woman who had literally changed Gabby's life, but Gabby had done the unthinkable.

Now Cate was paler still. Her eyes were dark. "You're scaring me, Gabby. What did I do to make you so upset?"

"You didn't do *anything*," Gabby cried. "It was me."

"I'll need more than that." Cate straightened her spine and glared. "I can't imagine you doing anything so terrible. Talk to me, Gabby. What's going on?"

Gabby was literally shaking. She'd spent a year and a half wrestling with this truth. The time had come to cleanse her soul. To make amends, if that was even possible.

She shredded her paper napkin and took another sip of tea. "When we were at UGA, I had a crush on Jason. You can understand that, obviously. He was gorgeous and friendly and good at everything. An incredible athlete. It was my little secret. But when you and he started dating, the crush died. Or I killed it. Whatever. The point is, you were engaged to Jason, and I was happy for you."

"I didn't know about your crush," Cate said, her face troubled. "You should have told me. There were plenty of guys I could have gone out with. I didn't have to hurt you."

"Stop," Gabby begged. "You were wonderful—you did everything—you changed my life. You deserved Jason. I knew that. Honestly, I did."

Cate simply stared. "You've lost me," she said, the words flat.

Gabby swallowed hard and braced for the final, worst confession. "When Jason called a halt to the wedding—at the altar—and then you ran out of the church, I was *relieved*. Maybe even happy. I'm so sorry, Cate. What kind of *friend* reacts like that? Later, I wondered if the way everything imploded was somehow my fault. If I'd created bad mojo…"

"Gabby—"

Gabby interrupted her. "Oh, God, Cate. I am so desperately sorry. I know I don't deserve it, but I hope someday you can forgive me."

For several long moments, their booth was an island of silence in the bustle of the restaurant. Gabby looked down at her plate.

She was startled when Cate stood and came to sit with her. Even as Gabby stiffened, Cate put her arms around her and hugged her tightly. "There's nothing to forgive, sweet girl. Clearly, Jason and I were not meant to be. Deep down, I knew it, too, but the wedding had strangled me into submission. I was too much of a coward to call it off. I desperately wish Jason had done it sooner, but at least he had the balls to prevent a disaster."

"Oh."

"Oh, nothing." Cate took Gabby's face in her hands. "I need you to hear me. You didn't do anything wrong. We can't help our feelings. You didn't betray me *or* our friendship. I love you,

Gabby. You're one of my dearest friends. That's never going to change."

Gabby stared at her. "You aren't mad?"

"Of course not."

Cate's simple forgiveness was like icy-cold water on a hot Georgia summer day. It made everything better. "Thank you," Gabby muttered, leaning her head on Cate's shoulder. "This has been a terrible year and a half."

Cate smirked. "Not so bad for me, at least not after the first few months. Harry changed everything. I'm a lucky woman." She stroked Gabby's hair. "Now, let's put this behind us and quit being silly."

When Cate returned to her own side of the table, Gabby picked up her fork. "Even though I felt what I felt, I was furious with Jason for hurting you so badly."

"He and I and Harry have made peace about what happened."

"Really?" Gabby hadn't gotten that impression from Jason at all.

Cate scrunched up her nose. "Well, Harry and I have tried. I know it's weird. The two of them have been best friends for years."

"Maybe Jason wants to mend fences but doesn't know how." Gabby wasn't about to tell Cate about everything that had happened in December. The weekend with Jason in Blossom Branch was on a need-to-know basis.

"I was hoping the passage of time would ease the awkwardness between the three of us," Cate said, "but that hasn't happened."

"Well, to be fair, you've slept with both men, so that was always going to be a little strange."

Cate flushed. "You think I don't know that? I screwed up big-time. Jason did, too. We almost ruined our lives. Both of us would have tried to hold the marriage together. That's the kind of people we are. But it would have been misery eventually. When it's not right, it's not right."

"That's why I'm probably going to be single forever. My job. My mom. Friends like you and Leah. Who needs a man anyway?"

Cate leaned back in her chair and smiled. "Clearly you haven't found the perfect guy yet. Harry makes me happier than I ever knew I could be."

"Well, you do have a lot in common."

Cate looked puzzled. "Do we? He's ten years older than I am. He's a recluse. He bottles up his feelings. I think he and I are a case of *opposites attract.*"

"But you both come from wealthy backgrounds. Similar worlds."

"I suppose." Cate shook her head slowly. "By that measure, Jason and I should have been a perfect match. We weren't, though. We equated friendship and affection with love and marriage. The consequences were almost disastrous." She paused and stared at Gabby intently. "Don't let what happened to me prejudice you against falling in love. It's not always as complicated as Jason and I made it. And besides..."

"Besides what?"

"Aren't we ignoring the critical part of your so-called confession?"

"I don't know what you mean."

"You told me that you once had a crush on Jason, but it *died*. Yet when he called off the wedding, you were relieved. Shouldn't we talk about that?"

"Oh, no," Gabby said firmly. "I've run into Jason a time or two. And yes, he's so gorgeous he makes my knees weak. Kind of like seeing a movie star. But that's the stuff of fantasy. I'm a grown woman now. I don't have a crush on him."

Cate cocked her head. "Then why were you relieved?"

Gabby waved a hand at the waiter to get their check. "Who

knows? The point is, I've confessed, you've forgiven me, and maybe now I'll be able to get in the Christmas spirit. Keeping that awful secret has been eating away at me."

"So you won't avoid me anymore?"

"No, I promise."

Cate cocked her head again and stared at Gabby. "What would you think about a double date? Harry and I could go out with you and Jason. I'll set it up. Maybe we could get tickets to one of the Christmas concert series events at the Fox Theatre. Have dinner before. That would be fun."

Gabby's mouth dried. How had she forgotten that one of Cate's superpowers was making things happen? But Gabby couldn't overreact. If she did, Cate would dig in her heels. Or else know something was up.

"That's really sweet of you," Gabby said. "But I'm slammed at work right now with end-of-the-year stuff. I'm toast when I get home in the evenings. Maybe January when things slow down."

What Cate didn't know was that she and Gabby would see each other at the gala if Gabby agreed to go as Jason's date. Suddenly, she realized she was keeping a secret from Cate *again*. She badly wanted to talk about her feelings for Jason, but to admit those feelings would make her current situation seem all too serious…and real.

Her friend nodded slowly. "Okay. I don't want to stress you out. But let's at least do a holiday brunch with you and me and Leah sometime soon."

"That would be lovely," Gabby said. "I can't wait."

# Chapter 12

Jason ached from his head to his toes. After the weekend with Gabby, he had attacked the remodel with dogged determination. Only by working himself into the ground was he tired enough to sleep every night.

Even then, he dreamed about her. Vivid, adult-rated sex dreams with color and sound and so much damn heat he woke up hard as a pike. It was a vicious cycle.

On the other hand, the house was coming along at a good clip.

He wasn't going to attempt the new wiring and plumbing. He knew his limits. But if he kept up this pace, he'd be on schedule to bring in the experts at the first of the year.

Gabby had been annoyingly uncommunicative since he left her apartment Sunday night. He'd kept his promise not to call from nine to five. But in the evenings, he had *tried* to initiate a text exchange or two.

Her answers were friendly but not wordy.

Wednesday night, he caved and called her.

When she answered after two rings, he tried for a casual tone. "Hey, it's me. How's your week going?"

"It's fine, Jason. Nothing out of the ordinary. How about you?"

"Dust and noise and a half a dumpster full of trash. About what you'd expect. Do you want to see it sometime?" He hadn't known he was going to say that.

She hesitated. "Sure."

"Gabby…"

"Yes?"

"I want to take you to the gala Saturday night. It would mean a lot to me."

Long silence. "Why?"

He rubbed the center of his forehead with two fingers. "Why not? Christmas parties are festive and fun. I like spending time with you."

"Does that mean sex afterward?"

She might as well have punched him in the gut. "I guess that would be up to you," he croaked. "But the invitation was just for the party."

"I'm not sure I have an appropriate dress to wear."

"Surely you've been to some Grimes & Hancock events with high rollers."

"A few."

"Look, Gabby. You'll be stunning in anything you wear. And besides, there will be several hundred people there. We can get lost in the crowd."

"But I'll have to say hello to your parents, right?"

"It would be the polite thing to do."

On the opposite end of the line, he heard a long-suffering sigh. "Fine," she said. "But I don't drink much alcohol, and I definitely don't dance."

"How about sitting on Santa's lap?"

"Is that a sex joke?"

He chuckled. "What do *you* think?"

"Good night, Jason."

"Good night, Gabby." He ended the call with a smile on his face. His week had just gotten a whole lot more interesting.

Thursday was a fantastic day. The sun was shining, his flooring was delivered two weeks early, and he had a date for the gala. Everything was going his way. Right up until the moment his doorbell rang. When he unlocked the dead bolt and swung the door wide, two familiar people stood on his small concrete stoop. Cate and Harry.

His stomach fell to his feet. "What are you guys doing here? How did you even know where I was living?"

Harry rolled his eyes. "It didn't take much detective work. I talked to your dad. He gave me an earful about your questionable life choices."

Cate swatted Jason's shoulder with her hand and eased past him. "We're here for an intervention," she said.

Harry followed her. "What she said."

Jason closed the door and watched as they assessed his living quarters. Cate's expression was horrified. Harry shot him an incredulous glance. Jason tried to look at it through their eyes. He had a decent mattress on the floor. The sheets and blankets were rumpled, but he wasn't picky. Nearby, he'd plugged in a minifridge and a microwave. Clean clothes spilled out of his duffel bag.

When they both stared at him, Harry shook his head slowly. "What the hell, Jason? Have you lost your mind?"

Jason folded his arms across his chest. "I bought a fixer-upper. That happens to be a perfectly acceptable thing to do. Dozens of cable channels devote entire hours of programming to this very activity."

Cate ran a hand along a dirty windowsill. "But you could hire somebody, Jason. Or twenty somebodies."

Harry nodded. "Do you even know what you're doing?"

"Maybe you both forget that I worked construction the summer between my freshman and sophomore years. Bubba's dad hired him and me. Remember?"

"That was almost a decade ago," Harry said. "And you're a brilliant man. I fail to see how this project is utilizing your many talents."

Cate dusted off a camp chair with her hand and sat down. "We think you're hiding out, Jason. And we don't like it. The past is in the past. We're living a whole new chapter. Harry loves me. But we both love you, too, and you've avoided us. It hurts."

Jason should have known this day of reckoning would come. He'd spent a little time with Cate and Harry in the last nine or ten months, but those occasions had been short and generally buffered by other people. "I don't know what you want from me," he said.

Cate's beautiful eyes were shiny with tears. "You've been my best friend forever, Jason. I have Harry now, but that doesn't mean I can just slice you out of my life. I want us to get back to where we were."

God, this was awful. He hadn't a clue how to respond. He had missed Cate, too. But how did a man relate to the woman who had once been his fiancée? Especially when she had married his mentor and dear friend.

He shot a glance at Harry. "Was this *her* idea?"

"Both of us, actually. You may have walked out of your own wedding, but you walked out on me, too. I think you're pissed that I married Cate. I'm not sure why. I adore her, and I'll spend the rest of my life making her happy. I fail to see how that's a bad thing."

Though Harry's words were even and quiet, Jason knew him well enough to hear the underlying frustration.

Jason rubbed the back of his neck. "I love you both. But I've kept a low profile because I didn't want the gossip. The three of us? Together again? We might as well sign up for some stupid reality show."

Cate nodded. "I get what you're saying. People are bound to talk. After all, they crucified you and me online in those weeks after we *didn't* get married. But that was a year and a half ago, Jason. We need to move on."

"*You've* moved on," he snapped. "And I'm happy for both of you. But I'm not sure you get the call on my life."

Harry moved to stand behind his wife. "Easy," he said.

Jason saw the other man put a protective hand on Cate's shoulder. Jason witnessed the almost palpable aura of love between his two friends. It wasn't a lie to say he was happy for them...and relieved that his actions hadn't ruined Cate's life.

But still he wrestled a sharp shard of bitterness that in their little triangle, he was now the one on the outs. He had begged Harry to look after Cate while Jason was in Peru. Never in his wildest imagination had he expected them to end up together.

"You both are important to me," he muttered. "Is that what you want to hear?"

Cate jumped up and flung her arms around his neck. "I want you to be happy," she cried. "It's killing me that you're all alone and living like a hobo."

Jason hugged her briefly, then put his hands on her waist and set her aside. "Pretty sure that word is obsolete."

Harry pinned him with a steely-eyed gaze, the same one Jason remembered as a child. If he'd done something stupid, his mentor and distant cousin had been there to jerk him back in line.

Harry shook his head slowly. "You know I've loved you since you were a punk little kid of five or six. There were times when loving you was the only thing keeping me sane when my screwed-up family made my life miserable."

For the inscrutable Harry, that speech was little short of astounding. Jason's chest hurt. He'd blocked out the feelings of loss and abandonment because he hadn't known how to come back into the fold. "You were always good to me," he muttered.

Harry cursed under his breath. "Don't make me beat the crap out of you. The three of us—Cate and me and you—are family. You made one lousy mistake, but Cate will tell you it was her fault, too."

"It was," she said, her cheeks damp with tears. "I knew something was wrong between us, but I was too scared to talk to you. We were getting married for all the wrong reasons. I'm so sorry, Jason. You saved us. You must know that's true." She wrinkled her nose. "June seventh last year was a day we'll never forget, but I won't let all that heartache ruin anything else." She hugged him again.

Harry joined the embrace. "You might as well listen to her," he said, his own eyes suspiciously bright. "She always gets her way."

Jason felt two sets of arms close around him. His gut response was a mix of longing and uncertainty. Was it really that easy? He returned the hugs, unable to think of a single word to say. Cate was visibly disappointed. Harry frowned.

"Thank you for coming," Jason said finally. "It means a lot. The next time you issue a dinner invitation or whatever, I'll do my best to be there. I swear."

Cate's smile returned. "That's good to hear," she said.

Harry got in his space, nose to nose. "What are you going to do now? In this new year that's coming? Besides putter with this house. I know you and Cate were going to do a gallery. That's still an option."

"No," Jason said. "I've sold a few of my Peru pictures. I might even have a show of my work. There are a few possibilities there."

"But?" Harry's interrogation was implacable.

"But nothing." Jason walked away. "I'm entitled to be aimless if I want. Nobody is depending on me. I'm taking time to make decisions."

"Are you?" Harry asked. "Or are you goofing around and wasting your life?"

"Piss off, Harry." He glared at his friend. "Not all of us can be wunderkind architects. Besides, I'm *way* younger than you. I've got time."

"Ouch." Harry grinned.

Cate got between them. "You two behave." She took Jason's hand. "I love you. Harry loves you. All our friends love you. Quit hiding out, Jason."

"Sure," he said.

His flippant reply made her sad. He saw it on her face and instantly regretted being an ass. He exhaled and pulled her into his arms, marveling that the two of them had ever been on the verge of matrimony. He kissed her forehead. "Honestly, Cate, I'm great. Maybe I haven't landed on a five-year plan, but I'm in a good place, I swear. And for the record, I'll *always* love you."

"Thanks for saying that," she said. "I'll always love you, too. We were kids playing at love, I guess."

Harry cleared his throat. "Let's not get *too* chummy," he groused.

Cate and Jason laughed at him. Cate went to her husband and kissed him right on the mouth. "You know I'm yours forever."

Jason made a gagging noise. "Get a room," he said, smiling.

Harry raised both eyebrows and made an exaggerated visual tour of Jason's less than impressive abode. "Maybe you're the one who should get a room." He sniffed the air. "Do you even shower?"

"Very funny. The bathroom is in full working order."

Cate glanced at her watch. "We should go, Harry." She turned back to Jason. "I thought you'd have a new girlfriend by now. Have you been seeing anyone?"

"No girlfriends," he said. It wasn't a lie. Gabby was a lover and maybe a friend. But she was certainly not ready to accept *girlfriend* as a descriptor.

Harry took his wife's arm. "C'mon, love. We've done what we came here to do. Jason isn't going into a decline anytime soon."

"Hysterical," Jason said as he followed them to the door.

When they were outside on the stoop again, he looked at two of his very best friends, realizing how lucky he was. "Thanks, guys. I mean it. Thank you for worrying about me. I might have lost my way for a little bit, but I'll be fine."

Harry nodded. "So we're good, man?"

Cate searched Jason's face. "Are we?"

He nodded slowly. "We're good. I love you both. Now get out of here and let me demolish something."

Saturday morning, Gabby wondered what it felt like to have a panic attack. The Christmas gala at Jason's parents' house was a little more than eight hours away. She was sure she had made a mistake, but she also knew Jason would never let her back out now.

She looked at Tanya sitting on the bed with the twins while Gabby tried on dresses. The boys were playing with hairbrushes. They had started out trying to style each other's hair. Now the brushes had turned into instruments of battle.

Tanya was unfazed. "So which one is your favorite?" she asked. "I think a woman always feels her best when she's comfortable but at the same time positive she's making a kick-ass impression."

"I do *not* want to stand out," Gabby said, feeling dread curl in her stomach. "These people will be rich and snooty. I want to blend in with the woodwork. I know nothing about their world."

Tanya shook her head. "Don't hand me that tired line. You've been best friends with Cate Penland for the last nine or ten years. I know you've been to her house a million times. This isn't some socioeconomic gauntlet."

"You're right about Cate's family. They're very well-off. But the Brightmans are next-level. Jason probably ate with a real silver spoon as a baby. Their house is big enough for two or three hundred guests."

"Take a deep breath," Tanya said, laughing. "Besides, I'm living vicariously through you. This evening is for both of us. Try on that first one again."

The sleeveless gown was from last year. Gabby had been asked to participate in a charity fashion show sponsored by Grimes & Hancock. She knew that her height and general size had gotten her the invitation. The whole thing had been exhausting.

But at the end of the evening, she got to keep the couture dress.

Now she stripped down again and changed back into the one Tanya suggested.

The bodice was red satin, fitted at the bust and waist. The long, narrow skirt was fashioned of high-end black velvet. The gown swished when she walked, and though she would never be a fan of spending a couple of thousand dollars on a dress, she had to admit this one made her feel like a princess.

"I guess it will do," she said, looking over her shoulder at her image in the mirror. Her butt did look nice in black velvet. Thinking about Jason seeing her in this dress made her heart race. Was she going to invite him to go home with her after the party?

She wanted to...more than anything. But such a move would be diving deeper into a relationship that was never going to work. Would Jason accept sex and nothing else?

And how would she feel if that arrangement was okay with him?

The five days she had asked for were over. Yet she was no closer to knowing what to do about Jason and their relationship.

Tanya waved a hand in front of her face. "Hello? Are you zoning out on me?"

Gabby flushed. "Sorry. I'm freaking about tonight."

"Well, don't," Tanya said firmly. "That's the dress you should wear. The boys and I are going to get out of your way now. We have Santa pics at twelve thirty. I'm going to feed them an early lunch and change their clothes."

"I could go with you," Gabby said.

"Nope. Get a manicure. Do your hair. Experiment with makeup. Tonight is going to be great. I can't wait to hear all about it."

At four p.m., Gabby nearly sent Jason a text bowing out of the evening. Only pride made her hesitate. She didn't want him to think she was a coward.

She *wasn't* a coward. Not really. But she knew her limits.

This party was going to be a marathon of societal torture. How long could she smile and nod and not give away the fact that she didn't belong?

Surely there would be women in attendance who were peeved that one of Atlanta's premier bachelors had brought a *nobody* for a date. Already she could feel the weight of disapproving glances. Gabby Nolan was the last person who should be hanging out with the gorgeous, extremely eligible Jason Brightman.

Why couldn't he see that?

When her doorbell rang at six, a sharp pain ratcheted through her stomach. She'd had chicken soup and hot tea for lunch. Now she was both hungry *and* nauseated. It was an uncomfortable combination.

Jason's expression reflected stunned appreciation when he saw her. That made things a tiny bit better.

He stepped inside and closed the door, keeping the frigid

air out. "Holy hell. You look amazing. Every man at the party will want to dance with you."

The panic mushroomed. "No dancing," she said firmly. "You promised."

"Did I?" he said.

He walked a circle around her, shaking his head slowly. "I'm afraid to touch you, Gabby. You look like a model, runway-ready."

"Oh, stop," she said, even as his words bolstered her self-esteem. "I should be the one impressed. Jason Brightman in a tuxedo? You're hot." She held out her arms. "I'm not wearing lipstick yet. Feel free to kiss me."

"Hell, yeah." He grabbed her up and held her tightly. When he lowered his head and found her lips with his, her body quivered. He was cold from being outside, but his kiss was hot and tender at the same time. Desire curled in the pit of her stomach. Her breasts ached. More than anything, she wanted to feel his naked body against hers.

He inhaled sharply and put at least six inches between them, but still held her, his strained breathing audible. "I want to stay with you tonight. Or we can go to my place. But that would be quite a comedown after my parents' house."

She frowned. "Isn't it your house, too? Didn't you grow up there?"

"No," he said, stroking her arms. "We used to have our place in Blossom Branch *and* a nice two-story in an established subdivision here in Atlanta. When Mom and Dad were fighting in earnest, they would separate. It's true I went to Blossom Branch Elementary, but my attendance there was sporadic. I mostly grew up in the Atlanta house—went all the way through school in the neighborhood. Had a slew of great friends. Memories, too, for that matter."

"So what happened?"

He released her and shrugged—his lips pressed together in

an almost grim line. "When I went off to UGA for freshman year, my father decided he needed to take a step up. To buy a home that reflected his burgeoning success. They listed our redbrick colonial, accepted an offer, and moved out. Packed my childhood bedroom in boxes and put them in storage. I never even had a chance to say goodbye. There's a time capsule buried in the backyard that my friends and I were going to dig up when we turned twenty-five. I suppose it's still under the dirt near the dogwood tree."

"*Jason.* That's awful. How could they do that to you?"

He shrugged again as if his tale was no big deal. "My parents aren't the sentimental type. To them, it was only a house. They were excited to find something new that showcased their social and financial standing."

She went to him and wrapped her arms around his waist, resting her cheek over the spot where his heart thumped steadily. "We don't get to choose our families, do we? I'm sorry your folks weren't the warm, fuzzy type." Her own mother faced challenges, but she had always made sure her daughter knew she was loved.

She felt his chest expand and fall as he drew in a heavy breath and let it out on a ragged sigh. He rested his chin on top of her head. "You don't have to go tonight, Gabby. I know I pushed you. It's not fair of me to make you uncomfortable."

An odd mix of emotions swirled in her chest. "So you're saying we would stay here instead? Cuddle in front of the TV?"

His laugh was hoarse and held little humor. "Oh, no. *I* still have to go. It's a command performance where I'm concerned."

Gabby walked away, pausing at the kitchen table to give him a frosty glare. "I said I would be your date for the party. I keep my promises. Besides, you went to church with my mother, so I owe you."

Jason's blue eyes were dark. He shoved his hands in his pockets, rocking back on his heels. His tux was clearly custom-made. It molded to his taut, fit body perfectly. His golden hair shone in the glare of the overhead light.

He lifted an eyebrow. "And you'll try to have fun?"

She chuckled. "*Now* you're pushing. How long do you think we have to stay?"

"A couple of hours maybe. Depends."

"If your parents have strong opinions about your career choices, they probably see you ending up with someone like Cate. Are you trying to show them who's boss?"

Jason frowned. "I'm taking you because I want to spend time with you. What my parents think of my love life is immaterial." He rolled his shoulders, betraying the tension he felt about the evening ahead. "If we agree to come back here later, it will give me something to look forward to."

"Nice try," she said wryly. If the evening was a bust, she might end up pulling the covers over her head and licking her wounds. "I'm not making any promises about *that*." She picked up her coat. "Let's go."

# Chapter 13

Jason helped Gabby into her knee-length black wool coat, pausing to lift her hair free of the collar. Silky strands clung to his fingertips. He wanted to grab handfuls and coax her onto the table so he could explore her body. Unfortunately, tonight was not likely to be about his wants and needs at all.

His companion's outerwear was classic but not new. It was the kind of garment a person could wear for several years and still fit in. Highly practical. Definitely Gabby.

When he tucked her into his car, he felt a jolt of *something*. Tonight's outing made him feel as if his life was almost back to normal. It wasn't. He still had a long way to go. But for once, the hollow feeling in his chest was filled with a warm certainty that things were better than they were a year ago during the holidays when he exiled himself to a solitary Christmas in Europe.

When he sneaked a sideways glance at his quiet companion, her expression was pensive. He reached out and took her hand in his. "Thank you," he said gruffly.

Her half smile was wry. "For what?"

"For being you. You're tough and resilient but also kind and forgiving. Having you with me tonight makes me feel…" He trailed off, not wanting to spook her.

"Feel what?" The slight frown she wore told him his caution was warranted.

He put both hands back on the wheel. "Happy," he said, the word light. "I never look forward to my parents' huge social events. I prefer smaller get-togethers. But you make this one bearable. That's all. You're a kindred spirit."

He hadn't lied. Every word of that explanation was true. But he couldn't articulate how he suspected Gabby was the woman he wanted. He doubted his own good judgment, and clearly, his date tonight was not ready to talk about any kind of serious relationship.

When he turned onto his parents' posh street, he sighed inwardly. Cars were lined up already, even though he had intentionally arrived on the early side. When it was his turn, he made a right into the driveway, rolled down his window, and spoke to one of the two uniformed security guards. "Hey, Dennis. How are things with you?"

The thin older man smiled and ducked his head. "Doin' alright, Mr. Brightman. You gonna park in the garage?"

"That's my plan."

"Big shindig tonight. You kids have fun." He bent down and whistled. "That's a nice-lookin' woman you got there." He winked at Gabby. She waved and smiled.

As they pulled away, Gabby frowned. "Where will everyone else park?"

Jason eased forward carefully. "Whenever Mom and Dad entertain on a large scale, Dad rents the outer sections of a couple of grocery store parking lots nearby. Guests hop out here at the front door. Valets take cars to the off-site spaces. Then, when anyone is ready to leave, they're ferried in minivans to where their vehicles are waiting."

"Wow." Gabby shook her head slowly. "But your car gets to stay here?"

"Yep. One of the perks of being related to the esteemed hosts."

He turned around the side of the house and used his garage opener to access the fourth of five bays. "We're here," he said.

His date for the evening was quieter than he would have liked. He wondered what she was thinking. There was no way to hide the wealth and privilege surrounding them. Everything he had learned about her came back to haunt him. The hunger. The barely functional early living spaces. The ridicule from cruel classmates. He tried to imagine the scene tonight through her eyes.

The Brightman estate was undoubtedly impressive. The house was constructed of mountain stone from the northern part of the state. But there was nothing rustic about the design. Copper guttering, slate roof. And inside—his mother had hired a decorator from Manhattan, supposedly a woman who had designed for the Rockefellers and the Kennedys.

The twelve-thousand-square-foot house was stunning. Jason liked it. But it didn't feel like home.

He helped Gabby out of the car and watched as she smoothed her hair. She looked up at him, her gaze guarded. "May I leave my coat here?"

"Sure." As he helped her out of it and draped it across the seat, he leaned forward and pressed a kiss to the back of her neck. The garage was quiet enough for him to hear the slight catch in her breath when he was naughty.

She turned to face him. In that split second, he was struck speechless by her elegance and beauty. He knew she wouldn't believe him if he said what he was thinking. When a woman's best friend was an actual beauty queen, perhaps it was hard to measure up.

Gabby put her hands on his shoulders, taking him by surprise. Her eyes were deep, mysterious pools of smoky gray. "We could skip the party and have car sex again."

He had a hunch she wasn't joking. "Well…" He rested his forehead against hers. "This entire area is covered in surveillance cameras. I'm guessing that's not your kink," he said as he traced her collarbone with his thumbs.

The little sound she made as she leaned into him and wrapped her arms around his waist had him hard and ready.

"You're right," she muttered. "Let's get this over with."

He chuckled. "Shall we sneak in through the kitchen or use the front door like everyone else? But remember, it's cold outside."

She stepped away from him, smoothed her hair, and lifted her chin. "I can manage a few steps around the house. Let's see if we can get lost in the crowd."

As they exited the garage, he took her hand. "I won't leave you, Gabby. This will be fun. Relax and let me show you off."

Her fingers were so tightly curled in his, he winced at the press of her fingernails. She might be trying to feign courage, but her death grip suggested otherwise.

As they rounded the corner of the house, he groaned inwardly. The interlude in the garage had given the trickle of early guests enough time to swell into a flood. He and Gabby joined the tide.

"Is there a receiving line?" she whispered.

"No. My parents usually take spots in one of the two sitting rooms on either side of the foyer so they can greet their guests. They won't be together, though. It will be a divide-and-conquer approach."

Gabby shot him a confused look but followed him into the house.

Immediately they were surrounded by noise and laughter. From the integrated sound system, Christmas music spilled over the crowd at exactly the right volume. Like the music, the holiday decorations were exactly right. This year, his mother had gone with fresh evergreen boughs, silver-and-gold ribbons, and red holly berries.

He and Gabby were flanked by a group of folks his parents' age. A few of them looked familiar, but he kept his attention on his partner. "We're going left," he said.

Part of the crowd saw his father and headed that way. Another gaggle of partiers went straight for the refreshments. For a split second, Jason could see that his mother was momentarily alone.

"Hey, Mom," he said. She had been facing the opposite direction, but when he put a hand on her shoulder, she whirled around.

"Jason!" Her face lit up. "Why are you so late?"

"I'm right on time, Mom. You know I wouldn't miss this," he said. "It's not the holidays without your party."

The attractive woman in her late fifties hugged her son. "And you've brought a date. I remember you. It's Gabby, right? Cate's friend?"

"Yes, ma'am."

"Call me Sheila." She beamed at Gabby. "I'm delighted, my dear. Jason has been a little too *hermit-y* lately. So nice to know he's rekindling his social life." She put an arm around Gabby's waist. "There's a lull in the crowd for a moment. Let's you and I chat. Jason, grab two champagnes for the women in your life."

Jason saw the color drain from Gabby's face and then rush back in a flush along her cheekbones.

"Mom, I—"

His mother waved a hand. "Go, son. For heaven's sake, I'm not going to poison her. Go. I'm thirsty."

Gabby knew on an intellectual level that Jason had no choice, but it was hard not to feel abandoned.

Sheila Brightman drew her deeper into the house to a small

study with book-lined walls. The older woman's silver lamé dress was tastefully sophisticated. She sighed and leaned a hip against the desk. "We always host these shindigs for business reasons, but the evenings are exhausting. I do enjoy it, though."

"Your home is beautiful," Gabby said. In fact, the house looked like something out of an architectural magazine.

"So, tell me about you and Jason," Sheila said, smiling archly.

"Nothing to tell," Gabby replied, her tone deliberately casual. "Understandably, he wanted a date for tonight. I agreed to accompany him. There's nothing romantic between us."

The other woman's gaze sharpened. "Are you sure about that? My son hasn't dated for a year and a half. He's wallowing in guilt."

"He *was*," Gabby said. "But I think he's coming out the other side."

"He told me all his friends sided with Cate after the wedding disaster."

"Is that true?" Gabby asked, frowning slightly.

"I'm not sure. It may be that he simply withdrew from them and not the other way around."

"It must have been terribly painful for all of you."

"Yes." Sheila straightened and paced the small room. "Cate would have made a fantastic daughter-in-law. But it wasn't meant to be."

Gabby stood mute and frozen. How long did it take to grab two glasses of champagne? "Don't feel like you have to entertain me," she said, feeling vaguely desperate. "I'm sure your guests will want to see you."

Sheila crossed her arms over her chest. "Jason needs to focus," she said sharply. "Did you know he received sizeable trusts from both sets of grandparents? They became available to him at age twenty-five. Perhaps you could coax him into reconsidering med school or law school. My only son is working like a common laborer to amuse himself. He's wasting his life."

"Um…" Gabby swallowed hard. "I don't have that kind of influence, I promise you. But I'm sure Jason has many options. He's taking time to decide what he wants."

"Have you seen that dump of a house?"

"No. Have you?"

Sheila sniffed. "I haven't been invited. But I looked it up online. It's dreadful."

"Maybe that's why he likes it."

"Because rehabbing the house is a metaphor for rehabbing his life?"

Gabby laughed, liking Jason's mother far more than she had expected. "I don't know that he's defined it like that. But sure… maybe."

Finally Jason appeared, his expression slightly frazzled. "I couldn't find you two," he said. He handed over the champagne, his gaze apologetic as he gave Gabby hers. "I said hi to Dad. He wants to meet you."

His mother sighed. "Richard has probably met Gabby on multiple occasions. Does he not remember she was a bridesmaid?"

Gabby's stomach tightened. "I'd be happy to say hello to him," she said. "I enjoyed chatting with you, Sheila." Big fat lie. "Perhaps we'll have another moment before Jason and I leave."

At last, the lady of the house exited the room. Jason slumped into a leather armchair. "I am *so* sorry. Was she brutal?"

"Not at all, really. I'm confused, though. I thought you didn't get along with your parents. But your mom is lovely, and she adores you."

He drummed his fingers on the arm of the chair. "I adore her, too. And I love my dad dearly. It's just that the *two of them* are oil and water. They're constantly in the middle of one skirmish or another. I don't know how they ever ended up together. The fact that I grew up surrounded by a thousand battles convinced me I wanted something more peaceful. I guess that's why I imagined marrying Cate would work. We never fought like my parents."

Gabby didn't want to think about Jason deciding to marry Cate. It made her both angry and sad. "Well, your mother hasn't given up on you being a doctor or lawyer. She asked me to use my influence with you. I assured her I had none."

He reached for her wrist and pulled her into his lap. "That's where you're wrong, Gabby. I value your opinion. Among other things."

When he slid his hand into her hair and angled her head so he could capture her lips with his, she groaned. This wasn't the time or place to fool around. But she could no more say no to him than she could walk naked through a ritzy Christmas party.

"Jason," she muttered, trying to breathe.

"What?" he asked, his thumb stroking her breast through red satin.

"Shouldn't we mingle?"

"I happen to know there are several lovely guest rooms upstairs."

For a nanosecond, she considered it. Then, shocked with herself, she tried to stand up. "Don't be absurd."

He held her tightly, finding her mouth again, shocking her with a carnal, desperate kiss. "Or I could lock that door behind you." It was pushed to but not completely closed.

Arousal, hot and sweet and wicked, rolled through her veins. The man was wearing a bespoke tuxedo. He was the epitome of sin on a plate. His hair was silky beneath her fingertips. She wanted to strip him bare and make all her Christmas wishes come true.

But sadly, she was a mature, responsible woman.

"Let me go," she said. When she sucked his bottom lip, he could surely be excused for not taking her seriously.

"Gabby…" He said her name with a ragged groan that echoed every one of her reckless fantasies.

She toyed with the crisp bow tie at his throat. "This isn't why we came tonight," she reminded him, whispering...aching. Beneath her hip, his eager sex made her rethink her good girl ways.

"I know." His eyes glittered with enough heat to melt her good intentions. Almost.

"I'm getting up now," she said.

"Okay." He ran his finger down into the vee of her bodice, raising gooseflesh all over her body. "You are so damned beautiful," he said softly. "I want you in my bed tonight. Or *any* bed—if my fixer-upper offends you. I could get us a room at the Ritz-Carlton."

"We don't have any luggage," she reminded him.

"Don't care."

When he nipped her earlobe with sharp teeth, she staggered to her feet and smoothed her hair, sucking in a breath and needing more oxygen than she could find. "This is a party. Your parents' party. You came here to see and be seen."

"Screw that," he said.

Before she could frame another cogent argument, the door opened. A female voice intruded. "Jason? Your mom said we could find you here."

Gabby froze, incredulous that she had forgotten the other awkward time bomb that awaited them. Cate stood framed in the doorway. Harry was right behind her.

Jason's face turned red as he struggled to his feet. "Um, yes. We had a few minutes with Mom to ourselves. It was nice."

Harry urged his wife forward. "And yet you're still here."

Cate tapped his arm. "Stop that, Harry. We're all mature adults."

He grinned at her. "Are we?"

Cate turned back to Jason, a slight frown creasing her brow. "You told me you didn't *have* a girlfriend."

Gabby managed a calm smile, though her insides were going berserk. "He doesn't. Jason and I ran into each other at a coffee shop recently. We caught up a little bit. He didn't want to come to this party alone tonight, so I agreed to join him. End of story."

Harry and Cate were neither stupid nor clueless. Jason's top shirt button was undone, and Gabby was certain her lipstick was smudged.

Cate straightened her shoulders. "Then now is our moment. Jason Brightman, we're going to wade out there in the middle of all those gossipy people and let them see there's nothing to talk about anymore. I'm married to Harry. You have a new female friend, and all four of us are simpatico."

Harry drew her back against his chest and curled an arm around her waist. "Jason and Gabby get a vote here, my love."

She slumped against him, her expression mortified. "Sorry. Harry is right. How do you want to deal with the situation? If you'd rather, Harry and I can go out ahead of you and avoid bumping into you completely."

Gabby didn't say a word. This wasn't her fight.

Jason sighed. "Atlanta has half a million people in the city limits. But the upper crust all move in the same circles. If we handle this right, word will spread that you and I aren't a story anymore. We might as well do it."

Harry sighed. "Absurd, but necessary."

Gabby made a face. "I'm a terrible actress. Cate knows that."

Jason touched her shoulder lightly. "No need to act. You're here as my guest. Cate is your dear friend. All we need to do is enjoy a few hors d'oeuvres and chat with my dad. In forty-five minutes, it will all be over."

Cate winced. "I'm sorry we're putting Gabby through this. You boys go first. She and I will be right behind you."

When the men walked out, Cate fixed her troubled stare on Gabby's flushed face. "Why didn't you tell me about Jason?"

Gabby lifted her chin. "There's nothing to tell. Look at this house, Cate. He and I are from different planets. Nothing important is ever going to happen between us."

"Jason's not a snob. He wouldn't care about your past."

"But *I* care. If I ever get married—and that's a big if—I'll pick an ordinary man, not the heir to the kingdom."

"You're being flip, but I know you, Gabby. You told me you once had a crush on him. Now you're his date tonight. That means something."

Gabby eased past Cate. "Come on. They're waiting for us. Besides, I'm hungry." Despite an aversion to being stared at by strangers, Gabby walked right across the center of the house until she spotted two tall, handsome men and a table laden with exquisite holiday treats. "Here we are," she said. "Have you scoped out the snacks?"

Harry chuckled. "*Snacks* isn't exactly the right word. Sheila has very high standards when it comes to catering."

"And everything else," Cate said ruefully.

The four adults loaded their plates and made their way toward the corner of the living room, where Jason's father held court. When he saw them, a broad smile crossed his face. "There's my boy." He hugged his son. "And Harry and Cate. I'm so glad you all came." He glanced at Gabby with kind eyes. "I know I should remember your name, but I don't."

Cate stepped up. "This is Gabby. She was one of the bridesmaids."

"Ah, yes." Richard Brightman smiled as he shook Gabby's hand, his grip warm and firm. She caught a glimpse of what Jason might look like in another twenty-five years. The older man seemed puzzled for a moment. "Am I allowed to point out my surprise that you're all together in the same room?"

Cate smiled brightly. "We're doing it on purpose. The gossip from the wedding that *didn't happen* is old news. If people see us all getting along, it won't be a big deal anymore."

"We hope," Harry said wryly.

Gabby had some opinions on the subject, but she kept her mouth shut. Beside her, Jason's body was braced and tense.

For ten minutes, the five adults ate and chatted, laughed and ignored the curious looks from other guests.

Finally, Cate sighed and set her plate aside. "That should do it, I think. Great party, Mr. Brightman. I promised Harry we would head home, put our feet up, and watch a movie."

"How old *is* your husband?" Jason teased.

Harry pretended to scowl. "Show a little respect for your elders."

Jason's dad excused himself. "You kids have fun. I'm going to work the room."

Silence fell. Gabby wondered if she was the only one who felt the strained undercurrents. She puzzled over the fact that Jason had told his two friends he didn't have a girlfriend. Was he being circumspect, or did he not see the two of them as having a relationship that could be defined so easily?

She should be glad about that. Really. She should. Being Jason's girlfriend was not a choice, even if he asked.

Besides, that word was so inadequate to describe the connection between them.

Cate slid her arms around Gabby's waist and hugged her. "We really are going to head home. I only made Harry come tonight because I want to stay on good terms with Jason's parents."

"And you like dressing up," Harry teased.

Cate's smile was brilliant. "I do," she said. She kissed Gabby's cheek and then Jason's. "Bye, you two."

As the other couple walked away, Gabby sneaked a quick sideways glance at her companion. Had he flinched when Cate kissed him? Or was Gabby creating drama where there was none? At least not anymore.

She touched his hand. "How long do you have to stay?" Now that Cate and Harry had departed, Gabby didn't recognize any of the guests, though it was a certainty that at least some of this

crowd had been sitting in the church eighteen months ago on
June 7 and had seen Gabby at the altar and read her name in
the program.

For the first time, something odd occurred to her. Many
people now chose to have weddings in fancy venues or at exotic destinations. Cate's family certainly had the resources to
throw a big bash like that. But Cate had chosen to get married
at the church where she had grown up.

Had it been the reverence of the moment that told Jason he
had to call it off? Would he and Cate be married now if the
ceremony had been in a converted barn or on a beach?

For some reason, the question bothered Gabby.

Even now, despite everything Jason and Cate had told her
individually, it was hard to understand why Jason Brightman
and Cate Penland hadn't been perfect for each other.

# Chapter 14

Jason grimaced. "I think we've done our duty. But I'll have to say goodbye to Mom before we slip out."

"Okay."

Even though they were in a roomful of people, Jason took her wrist and stroked the beat of her pulse with his thumb. "One question, though…"

She raised an eyebrow. "Oh?"

"Where are we going when we leave here? I only ask because my bed is a mattress on the floor. And you told me your nosy neighbors think you're pure as the driven snow."

"I never said that." She laughed softly. "I'm sure your little bachelor hovel is entirely adequate, but I have a full-size fridge and a big-screen TV. Besides, I may have overstated my neighbors' interest in my overnight visitors."

A tiny smile tipped the corners of his kissable lips. "And why did you do that?"

"To keep you at a distance."

He winced theatrically. "Wow. I suppose I should appreciate your honesty, but that stings, Gabby."

"I'm warming up to you," she said, running her hand from his shoulder down to his wrist. Even beneath a layer of expensive fabric, the muscles in his arm were impressive.

The party swirled around them. Somewhere in the distance, a woman's voice sang of being home for Christmas. That song always made Gabby's chest ache. She had never known the make-believe world those verses described. Nor could she identify with TV commercials where somebody returned from college and the whole family celebrated.

Most years, as she grew up, there had been no Christmas cookies or wrapping paper. Sometimes not even a stocking. As a young child, she had been confused about why Santa Claus always skipped over her in his once-a-year rounds. Only later—when she made it to third grade and one of her classmates announced that Santa wasn't real—did she finally understand the bitter truth. Storybook Christmases were produced by storybook families.

There was nothing storybook about Gabby Nolan's existence. But she had never resented her mother. Gabby never railed at fate for placing her in a hard, barren life.

Dahlia and her daughter survived the hard times. Somehow. And Gabby was the stronger for it.

"Gabby?"

Jason's low, concerned voice broke her introspection.

She summoned a smile. "Sorry. I zoned out for a minute."

He frowned slightly. "I could tell. Are you okay?"

She squeezed his hand. "I'm great. Honestly. Let's find your mom so we can leave."

Jason could think of only one thing—getting Gabby naked. In fact, he should win a freakin' award for making it this far without doing something entirely inappropriate. He was obsessed with the woman he'd brought to the party, and he didn't know what to do about it.

Especially because the obsession might be one-sided.

As they wound their way through the crowd, searching for his mom, Jason battled regret. He had wanted so badly for Gabby to be his date tonight. What he hadn't counted on, though, was the fact he might have reinforced every one of her reservations about them being a couple...any kind of couple.

She was hung up on the idea they were from different worlds, and now, tonight, he'd been the one to press the point home.

It hadn't been his intention. All he'd wanted to do was spend time with her.

But it might have been a huge mistake to let her see his parents' house.

In contrast with the things Gabby had revealed to him in Blossom Branch, tonight's party was almost painfully over-the-top.

His stomach churned when they finally located his mother, almost in the same spot they had encountered her earlier. Sheila greeted them with a smile and a pout. "You're not leaving already?"

Jason kissed her cheek. "We are. Gabby and I have both had long weeks. I think we're calling it a night."

Gabby, cool and serene, nodded. "It was a great party. Thank you for your hospitality, Mrs. Brightman."

Sheila cocked her head, her gaze darting from Gabby to Jason and back again. "I saw you both with Cate and Harry. What was that all about?"

"Um..." Now Gabby was visibly flustered.

He grimaced. "Cate thought we could put an end to the gossip if the four of us appeared to be on good terms."

"But you're not?" His mother frowned.

"Yes, we are. Of course we are." He pinched the bridge of his nose. "But this seemed like an opportune moment to put our mended relationship on display. Everybody has moved on. Your guests saw us chatting amiably. I think Cate was right. Hopefully, our canceled wedding will be old news now."

His mother, in an unusually public show of affection, hugged him tightly. "I'm sure it will. I'm happy for you, son."

She took Gabby's hand. "I'd like to know you better, dear. What if I take you to lunch Monday?"

Jason saw the panicked look Gabby sent him. "I...uh..." she said.

He intervened quickly. "Gabby's job is very demanding, especially at year end. She has a hard time getting away."

Sheila waved him off. "Nonsense, Jason. Everyone needs to eat." She patted Gabby's flushed cheek. "I'll pick you up at noon and have you back to your office in an hour. Surely that can't be a problem?"

The bland look his mother gave them both did nothing to fool either Jason or—he was certain—Gabby. His mother had an agenda. God help the hapless individual who tried to side-track her mission.

Gabby was stuck—unless she could manufacture a convincing lie. But he had a hunch that outright deception wasn't Gabby's strong suit. She might guard her secrets and her emotions, but she wasn't an accomplished liar, not even with the little white ones.

After a few beats of silence that felt like an hour, Gabby smiled. Perhaps only he saw beneath it to the fact that she was freaked out by his mother's invitation.

"That would be lovely," Gabby said. "Jason can text you my building address and my phone number. Hopefully nothing will pop up on my schedule."

"Wonderful." Sheila beamed.

Jason intervened before things could get worse. "Good night, Mom."

Another guest appeared, making it possible for Jason and Gabby to slip away without further drama.

Outside, the night was crisp and cold. He shrugged out of his jacket and wrapped it around Gabby's slender frame.

She shot him a glance. "It's only a few steps to the car, but thanks."

"I can't have my best girl catching a cold," he said lightly as he steered her around the side of the house.

Gabby chuckled, her breath visible. "Colds are caused by germs."

He stopped and put his hands on her shoulders, bending down to steal a kiss. "Humor me."

Her lips clung to his. "Yes, sir."

When they made it inside the warmth of the garage that smelled of car wax and cedar beams, he stared at her. "I want to make love to you."

She blinked once, perhaps taken aback by the intensity in his words.

He'd been trying for casual, but that was never going to happen. Not right now.

Gabby nodded slowly. "I want that, too. Shall we stop by your place so you can pack a bag?"

His heart slugged in his chest. "Do I need a bag?"

Her tiny smile was half tentative, half siren. "If you'd like to spend the night."

All evening, he had battled a potentially embarrassing erection. Now it throbbed, hard as iron. "Yes," he croaked. "I do."

He opened her door, waited for her to sit, and then carefully tucked her skirt inside so the door wouldn't catch it. As he leaned down, she put a hand on his cheek. "If we had a bottle of paint, we could spray all those pesky cameras. Then you could lift my skirt and take me over the hood of the car."

When he jerked upright, he whacked his head on the door frame. Hard. Pain radiated throughout his skull. "Don't say things like that, Gabby. I'm barely holding it together right now."

She batted her eyelashes. "I was only teasing. Fantasies aren't real."

He stared at her, his hands fisted at his sides. "When you say the words, they sound real enough to me. Let's get out of here."

He ditched his bow tie and slid into the driver's seat. Unfortunately, they were hindered by other partygoers also heading home. The line of cars and vans waiting to load passengers blocked the driveway.

Jason clenched the wheel, his body quivering with *something*. Lust? Desperation? Whatever it was, the feeling was all-consuming.

Beside him, Gabby was silent, her hands folded in her lap.

What was she thinking? Did she see him as a fun sexual blip in her otherwise carefully managed life?

He didn't want that, did he? Was it okay that they were both caught up in a holiday romp? That they had plunged into physical intimacy with no regard for the future?

The one thing clear to him was that his focused and hardworking Gabby had a five-year plan. Hell, maybe a ten-year plan. She had goals and responsibilities that didn't include him. Yet somehow he'd found a chink in her armor.

"You don't have to have lunch with my mother," he muttered. "Text her Monday morning with an excuse."

"I don't really mind," Gabby said, her words calm. "I understand. She's a mother looking out for her son. I'll reassure her."

His head snapped in her direction. "What the hell does that mean?"

Gabby shrugged. "It doesn't mean anything." She pointed out the windshield. "We can go now."

Jason eased the car forward and merged into the line of cars exiting his parents' long driveway. Once they were on the route back to his house, he exhaled. "You don't have to come in at my place. I'll grab a few things. Won't take me long."

"I'd like to see what you've been working on."

"The place is dusty, and there are all sorts of tools around."

Gabby reached across the small space separating them and splayed a hand on his thigh. "I don't mind a little mess."

His brain short-circuited. Sure, he wanted her to see his house. Eventually. The only people he'd allowed inside so far were Cate and Henry—and that hadn't been his choice. Not really.

"It's more than a *little* mess," he muttered. "But sure…if you can't wait. Don't say I didn't warn you."

When he parked in the driveway twenty-five minutes later, he tried to see the house through Gabby's eyes. The single-story brick rancher was emblematic of entire Atlanta neighborhoods from the 1970s. Surrounded by pine trees and seeming to nestle close to the ground, the house was comfortable and appealing, at least to him.

Granted, the soffits were rotten in several places, and he needed to replace the roof, but the bones of the structure were good. Large, mature azaleas would be glorious in the spring. Not to mention the many daffodils and a half-dozen dogwood trees.

Gabby got out of the car and quickly donned her heavy wool coat. She looked around with interest. He had left the porch light on, so there was some illumination, but not much. She didn't say a word as they walked to the front door. He fished in his pocket for the key. "Welcome to Casa Brightman."

Inside, Gabby tossed her coat on a small table in the foyer and looked around with interest. His mattress was at her feet, the covers tumbled. Having a beautiful woman in a couture gown standing in the middle of construction debris made an odd picture.

"Why is your bed not in a bedroom?" she asked.

"The three bedrooms are all torn apart. It's easier to sleep here in the living room." His college-size fridge was plugged in nearby.

Without saying another word, she walked from room to room.

Her silence bugged him as he followed behind her. "There won't be a formal dining room anymore," he said. "I'm knocking out the wall over there and making the kitchen larger."

"And the garage?"

"I'll combine that space with the living room and maybe include a screened-in porch. One of my buddies is an architect, so he's keeping me from going too far off track."

"I see."

He couldn't read her face. Did she hate it? He had to admit that things looked dismal right now. Not a single spot in the house was close to being finished. But he made progress every day. Good progress.

At last, they ended up back where they had started. When Gabby still didn't say anything at all, he grabbed a duffel bag, stuffed it with sneakers and a few items of clean clothes, and ducked into the bathroom to retrieve his shaving kit.

When he came back from the bathroom, she was right where he had left her, arms wrapped around her waist and a tiny frown creasing the spot between her brows.

"What?" he asked, exasperated. "Your brain is going a thousand miles a minute. You might as well say what you're thinking."

She looked at him, still with that puzzled frown. "Why, Jason? You could afford to buy literally any house in Atlanta. What is the point of all this?"

Harry and Cate had responded in a similar fashion, though maybe not with those exact words. How could he explain where he was mentally? Was he ready to be open with this woman who kept so much of herself under wraps?

He swallowed, shifting from one foot to the other. "My

whole life was easy up until eighteen months ago. A charmed childhood. A successful college experience, both academically and athletically. A wide circle of interesting friends. A woman who was fun to be with. A plan for the future."

"I'm not sure I follow, though yes, all of that seems to be true." Gabby's expression was neutral.

He shrugged, feeling the faint sting of bitterness. "I never had to work too hard for *anything* in my life. I was surrounded by people who doted on me and cushioned me from the real world. Everything I wanted was handed to me on the proverbial silver platter, particularly because my parents used gifts to their only child as part of an ongoing competition. So when I ran smack into an honest-to-God, complicated adult problem for the first time, I screwed up. Royally."

"I think you're being too hard on yourself. You didn't choose to be born into your family's wealth. That was the luck of the draw. And I don't see you as arrogant or conceited, though you certainly could have been. Despite your upbringing, I'd say you turned out to be a decent person."

"And the wedding?"

Gabby winced. "Well, yes. That was bad. You messed up bigtime. But how long are you going to punish yourself for that?"

He kicked a crumbling baseboard. "I'll let you know," he muttered.

This wasn't how he had planned for their romantic evening to progress.

His companion unfolded her arms and closed the distance between them. She was tall and graceful and lovely, even more so with the juxtaposition of his unruly building project framing her. She stopped shy of touching him but waved a hand. "I'm missing something. How does the house fit into what you just told me?"

He might not have been able to answer that question six months ago, but he was learning along the way. "I wanted to do something hard. Something that would push me to the edge of my talents and capabilities. I needed to create something that was *mine*. This crazy project is clearly more than a simple renovation. I'm basically starting from the ground up. But I love the challenge. And I feel as if I'm finally seeing clearly. When and if I eventually finish this, I'll have a house that's my home. *My* home."

"And your photography?"

"That's the great thing. I can move at any pace. It may sound crazy to you, but the photography and the remodel are similar."

"How?"

"Well, when I travel, I see things worth framing with my lenses, and I get excited when I can capture an image that is unique."

"And the house?"

"I'm changing it bit by bit to fit the vision in my head. I see something in this place that no one else sees."

Finally she smiled. "Okay, I think I get it. Thank you for sharing that with me."

"But we've killed the mood, haven't we?"

Gabby's smile lit up the room. "Not necessarily. Grab your bag, big guy. Let's head over to Peachtree Court and have a little Christmas party of our own."

Gabby felt both relieved and melancholy. Jason's willingness to be honest with her had crushed any burgeoning dreams she might have entertained in private. He was probably still going to travel the world. Footloose and fancy-free. Coming home only to work on his very special project.

Nothing in what he had told her made room for a partner. Nor did she want to be in a long-term relationship with a man who might pick up and leave at any moment. She knew herself well enough to accept that she had a craving for certainty and permanence. After years of upheaval and turmoil, she had created a foundation for herself and her mother that felt comfortable. Reliable.

So she was not going let herself fall in love with Jason Brightman—but there was no reason at all to deny herself the pleasure of his company in the short term.

At her apartment, they climbed the stairs together. She was chilled to the bone, even wearing her coat. Thankfully, she had not turned the heat too far down when she left for the party. The apartment was warm and homey, even without a Christmas decoration in sight.

Jason slipped out of his tux jacket and tossed it on a chair. "We could get you a tree tomorrow," he said. "I'm free."

She hung her coat in the hall closet. "I don't know, Jason. We're well into the month already. Seems like a lot of trouble for a short time. Besides, I'll be in Blossom Branch for the holiday."

"Oh." He frowned.

"What?"

His jaw stuck out with a hint of belligerence. "I thought you and I might be together on the twenty-fifth."

That idea was so incredibly appealing she almost gasped. Instead, she straightened her spine and smiled. "I doubt that. We both have family commitments."

"What if I'd rather spend time with you than with my folks?"

"Sometimes we have to make other choices. The right choices. Christmas is about home and family. You and I barely know each other."

"That's a damn lie." His eyes sparked blue flames. "I saw something in you I wanted when we were in college. I'm thinking that's been buried all this time, and now we've come full circle. Don't push me away, Gabby. Please."

"Okay, fine," she said, huffing. "We're not strangers. Is it time to adjourn to my bedroom?"

His jaw tightened again. "You're deliberately changing the subject."

She lifted her chin, staring him down. "I thought you *wanted* to have sex with me. My mistake."

His body language relaxed, and he laughed out loud. "You're a piece of work, Gabby Nolan. Stubborn. Brilliant. And if I'm honest, infuriating at times. But I want you too much to argue anymore. At least not tonight." He held out his hand. "Come here, woman."

What would it be like when all this was over? Would she survive having Jason and then *not* having him? The part of her brain that always weighed risk and reward knew the answer. He was going to break her heart.

Even so, there was no way she could walk away from him now. It was far too late for that.

They both kicked off their shoes. Urgently. He kissed her all the way down the hall, showing an impressive knack for walking backward and never letting her go.

In her room, he stopped and kissed her some more. "Thank you for going with me tonight."

She wrapped her arms around his neck and played with the hair at his nape. Then she tipped back her head to lose herself in those incredible blue eyes. "It wasn't as bad as I thought. Your parents are nice, and their house is incredible."

He found her zipper and lowered it slowly. "You're not wearing a bra?" The question was hoarse.

"It didn't seem necessary. The satin isn't thin."

He took the zipper all the way down and held her hand as she stepped out of the dress. "Hanger?" he asked. "I don't want to be responsible for ruining this."

"The chair," she whispered, leaning into him and pressing her breasts against his hard chest.

Jason stepped away from her for three seconds and took her in his arms again. He stroked her bare back. "I've been imagining this moment all day."

"Me, too." Was sex with Jason the only reason she had agreed to be his date for the party? Or did she simply want to be with him in every way? She started unbuttoning his shirt, revealing smooth tanned skin.

When Jason shuddered hard, she stared at him. His eyes were closed. His fingers dug into her hips. Desperation was written on every plane of his face. Was this a natural male reaction to unfolding sexual pleasure, or did he really want *her*?

She tapped his cheek. "Help me with the cuffs."

His eyes opened slowly, his expression dazed. "Cuffs?"

"On your shirt. I can't undo them."

Quickly he removed his silver cuff links, and the two of them ripped off his shirt. When her bare breasts nestled against his bare chest, they both groaned.

Gabby felt his thundering heartbeat beneath her cheek. "Merry Christmas to me," she whispered.

# Chapter 15

If Jason was having a sex dream, he never wanted to wake up. Gabby was in his arms, naked except for a tiny pair of black undies.

He cupped her ass in both hands and dragged her closer. "You were the most stunning woman at that party tonight."

When his partner stiffened, he knew he had said the wrong thing.

Gabby shook her head slowly. "You don't need to give me words like that. I don't expect compliments."

He ground his teeth. "Is this about Cate?"

"Not specifically, but good grief, Jason. Your ex-fiancée has a regal Grace Kelly beauty. I know you're attracted to me, but the truth is the truth."

"So I can't think you're beautiful, because of Cate?"

"That's not what I said."

She made him frustrated and crazed in equal measure. He took her wrist and dragged her to the bed. He wanted to get undressed, but they had to sort something out first. When he pulled back the covers and gently shoved her onto the mattress, she clutched the sheet to cover her breasts.

Shaking his head wryly, he flopped down beside her and rested his head on his hand. "You're an incredibly lovely woman, Gabriella. Just looking at you makes me ache. Your creamy skin is smooth and warm. Smoky gray eyes hold secrets. Hair so soft and silky I want to wrap myself in it. And your body. Damn, woman. Curves in all the right places. I can't even *see* anyone else when I'm with you. I'm breathless."

Her eyes rounded during his speech. A hint of pink bloomed across her cheekbones. She searched his face. "You really mean that, don't you?"

He traced her lips with a fingertip. "All that and infinitely more. But until you tell me you understand, I'm not taking off a single other piece of clothing. You can't have me, Gabby, unless I know you hear me loud and clear."

Her lips twitched. "I bet I could seduce you."

His pulse kicked. His mouth dried. He smiled. "Maybe so. But you'd hate yourself in the morning."

She reached up with the hand that wasn't clutching the sheet to run her fingers through his hair. "I do believe you. I'm not sure how it happened, but I believe you."

"And what do you think about me?" He closed his eyes and rolled onto his back. "Did my masculine butt win you over? Or my broad shoulders?"

When he didn't hear an answer, he opened his eyes and frowned. "Gabby?"

Her smile was wistful. "It was your heart. I loved the way you talked to my mother and did things for her. And the same goes for how you treat your own mom. Nothing about a man can be any sexier than a caring heart."

For once, he was taken aback. Speechless. Her words touched him deeply. He'd spent so much time beating himself up recently, it was incredibly healing to know that Gabby liked and respected him. "I'm glad you think I qualify," he said gruffly.

She was on her elbow, still holding the sheet. "I do," she said quietly. "*Now* can we undress you?"

His heart pounded. This entire day…this interminable evening…all the hours adding up to this moment had finally led him here. To Gabby's bed. He rolled off the mattress and onto his feet. "Whatever the lady wants."

Removing his tux pants and kicking off his socks was no problem. Having Gabby stare at him when he was down to his boxers made his sex twitch. No man could object to his woman appreciating the show.

"Close your eyes, Gabby," he said.

Her eyelashes flew wider. "Why?"

"I'm too close to the edge. You looking at me like that is fuel for the fire. I don't want to come too soon."

"Okay." She settled onto her back. Instead of closing her eyes, she squinched them shut. Both her hands were white-knuckled on the edge of the sheet.

His heart thumped hard at his sternum. This woman was the most intriguing mix of confidence and vulnerability. She carried a gut-level innocence that humbled him.

When he lay down beside her, she flinched. "Easy, sweetheart," he said. "I won't do anything you don't like. I promise."

Now her eyes were open, the pupils dilated. "I believe you."

This time was for him, though that was probably selfish. It was an unimaginable privilege to stare at her. This was her bed. Her room. Her sanctuary. The space was elegantly feminine. Not frilly at all but filled with soothing colors and tantalizing scents.

Experiencing Gabby in this very personal environment was another layer in knowing her intimately.

He reached beneath the covers and drew her panties down her legs and completely off her feet. Gabby's ragged sigh as he tossed them aside made him smile. Carefully he reached under the sheet a second time, found her flat belly, and stroked it. Her whole body was tense and braced.

"Relax, Gabby," he whispered. "Let me touch you."

Muscle by muscle, he coaxed her into enjoying the moment. It was a careful choice on his part to avoid her sex for now. He needed her to trust him, wanted her to feel uninhibited and free.

Instead, he learned every inch from her throat to her shoulders, rib cage to navel. He kissed her forehead and her eyelids. The little sounds she made pushed him closer to the limits of his control.

When the time was right, he gently tugged the sheet away. Seeing Gabby warm and wanton and naked was a kick to the chest. He was so hard, he ached. When he pressed his cheek to her stomach and kissed her there, his lover's ragged sigh echoed in his brain.

He slid a hand between her thighs and found her damp and ready for him. Because he wanted this moment to be perfect, he decided to give her first dibs on the orgasms. He didn't want to disappoint her.

Gabby arched her back with a breathless keening cry when he stroked her in the one spot that centered her pleasure. "I want to watch you," he said.

His guttural words did something to both of them—it was a big ask so soon in their sexual relationship.

She stared at him with a hazy expression that combined confusion and alarm and need. "Jason, I—"

He repeated the focused caress, and she came apart. He captured her cries in a desperate kiss. "All the way, Gabby. All the way."

Her climax was a gift to him. He held her close as she trembled in the aftermath. The feel of her in his arms was like finding a path in the darkness. Gratitude and wonder washed over him in equal measure. Against all odds, he had found redemption.

After her breathing stilled, he stroked her hair. The words *I love you* trembled on his lips. He wanted so badly to say them. Wasn't this the universe giving him a second chance? Gabby had appeared unexpectedly in his drab world and brought life and depth to his two-dimensional existence.

He had almost forgotten what it felt like to be truly happy.

But he was neither a fool nor an idiot. The woman in his arms was not where he was on this journey. Her life had been just fine before he arrived. Orderly. Productive. Admirable. It was no secret that his Gabby liked to be in control. No surprises. No big changes.

She was attracted to him—he knew that. She even enjoyed his company. But it might not be enough.

Pushing aside the uncomfortable thoughts, he kissed her temple. "That was fun," he said lightly. His chest was tight, but he had to keep things easy and carefree.

Gabby yawned. "Understatement. You have a gift, Mr. Brightman. I'm impressed." Her impish grin eased some of his turmoil.

He dragged her closer and let the kiss go deep, his tongue tangling with hers. "I haven't even showed you my best work yet," he said, trying to breathe.

When they kissed, it was a connection almost as intimate as sex. Their lips clung. Her tongue urgently dueled with his. She bit his lip and whispered his name until he was almost insane with the need to take her hard and fast.

Without warning, she scooted down in the bed and slid both hands inside his knit boxers. She palmed his butt. "Time for these to go," she said. The smug satisfaction in her words told him she recognized his shuddering need.

When she pressed a kiss to the head of his sex through the cloth, he cursed, his hips arching off the bed. "No," he said sharply. "Let me have you."

She sat up without warning and stared at him, her gaze hot

with an emotion more akin to annoyance than passion. "I thought this was an equal exercise. I'm not your little innocent protégé, Jason. I'm a full-grown woman with a few fantasies of my own. Are you threatened by that?"

He put a hand over his face and groaned. "Hell, no. But this is only our third time to..." He waved a hand.

"Fuck?" Her gaze was still pissed.

"Don't talk like that," he said, his teeth clenched. "It's not you."

Storm clouds gathered in her gray eyes. "Maybe I say the *F* word twenty times a day. You don't know me."

He sat up and faced her. "Yes, I *do* know you. And my knowing makes you uncomfortable. You don't like it."

Silence fell between them. A succession of emotions flitted across her face. Shock. Chagrin. Reluctance. She inhaled sharply and let the breath out slowly. She shot him a look from beneath lowered lashes. "I suppose I don't. I'm sorry, Jason."

"Am I really that scary?" he asked. His erection had deflated, which was probably best under the circumstances. The pit of his stomach curled, and not in a good way.

"The truth?"

His stomach tightened further. "Yes, please."

"You *are* scary," she said quietly.

His eyes burned. "Is this because you think I'm a flight risk? That I might hurt you like I did Cate?"

She stared at him for so long he almost climbed out of bed. Just when he was ready to admit defeat and call time of death on this relationship, Gabby shook her head slowly. "No. It's not that. I think what happened with your and Cate's wedding probably taught you some valuable lessons about yourself."

"Then why are you afraid of me?" This time, he was the one to find shelter behind the sheet. He scooted up in the bed and propped his back against the headboard, the covers over his lap.

Gabby copied his posture, her hands twisting. "When you

and I were in Blossom Branch, I shared some things with you that even Cate and Leah don't know."

"And why was that?"

She chewed her bottom lip, her face pale and haunted. "I thought it would chase you away."

"But it didn't."

Her breath hitched audibly, half sob, half rueful chuckle. "No, it didn't. You seem to be a particularly stubborn man."

He reached for one of her hands and twined his fingers with hers. "Only where you're concerned." He lifted her hand to his mouth and kissed her fingers. "If you tell me to leave you alone, I will. But I don't want to walk away from this. Just so we're clear. I think you and I might be perfect for each other."

She closed her eyes, sighed, and dropped her chin to her chest. "No," she whispered. "We're not."

"Why do you believe that, Gabby?"

After uncurling her fingers from his, she rested her elbows on her knees and put her head in her hands. Her voice was muffled when she spoke. "Couples need at least something in common. You and I are too different. You were born with that shiny silver spoon in your mouth, and I—"

She stopped short.

"You're what?"

"I pinch pennies." She sat up and stared at him, her eyes shiny with tears. "I worry about the future. I wonder if any of my mother's mental health issues are hereditary. I'm cautious and not spontaneous. I always count the cost of any endeavor, both literal and emotional. The farthest I've ever traveled from Atlanta is Macon for a work conference. Once the sexual fire between you and me burns out, you'll discover that I'm boring as hell. And although you haven't brought it up, I don't even know if I want to have kids."

He blinked, trying desperately to process the flood of information. "I see."

"I only wanted to have sex with you, Jason. I'm lonely, and I've always liked you. But you keep dangling the prospect of more, and that scares me to death."

For the first time, he understood the full scope of the obstacles in his way. "Do I?" he asked weakly, struggling for the words to make this better. "Dangle things?"

Gabby shot him a wry look. "You introduced me to your parents."

He winced. "And my mother is taking you to lunch Monday."

"Indeed."

Inwardly he floundered, embarrassed at how badly he had approached this relationship with the woman who had him tied in knots. "I understand what you're saying. I do. And maybe you're not wrong. We *are* very different. But…"

"But what?" The naked yearning on her face gave him a sliver of hope.

"But we could take things slowly. Not the sex, obviously." His laugh was not filled with humor at all. More like rueful awareness that no matter what happened, he would take whatever crumbs she was willing to give him. "Let me be your lover, my beautiful Gabby. The other…well…"

Her chin lifted. "Well, what?"

He shrugged. "There's no clock ticking. You have your job and your mom. I have the remodel from hell. In between, let's be together. We gave ourselves five days, almost six, to think this through. Is sex with me something you want?"

This sweet, gorgeous woman was the queen of awkward pauses. Even now, she didn't blurt out an answer. She studied his face, her gray eyes pools of mystery. After an eternity, she nodded. "Yes."

Like a shock to the heart, that single affirmative syllable breathed life into him. Jubilation swelled in his chest, even though he was only now accepting how badly she could hurt him. The end of his wedding plans with Cate had been traumatic. If Gabby decided he wasn't worth the effort, walking away from her would wreck him.

He swallowed hard. "Good. I feel the same."

"So we'll have an affair?"

Anxiety echoed in her question.

"Does anybody really use that word anymore? Well, maybe when it's a politician and a married woman. But other than that, I think what we do in private is our business only. You can tell people or not tell people. I'll play this your way, I promise. All that matters is our friendship."

Finally, a real smile lit her face. "Friends with benefits."

"Something like that."

More silence gathered. Like an actor who had forgotten his lines, Jason had no idea how to get off the stage. "I should probably go," he said, trying to disguise his utter misery at the thought.

Gabby scooted closer, shaking her head. "Don't go. I swear I won't squabble with you anymore. I want you, Jason. That's not going to change anytime soon." She cupped his cheek in her hand. "You make me laugh. You make me yearn. We may not have forever, but we have now."

It wasn't a perfect speech, not to his way of thinking. But he was wise enough to know when it was time to regroup. "Yes, we damn well do," he said quietly. She had invited him to spend the night. That was huge. Yet he had almost ruined things.

Together, they eased down into the bed, wrestling with covers. Studying each other with sideways glances that were edgy and uncertain.

When they were on their backs, he shucked his boxers the rest of the way and tossed them on the floor. "I have protection," he said. "If you're ready."

She moved half over him, one hand on his chest, her palm

covering his heart. "I'm ready." She smiled sweetly. "But I'd really like to touch you. Is that okay?"

He gulped. "Sure."

This time, she didn't move much at all. With her gaze locked on his, she found him beneath the covers and stroked him gently. Her smile was more naughty than sweet. "You have a most impressive body. Even better than in college when I watched you jogging shirtless across the quad."

His eyebrows shot up. "You watched me?"

"Only freshman year," she said quickly. "Not when you and Cate started dating. That would have been creepy and gross."

When her fingers wrapped around his reenergized erection, he gasped, his forehead damp. "Feel free to watch all you want."

"I think I'll watch your face instead," she teased. "To see what you like."

"I swear, darlin', if you're doin' it, I like it."

She leaned down and pressed her lips to his. A baby kiss. An innocent kiss. It shouldn't have revved his motor, but it did. He curled a hand behind her neck and pulled her closer. "Kiss me like you mean it."

She took him at his word. Having Gabby in his arms, eager and lush, made him ravenous. He pulled her on top of him and took the kiss deeper still. Her body nestled against his perfectly. He ran his hands from her shoulders to her ass, barely able to breathe.

She splayed her hands on his collarbone. "Hurry, Jason."

"Give me half a sec." He reached for the bedside table, grabbed a condom packet, and ripped it open. Honestly, he had never reconsidered protection at any point in his life, but for a split second, the image of a pregnant Gabby filled his brain.

Shaking off the disconcerting thought, he took care of business and rolled back to her. "You want to be on top?"

She blushed. "No thanks. Boring, remember?"

He smiled, moving over her and settling between her thighs.

"Never." He held her gaze and held his breath as he entered her slowly. "I've thought about this all week."

"Me, too." Her breath caught audibly when he surged deeper.

Being inside her felt more perfect and right than anything he had ever experienced. The way she looked at him tightened his chest. His Gabby might think they were too different, but how could she doubt this?

He tried to take things slowly. It was late, though, and he had wondered if this moment would ever happen tonight. The need to come clawed in his gut. "I can't, I can't…" he groaned.

Gabby wrapped her legs around his waist. "Don't hold back. I've got you."

When he came, he lost himself for long, wrenching moments. Gabby's embrace tethered him, bound him to her whether she wanted it or not.

He knew she hadn't come this time. How could she in such a rush to the finish line? When he mumbled as much with his face pressed to the curve of her shoulder, she stroked his hair. "We're one for one. I'm good."

Sleep claimed him. When he roused eons later and glanced at his watch, it was almost two. *Shit.* How could he check out with so much at stake?

Gabby was on her side, facing away from him. His body spooned hers. One of his arms had settled loosely beneath her breasts.

He inhaled deeply, breathing in the scent of her hair and the fragrance of warm skin and sex. "Gabby?" he whispered, not sure if she was as out of it as he had been.

Immediately she rolled onto her back. "Yes?"

"Have you slept?"

Her smile was heavy-lidded. "Dozed. On and off."

His eager cock nudged her hip. "Again?"

"Oh, yes…"

This time, he didn't ask her preference. After donning a second condom, he lifted her on top of him without thinking and thrust wildly. There was a tiny second of uncertainty on his part. Maybe a tendency to freak out. Because, hell, this carnal desperation was wild and agonizing. Unprecedented.

He fucked her with everything he had. Soul, mind, and body. She leaned forward, her fingers gripping his shoulders. Though he loved the way her hair brushed his face, he wanted to see her eyes.

"Sit up," he croaked.

"Okay."

He steadied her with his hands on her hips as she did what he asked. But now she was still. Her gaze was guarded.

Inside her, his sex trembled and swelled impossibly more. "Touch your breasts. How you would if you were alone."

Something flickered in her gaze. But she cupped the creamy mounds of flesh and pressed them together.

"Now the nipples."

Her jaw dropped. Even in the dim light, he was certain her cheeks turned pink. She used two fingers to bracket her left nipple. It was pert and taut.

"Ah, Gabby..." He touched her where their bodies joined. She gasped, wiggled closer, and then cried out when she hit the peak. He held her through the storm. Then, when her body went lax, he rolled her under him and took her hard and fast until his own climax roared through him like a tornado obliterating everything in its path.

When he could breathe, he shifted to one side, afraid his weight was too much for her. But he rested his cheek on her shoulder and pressed his hand flat on her stomach, as if he could keep her from leaving him.

Gabby sighed. "Good night, Jason." Her voice was slurred with exhaustion. No wonder. She had probably been up for hours.

"Good night, Gabby." He reached down and pulled the sheet

and blanket and comforter to cover them. His eyes were heavy already when she lifted his hand from her stomach, kissed his fingers, and then rolled to her side away from him.

He pulled her bottom into his groin, shuddered with satisfaction, and let the darkness claim him.

# Chapter 16

Gabby opened one gritty eyelid and tried to remember what had happened. First there was the fancy society party. Later a stop at Jason's house. An argument at hers. And then sex. *Oh, the sex.*

A blush spread from her throat to her hairline, though there was no one to see. The woman who had made love to Jason in this bed with reckless abandon—for hours—was her hedonistic, unfamiliar twin. That other female looked like Gabby. She talked like Gabby. But her willingness to be free and open was unfamiliar at best.

One thing was clear. A big, warm, tempting-as-hell Jason Brightman was still asleep in her bed. And to be honest, he showed no signs of rousing.

She would die before admitting to him that she had never spent an entire night with a man. He already thought of her as innocent and naive when it came to physical intimacy. The fact that they had indulged in sex half a dozen times during the night might have advanced her experience considerably, but she didn't want to let him know she had issues relating to this kind of situation.

For one thing, *the morning after* was new to her.

She needed to pee. And she craved a shower.

But what if she accidentally woke him up? Shouldn't she at least brush her teeth before they got involved again?

Inch by inch, she slid her body away from his side of the bed, lifting his arm slowly and substituting a pillow beneath it. When she was ready to stand up, she took an entire ten seconds to listen to him breathe. Not quite a snore, but close. He was dead to the world, his body completely relaxed.

She smirked. No wonder he was comatose. The man had burned a whole lot of calories during the night.

When she stood, her head spun dizzily. Maybe she, too, was going to feel the aftereffects. Her thighs ached pleasantly, and her body was the tiniest bit stiff.

Opening a drawer to get jeans and a top seemed too risky. Instead, she grabbed a clean pair of undies from the laundry basket on the floor of her closet. Her knee-length pink chenille bathrobe would have to do. Her feet were freezing now that she was out of bed, so she grabbed the matching pink scuffs and carried her armor to the bathroom.

After carefully locking the door, she used the bathroom, turned on the shower faucet, and stared at herself in the mirror as she waited for the water to heat. She had a smudge of mascara under one eye, but other than that, not too bad.

It was the glow that alarmed her. She looked happy and satisfied. Her usual guarded expression was nowhere to be found. Shouldn't that worry her?

She bit her lip but couldn't erase the smile that lifted her mouth into a smug curve. Last night with Jason had been incredible. She couldn't even whip up any desire to kick him out of her apartment. It was Sunday. There was no rush.

Astonishingly, the clock said it was almost noon. She couldn't recall the last time she had stayed in bed so long. Maybe a year ago when she'd had the flu?

Quickly she showered and washed her hair. After wrapping her head in a towel, she brushed her teeth. Then she finished drying off and slipped into her robe, belting it tightly around her waist.

When she opened the door, the apartment was still and quiet. After taking a peek at her guest—who was still sound asleep— she made her way to the kitchen, prepped the coffeepot, and turned it on. She owned one of those single-pod machines, but she had company today. It was bound to be a more-than-one-cup morning for both of them.

As she cradled her first mug between her palms, she heard the bathroom door open and shut. Then the water running. Thank goodness. She hadn't wanted to be responsible for waking him up. No telling what might have happened.

She trembled—all alone in the kitchen—and knew she was in trouble. Fun, delightful, satisfying trouble, but trouble nevertheless.

When Jason finally walked into the room, she was standing at the sink looking out the window at the squirrels who always managed to steal her neighbor's birdseed from the feeder. Gabby looked over her shoulder at him. "Good morning, sleepyhead."

If life were fair, he should have looked slightly hungover. Or at least haggard. But the man with the crystal-blue eyes was as stunning as ever. He wore jeans and thick wool socks, but he was bare from the waist up.

He came up behind her and nuzzled the back of her neck, pressing his lips to her nape. "I deserve that. Why didn't you wake me up?"

She turned in his arms and kissed him lazily. "I thought you needed the sleep. You want me to make you some toast? Or eggs?"

He smiled, his eyes heavy-lidded. "How does brunch sound? I know a fun place. And I need to do an errand at the mall while we're out."

She poured him a cup of coffee and watched as he doctored it with cream and two sugars. "An errand?" she said. "You want to go to a mall the weekend before Christmas? Are you mad?" She knew he was referring to Lenox Square. It was the large, upscale property in the heart of Buckhead. Even though the twenty-fifth was still six days away—next Saturday, to be exact—malls everywhere were sure to be crowded with shoppers.

"It won't take long." He drained half the cup.

"What are you going for?"

He smiled ruefully. "My mom's parents retired to a condo on Marco Island in Florida a few years back. They usually come up for Christmas. But Granddad has been ill, so they've decided to stay put for now. I'll probably fly down there one weekend in January and do some fishing with them."

"And how does that connect to the mall?"

His smile was abashed. "My grandmother bought me a present from Neiman Marcus. She hates getting out to mail things, so I'm going to pick it up."

"Wouldn't Neiman's have shipped it for her?"

"They would, yes, but she was afraid that she ordered too late, and she doesn't trust any of the shipping companies. I could tell she was fretting about it, so I promised I would pick it up in person."

Gabby patted his cheek. "What a good grandson. And yes, I'm starving. Brunch it is. I can be ready in fifteen minutes."

While Jason lingered in the kitchen for another cup of coffee, Gabby dashed into her bedroom to get dressed and blow-dry her hair with a round brush. She threw on a pair of slim black pants with a red sweater and black flats. Because her hair cooperated, she soon had it curving at her chin in a familiar style.

She had friends who loved changing their color and cut often. No, thanks. Gabby's hair philosophy was *if it ain't broke, don't fix it*.

When she was done, she dashed back to the kitchen. "I'm ready," she said, breathless and still somewhat flummoxed that

Jason now seemed at home in her apartment. "But I think you have to wear a shirt."

He grinned. "Yes, ma'am." After setting his coffee mug in the sink, he yawned and stretched. The muscles in his abdomen moved subtly, mesmerizing her. "Give me two minutes," he said. On the way to the hallway, he paused to kiss her.

His lips were firm and warm and coaxing. He smelled like sleepy male and a trace of evergreen scent she had noticed last night. She leaned toward him and tried to pretend that kissing half-naked men on a Sunday morning was nothing new.

Their lazy wake-up routine suddenly became edged with danger.

Gabby was embarrassed to hear the needy sound she made when he pulled her close and took the kiss deeper.

Jason groaned. "I could do my errand tomorrow."

She put both hands on his chest and shoved, her fingertips tingling from contact with his warm, smooth skin. "Oh, no. We can't stay in bed all day."

"Because?"

She felt her face go hot. "Well, honestly, I'm a little…um…"

He grinned. "Chafed? Sore?"

"Something like that," she said wryly, wishing she could match his nonchalance. Her whole reality felt slightly off-kilter. As if all of this was a dream, and she was eventually going to wake up.

"Fine," he said, pretending to grumble. "Be a spoilsport. Let me grab my shirt and we'll be on our way."

When he returned, it was hard to breathe. How did he do that? He was wearing the same pair of trendy dress jeans and the woolen socks. But he had added a thin black cashmere V-neck sweater over a black-and-white-checked shirt. Expensive ankle boots in dark brown leather completed his ensemble.

Though everything had been stuffed in his duffel bag willy-nilly, and he hadn't even taken the time to shave, he looked like an ad for *wealthy guy enjoys the weekend*. It wasn't fair at all.

She told herself clothes didn't make the man. Jason was genuine and caring. Since he clearly had a thing for her—at least now—she needed to get over her squeamishness about his money. His natural masculine confidence was not an attempt to impress Gabby, or anyone, for that matter. He was who he was.

Over brunch they talked books and movies and podcasts. She asked questions about his photography and smiled inwardly to herself at his boundless enthusiasm for lighting and composition.

His offhand mentions of exotic locations drove home to her how limited her global experience was. She *wanted* to travel. And she had recently reached a point financially where a big trip wasn't out of the question. But the thought of leaving her mother behind stalled Gabby every time. Dahlia would barely escape Blossom Branch for a day trip to Atlanta, much less exit the state or the country.

As they left the restaurant and climbed back into Jason's car, she groaned. "You let me eat too much. The bacon and eggs were amazing. But those Belgian waffles with the chocolate sauce were over-the-top."

He chuckled as he pulled out onto Peachtree Street. "Well worth it, though. We can go for a run later this afternoon. Offset all those calories."

Gabby mulled that statement. Did he assume they were spending the day together? Based on last night's activities, that wasn't altogether out of the question. But was she okay with his moving into her life so easily?

She'd been honest with him. The way she felt about Jason was scary. He made the world brighter, more fun. If Gabby let herself rely on him, how broken would she be when they parted company?

Her dark thoughts occupied her all the way to the mall parking lot. Jason had to circle three entire levels before they found an empty space. The sheer volume of cars was staggering. Finally they made it inside.

Neiman Marcus was down a wide corridor off the center section. Overhead, holiday decorations added to the festive air, as did the hordes of happy and not-so-happy customers. Christmas brought out the best in most and the worst in some.

In Neiman's they made their way through the array of fancy cosmetic counters at the front of the store. Gabby had brought her mother here one day so the two of them could collect samples. Dahlia had thought the whole thing was a great lark. She never used any of the products.

Now Jason and Gabby took the escalator down to the floor below, where an extensive men's department was located. "I'll ask that guy," Jason said, heading for a discreetly placed sales register.

The poor store clerk was visibly harried. The line of people waiting to speak to him was four deep when Jason joined the queue. Jason gave Gabby a wave with a rueful expression that made her smile. Served him right for thinking he was immune to the difficulties of holiday shopping.

Gabby hovered at a distance, not wanting to seem curious. She crisscrossed the area, pausing to touch the sleeve of a charcoal wool-blend suit that cost more than a month of her rent. If she had an iota of artistic talent, it would be fun to work here and showcase the designer goods. There were shirts and belts stacked gracefully around white reindeer. Italian dress shoes filled with colorful Christmas ornaments.

Her favorite display was an eye-catching assortment of men's silk boxers and neckties. The center of the table supported an artfully snowy mountain. The underwear and ties had been layered beautifully in a cascade down the sides of the faux hill. Some items were navy with a tiny green Christmas tree print. Others red with white snowflakes. And of course the more traditional paisleys and stripes.

When she looked, Jason was still one back in the line waiting for help. He had his phone in his hand, probably reading email. To entertain herself, she picked up one of the pairs of boxers at the bottom of the mountain and glanced at the price tag. A hundred seventy-five dollars? *Good lord.* For underpants?

She knew this wasn't her kind of store. Even with her current job. But thriftiness ran deep in her psyche. Maybe she was being prissy and judgmental. People could spend their money however they wished. It wasn't up to her to police the world.

Still, it was hard to swallow.

Finally Jason was done. He returned to her side carrying a silver box tied with a burgundy bow. "Sorry about that. I didn't think it would take so long."

"Are you going to open it?"

He chuckled, putting a hand at her back and steering both of them toward the escalator. "Not now. I already know what it is."

When they were back in the car, she watched him toss the package in the back seat before starting the engine.

"Obviously not breakable," she said, fastening her seat belt.

Jason backed out of the space and was nearly caught between two cars duking it out for the newly vacated spot. He eased around three more cars in the narrow aisle and headed for the exit. When they were finally out on the road and merged into traffic, he exhaled. "Remind me never to do that again."

"So you're not going to tell me?" she said, teasing him.

He shot her a laughing glance. "Tell you what?"

"About your present."

"Oh, that." He braked hard when the car in front of them skidded to a stop at a traffic light. "Let's hope we get home in one piece," he said. Then he grinned. "Since you risked life and limb with me to pick up the box, I guess I can tell you. When I was a teenager, my grandparents bought me all the usual electronic gifts. Tablets, phones, you know. But the first Christmas after I turned eighteen, my grandfather told me it was time to embrace an adult man's luxuries."

Gabby raised her eyebrows. "I'm almost afraid to ask."

"Exactly. I had the same initial reaction. My grandmother

pretended to be scandalized, but in reality, she thought it was fun. They gave me silk boxers for Christmas. It's become a kind of tongue-in-cheek family joke, but every December 25 for a decade now, the gift is always the same."

"I see," Gabby said faintly. "I'll have to admit, a pair of silk boxers is a bit odd coming from the older generation."

"Oh, no," he said, still grinning. "It's *half a dozen* pairs—in a collection of colors—every Christmas."

She felt her stomach twist unpleasantly. Jason's gift cost over a thousand dollars? For boxers? Still, what was in the beautifully wrapped present might *not* be the same as ones in the display she had seen. Maybe the boxers in his beautifully wrapped present were *only* a hundred bucks a pair. It didn't really matter. The fact was, this family could afford to gift their beloved grandson with a completely unnecessary luxury.

But wasn't that the point? Luxuries *weren't* necessary.

The whole incident left her unsettled. It seemed to reinforce the myriad of differences between them. Her friend and lover had never known financial hardship. That wasn't his fault. Nor was it something to be pursued.

At the next traffic light, Jason reached across and squeezed her hand. "You okay? You got awfully quiet."

She nodded. "I'm fine. Probably all those waffle carbs making me sleepy."

Back at her apartment, she felt a knot grow in her chest. As much as she would have liked a repeat of the night before, another part of her needed Jason gone. Everything was going too fast.

In her kitchen, she gave him a cajoling smile. "The past twenty-four hours have been wonderful, Jason. I've loved every minute with you. But to be honest, I have a few Sunday evening routines to get ready for the workweek. Grocery shopping. Food prep. Laundry. I hope you understand."

The lighthearted expression on his face disappeared. His gaze narrowed. "You're kicking me out." It wasn't a question.

"Not kicking you out," she protested. She made herself approach him and kiss his cheek. "Just needing some time at the end of a long weekend to prepare for tomorrow."

Her smile was genuine. Even affectionate. She didn't think she had revealed any of her unsettled emotions.

Jason was visibly disgruntled. "Is something wrong? Are you upset about having lunch with my mother?"

"I'm fine with your mother. She doesn't scare me. Lunch will be short and sweet. Don't you worry about it."

He folded his arms across his chest. "I've bought you a Christmas present," he said bluntly. "No need for you to reciprocate. Besides, I know you'll say it's *too soon* or *not necessary*. When can I give it to you?"

This was a curveball she hadn't seen coming. Certainly not the bold, head-on question. "Um…can I text you in a couple of days? Work is crazy this week. I'm not sure when I'm heading to Blossom Branch."

What she didn't say was that the sex they had shared was so incredible, she was torn. Did she encourage a repeat performance, or should she step back before she ended up far too involved? If she eased away from Jason now, that would be the end of it. He was a gentleman. He wouldn't pursue her if she made it clear she wasn't interested.

But that was a huge problem. Jason *knew* what things were like between them. He *knew* Gabby was head over heels in lust with him.

She wouldn't let herself think beyond that truth. It made perfect sense that she enjoyed him in bed. He was stunningly masculine, but sweet and tender, too.

This was a bad time to admit she might be in love with him. In fact, she had probably been in love with Jason Brightman for a decade in one way or another. No other man ever came close to being so perfect and yet so completely wrong for her.

Jason took her wrist and pulled her into his arms. "So you're saying you don't want to be naked with me one more time today?" He stroked her hair, his smile gentle as if he knew she was fragile in this moment.

"I *want* to have sex with you," she said firmly. "I do. But we both know what will happen. It would be last night all over again."

He ran his thumb across her cheekbone, his eyes lit with a tiny blue flame that betrayed his arousal. "And that's a bad thing?"

She rested her cheek against his shoulder, inhaling his scent. Memorizing the feel of his big arms wrapped around her. "It's a wonderful thing. But your current *job* caters to the schedule you want. Mine doesn't. I'm sorry."

"Don't be sorry." He bent and kissed her lips, then stepped away quickly as if he was afraid to linger. "I understand, Gabby. You've given me so much this weekend. I won't push for more. I respect your work ethic and your sense of responsibility."

She winced. "I've been called a stick-in-the-mud. A party pooper. Debbie Downer. Not everyone appreciates a person who is incapable of throwing caution to the wind. I'd like to be that woman. I've tried at times. But it's not who I am."

"I like you exactly the way you are, Gabby." He shoved his hands in his pockets, his jaw outthrust. "Don't assume I'm trying to change you. I'm not. I can't help it if you're so sexy and desirable that I want you 24/7."

Her gaze widened. "You're exaggerating," she said, the words strangled with disbelief and embarrassment at his raw pronouncement.

"No." He stared at her. "You're everything I want in a woman. I could make a list if you like."

She managed a rusty chuckle. "Thanks for the offer, but no. I believe you. You must know how much I want you, too."

"But wanting isn't enough, is it?" he asked, the words low and rumbly. As if he hadn't meant to say them at all.

She thought about that. "Well… I suppose it depends on the

end goal. If you and I choose to give and receive pleasure as lovers, then maybe all the ways we're different won't matter so much."

He straightened, his posture stiff. "And if the goal is far more visceral—deeper, more significant?"

She shifted from one foot to the other, wishing she were sitting down. "I don't know what you mean." That was a lie. Of course she did. He was talking about the two of them as a couple. For real.

The thought of that sent a rush of emotion through her veins—a combination of delighted anticipation and flat-out terror.

Jason saw through her pathetic attempt to misunderstand him. His smile was grim. "Don't worry, Gabby. You look like you're going to faint. I'll be as patient as I need to be, I swear."

If his patience was all she needed, his promise would have solved everything.

But what if there *was no* answer? What if there would *never* be an answer? This whole thing might be temporary at best. What if Jason Brightman and Gabby Nolan had no long-term alignment? What if they were bound for disaster?

Gabby wasn't the only one with vulnerabilities. She didn't want to be Jason's rebound fling. That wouldn't be good for him because of his relationship with Cate…and Gabby's with Cate, as well. If things blew up, life would be very complicated.

"We have time," she said weakly.

His face darkened, though he nodded slowly. "Sure," he said curtly. "Let me know when we can see each other before Christmas."

Before she could say another word to him, he opened the door and walked out.

# Chapter 17

Jason didn't start the engine. Instead, he sat in his car in the parking lot of the Peachtree Court apartments and conceded reluctantly that he didn't belong here. Not that he didn't *want* to be here...but that he was an outsider. Someone who had never lived a life of financial stress.

Gabby had told him so many stories about her neighbors. He'd even met a few of them in passing. He couldn't think of a single person or family in this complex who didn't struggle in one way or another. Childcare issues. Elderly folks with no support system. Teenagers with dreams that were curtailed by the financial realities of their parents.

Shame filled him, but for what, he didn't know. He liked to think he was generous with his money and his resources. He hoped his friends knew they could always come to him for help. Still, he realized for the first time that although he had often brushed aside Gabby's concerns, she was right. Their backgrounds were opposite sides of the moon.

How could he understand and love her when she had overcome almost insurmountable obstacles in life? She needed a man who would appreciate her strengths and shore up her hidden insecurities. A person who recognized what those early years had done to her…how they had shaped her.

His eyes stung and his chest ached. Finally he knew what he had to do.

He pulled out his phone. Hit a number. Waited.

When the person on the other end answered, he cleared his throat. "Are you guys home? Can I come over and talk to you?"

The affirmative from the man who was his de facto brother helped him breathe.

"I'll be there in twenty minutes," Jason said.

Harry's penthouse apartment was luxurious in every way. But homey, too. Cate had added a few feminine touches when she moved in.

They both greeted him at the door when he got off the elevator.

"Are you okay?" Cate asked anxiously.

Harry put a hand on her arm. "Give him a minute, love. He just got here." Harry shot Jason a rueful smile. "My wife is a worrier, as you know. We ordered pizza. Thought you might be hungry. It should be here soon. Come on into the den."

Jason breathed a little easier. Maybe he had come close to having a panic attack. That was a hell of a thing for him to admit. But he was struggling suddenly in high weeds, and he needed help.

The pizza arrived even before they were all seated. Harry offered him a beer. Jason chose Coke. He was too wound up to drink. He needed a clear head.

Cate and Harry didn't question him right off. Jason offered no explanations for his sudden appearance. They ate and drank. Discussed the weather. Bemoaned the stock market. Talked winter sports.

At last, Cate was incensed. "Stop it, you two. Jason is here for a reason." She smiled at him sweetly. "Go ahead. We're listening."

Jason bounded to his feet and paced. The pizza churned in his stomach. Finally he stopped with his back to the fireplace, shoved his hands in his pockets, and stared at his two friends. "I'm in love with Gabby."

*Damn.* That wasn't how he'd meant to start this conversation. But the words had been bottled up inside his chest since yesterday. He sure as hell couldn't have said them to Gabby. He knew instinctively that a declaration like that would have sent her running.

Telling Cate and Harry was the next best thing.

Cate burst into tears immediately. She jumped to her feet and hugged him. "That's wonderful news."

Over her head, Jason and Harry exchanged a grim look.

Harry sighed. "Easy, love. I don't think it is."

Cate sat down, wiped her face with a tissue, and glanced back and forth between the two men. "Why not?"

Harry looked at Jason. "Like she said. We're listening."

Jason sat on the hearth and rolled his shoulders. "Cate...you don't know this, but I asked Gabby out back in college. Long before you and I started dating. She shot me down right away. I'll admit. It hurt my pride."

Cate nodded slowly. "I'm not surprised she would have said no. She wasn't at all social back then. I had to drag her to parties and get-togethers. Gradually she loosened up, but that reserve she has will always be there, I think."

Harry nodded. "Gabby isn't an easy person to get close to. I suppose you know that already." His sympathetic expression as he spoke made Jason feel worse.

"Oh, I do know," Jason said. "From the moment we ran into each other earlier this month, she's been telling me why we could never be a couple. Because we're too different." Jason shook his head slowly. "But the truth is…" He trailed off, feeling disloyal to his lover. Should he even be talking about their private lives? On the other hand, Cate and Harry knew better than anyone how tricky this was.

"The truth is?" Cate wrung her hands. "Don't stop there. I'm worried about both of you. What happened? You each seemed happy at your parents' party yesterday."

Jason cleared his throat, feeling his face go hot. "We had an amazing night. *All night.* She was open and sexy and funny, but…"

Now it was Harry's turn. "But what, Jason? Did you upset her?"

"No, damn it. Everything was perfect. Until today, I think I screwed up and didn't even know it."

Cate poured herself another glass of wine. "I think you'd better start at the beginning. We can't help if we don't know what's going on."

Jason rubbed his eyes with the heel of his hands, suddenly feeling the sleep deprivation from the night before. "I took her to brunch, and we stopped by Lenox. My grandmother wanted me to pick up my gift from her at Neiman's since she and Granddad aren't coming at Christmas."

Cate snickered. "The silk boxers, right? Your grandparents are a hoot. They get you those every year."

"Yeah, the boxers." Jason grimaced. "I think Gabby saw a price tag and…" He swallowed hard.

He still felt a little sick at his lack of understanding.

Harry was a brilliant man. He caught on immediately. "Gabby saw you holding a box of ridiculously priced silk underpants, and it proved her point that the two of you should never end up together. Period."

"That's about it," Jason said. "The truth is, I'm finally beginning to understand that she may be right. I don't care about her past. Other than to admit it hurts like hell to think about what she endured as a child and a teenager. I love the woman she is now. But I may not be the man I need to be for her."

"Why not?" Cate asked indignantly.

Jason shrugged. "She's told me about a few of her neighbors. The single mom with two young sons. Daycare eats up a third of her paycheck. And then there's the older lady who has mobility issues and survives on a fixed income. The compensation package for Gabby's job means she could live lots of places in Atlanta, but she *chooses* to stay at Peachtree Court, because she *belongs*. Those are her people. In fact, she's experienced far worse in life than most of her fellow residents."

Harry nodded. "Empathy. Our Gabby has it in spades. She *feels* things deeply. Her caring heart endears her to everyone in her orbit."

Jason looked at Cate. "I know you and Leah are her dearest friends. And she is so very grateful for all you did to take her under your wing at UGA. But when we were in Blossom Branch recently, she showed me things and told me some about her past that she says even you guys don't know."

Cate's gaze was wide and worried. "Why would she do that?"

Harry rubbed his jaw. "Because she feels close to Jason? Romantically?"

Jason snorted. "I wish. No. She was trying to push me away. When I questioned her about that very thing, she admitted it."

"So what are you going to do?" Cate asked.

"Give her time?" Harry frowned.

"It's not as simple as time," Jason said. "That's why I'm here. I need to talk this through. You two know Gabby as well as you know me."

"What's there to talk about?" Cate said. She kicked off her shoes and curled her legs beneath her. "Gabby needs a man who will love and care for her. She deserves that—more than anyone I know."

Harry shook his head slowly. "I don't know that I agree with you, sweetheart. Gabby is incredibly strong. She doesn't need someone to take care of her. Love her, yes. But she can chart her own life."

Jason resumed his pacing. "I want to be with Gabby. I want to love her and spoil her and fight with her and...well, everything."

"So what's the problem?" Cate asked. She and Harry stared at him.

"That's just it. I'm not sure. Maybe a guy like me can't be the man she needs. I've never faced a single day where I worried about money. Gabby, though, went to bed hungry on multiple occasions in her young life. Do you see how that looks from her side? There are so many layers to her, maybe I *never* can understand. I might end up failing her because of my ignorance."

Jason had been hoping Cate or Harry or both would jump in and convince him that everything was going to be okay. Instead, they sat in silence, clearly processing his words, their expressions troubled.

Harry stood up as well and stretched. "What's the harm in trying?"

Jason swallowed hard. "If this relationship with Gabby is a possibility—if I want her in my life permanently—I have to be sure. I nearly ruined Cate's future. I can't do that to another woman."

"Don't be stupid," Cate said indignantly. "You and I were both to blame for our mismatch. You didn't ruin it. We were both afraid to admit the truth."

"It was the biggest mistake of my life, Cate. I knew there was something wrong, but I waited until literally the last minute to back out of our wedding."

Harry scowled. "We've both said this to you, Jason, but you're not listening. That's in the past. Yes. You made a mistake. Get over it."

His throat hurt. "What if being with Gabby is an even worse

mistake? I can't do that to her. She's dealt with such hard things in her life. I don't want to be another crisis. I don't want to cause her more pain."

Cate crossed the room and took his face in her hands, her expression pained. "The decision isn't entirely up to you, Jason. Gabby gets to have a vote. You can't presume to know what's best for her." She kissed his cheek and went back to her seat. "Men tend to *fix* problems. Sometimes we women appreciate that. But in a situation like this, I think Gabby will have to take the lead."

"There's more," Harry said. "You may not want to hear it."

"Oh, great. Go ahead." Jason braced inwardly.

Harry shook his head slowly. "I've been a closed-off bastard for a lot of my life. I let *you* get close when you were a scrappy six-year-old kid and I was sixteen. We kept that bond and still have it to this day. But when I was in love with Cate, I was a chickenshit coward. I hated to see her hurting so badly. I took care of her. Loved her in silence. Despite all that, when the time came, I was afraid to tell her how I felt. I could have easily lost her forever."

"What are you saying?" Jason asked, trying to follow Harry's explanation.

"I'm saying you may have to lay your heart at Gabby's feet and risk letting it get stomped on. You may have to be more vulnerable than you ever have been in your whole beautiful, golden, entitled, easy life. But when that terrifying moment occurs, remind yourself of everything Gabby has endured."

In a startling moment of clarity, Jason saw the truth. Harry and Cate were right. If Jason wanted Gabby in his life, he had to let Gabby call the shots. He had to step back. He had to wait and hope and pray that she would come to him.

It wasn't what he wanted to hear. It wasn't what he wanted to do.

But it was the only way.

"Thanks for the advice," he said gruffly. "I've got a lot to think about."

"You're welcome to stay and watch a movie with us," Cate said.

Jason knew he wasn't doing a good job of covering up his emotional state. "I appreciate the invitation, but I think I'll head to the house and sledgehammer a few things."

Harry grinned. "That dump of yours is better than therapy, right?"

"You could say that." He hugged both his friends and headed for the door. The urge to drive back to Gabby's apartment was almost overwhelming. But he knew he couldn't. "I'll keep in touch," he said. "Good night."

Gabby hadn't expected to miss Jason so badly. Her apartment felt empty and cold without his presence. Even though she had been the one to send him on his way, and even though her decision was the smart thing to do, she felt sad and wrapped in regret.

The late afternoon and the evening stretched on forever. She ran through her list of Sunday night chores automatically. A trip to the grocery store. Back home to wash fruit and start a load of laundry.

When she picked out what she would wear Monday, she was mindful of her lunch with Sheila Brightman. Everyone at Grimes & Hancock adhered to a classy dress code. Any of Gabby's work outfits would have been fine for tomorrow.

Even so, Gabby picked out one of her newer tops. It was a sleeveless apricot silk shell that looked feminine and flattering beneath her charcoal-gray, waist-length jacket. The matching pants showed off her long legs. Often she wore skirts to work, but the temperature was supposed to tumble during the night.

At ten o'clock, she was ready for bed. After getting so little sleep last night, she was ready to crash. But her bedroom was a problem. She could swear Jason had left an imprint in the space. She could see him in her bed. Amused. Aroused. Focused on her pleasure.

Some women might have climbed into the rumpled bed and inhaled the faint remnants of his aftershave on the cotton sheets. Gabby was the opposite. She was determined not to weave silly, pitiful fantasies.

Doggedly, she stripped the bed, tossed the pile of linens on the floor of her small laundry room, and reached into the closet for clean sheets. When the bed was made and the covers smoothed perfectly into place, she breathed more easily.

Jason hadn't disrupted her life. He'd taken her to a fancy, fun party. At her invitation, he had stayed over at her place. They had indulged in incredible, crazy sex. She had enjoyed last night immensely. But tomorrow would be the moment when Gabby Nolan went back to the real world and reclaimed her no-nonsense, predictable life.

She was almost ready to turn out the light when her phone buzzed. She picked it up. "Hey, Jason." She tossed her book to one side as she answered. "What's up?"

"Nothing really. I'm calling to say good-night."

His voice sounded different somehow. Maybe he was hoarse. She curled on her side. "That's nice."

"Do you miss me?"

She gripped the phone. Her breasts ached and her nipples tightened. "You know I do." She was in bad shape if nothing more than hearing him on the phone made her feel so restless and desperately alone.

"I miss you, too, Gabby." He cleared his throat. "Lucas texted me a little while ago. He's off tomorrow and asked if I wanted to take a tour of the camp. Leah, too, of course. I'm excited to see it."

"That sounds like fun," she said wistfully.

"I'll happily reschedule if you'd like to go with us."

"That's okay," she said. She swallowed her weirdly emotional response to hearing that her friends would be socializing without her. Leah and Jason had known each other forever. And Gabby had been to the camp many times. She didn't need to be included.

Jason moved on. "I hate to bring up a potentially sore subject, but are you fretting about lunch with my mom?"

"Not at all. I told you—I like Sheila. It will do me good to get out of the office. I eat lunch at my desk far too often."

"I hope she behaves."

"Maybe *you're* the one who's nervous," Gabby teased. "I promise to say only good things about you."

"Thanks. I think." His voice lowered. "Last night was insanely hot. You made me lose my mind, and I didn't even care. We're good together, Gabby."

"Good in bed." Was she trying to pick a fight?

She heard him laugh wryly.

"It's more than that, and I think you realize it deep down," he said. "You know I want to see you for Christmas. I'll try to be a patient man."

"So I'm supposed to pick a time?"

"Is that so surprising? I'm flexible. I know how hard you work. I'll drop everything when you call."

"Don't say that, Jason. It makes me feel weird."

"Weird, how?"

"Like I'm playing hard to get. I'm not. You remember last night? I *invited you* to spend the night. We were in *my* bed when we…"

"Explored our mutual fantasies?"

She flexed her toes, feeling his phantom touch even when he wasn't with her. "You could say that." When her breath came more quickly, she knew it was time to end the call. "I need to go. Good night, Jason."

"I'll let you sleep," he said. "Though I doubt I will. Good night, Gabby. Sweet dreams."

On Monday morning, Gabby made it to work twenty minutes early. Even her ambitious intern, Jamie, hadn't arrived. Gabby hadn't been willing to risk another emotionally hungover Monday.

Thankfully, she had slept straight through until her alarm rang. Her exhaustion from Saturday night had helped with that. Now she'd had two cups of coffee. Her daily calendar was neatly planned. Even the upcoming lunch with Sheila wasn't bothering her.

The familiar routines of her work were comforting.

A ten o'clock meeting with her immediate boss took a surprising turn. When she showed up in his office, he shut the door. "Have a seat, Gabby."

She wasn't alarmed. Bradley was lazy and a bit too full of himself. He could be goofy and annoying on occasion. But he had never done anything that could remotely be construed as inappropriate. They had a good relationship. Gabby brought in new clients and made them feel important and comfortable with the services they received. Bradley racked up the credit.

"What did you need to see me about?" she asked.

He leaned back in his chair, flipped a page or two on his fancy leather-bound agenda, and gave her an odd look. "This is not to be shared," he said, lowering his voice. "But I'm leaving town."

Her jaw dropped. This silly, pretentious man had it made. Why would he give up such a cushy position? She swallowed all the inappropriate questions that trembled on her lips. "Where are you going? If I may ask? I thought you were very happy here."

"I have been." For once he looked moody. "My wife has been offered a big fancy job at a headhunter firm in Orlando.

It's what she does here in Atlanta. This will be more money, though, and a promotion. She'll be in charge of her own department."

"Wow. That's wonderful," Gabby said. "Please give her my congratulations."

"Sure," he muttered. His gaze was focused out the window. Finally he spun his chair again so he faced Gabby. "The big cheeses here have asked me to consider starting a branch of our company in Florida."

Her jaw dropped briefly before she snapped it shut. "Again. Wow. You must be flattered that they think so highly of you."

"Yeah. I guess." He tapped a pen on his blotter, then shot her a calculating look. "I wondered if you would consider going with me. I'm not a fool, Gabby. I don't have what it takes to do something like that. You're the smart one. I'd give you a huge increase over what you're making here. And a title that reflects your worth. What do you think?"

"Um…" Her head spun. If Grimes & Hancock was her passion, this might be very tempting. But her work here in this building was only a job to her. A means to an end. "I appreciate your trust in me. I do, Bradley. But my answer has to be no. My mother lives alone. I have certain responsibilities with her."

"Move her to Florida, too," he said, the words impatient.

"She wouldn't go, unfortunately. I haven't even been able to get her to relocate to Atlanta. She's a very stubborn woman," Gabby said with a smile.

"I thought this would be your answer," he grumbled. His expression was morose. "You got any suggestions? Preferably someone without kids who wouldn't have to worry about the school year. This thing is going down ASAP."

"Well, Timothy is single and very competent. He might be interested. Or Geneva. She's a widow. Also super sharp. She would be more than capable of setting up a new cast of team members and supporting you."

"Got it." He jotted a couple of notes on a slip of paper and shot her a cajoling glance. "Any chance you might think about this overnight and change your mind? They've given me a huge budget. I could make it worth your while."

She smiled at him kindly. "Thanks, Bradley. But no. I'm settled here in Atlanta."

He sighed. "I understand. I don't like it, but I understand."

When she made a move to stand up, he waved a hand. "Don't go yet. There's one more thing."

"Okay." She settled back in her chair.

"To be honest," he said, "they'll probably offer you a shot at my job as I'm leaving. Don't let them jerk you around. I'll tell you what they're paying me. You ask for more and don't budge. They'll have three or four names on the short list. You'll be my recommendation." He shrugged. "You deserve it, Nolan. You work twice as hard as anybody here."

"I appreciate your vote of confidence," she said faintly, her head spinning. For a moment, she wondered if getting Bradley's job could change how she felt about fitting into Jason's world. She would be an executive at a prestigious company. But she would have even less time to care for her mother. And truthfully, the work at Grimes & Hancock often felt like drudgery. "Thanks for the head's up," she said.

"You're welcome. That's all I've got for now," he said. "But if there's an overnight miracle and you have a change of heart, let me know."

# Chapter 18

At eleven fifty-five, Gabby's phone buzzed, startling her. The text from Jason's mother was short and sweet. I'm here. At the curb out front. Come when you're ready.

*Here we go*, she thought to herself.

Sheila wouldn't have been able to come upstairs. Building security was tight. Although Jason had sweet-talked his way past the cop on duty several weeks ago, Sheila probably didn't see the need. That meant Gabby hurried downstairs to meet her lunch date. This was better all the way around. No need to invite Sheila to her office for a chummy tête-à-tête that might lead to awkward questions from coworkers.

Jason's stylish parent was standing beside a dark Secret Service-ish sedan. Like Gabby, she had chosen to wear pants in deference to the colder weather. Her outfit was topped with a thigh-length fur coat. Real, not faux. Gabby winced inwardly. A fur coat in Georgia was only appropriate for a handful of days each winter. It was the most pretentious and unnecessary of all the expensive female adornments in the South.

But as she had reminded herself before, people with money could spend it however they wished.

Sheila hugged her quickly. "I made a reservation at Athena's. My driver will drop us there and pick us up whenever you say."

Gabby slid into the back seat and scooted across to the other side. The restaurant was barely a third of a mile away. They could easily have gone on foot. Maybe Sheila didn't like walking in dress shoes. Or maybe the cold was to blame.

Either way, it was going to be a short trip.

When they entered the restaurant, the maître d' greeted them warmly and showed them to a cozy table in the back. It was tucked in a corner and surrounded by pots of hibiscus plants staked to narrow wooden trellises.

The waiter took their drink orders, read them the specials, and departed.

Gabby gathered her courage. "Mrs. Brightman... Sheila. I think I know why you wanted to have lunch with me today. And I believe I can put your mind at rest. I'm not after a wedding ring *or* Jason's money. We're having fun together. But nothing more. I promise I'm not a threat to you or your son."

Sheila leaned back in her chair and smiled. "You're way off base, my dear. I think you're wonderful. Particularly for Jason."

Gabby frowned. "You said at the party that Cate would have been the perfect daughter-in-law. I'm nothing at all like her. So I don't follow your logic."

The waiter returned with beverages. Sheila took a sip of her gin and tonic. "I've never seen Jason happier, at least not in the last year and a half. It was very hard for his father and me to watch him suffer after the aborted wedding. My son was trapped in a dark pit. There were days I wondered if he would ever find his way out. But recently—" She smiled. "Jason's almost himself again. I have reason to believe that's all you, Gabby."

"Oh, no ma'am," Gabby said, feeling rattled. "What you're

seeing is probably the fact that he and Cate and Harry have reconciled...made peace between themselves."

"You're too modest, dear."

The lunches arrived about then. Large Italian salads. Small servings of lasagna. As they ate, the conversation was far less personal.

Gabby breathed an inward sigh of relief, but as her small glass of rosé calmed her nerves, one thing became clear. This was a chance to better understand Jason via his mother.

"Tell me about Jason growing up."

Sheila smiled wistfully. "His father and I were a bad match from the beginning. Both of us too stubborn, both of us spoiled by our families. But when we had Jason, it was as if the angels smiled on us despite our rocky marriage. I know you'll think I'm biased, but at every age, people have loved Jason. Where some teenage boys go through a moody, rebellious stage, Jason was always a calm, steady rock."

"I see that in him," Gabby said quietly.

Sheila went on. "My son was often surrounded by boys and young men who wanted to emulate him or girls and young women who wanted to catch his attention. Even as a child of ten or twelve, he had an uncanny ability to talk with adults as well as his peers. Perhaps that was a result of being an only child. I don't know."

"You must be very proud of him."

"I am," Sheila said. "It took great courage to call off that wedding. His timing sucked. No one denies that. But he did the right thing."

"Yes."

"I can't explain it," she said, "but Jason inherited the best of his father and me, yet none of our failings. He deserves to be happy. Did you know that in high school, one of his teammates suffered a terrible injury during a football game? Jason organized a blood drive when it was needed and rounded up more than two hundred volunteers. He was an Eagle Scout. His college fraternity won awards for community service, most of which was driven by Jason. You would have to search far and wide to find anyone who dislikes him."

"I believe you," Gabby said. "Which is why he should end up with a woman who can be his equal."

Sheila frowned. "You work for one of the most prestigious firms in Atlanta. You dress beautifully. You're poised and sophisticated and successful. I fail to see how you aren't perfect for him. I've heard snippets over the years that you had financial difficulties when you were at UGA. None of us care about that."

Gabby didn't want to open a vein and expose her painful roots. But Sheila needed to know the truth so she could steer her son in another direction. Gabby laid down her fork and folded her hands in her lap.

"It's more than that, Sheila. My mother was pregnant when her boyfriend was killed. I was born when she was sixteen. The state nearly took me away from her. My mother has battled mental illness for years. We weren't poor when I was a child. We were destitute. Everything I've accomplished in my adult life has been so I could take care of her. You and your family are lovely people, but we have no life experience in common. You need to introduce your son to daughters of your society friends."

"No," Jason's mother said. The word was flat. "I need *you* to help him focus. He clearly thinks the world of you. He *wants* you. Use your influence, Gabby. Remind him that with great privilege comes great responsibility. He's not too old to go back to school. Start a new career."

"Why can't he take his time?" Gabby asked. "This house he bought is important to him. Ask him about it. He'll tell you."

Sheila scowled. "I don't care about the house. I want grandchildren. And I want my son to have a good life. A settled life."

"He plans to travel the world. Take more pictures. He's not your sweet little boy anymore. He's a complicated man. Surely you see that."

Sheila waved a hand at the waiter. "I'll have another drink," she said to him. Then she stared at Gabby once more, her eyes narrowed. "You care about my son. Maybe more than you realize. That party at my house this weekend was not somewhere you wanted to be. But for Jason's sake, you went along as his date. When I criticized his recent behavior, you defended his choices."

"Well, I—"

Sheila didn't let her finish. "My son won't appreciate me interfering in his love life. I get that. So today will be the only time I talk to you about this. Please help Jason find peace and happiness in his life. Be the woman he needs. Give him love, Gabby. That's something money can't buy. Believe me. I learned that lesson the hard way."

"I don't know what to say," Gabby muttered. She glanced at her watch. "I don't mean to cut you off, but I need to get back to the office."

"Of course, you do. All I'm asking is that you give my son a chance. Give yourself a chance. The two of you could have a wonderful future together. There's more to life than work and duty. Cut loose. Roll the dice."

Gabby shook her head slowly. "You don't know me very well at all, do you?"

"Change isn't easy. It never is. But I believe it's possible."

Jason made the trip to Blossom Branch on Monday, wishing like hell that Gabby was by his side. It didn't seem right for her to be in Atlanta and not here with him. It was impossible not to remember every detail of their recent visit and all its interesting twists and turns. Being in Blossom Branch with her had rekindled a host of feelings.

When mental images of the two of them in the back seat of his car went straight to his gut and made him burn with frustrated longing, he ground his jaw and resolved to forget about Gabby for the next few hours. He knew it was a futile choice, but a man had to have *some* pride. Even if he was in deep water and perhaps going down for the third time.

Leah and Lucas met him at the front gate of Camp Willow Pond. "We're so glad you came," Leah said when he climbed out of his car.

Lucas nodded. "I think you're going to be impressed."

"I'm impressed already. I can tell you've done a lot of work here."

For the next hour, the three of them walked the property. The day was cold and windy, but Leah's enthusiasm bubbled over as she and Lucas showed him around. Lucas let Leah do most of the talking. He was clearly supportive of his wife's dream.

Jason was fascinated. "So your first summer was a clear success?"

"It *was*." She grinned. "Not to say we didn't hit a few rocky spots. I'm lucky to have such great people in my life. As you probably know, Cate volunteers at the art museum with underprivileged kids. Her contacts at social services helped us identify prospective campers. Gabby has guided me in finances and planning."

"Anything new for this summer?" he asked.

Leah nodded. "A few tweaks here and there. The thing is, summer is far too brief. Because we live in Georgia, we theoretically have the option of winter camping, at least on the weekends. So that's my biggest problem right now," she said. "We have to decide whether it's cost-effective to winterize the buildings we already own. Or if not, we could construct new facilities that are insulated correctly and later decide how to fully utilize those spaces in the summertime, too."

Jason stared out across the property. They were standing on the porch of the owner's house. It was a modest but nice place, not unlike the one he was renovating. "The possibilities are endless, aren't they?"

Lucas chuckled. "As long as money is no object."

Leah slugged his arm playfully. "Be nice. I was a novice all the way around when I started this project. I often get ahead of myself financially, but I'm learning."

"This is exciting," Jason said. "I might be able to help if you're open to having other fingers in the pie."

"How so?" Leah asked, bouncing on her feet to keep warm.

"My parents are well-connected with the nonprofit community in Atlanta. They enjoy supporting various charities, hosting fundraisers, strong-arming their friends into giving. Because of all that, they know a ton of the right people. There might be grants available to you that you haven't come across yet. Is it okay if I do some digging?"

Leah beamed. "That would be awesome. Thank you, Jason."

Lucas nodded. "Anything you can do would be great. The kids we met this past summer came from all kinds of tough situations. Makes your heart hurt. Leah and I are determined—more than ever—to make Camp Willow Pond a long-term success." He smiled. "I'm going to spot-check a couple of things before we leave. I'll be right back."

When he was gone, Leah touched Jason's arm. Her brown-eyed gaze was concerned. "How are things with you and Gabby? Maybe you don't want to talk about it, but I really want to know."

He shrugged. "Let's just say that your brilliant and beautiful friend can be a frustrating woman at times."

"That's very true. But I think she likes you. Seriously, I mean."

"I'm not so sure." He kicked at the porch railing. "Every

time I feel we're making progress, she pushes me away. Says we're *too different*."

Leah nodded. "I understand why she thinks that."

"You do?" He frowned.

"At times, Cate and I felt the difference keenly when we were in college. Gabby was academically confident but so socially awkward as an eighteen-year-old. We remembered her vaguely from elementary school. But at UGA—as she began to trust Cate and me—she gave us snippets of what her childhood was like."

He sighed. "She's shared things with me, too."

Leah beamed. "Well, that's a good sign."

"Unfortunately, I don't think so. In my case, it's been her attempt to push me away. She says she enjoys having sex with me. But that's as far as we're going, apparently. Gabby has no intention of building anything significant with me."

"Oh, Jason. I'm so sorry."

He scowled. "The worst part is, I have no idea what I'm supposed to do in this situation. Give up? Walk away? Or be patient and hope she'll surrender to my charm and persistence one day?"

His attempt at humor fell flat, even to his own ears.

"Never mind," he said. "Here comes Lucas. Please don't tell Gabby we talked about her. She's so private. I get that. She's probably had to be over the years."

"Yes," Leah said. "But Cate and I have worried that all those secrets and feelings she holds inside might harm her. You've made a powerful connection. If she trusts you with her body, maybe the rest will follow."

"I don't know," he said. "That was my hope in the beginning. Now I'm not at all sure she wants me in her life."

Grimes & Hancock always closed their offices during the week between Christmas and New Year's. It made sense. Clients were otherwise occupied during that time.

The only downside was the frenzy of work in the days leading up to the break. Gabby knew she would be putting in ten-hour days and eating lunch at her desk. That was one reason she had been willing to meet up with Sheila on Monday. She knew the remainder of the week would lurch into fast motion.

Monday night she debated calling Jason. He was probably curious about what his mother had to say. Who could blame him? Parents were notoriously unpredictable when it came to their children.

Before she could act on that impulse, Jason texted her...

How was lunch with my mom? Did you survive???

Gabby grinned. She wants grandchildren.

This time, there were no text dots. Her phone rang. Jason's name showed up on her screen. Her heart sped up predictably. But she took a deep breath and answered.

"Hi, Jason."

"Grandchildren? Really?"

"What can I say? You're her only kid. She has big plans for you."

"Great," he muttered. "What did you say to that?"

"I told her we were just having fun and that she needed to introduce you to her friends' daughters."

A long silence ensued on his end. Finally he spoke, his tone sharp. "I don't need you pimping me out on the social circuit, Gabby."

"Sorry," she muttered. "I was only trying to distract her. Besides, I stood up for you. I told her you wanted to continue traveling the world and taking pictures. And that she should let you be you."

"I see."

"What's wrong with that?" She wasn't willing to tell him everything his mother said. It was embarrassing to know that

Sheila believed Gabby had special influence with Jason. She didn't. Not at all.

"Nothing, I suppose. But I never actually said I was going to travel the world. At least not like I have the last year and a half."

"Oh. I just assumed you would. For your photography."

"I'll take some trips. When the time is right. But the whole reason I'm redoing this house I bought is because I want to settle down. I need to have a home base. A place where I feel grounded."

"Breaking up with Cate changed your whole life, didn't it?"

Another long space of quiet. His voice was low when he finally spoke. "Cate and I were too young when we made the decision to get married. Not that age is everything. But we were still figuring out who we were as individuals. When the wedding didn't happen, I was forced to decide what I want from life."

"And have you?" she asked.

He chuckled. "I'm working on it."

"You're lucky to *have* choices, Jason."

"I know that." He cleared his throat. "Any word on when you and I can get together before Christmas?"

She wanted so badly to see him that she nearly told him to come over on the spot. "Not really," she said. "I'm spending ten hours a day at the office. We close at two on Friday, but I'll be heading down to my mom's house for Christmas Eve."

"I miss you, Gabriella."

The ragged statement made her heart clench. And somehow, because he so often called her *Gabby*, as she had requested, the longer version of her name sounded intimate. The deep masculine timbre made her thighs clench and her heart race.

It was all up to her. All she had to do was say *yes*, and Jason would be in her bed tonight. Holding her. Making love to her.

"I miss you, too," she said.

"I have a feeling there's a *but* in there somewhere." His reply held resignation. That resignation made her feel guilty.

"I go to bed early on work nights. My job is stressful. I need my sleep to keep up with the workload." She could have told him about her conversation with Bradley, but she didn't. It was too complicated, and her feelings too unsettled. Because her willpower was dwindling, she gripped the phone and did the smart thing. "I need to go now. Good night, Jason."

"Do you remember that I have a Christmas present for you?"

"I have one for you too," she said. Technically, the gift wasn't in her possession yet. But she had tracked it down. "We'll have time after the twenty-fifth if not before."

"I don't like that at all," he grumbled. "Christmas is a time for magic, and you're the magic in my life, Gabby. I'll be sad if I can't see you."

"Good night, Jason…"


Jason ended the call with a sick feeling in the pit of his stomach. If he had to run the odds at this very moment, he'd have to admit that his relationship with Gabby had a less than fifty-fifty chance of succeeding. Why was he doing this to himself?

There were at least a dozen women in Atlanta who might welcome a phone call from him—even knowing what he had done to Cate. Was it time to cut his losses? If Gabby really cared about him, wouldn't she have softened by now?

Yes, she'd had a sucky childhood and adolescence. And no, he hadn't. But was that reason enough to throw away a potentially good relationship? He had some thinking to do. Some long and hard thinking, along with a healthy dose of self-reflection. Fortunately, sweaty, dirty labor offered plenty of opportunity for that.

The week was wide-open. No commitments of any kind.

He had assumed, perhaps, that he would be spending the nights in Gabby Nolan's bed. Now he knew how arrogant and deluded his suppositions had been. She had shored up the walls between the two of them.

As he walked around the block in the dark, trying to convince himself he could sleep without her, he faced a hard truth.

Breaking up with Cate had nearly broken *him*.

Would Gabby finish the job?

Surely he wasn't a masochist. Was he destined to choose women who were all wrong for him? Why couldn't loving someone be easy?

Part of his trouble now was how successfully he had isolated himself for the last year and a half. Some of his friends had reached out to him after the wedding imploded. But first he had left the country. Then, when he returned, he hadn't answered calls or texts.

His emotions had been raw.

Embarrassment. Guilt. Depression.

All the negativity and heartbreak had seemed better handled in private.

Most of those dark, self-destructive feelings were in the past. He had now reached a time when he wanted to hang out with the guys, drink a beer, and maybe (one-on-one) admit that he was floundering. Several of his college buddies had married. Surely they would have words of wisdom to share.

In years past, Harry would have been the main person Jason talked to about his complicated love life. But despite all the positive steps Jason had made with his best friend and his ex-fiancée, it was still weird. Which meant that Jason felt isolated and alone.

It was his own fault. He had made the choices that brought him to this complicated point in his life. Now he had to be the one to find a way through.

For better or worse, Christmas felt like a line in the sand. He wasn't going to let the day pass without facing Gabby. He felt in his gut that it was important.

The confrontation could go several ways. He'd like to think he had a shot at a holiday-worthy rom-com happily-ever-after. A guy could hope.

Unfortunately, the part of him that had battled a few hard knocks knew that Gabby wasn't likely to be a pushover when it came to romance. She was the most pragmatic, steely-edged woman he had ever met.

She'd spent a lifetime developing her defenses. Her heart was undeniably wide and deep. But she reserved her softer emotions for the people in her life who needed help.

When Gabby looked at Jason, she saw nothing but his privileged upbringing and his cushy financial spreadsheet.

Seducing her wasn't enough. Nor was the undeniable connection they shared in bed. He knew she *wanted* him. But what about respect?

He wasn't at all sure he had earned that. Not from his wide circle of friends. Not from Cate and Harry. And most importantly, not from the woman who made him believe in hope and redemption and miracles.

It was only days until Christmas. He would bide his time.

Maybe between now and then, he could decide whether he and Gabby were a perfect match or another painful mistake.

# Chapter 19

Gabby felt as if time was standing still. The hours at work were torture. She wanted to see Jason. Hear his voice. Look into his gorgeous blue eyes. Feel his arms wrap around her and convince her that happiness was in reach.

Instead, she was mentally exhausted from checking spreadsheets and answering emails.

It was almost Christmas…didn't people have things to do?

After Monday's late-evening text and subsequent call, her phone had been eerily silent. Either Jason was deep in his remodel project, or his family had lured him home, or he was out on the town with another woman. Perhaps a female who was lighthearted and fun and easy to be with…in other words, not Gabby.

She didn't call or text *him*. If she wasn't willing to extend an invitation, it seemed unfair to have the equivalent of G-rated phone sex.

Jason was a man in his prime. How long would he wait for her to get her head together? And was it even possible?

The only way she had navigated life up until now was to keep her goals simple, clear, and obtainable. Finish her degree. Get a good job. Care for her mother physically, financially, and emotionally.

On a side note, she did her best to be a good friend and neighbor.

But getting into an intimate, committed relationship with a man? *Especially* a man like Jason? That wasn't a goal. That was a fairy tale.

Tuesday night she wrapped his Christmas present and set it in the middle of her kitchen table. Every time she passed the spot, her heartbeat staggered. If she tried hard enough, she could almost imagine a warm, cozy holiday movie where the two of them exchanged presents and kisses and so much more when the TV screen faded to black.

Could fiction ever morph into reality?

Wednesday evening, she cooked for Mrs. Rabinski in 3C. Then she cleaned up all the dishes and fell into bed. Thursday night she swapped goodies with Tanya and the twins, packed her suitcase for the weekend, and tucked her mother's presents into a large red tote. Dahlia preferred lots of little gifts instead of anything pricey or extravagant. Gabby indulged her mother's preferences gladly, even if it meant wrapping a dozen boxes.

When the alarm rang Friday morning, she knew her time had run out.

She hadn't called Jason. She hadn't made plans to see him today. And she had more or less insisted they each spend Christmas Day with their parents.

His present mocked her every time she saw it. Finally she stuffed it deep in her tote and tried not to feel guilty.

By the time she made it to the office, she wanted to climb back into bed. Instead, she greeted her intern, Jamie, gave her a sizeable gift card to her favorite upscale department store, and handled half a dozen last-minute items that couldn't wait until the new year.

Grimes & Hancock still embraced the traditional office Christmas party. It started at noon with a holiday DJ, a buffet, and an open bar. Gabby dreaded the event every year. Though seventy percent of her male coworkers were perfect gentlemen, the other thirty percent were *handsy*. Even more so when they'd had a few drinks.

Jamie had been invited to the party, but Gabby had given her a dispensation to leave with her handsome boyfriend. The two of them were driving all the way to St. Louis to be with both their families. They needed to get on the road.

That left Gabby to mingle and smile and pretend that she enjoyed mediocre food, loud talking, and socializing with her coworkers. It wasn't that she didn't like people. Most of her colleagues were decent and fun. But she preferred one-on-one interactions.

At one forty-five, she escaped.

She had loaded everything in her trunk so she could get on the road immediately. Even so, the traffic was nightmarish. Christmas Eve Day was a dreadful time to travel.

The trick was to pick good music and find a zen state of mind.

By the time she reached Blossom Branch, she was tired, but satisfied. The trip had taken forty-five minutes longer than usual, but it could have been worse. She'd seen not one but four fender bender incidents along the way.

Just for fun, she didn't go straight to her mother's house. Instead, she drove right into the center of town and did a circuit of the quad. She wanted to enjoy the tree and Santa's sleigh and all the hustle and bustle of last-minute shoppers.

Cate's cute shop was overflowing. In fact, there was a line to get inside.

Even though it was winter, the ice cream store was open.

And the diner, the Peach Crumble, had a sandwich board out front that said, "Closing at seven p.m. tonight—Merry Christmas!"

Gabby hadn't expected to feel Jason's presence so keenly. He was eighty miles away in Atlanta. Doing who knew what.

He'd asked to spend time with her this week, but she had shut him down. Now here she was, back in Blossom Branch, realizing that this little town was always going to make her think about him. Every bit of her childhood and her past that she had exposed to him had been received on his part with compassion and an attempt to understand.

She couldn't fault him for not understanding *everything*. Unless a person had lived through what Dahlia and Gabby had, it was hard to fathom the extent of their vulnerable, on-the-edge existence.

As a very young kid, Gabby had known nothing else. But when she started kindergarten, she began to see the wide gap between what her life was like and how her classmates lived. That realization had grown slowly. At first with confusion.

She had blamed herself in the beginning. Surely six-year-old Gabby had done something wrong. Her mother's odd moods and crying jags must have been her fault.

More than one teacher along the way had treated her with exquisite care and kindness and empathy. There had been women who stayed late after class to help with homework, presumably because they knew Dahlia's limitations.

Gabby knew she was lucky to be a good student. She had worked hard and never done anything remotely out of line. Even in elementary school, she had recognized that her brain and her ability to fly under the radar would be her best chances to improve life for herself and her mother.

Tonight she and Dahlia would exchange gifts. That was their tradition. Even in the leanest years, Dahlia had wrapped tiny, insignificant gifts for her baby girl and offered them on Christ-

mas Eve. Christmas morning would be a home-cooked breakfast and stockings filled with fruit and candy, some of which
had come from the food basket they received.

Only much later in life did Gabby realize that the "let's do
presents on Christmas Eve" suggestion had been Dahlia's way
of drawing attention from Santa's absence. He never visited
their house.

She shook her head slowly, trying to dislodge the disturbing memories.

Moments later she found an empty parking spot at the curb.
After pulling in and shutting off the engine, she called her
mother.

"Hey, Mom. I'm in Blossom Branch. Just checking to see if
you still want pizza."

"Oh, yes," Dahlia said. "And please don't forget the garlic
knots."

"Got it."

"Is Jason with you?"

Gabby winced. "No, ma'am. He's probably spending the
weekend at his mom and dad's house."

"Oh." Dahlia's response sounded deflated. "I was hoping we
might play some games tonight."

"It will be just you and me watching our favorite Christmas
movies," Gabby said lightly. "Like always. I'll be there soon."

When Gabby pulled up at her mother's modest house and
unloaded the car, Dahlia came out to help with the pizza box.
She was smiling and bubbly, sounding much more upbeat than
she had on the phone.

Gabby was relieved. "I love your new haircut," she said.

"Thanks, darlin'. I even treated myself to a mani-pedi. Several residents at the nursing home chipped in and gave me a
gift certificate for my Christmas present. Wasn't that a lovely
thing to do?"

"It definitely was. I know how much you mean to them."

After dinner, they moved into the living room. With the fire going and the tree lights gleaming, Gabby felt her Christmas spirit revive. Life was good. With or without Jason, she had nothing to complain about. She and her mother were a tight unit.

The truth was, Dahlia *had* improved over the years. Newer drugs with fewer side effects. The hours of professional counseling Gabby had paid for. And simply the passage of time. Her mother was doing well.

It was a good feeling to know that she had kept her mom safe.

Around eight, they opened presents.

"You first, Mama. You can start anywhere."

It was a treat to shop for someone who was so appreciative of *everything*. A new nightgown, robe, and slippers. Two sweaters. A soft velour throw for the sofa. Costume jewelry to match the sweaters. New novels by her favorite authors.

Dahlia's cheeks were pink with excitement when she finished. "You spoil me," she said, leaning over to kiss Gabby's cheek. "I'm so lucky to have you for a daughter."

"I'm lucky, too," Gabby said. "I love you, Mama."

"Now it's your turn." Dahlia practically bounced in her spot on the sofa. Excitement made her beautiful. Gabby's soul pinched, thinking of everything her mother had missed out on in life. She'd been forced into adulthood. Motherhood. Dahlia had a pure heart and gentle spirit. She deserved so much more.

The box she handed over was shirt-size, but thick. It was beautifully wrapped in red foil paper stamped with sprigs of holly. "Such a pretty package," Gabby said. "I almost hate to open it." She slid a fingernail under one piece of tape and popped it carefully.

"Oh, pooh," Dahlia said. "Open it. Open it."

Gabby relented and tore into the wrapping, tossing the shiny paper aside. When she took the lid from the box and folded back the tissue, she frowned inwardly, confused. What was she looking at?

"Mama?" She lifted out one of two light, fluffy items. They were rectangles—one blue, one pink—each about three feet wide and four feet long. The yarn was so fine and soft, it was like holding a cloud. "This is beautiful work, but what is it?"

Dahlia beamed. "You know how my neighbor has been teaching me how to knit? Little items for the animal shelter?"

"I remember." Gabby nodded.

"Well, I wanted to make you a sweater or a hat or something, but I'm not very good yet. So I made these two baby blankets."

Gabby's jaw dropped. "Baby blankets?" Was she being punked? This was surreal. Surely her mother wasn't having a break with reality.

Dahlia stared at her daughter with a resolute expression. "I want grandchildren, Gabby. You're not getting any younger, and neither am I. Well, truthfully, because I had you when I was only sixteen, I'm the age now to really enjoy a granddaughter or a grandson. And I would be a great babysitter."

"Mama, I thought you and I were happy with our own little family."

"Things change, baby girl. Life moves on. You've carried the responsibility for me far longer than you should have. But I'm good now. Really good. I want you to hook up with that sweet Jason boy. Get married. Start a family. I won't be with you always. I want you to have other people to love."

Gabby panicked. "Are you sick? And you haven't told me?"

Dahlia rolled her eyes. "I'm not sick. I'm great. You, on the other hand, do nothing but work and look after me."

"That's not true," Gabby said. The words were weak.

Her mother sobered, twisting her hands in her lap, her expression almost bleak. "I gave you a terrible start in life. It wasn't all my fault, but still. No little girl should have been watching over me at age ten. My shortcomings made you too serious.

Too responsible. You never asked for anything frivolous or fun. In fact, you never asked for much at all."

Gabby's mouth was dry, and her heart hurt. "Have I smothered you? Is that what this is about? Do you want to be more independent?"

Her mother dropped her head back on the sofa and bumped her fists on her forehead. "Sweet Jesus, no. You're not listening, hon. This is about *you*. My wonderful only daughter." She sat up again. "I know better than most how short life is. I loved your father with all my heart. He was ridiculously smart. That's where you get the brains. I knew he and I would be going places in the world."

"I'm so sorry he died, Mama."

Dahlia grimaced. "Me, too. I didn't think I was strong enough to survive, but I did. And look what I got as a prize. You, Gabriella Elizabeth Nolan. You're tough and brilliant and kind. No mother, no parent, could ever ask for more. You've made me so proud."

Gabby was near tears. She hadn't anticipated this turn in the conversation. "I'm glad," she said. "You took care of a baby when you were grieving and struggling. If I'm strong, it's because I learned it from you."

"So you'll give me grandchildren?"

"I'll at least think about it. How's that?"

"I suppose it will do." Her mother's impish grin signaled victory.

Gabby's head was awhirl with confusion and shock. The grandchildren topic had never come up before. What had prompted this outpouring of emotion from her mother? And the baby blankets? Was this all about Jason?

She knew her mom had bonded with him, admired him. But surely one weekend together hadn't prompted the unusual gift and the plea for babies.

As part of her and her mom's final Christmas Eve tradition,

they fixed popcorn and hot chocolate and settled in front of the TV to watch their favorite Christmas movie. It was one they had seen a dozen times. Maybe more.

Dahlia's attention was glued to the screen. Her tittering laugh lifted Gabby's spirits. She would do anything in the world for her mother. But babies? That was a big ask.

It was closing in on midnight when they were done. Gabby yawned as they carried dishes to the kitchen sink.

She noticed her mother had already hung a packed-to-the-gills stocking on the right side of the fireplace mantel. The familiar long red sock—the same one from Gabby's childhood—was full of odd and intriguing bulges. On the opposite end of the hearth, Dahlia's matching stocking dangled pitifully empty. Gabby had brought all she needed to fill it as soon as her mother fell asleep.

After Gabby graduated from college and the family finances finally improved, she and her mother had progressed beyond candy and fruit to more interesting items.

When the house was quiet and her stocking chore done, she took care of the few remaining coals in the fireplace. Then she perched on the edge of the sofa and stared at the beautiful tree. She remembered Jason's genuine delight in helping them decorate the fragrant fir. He had attacked the project with enthusiasm and had enjoyed every moment.

How would tonight have been different if he had joined them? She couldn't imagine that Dahlia would have forged ahead with the baby conversation.

Gabby missed him with a raw ache unlike anything she had ever experienced. The hands on the clock were far past midnight. It was Christmas now. She couldn't lie to herself any longer, not on such a holy and auspicious day. She had almost certainly fallen head over heels in love with Jason Brightman.

The feeling in her chest was a combination of incredulous jubilation and sick fear. It was easy enough for her mother to advocate pregnancy and childbirth with one of Atlanta's premier bachelors. Dahlia's outlook could be simplistic at times.

Her mother certainly couldn't understand Jason's world.

For a time, Gabby had wondered if her own reluctance to let Jason slide into her life was based on a fear that he might be emotionally hung up on Cate. But she had seen enough to know that wasn't true.

She wasn't even worried that his pursuit of her was a rebound relationship. It had been eighteen months since the almost-wedding. If he was going to have a rebound fling, he would have done so long before now.

Jason's genuine physicality had convinced her that he was attracted to her and honestly wanted a relationship. She believed everything he had said and done. In his sexy smile she saw a future that might exist for *some* woman.

That was the terrifying reality she faced.

She wanted him in the very same way.

But it made no sense.

In the short term, physical lust could obscure any number of problems. Those pesky realities would rear their heads sooner or later, though. Wasn't it better to give him up now with her heart mostly intact? There would be other men…if she wanted babies.

Ending things with Jason would hurt. A lot. But neither of them had made declarations from which they couldn't walk away. Not yet.

If Gabby ended things immediately—before she let him work any more of his magic on her with those blue-flame eyes—she and Jason would survive. In the future, they would both be able to exchange bland, unemotional smiles on the few times their paths crossed. Perhaps a baby shower for Cate. A birthday party for Harry. An opening day at Camp Willow Pond to celebrate Leah and Lucas's exciting venture of building winterized cabins.

Gabby and Jason could skate around the edges of their social circle and never reveal that they'd had wild, breathless sex in the back seat of Jason's car while they were both visiting Blossom Branch.

Who would have believed them anyway?

Gabby was a rule-follower. Not a risk-taker. She was a careful, measured, never-spontaneous woman.

Even a man as stunning and appealing as Jason shouldn't have been able to sway her from the path.

But he had.

To make matters worse, Gabby's own mother was advocating *having fun, making babies.* Finding other people to love.

Madness. Sheer madness.

Gabby went to bed, but it was a long time before she fell asleep. Christmas Eve and Christmas Day had always elicited complicated emotions. The disappointments of her childhood had created an adult woman with a strong need to manage expectations.

There was nothing special about today or tomorrow. Not really.

December 24 and 25 were merely two days on the calendar.

Santa wasn't real, and he surely wasn't infallible. He'd skipped over her home year after year. She had learned to do life on her own. Make her own celebrations. Buy her own presents. Care for her own mom.

She didn't want anyone to feel sorry for her. Life was what you made of it. Her world—centered around work and Dahlia—was pleasant and secure. She didn't need anything more.

A lie was a lie even when you told it to yourself...

Gabby awoke Christmas morning in a much better mood, feeling calm and happy. Despite the über-practical voice inside her head, she grinned. She wasn't stuck in the past. Life was good, and she was going to enjoy the day with her mother.

Already, the smell of bacon and coffee filled the air.

Plus, Dahlia had popped the first batch of homemade cinnamon rolls into the oven by the time Gabby walked into the kitchen. They were labor-intensive, but the dough could be made the day before.

"Merry Christmas, Mama," Gabby said, hugging the cook.

Her mother turned and hugged her in return. "Merry Christmas to you, too, sweetie. Sit down and talk to me. Breakfast this morning is my treat."

Gabby frowned when she saw her mother's face. Dahlia looked haggard, as if she hadn't rested at all. The health worries came rushing back.

"Are you okay?" Gabby asked. "Did you sleep?"

Dahlia wiped her hands on a dishcloth. "Tossed and turned a bit. I'm fine." She lifted the last of the bacon onto a paper towel, turned off the eye on the stove, and poured herself more coffee. Then she joined her daughter at the table. She shredded her paper napkin into little pieces, her gaze downcast. "I was supposed to talk to you about something last night," she said. "I chickened out."

Gabby's stomach clenched. "You can talk to me about anything, Mama. Anytime. You know that."

Dahlia lifted her chin as if bracing for something unpleasant. Her lower lip trembled. "Dave Langford and I have been seeing each other, ever since that Sunday we all had lunch here."

It took every bit of Gabby's acting skills, but she held a smile. "That's wonderful. I'm so happy for you."

"There's more."

"Okay."

Dahlia patted her hand. "Don't be mad, please. I'm leaving today at one."

"Leaving?" Gabby parroted the word. "I don't understand. Leaving to go where? It's Christmas."

Her mother stood again and fluttered around the kitchen. "Dave has a small place down near the Florida panhandle. It's nothing much, but it's in walking distance of the beach. He always stays down there for January and February. He's asked me to go with him this time. He's going to teach me how to fish. My neighbor has agreed to check on my house a couple of times a week while I'm gone."

Gabby heard a roaring in her ears. She couldn't overreact. This was a huge step for her mother. But was it a good step or a bad step?

"Do you feel comfortable with him, Mama?"

For once, Dahlia looked confident and happy all in the same moment. No doubts. No fears. "I do," she said. "He's been very sweet to me. I know I should have told you sooner, but I suppose I was embarrassed."

Gabby pulled herself together despite her rioting emotions. "Don't be embarrassed. This is lovely. Truly it is." She stood and wrapped her mother in her arms. Dahlia felt thin and frail and small. Gabby was terrified for her, but her mother was a grown woman who had conquered demons. She was a survivor. This thing with Dave was Dahlia's shot at a relationship that could carry her into middle age and beyond. If this was what she wanted, Gabby prayed it was the right thing.

Dahlia dabbed her eyes when they separated. "I assumed you and Jason would be spending part of the holiday together, or I never would have agreed to leave so soon. Will you be okay, baby girl?"

Gabby smiled brilliantly, gritting her teeth against one shock after another. "Of course I will. After you and Dave are on the road, I'll drive on back to Atlanta and put my feet up. Work has been crazy since before Thanksgiving. The thought of kicking back and relaxing is wonderful." The lies rolled off her tongue.

Breakfast was delicious, but Gabby had to force herself to eat. Then it was time to clean up the kitchen and help Dahlia finish packing her suitcase. Finally they sat down to open their stockings.

The familiar ritual rang hollow for Gabby as they each ex-claimed over small, thoughtful gifts. She tried not to feel hurt and abandoned. She was a grown woman, too. But it felt as if the proverbial rug had been tugged out from under her feet.

At twelve thirty, Dave Langford showed up.

"Merry Christmas, Gabby." His greeting was warm. "I hope you don't mind me stealing your mother away. I predict she'll love the beach."

Dahlia put her hands to her mouth and blushed. "I've never even seen the ocean," she said. "Isn't that awful? I'm ready to go. But let me make one more pit stop. Gabby, give him my suitcase. I'll be right back."

As soon as she left the room, Dave sobered. "I care deeply about your mother, Gabby. I give you my word that I'll look after her as carefully as you have all these years. She knows how to FaceTime. I've got Wi-Fi connected at my place while we're down there. Check in on us as often as you like."

"She's thrilled to be going," Gabby said quietly, knowing it was the truth. "I'm happy she's doing so well."

"I'll make sure her meds are in order. If there's any sign of a problem, I'll seek medical help. You can trust me, I swear."

Gabby nodded slowly. "I know. The folks in Blossom Branch think highly of you, Dave. If you make my mother happy, that's all the promise I need."

Fifteen minutes later, Gabby watched through the open drapes as Dave Langford's navy SUV pulled out of the drive-way and headed south.

Then she sat down on the sofa and cried.

# Chapter 20

Jason hadn't lost his Christmas spirit. It was worse than that. He'd never found it to begin with...

This made two years in a row that Christmas Day had been difficult, confusing, and lonely. He wasn't *alone*. Not like last year. Today there had been plenty of people at his parents' house. His mom and dad loved including friends and neighbors who had nowhere to go on the holiday.

Christmas morning and the noon meal had included great food, lively conversation, entertaining presents, and plenty of *goodwill toward men*...and women.

But Jason had yearned to be with Gabby, so he felt lonely even amidst all the chaos and celebration.

He made himself stay until three in the afternoon. After that, he went home and collapsed into a camp chair to mindlessly watch football and contemplate the morass that was his life. What was wrong with him?

He'd managed to wrestle this house into submission...or at least he was well on the way to success. But his relationship with

Gabby was far more difficult to wrangle. She wasn't Sheetrock he could demolish or a wall he could relocate. There were no easy answers. No guarantees.

He had blueprints of what his finished home might look like. But his future with Gabby was far less clear.

Did he even have one?

In a time when men were rightly being held accountable for bad behavior toward women, Jason had tried to honor her independence. Though he'd wanted to spend every night in her bed, he hadn't pushed when Gabby made excuses.

He had to face the nausea-inducing possibility that he might be more invested in the relationship than she was. That sucked. Big-time.

But when he remembered the look in her eyes as he held her close and made her come, he felt a glimmer of hope. That had to mean something—surely. Gabby didn't sleep around. She was fastidious and guarded. If she had shared intimacy with him, she must have *some* feelings that were more than physical.

Unfortunately, she was hung up on his money. She saw it as a deterrent to anything permanent between them. To Jason, the money didn't matter. But until Gabby trusted him—completely—his bank balance would continue to shadow their relationship.

Around five, he jumped to his feet and grabbed his keys. He couldn't sit around one second longer. It was Christmas for a few more hours. He wanted to see Gabby. He wanted to kiss her and make her laugh and give her the present he had picked out. He needed her desperately.

Surely Dahlia wouldn't mind him showing up and interrupting their celebration this late in the day.

He drove to Blossom Branch on autopilot. He set the cruise control so he wouldn't make stupid mistakes. The radio played in the background.

Though the trip normally felt brief and easily navigated, tonight it was a million miles long. It didn't help that the shortest day of the year was barely past. Darkness fell early and stayed late.

The roads weren't empty, but on December 25, traffic was light. Headlights from oncoming cars made him blink. His fingers ached, so much so that he forced himself to loosen his grip on the steering wheel. He'd grabbed a bottle of water on the way out the door. Now he sipped from it every few minutes, struggling against a dry throat.

Sadly, water probably wasn't the solution.

Until he cleared the air with Gabby, he was going to feel like a man stranded out at sea. No land in sight. No help anywhere.

At last he pulled up in Dahlia's driveway. The drapes were open. The Christmas tree shone brightly, its colored lights piercing the night.

But the house was dark and seemingly deserted. He frowned. Gabby's car was parked in the driveway in front of his. Where were Gabby and her mother? It wasn't even eight yet. Surely they hadn't gone to bed.

Feeling a weird sense of foreboding, he got out, strode up to the house, and knocked on the door. "Gabby. Are you in there?"

Wild thoughts of gas leaks and home invasions flitted through his head.

Something was wrong. He felt it in his gut.

He knocked a second time, his heart pounding. "Gabby. Open up."

Without fanfare, the door suddenly swung inward. The woman he wanted, the woman he needed, stood framed in the opening. Because the porch light wasn't turned on, her face was in shadow. He could see that she was wearing a soft green sweater and dark knit leggings. Her feet were bare despite the chill.

She stared at him. "Jason? What are you doing here?"

He shrugged. "It's Christmas. I wanted to see you." He held up a small box. "And I brought your present. May I come in?"

There was no answer to his question, but she backed into the house, and he followed her, pausing only to slam and lock the door behind him.

As they stepped into the living room, he saw Gabby's nest on the sofa. She'd had a blanket for warmth and a cup of tea on the nearby table. The fireplace was empty and cold. A box of tissues flanked the teacup. On the floor lay a mound of used Kleenex.

He dropped the box on the table, slipped out of his jacket, and turned on a lamp. "Gabby. Honey. Where's your mom?"

Gabriella would be beautiful under any circumstances, but her mascara was smudged, and her eyes were red from crying. She didn't answer him. Instead, she resumed her stakeout on the sofa. After sitting down, she pulled her knees to her chest, circled her legs with her arms, and buried her face.

Seeing her so upset killed him.

He sat beside her. "Tell, me sweetheart. Where's Dahlia?" Was she in the hospital? Oh, God, he hoped not. But that didn't make sense. If it were true, Gabby would be at her mother's bedside.

This approach was getting him nowhere. He put an arm around her and pulled her close, kissing the top of her head. "Whatever it is, we'll figure it out. I'm here, Gabby. I won't leave you."

After a moment, he realized she was crying again. Silent, dreadful tears that barely shook her shoulders. His arm tightened. "You're scaring me," he said quietly. "Please tell me what's wrong."

She raised her head suddenly and looked at him, her expression wry, her face wet with tears. "I had a big Christmas morning surprise. My mother's been keeping secrets. Apparently, she was afraid to tell *me*—her only child—that she's been seeing Dave Langford. Very seriously. They left this afternoon, right after lunch, for two months in Florida."

"Oh, Gabby. And you've been sitting here alone all this time?"

Now she glared. "Don't you dare feel sorry for me. I'm fine."

His heart shattered into a hundred jagged pieces. He stroked her hair, tucking one side behind her ear. "Of course you are, my brave girl. Of course you are." This time he pulled her all the way into his arms and held her as she fell apart.

The thought of Gabby crying in the dark on Christmas was more than he could bear. And of course, Dahlia had done nothing wrong. Not really. Nothing except take a huge step forward in her personal life, but perhaps in the process unwittingly make her daughter think she wasn't needed anymore.

At last, Gabby's emotional storm wound down. She sat up and reached for another handful of tissues, wiping her face and blowing her nose. "I'm okay. Honestly. It was just a shock. Everything is changing. It scares me."

"I can only imagine. Do you think this trip will go well?"

"I hope so. Dave promised me he would look after her as carefully as I do. I believe him. I do."

There was not much Jason could add to that. Perhaps it was time to change the mood. He reached for the package he had brought with him and handed it to her with a smile. "Merry Christmas, Gabby."

She touched the shiny paper with a fingernail. "This is pretty."

"The present is inside," he said, giving her a droll look.

"Very funny." She opened the paper with the precision of a special-ops soldier defusing a bomb.

"It's not breakable."

"I enjoy the process," she said, not speeding up one iota.

"Ohhh. You're one of those."

Finally she gave him a genuine smile. "What's the purpose of fancy wrapping paper if the recipient doesn't appreciate the beauty of the presentation?"

"Fair point," he conceded.

She opened the small leather box and gasped audibly. "Oh,

Jason. They're gorgeous." The diamond stud earrings sparkled in the lamplight. She shot him a look. "But this is too much."

Her reaction was not a surprise. He sighed. "They're only half a carat each. I knew you wouldn't let me do anything more."

She shook her head slowly. "*Only* half a carat? Good grief."

He picked up her much-too-cold hand and kissed her fingers. "Will you wear them, Gabby? For me?"

Dahlia had a wood-framed mirror hanging over the sofa. As Jason watched, Gabby stood and inserted first one and then the other of the flawless stones, peering into the glass. She didn't need to know how much they cost. Only that they suited her. Fortunately, her tiny, pleased smile spoke volumes.

He stood at her elbow.

She turned her head side to side, staring at her reflection. Even partially shielded by the curve of her hair, the diamonds shot fire. "I love them, Jason. Thank you." She turned and kissed him sweetly, shocking his system. It seemed like months instead of days since he had tasted her lips.

"You're welcome," he said gruffly. If he had his way, he would drape her naked body in diamonds and pearls and never let her leave his bed. There were definite drawbacks to being a twenty-first century male.

Gabby cupped his cheek briefly. "Sit back down. Let me get *your* gift."

He was too revved to sit. Instead, he paced in front of the Christmas tree. Tonight felt like a momentous occasion. How would the evening end?

Gabby was back in a heartbeat. She handed him a package that was flat and heavy. Her expression was anxious. "I have a friend, a client from work. He runs a rare book business in Atlanta. When I told him what I was looking for, he came up with this. I hope you don't already have it. But if you do, it's okay to tell me. I can take it back."

Jason unwrapped his gift and stared in astonishment. It was a coffee table book of Hiram Bingham's incredible Machu Pic-chu photographs from 1911. The Harvard-and-Yale-trained thirtysomething explorer had led a dangerous and adventur-ous expedition under the auspices of National Geographic and brought images of the stunning site to the world.

Jason flipped through the first pages slowly. "Gabby. This is incredible. I've read articles about these photographs, but I've never actually seen the original book."

She gnawed her lip, her arms wrapped around her waist. "It's a first edition. You're a hard man to buy for, but I thought you might like it."

He shook his head slowly. "I love it." He stared at her. "I've never received such a thoughtful gift. Ever. Thank you."

"You're welcome."

Carefully he set the book on the coffee table, a safe distance away from Gabby's teacup. "I *would* offer to take you out to dinner, but nothing's open."

Her grin was wobbly. "I'd rather you take me to bed."

His whole body tensed. "I'd like that."

"Me, too." Her smile finished him off. He had no defenses against her irresistible pull on him.

In two quick strides, he crossed the room and scooped her into his arms. "I've missed you so much."

She rested her cheek over his heart. "I've missed you, too," she said.

In the bedroom, he set her on her feet. They stared at each other. The house was small. Small enough that the lamplight from the living room shone across the hall. They didn't need more than that.

Gabby cocked her head. "Did you bring an overnight bag?"

He winced. "No. I left in a hurry. An impulse. In retrospect, that probably wasn't too smart."

Her siren smile made his knees weak. "You're welcome to

share my toothbrush. Or we can go back to Atlanta after..." She waved a hand at the bed.

Jason swallowed hard, his chest tight. "Would you mind if we discussed our later plans...*later*?"

She tugged his shirttail from his jeans. "Whatever you want, Jason. I'm feeling particularly fond of you at the moment." She touched one of her new earrings. "These are far too extravagant, but I'm not giving them back."

He chuckled as he unbuttoned his shirt and tossed it aside. "I'm glad."

The undressing progressed in fits and starts, interrupted by kisses that were carnal and desperate. They worked on their own clothes at first and then each other's and then their own again.

When they were both naked, he struggled to breathe. His lungs were on fire, as if he had run a marathon or climbed a mountain.

His hands and arms tingled. "I don't want to pounce," he said. "You deserve romance. Especially at Christmas."

Color bloomed on her sharply etched cheekbones. "Pouncing is allowed. Besides, you're my favorite present."

"More than the earrings?" he teased.

"Let's call it a tie."

Her gray eyes were dark. She faced him with bravado, her slender, fit body a feast of feminine curves and temptation.

"Ah, Gabby," he groaned. When he tumbled her onto the bed, they both moaned and clung. He buried his face in the curve of her neck and shoulder. "Are you sure you're okay?" he asked, his breath sawing in and out. "You've had a rough day. I don't want to take advantage of you when you're at a low spot."

She pinched his arm. "I choose you. Quit being such a Boy Scout."

He felt her hands in his hair, stroking his ears, massaging his scalp.

His eyes stung. What had he done to deserve this incredible woman? She was physically and emotionally strong, but so beautifully delicate in his arms. Fragile. Like an orchid that couldn't be roughly handled. Rare. Stunning.

Her breasts were warm in his hands. He squeezed them reverently, thumbing the crests, kissing her wildly when she cried out with pleasure.

Almost lost to reason, he reached at last for his discarded pants and found what he needed in the pocket. Gabby watched him roll on the condom. Her intense regard came close to shattering his tenuous control.

"How do you want me?" he asked hoarsely.

Her pupils were dilated. Her bare pink lips parted in a naughty grin. "Dealer's choice." She touched an earring again. "Maybe I'm a bored saloon girl looking for an interesting man. After weeks and months in the wilderness, you've rolled into town to celebrate Christmas tonight."

He blinked, feeling his cheeks heat as his erection swelled even harder. "Got it, little woman. Merry Christmas."

Gabby sprawled on her back gracefully and welcomed him into her embrace. When he thrust inside her, slender thighs wrapped around his waist. "Oh, Jason…" She caught her breath. "Oh, yes."

He took her hard. Everything conspired against him. Their separation. The heightened emotions of the evening. A Christmas miracle in his grasp at last. He came too fast, but not before Gabby found her release as well.

After he rolled onto his back, they lay side by side, panting. "Sorry," he said. "I meant for that to last longer."

Where their hands touched, she linked her fingers with his. "No complaints from the saloon girl." Her stomach growled.

"Uh-oh," he said. "I think I need to feed you."

"I'm pretty sure a grilled cheese is the best we can do."

"Works for me."

They dressed slowly, stopping to smile and kiss and laugh. Jason felt good about his decision to come to Blossom Branch.

By the time they finally made it to the kitchen, his stomach was growling, too.

Gabby pulled out half a loaf of bread. In the fridge, they found butter and cheese and a single apple. "We're lucky to have this much," she said. "When a person goes out of town for two months, it's standard procedure to use up all the groceries."

The sandwiches came out of the skillet golden-brown and oozing cheesy goodness. Jason cut up the one apple and put half the slices on Gabby's plate.

The drink choices were limited. They settled for ice water.

The kitchen was quiet as they ate. Jason felt something inside him that had nothing at all to do with Christmas. It was warmth and happiness, and *certainty*.

But because he still wasn't sure where Gabby stood emotionally, he kept his thoughts to himself. For now. "Tell me how your week went at work," he said, smiling.

Gabby rolled her eyes. "Wretchedly long and boring days. But now we're on break until January 3. I feel light as a feather. How about you?" she asked. "Did you get things done at the house?"

"I did," he said. "I had a dumpster delivered Tuesday. I've made a million trips back and forth with the wheelbarrow."

"Sounds painful for your back."

He chuckled. "More than I care to admit. The weather's looking good for the first half of January, so that's when I'm having the roof replaced and all the windows swapped out with new ones."

"I can't wait to see it."

Something happened to him then. The thought of Gabby wandering from room to room seemed so right. He wanted to show off his progress, to impress her. He needed to hear her say that she liked the home he was creating.

He wiped his fingers on a napkin and took her hand. "Gabby?"

She looked up from her plate, her smile gentle and sweet. "Yes?"

"I'm in love with you."

He hadn't meant to say it. But the words tumbled out eagerly.

His dinner companion froze. The color drained from her face. Her gaze was haunted. "Don't," she said. "Please don't, Jason."

Her response stunned him so much he did little more than release her and fall back into his chair. The searing pain was almost more than he could bear. "Don't what?" He heard the sharp-edged question. It sounded bitter even to his ears.

Her lower jaw wobbled. "Don't ruin tonight."

"Ruin?"

"We were having fun. I'm really glad you came to Blossom Branch. You've made me feel so much better."

"I said *I love you*. I was hoping you might love me in return. Do you, Gabby? Do you love me?"

Now she looked as if she might faint, but she was sitting down. The agony in her eyes was his answer. He'd been so sure about her feelings, but he was wrong.

Gabby stood and began clearing the table. "It doesn't matter," she said. "It doesn't matter if I love you or not. I can't be the woman in your life."

"Can't or won't?"

She put her back to the sink and leaned against it, as if needing the support. "I think you should go," she said. Tears trickled down her cheeks again. This time they didn't move him. Not even a little.

He was frozen inside. Paradoxically, anger bubbled up in his gut like raw lava waiting to gush forth, obliterating everything in its path.

"Pack your bags, Gabby."

She frowned at his stark command. "Why?"

He scowled back at her, feeling both furious and frustrated. Heartbroken, too, but he shoved that razor-sharp pain aside out of sheer self-preservation. Anger was so much easier than desolation. "I can't stay here in this house with you, and I'm not leaving you alone. I'm going to follow you back to Atlanta and make sure you get to your apartment safely."

"And then?"

How dare she ask him such a question? And how dare she lie to him about love? She hadn't said she *didn't* love him. But she sidestepped his question, refusing to offer the words he so desperately wanted to hear. He ground his jaw, lifted his chin. Gave her an icy stare.

His chest was an aching, empty cavity. His heart a wretched stone in his belly. It was over. He'd never really had a chance with her at all.

"And then I'll drive away and leave you alone. Exactly the way you like it."

# Chapter 21

Gabby was in shock. She knew she shouldn't attempt driving, but Jason gave her no choice. In half an hour, she had gathered her things, set the thermostat, unplugged the Christmas tree, and closed the drapes.

After one last check of the bathroom and laundry room, Gabby returned to the kitchen. As far as she could tell, Jason hadn't moved, other than to stand and rest a shoulder against the door to the outside.

His handsome face was entirely devoid of expression.

"Are you ready?" he asked curtly.

"Yes."

They exited the house in silence. He carried her bags. She locked the door.

At last, they stood and faced each other in the driveway. The harsh glare of a streetlight painted the planes and angles of his face in foreboding shadows. "Anything else we need to do for your mother?" he asked, no inflection at all in his words.

"No," she whispered.

"Then get in the car, Gabby. Let's get the hell out of here."

She climbed into her vehicle and closed the door. It took her three tries to get the seat belt fastened. Tears still tumbled down her cheeks. She had cried more since lunch than she had in the last two years.

Jason didn't seem to care. Not anymore.

He backed out of the driveway and far enough up the narrow street for her to get in front of him.

Her hands shook from the cold or her nerves or both. When she put the car in Drive and headed toward town, he was right behind her.

In a flash of incredulous, dark humor, she realized this might have been her last overnight visit to the house where she had spent a big portion of her childhood. If things in Florida went well, Dahlia might move in with Dave and sell the unassuming structure in the rearview mirror. Another crack opened in Gabby's heart.

That house had seen its fair share of sadness and pain, but it was home.

The drive to Atlanta was a blur. Though she kept her focus on the road, each time she glanced in the rearview mirror, there he was. Jason. Keeping her in sight and shepherding her home, even though she had been a coward and a liar.

*Of course* she loved him. How could she not?

She had probably been in love with him at some subterranean level since she was eighteen and Jason flashed across her path like a fiery meteor.

When he asked her out on a date all those years ago, she had been young and timid and scared. Jason had been like the gorgeous alpha hero in the movies. All smiles and laughter and brilliant light.

What was her excuse now?

Jason wasn't willing to "date" her or court her or flirt with her. Or at least not only that. Those were superficial interactions. The relationship between them had moved far beyond lighthearted fun. He wanted more.

Finally, after an interminable drive, they ended up at Peachtree Court. A headache from stress and crying crushed her skull.

She made herself get out of the car and face him. "Good night. Thanks for the company on the way home."

The words nearly stuck in her throat. She wanted to throw herself in his arms and tell him the truth. She was madly, wretchedly, hopelessly in love with him.

But she had endured one too many shocks today. Her emotions were fragile as spun glass. It would be dangerous to blurt out the truth without considering the consequences.

She always weighed the consequences...

Jason popped her trunk. "I'll carry your bags."

She was under no illusion that he wanted to come inside. His terse words made that clear. Instead of protesting, she picked up her purse and a couple of lighter totes and followed him up the stairs. When she unlocked her door, he set the two small suitcases inside and stepped back.

They were at an impasse. An awkward, here-comes-the-end confrontation.

"I'm sorry I made you angry," she said.

His expression was impassive. "I'm not angry, not anymore." He shoved his hands in his pockets and stared at her. "You and Dahlia have conquered unimaginable obstacles in your life. And you've come out the other side. I know it's impossible for me to understand exactly how hard that was, though I've tried. When you let me. Now..." He shrugged. "None of your life experiences matter to me—other than to feel gut-deep sorrow that you faced so much hardship at such a young age. I don't care about your past. But the problem is...*you* care. Far too much for you and me to have a shot at anything real and lasting."

She opened her mouth to say something.

Jason waved a hand. "I'm not finished," he said. "I think

you love me. I'm pretty sure you do. But I can't be the one to make you feel safe and comfortable and accepted. That can only come from inside you. So here's the deal, Gabby. I won't call you. I won't ask you out. I won't send you texts. I won't contact you in any way. I love you too damn much to be nothing but a fuck buddy."

She winced. "That's not what you are to me," she whispered.

His expression was bleak. "Feels like it from where I'm standing." He sighed. "If you ever want more from our relationship, you know where to find me. I'll still love you in a day or a week or a year. But I'm not willing to accept less than a hundred percent. Do you understand what I'm saying?"

"Um…"

"I want *you*, Gabriella. All of you. A woman who will be at my side for better or worse, for richer or poorer. A wife. The mother of my theoretical children. A lover who will keep me warm at night. If my wants and needs ever line up with yours, come and get me. No more hiding. No more insecurity."

For the first time, his stoic expression cracked. She saw the utter devastation and pain in his gaze. "Good night, Gabby. Merry Christmas."

Gabby had thought one of the most dreadful days of her adult life was standing near the altar and watching Jason prepare to marry Cate Penland.

Turned out there were worse moments.

She was living a nightmare now.

How could he ask that of her?

Ignore her past? Act as if she belonged in the world Jason inhabited?

It wasn't possible.

Somehow, she made it through the holiday week by watching TV and eating junk food and texting with her mom. Dahlia was over the moon with excitement. She loved Florida. She had caught two fish so far.

New Year's Day was spent much like every other day since Christmas. Although Gabby did watch parades and clean out a few drawers. Despite the brand-new calendar on the wall and the pristine date, she refused to make even one tiny resolution.

Resolutions were for people who focused their hope into the new year.

She had nothing to hope *for*.

Returning to work on Monday was a welcome distraction from her personal life. She relished the busy pace, the nonstop demands.

For two entire weeks, every day was the same. Then, when she thought there were no more surprises, her mother Face-Timed one evening.

"Hey, Mama," Gabby said, feigning cheerfulness. "How are you doing? Wow, you've got a suntan."

Dahlia beamed. "I know. Isn't it great? Dave and I spend most of every day outside. And the fish we're eating...so good."

"I'm glad."

"Anything new in Atlanta?" her mother asked.

"No. Just working." On another, earlier call, Gabby had mentioned in passing that she and Jason weren't seeing each other anymore. Her mother had been visibly disappointed but hadn't pressed the issue.

Dahlia wrinkled her nose. "*I* have some news," she said. Anxiety colored her expression now.

"What is it, Mama?"

"Dave and I got married today. I started to feel bad about, you know, *living in sin*." She lowered her voice as she said it. "So we popped over to the courthouse and tied the knot. I'm Mrs. Langford now."

The man in question eased Dahlia to one side so his face appeared in the frame. He grimaced. "If I had known how she was going to feel, I would have married her in Blossom Branch before we left. I even offered for us to turn right around and go home for a few days so you could be with us, but your delightful mother is stubborn."

"Don't I know it." Gabby smiled. "Congratulations to you both."

Dahlia held up a bare left hand, bouncing in that way she had when she was excited. "I knew my baby would understand. And by the way, we did this so fast, we had to fake the ring part. We're going shopping tomorrow."

"Sounds fun," Gabby said. "I can't wait to see the new jewelry."

She had a hunch Dave saw through her lightly worded response to the shock and worry she was feeling. He leaned into the camera. "She'll want to have a party in the spring. When we get home. I'm sorry you weren't here, Gabby." His expression was troubled. "I hope you'll forgive me for stealing her away."

"I'm happy for you both," she said. "Truly, I am."

A few moments later, they all signed off.

Gabby sat on her sofa and stared out the window, feeling numb and surreal. How many more shocks could she take? After all these years, her mother was married. For the very first time. To an adult man, not a boy. A husband who would make her his priority. Who would love Dahlia and watch over her.

After tragedy and illness and heartbreak, Dahlia's mental health had improved. Jason had been right about that. Gabby had been too close to the situation to recognize the incremental changes in her mother. Dahlia was moving on with her life.

Gabby was not.

The empty feeling in her chest frightened her. She glanced at the clock on the wall. The twins would be in bed by now. She sent Tanya a text. Any chance I could come over for a few minutes?

Tanya replied immediately with a thumbs-up emoji.

When Gabby knocked at her friend's apartment and the door swung open, Tanya's eyes widened. "Come in, hon. What's wrong?"

Gabby sniffed as she sat down on the sofa, angry with the tears that seemed to be her constant companion these days. "I'm *not* a crier," she insisted.

Tanya took a chair nearby and wobbled her ankles as if they hurt. "Nothing wrong with crying," she said. "We all do it. Tears are good for watering whatever is going to grow next when our lives take a turn."

Gabby gave her a shaky smile. "That's beautiful. Who said that?"

Tanya smirked. "I made it up on the spot. Not bad, huh?" She cocked her head. "Something happened today?"

"My mother got married. In Florida."

"Oh, hon. I'm sorry."

"You don't have to be sorry," Gabby said.

Tanya frowned. "I'm sorry you weren't there to be part of a very special moment in your mom's life. That's what I meant."

"She's not an inconsiderate person." Gabby felt protective of her mother even in this context. "But she can be impulsive at times. I think she got down to Florida and began to wonder what the ladies at church might think of her. She was fretting about *living in sin*, so she and Dave went to the courthouse today."

"Well, that's a heck of a way to start off the new year."

"I should be thrilled," Gabby said, blowing her nose.

"And are you?"

"I'm trying to be..."

Tanya propped her feet on an ottoman. "So why are you here? Besides your news, I mean. You know I'm happy to listen anytime. But I get the feeling you want more than listening."

Gabby took a deep breath. "Will you tell me about your marriage?"

Tanya had never brought up the details, and Gabby—a private person herself—had not wanted to pry.

Tanya grinned. "What do you need to know? I've been divorced almost four years. It's old news."

"Were you in love with him in the beginning? When did you fall out of love? Would you ever get married again?"

"Whoa, whoa." The other woman held up both hands. "One thing at a time."

"Sorry."

"That first question is the hardest one, I guess. I didn't date a whole lot in high school. No college for me. I went straight to cosmetology school and then got a job at a hair salon. Made decent money. Not great. I'd been there ten years when Jimmy came in to get a haircut one day. I thought he was the cutest guy I had ever seen. There were pheromones bouncing all over the place. He asked me out on the spot. I said yes."

"And after that?"

Tanya shook her head slowly. "If we weren't at work, we were together. We had sex like rabbits. I didn't even know all that much about him, but he made me feel like the most desirable woman on the planet."

"So he asked you to marry him?"

"Not then. We'd been dating about eight or nine months when we messed up. Had too much to drink. Did it without protection. I ended up pregnant."

"Oh." Gabby's mind raced. It was hard to reconcile her oh-so-practical neighbor with this tale of wild, irresponsible intimacy.

"Oh, indeed." Tanya snickered. "That's when we got married. To be fair, Jimmy tried to do the right thing. But when the boys came along and they were twins, he freaked out. Even with neighbors and a family member or two to help, those first months with *double* little ones are kind of a nightmare."

"I still can't believe he deserted his family." Gabby was indignant.

Tanya shrugged. "Yeah. Said he didn't sign on for babies. Especially not two of the little stinkers. He paid child support for six months, and then he disappeared. I don't even know where he's living."

"How can you be so calm about it?"

"Because I have those two adorable babies asleep in the other room. They're my heart and soul, Gabby. Jimmy's missing out on all that. Even worse, he has no clue how wonderful they are."

"I see."

"Tell me the truth. Why the sudden interest in my dismal marriage? Is this about your beautiful man, Jason? I haven't seen his car around here since Christmas. What's the status with him?"

Gabby rubbed her hands over her face. "He told me he loves me."

"That monster." Tanya's smile was chiding but sympathetic.

"You don't understand," Gabby said. "He thinks it doesn't matter that I grew up without shoes sometimes. Or that Mama and I lived off restaurant leftovers the neighbor's husband brought home from the diner."

"You had a hard life. I get that. And I'm sorry. But what does that have to do with your Jason?"

"His family is wealthy. Both sets of grandparents are wealthy, too."

"So?"

"He was once engaged to Cate Penland, a beauty queen. I've told you about that wedding. Her family has money, too."

For the first time, Tanya sobered. "May I ask you a personal question?"

Gabby laughed softly. "I think the answer is yes. Considering I've made you dissect your marriage."

"Ever since I met you, I've heard about your two best friends, Cate and Leah. Why didn't you call one of them tonight? Why call me? Is it because they're more like Jason than you are? You think they'll take his side?"

*Whoa.* Gabby hadn't even admitted it to herself. "There might be some truth to that. If I talked to either of them, they wouldn't understand how I feel. They don't know what it was like for me. And they love Jason. Both of them would tell me to get over myself and give him a chance."

"Ah. So you came here because you think my opinion will be more sound."

"Something like that."

"Because I'm solidly blue-collar, and I live paycheck to paycheck."

Gabby's eyes widened in alarm. "I'm sorry if I've offended you. I think you're wonderful, Tanya. But yes. You at least know about things like food stamps and government assistance."

"Hmmm." Tanya's expression indicated deep thought. Finally she nodded her head. "Here's the thing, sweet girl. I'll have to side with Cate and Leah on this one. You have a fantastic job. You've looked after your mother all these years. You're an amazing person. It makes perfect sense to me that Jason is in love with you. What I *don't* understand is why a woman as smart as you are could be so ignorant about love."

"Ouch." Gabby gaped at her friend. "That's a little harsh."

"The truth sometimes is. You asked me if I would ever get married again? Definitely, girl. If I meet a man who loves me and my boys, I'm all in."

When Gabby stood, her knees felt wobbly. "I should go. It's late. Thank you for letting me cry on your shoulder."

"But you don't believe a word I've said, do you?"

Gabby smiled and reached for her coat. "Good night, Tanya. Sweet dreams."

January crawled by. The weather blew hot and cold. Literally. One day there was ice on the shrubbery. The next weekend, crocuses were popping up, and the thermometer hit sixty degrees. Then the chill returned.

On the twenty-fourth of the month, Mr. Hancock came to Gabby's office. A wide-eyed Jamie showed him in before making herself scarce.

Gabby stood politely, but he waved her back to her seat. "Sit, sit, young lady."

"Yes, sir." Since Mr. Hancock was almost ninety and not likely comfortable on his feet, she sat.

He took the armchair on the other side of her desk, lowering himself into it with a wince. "Getting old is the pits, Ms. Nolan. Avoid it as long as you can."

"But it beats the alternative," she said lightly. "Right?"

His chuckle was rusty, as if he didn't laugh very often. "I suppose."

"How may I help you, sir?"

He rubbed the bridge of his nose. "Now that Bradley is off to the Sunshine State with his wife, I need to fill his position. I think you're the person for the job." He slid something across the desk. "Here's the salary and benefits package."

Gabby picked up the sheet of paper. The base salary listed was fifty thousand over what Bradley had shared with her about *his* compensation. She cleared her throat. "This is a very generous offer," she said. Admitting that probably wasn't good negotiating strategy, but the numbers would double her current pay.

The old man nodded slowly. "Let's be honest. We all know that you've carried Bradley since you've been here. You're intelligent and empathetic. We have prospective new clients who call every week asking for you by name. They've heard from friends that you can talk about money in layman's terms and that you're extremely knowledgeable about the products and services we offer. Grimes and I are officially offering you this position with a commensurate financial boost and a new title.

You'll be the very first senior female staff person in the building. Congratulations."

Gabby's mind spun. She should be elated—right?

She tried to swallow, but her throat was dry. "Is it possible
for me to think about this before I give you an answer?"

Shock flashed across his face. He frowned. "Is somebody trying to poach you? Hell's bells. How much are they offering?"

"No, sir. That's not it. But this is a big step. I'd like to mull
it over before accepting so much responsibility."

"You've been doing the bulk of the work anyway. Might as
well get paid for what you're accomplishing."

"Please, Mr. Hancock. May I think about it?"

"One week," he said curtly. "One week. And if there's another company trying to steal you away, I want to know about
it. We can sweeten that offer if necessary. I'm not losing you
to the competition."

The meeting was clearly over.

She pretended not to notice how much effort he expended
rising to his feet. "Thank you, Mr. Hancock. I appreciate the
offer. I'll give it my utmost consideration."

He harrumphed. "Indeed."

The remainder of the workday passed in a haze of business
details and introspection, at least on her part. Jamie was understandably curious. Gabby didn't breathe a word to any of
her colleagues.

At home, she paced the floor. She had never believed in
*Fate* as a real concept. Things didn't fall out of the sky. She
worked her butt off week after week, and now all her efforts
were being rewarded.

She should have been over the moon.

But somehow, her mood remained flat. Was she struggling
with regret over not seeing her mother wed? Grief over missing Jason? Or something else entirely?

This was the moment when she really should have called Cate

and Leah for lunch and a meeting of the minds. They would help her look at the pros and cons of this new G&H position. Be sounding boards as she talked it over aloud.

She *wanted* to call them, but she couldn't. If she sat down at the table, face-to-face with her two best friends, they would understandably have questions about Jason. Gabby wasn't ready for that.

They might offer sympathy. Or maybe criticism. Neither would be helpful right now. Now—like it had been for most of her life—the hard stuff was up to her.

No one else understood the stakes. No one else understood what was in her heart. She had a week to decide what to do. Hopefully that would be enough.

# Chapter 22

Groundhog Day was an oddly American holiday. Gabby had a few clients from outside the US who were puzzled when February 2 rolled around every year. Punxsutawney Phil might have seen his shadow in Pennsylvania this morning, but the weather was bleak in Atlanta. Technically, that meant spring was right around the corner.

For the first time, despite every terrible thing that had happened with Jason, Gabby felt hope.

She *had* to see him. Soon. She'd chosen this day on a whim. After watching the movie *Groundhog Day* half a dozen times on late-night TV in years past, this week she felt a great deal of sympathy for the frustrated Bill Murray. Ever since Christmas evening when she and Jason called it quits, her days had been stuck in a repetitive and lonely loop.

Unless she made some changes in her life, she had no chance at all for a happy ending. Truthfully, she wasn't sure she believed in those.

Some people got them. But maybe not in a forever kind of way.

Was she willing to take a chance with Jason, knowing it might not last?

For days and weeks, she had told herself *no*. But now, like the first signs of spring emerging from winter, her heart had begun to change.

How to broach this confrontation was a problem. It didn't seem fair to corner him in his house when he would likely be covered in dust and dirt. But if she waited until later in the day, he might have commitments. He might be *out*.

She took a half day off from work and raced home to eat lunch, shower, and change clothes. Nothing fancy. Jeans. A soft lavender sweater that reminded her of the crocus she had seen in a nearby yard. When she slipped on her ballet flats, she had to smile. It was still winter. Jason would probably chide her for not wearing socks.

Her moment of humor was only that. A moment. She hadn't seen Jason in thirty-nine days. Hadn't talked to him. Hadn't read a funny text. Hadn't inhaled his scent, though that was still imprinted in her brain.

Anything could have happened in the interim.

He had said the ball was in her court. That was frankly terrifying.

Situations changed. People changed. For the first eighteen years of her life, Gabby had lived with inconsistency, lack of control, and last-minute *changes*. There had been no stability. No assurances. No promises of good things to come.

Life had kicked her in the stomach time and again.

That sick feeling had stayed with her even as an adult.

Maybe now was the time to exorcise the demon. Take away its power over her. Recognize that she was stronger than she knew.

Bad things could happen, even now.

Jason might not want to see her. Perhaps he was no longer interested in a woman who was high-maintenance. Not when it came to clothes or makeup or housing or cars. But with emotions.

He could have moved on. Like Dahlia. Like the whole wide world turning on its axis.

Gabby was tired of being stuck.

She wanted more. She wanted him.

Her body alternated between hot and cold as she made her plans. So far there was only Step One. *Go to Jason's house.* After that, she would have to wing it.

When she pulled into his driveway, she saw a familiar car. That was good—right? She got out and stared. Beautiful windows gleamed in the afternoon light despite a day that was gray. The roof was pristine, too.

So much had changed since the last time she was here.

Though it was difficult, she forced her feet to move. When she stood on the tiny stoop, she rang the doorbell.

He must have seen or heard her arrive. The door opened instantly.

Something flashed in those sea-bright eyes. Heat. Interest.

Or maybe she imagined that reaction.

When she chanced a look at him again, the expression on his face was impassive. Polite. "Gabby. Would you like to come in?"

"Um, yes…"

He stepped back and waved his hand. "Still no furniture. You can have the camp chair. I'll stand."

A mattress with rumpled covers lay on the floor near their feet. Things happened on mattresses. But not today.

Gabby scooted past him, looking around the open area. There were no walls in Jason's house yet, but two-by-fours that smelled of new wood gave a good idea where one room might end and the next one begin. "It's a lot cleaner now."

He shrugged. "All the demolition is done. I kind of miss it." His lips twitched. "Pounding things was good for stress relief."

"Pounding things?" Gabby's eyes widened.

His face turned red. "You know what I mean."

"Oh. Sledgehammers."

He stared at her. "Why are you here, Gabby?"

"I wanted to wish you a happy Groundhog Day."

He glanced at his watch. Checked the date. "So it is." He frowned. "I must be missing something. I wasn't aware you were a fan of rodent holidays."

"Stop being a smart-ass," she huffed. For a man who claimed to love her, he was remarkably unwelcoming. He wasn't dirty and sweaty, more's the pity. His button-down white shirt and leather jacket with dark khakis made him look like a fighter pilot in a World War II movie. Give him a pair of aviator sunglasses and he'd be a taller, broader Maverick.

She ignored the camp chair, unable to sit while Jason was on his feet. If they were going to make progress, she had to meet him on equal ground.

He folded his arms across his impressive chest. "How's Dahlia doing?"

"My mother is married," she said, still having trouble with that thought.

Jason's wooden expression slipped, revealing shock. "You're kidding. How did that happen?"

"When she and Dave got down to Florida, Mama felt guilty about *living in sin*. So they went to the courthouse. Dave felt bad, I think, about leaving me out."

Jason's face softened. "I'm sorry, Gabby. That must have hurt."

She wrinkled her nose. "It did. But in a way, it's a good thing that she felt confident enough to move ahead with marriage. Her *first* marriage. I've spent most of my life trying to take care of her. This is progress…even if I would have done things differently."

"I think you're right."

The silence built between them. Heaps and piles of uncomfortable silence.

Now that she was here, she honestly didn't know what to say. Was she supposed to throw herself in his arms and beg for another chance?

That seemed needy and scary.

It would be much better simply to state her case.

She hadn't expected it to be so hard.

Finally Jason glanced at his watch again. "I don't mean to be rude, but I have an appointment. Was there something else you wanted to say?"

Looking at him brought back familiar feelings. Like being a child and peering through store windows at shiny, beautiful treats that would never be hers. Pretty dresses. Expensive toys. Delightful foods. Standing on the outside looking in. Knowing that hoping and wishing weren't enough.

Now, though she tried desperately to read Jason's mood, it was impossible. He seemed as distant as the moon. And despite his dazzling masculinity, he was as cold as the moon.

"I was offered a new job," she blurted out.

Jason blinked. "Oh?"

Quickly she told him about Mr. Hancock's unexpected visit to her office. "It means a huge step up. I'd be the most senior female staff in the building. And the salary is double my current pay."

He shifted from one foot to the other and rubbed the back of his neck. "Congratulations. Your mother must be very proud."

"She doesn't know about the offer." Gabby said it bluntly.

Jason cocked his head. "Why not?"

"Because I turned it down two days ago. In fact, I quit entirely. I have enough in savings to take a little time off. Figure out what I really want to do."

Jason inhaled sharply and glared, visibly uneasy. "I don't know why you're here, Gabby," he said. "And I don't know why you're telling me these things. In case you forgot, we ended our relationship."

Panic stabbed sharply in her belly. "But you said I could come find you."

His eyes blazed. "Under one condition only."

"Please," she said. "I have some things to say. Let me say them."

"Why?" His scowl was dark and foreboding.

"Jason..."

"Fine," he said. "Talk."


Jason was in hell.

He'd spent long weeks convincing himself he could live without Gabby Nolan. Now she had walked right into his house and immediately exposed the lies he'd tried to believe.

He ached to hold her. But he dared not. This didn't seem to be anything close to a reconciliation. More like an information dump. Or someone cleansing her soul.

That sucked. He didn't want to be Gabby's sounding board. Not anymore. He couldn't handle it. Already his sex was hard, and his chest hurt.

His fists clenched in his pockets. Gabby's face was pale, her eyes huge and filled with some negative emotion—a combination of fear and dread and pain. Not the look of a woman who wanted him. "Talk," he demanded sharply. "I have thirty minutes, max."

There was no appointment. Maybe Gabby realized that. But he wasn't going to let her trample him again indefinitely.

She took three steps in his direction. Stopped. Pressed her temples.

Then she took a deep breath.

"I'm not good at letting people in," she said bluntly. "My default is to protect myself by not letting anyone witness my insecurities. I've spent my whole existence covering things up. It became a habit, even when it was no longer necessary."

He shrugged. "Okay. Not really a surprise."

She winced. "My life as an adult is predicated on being able to control my environment. Structure. Schedules. Doing the same things. Over and over. That may be incredibly boring to you, but it represented safety to me. Then you bumped into me at that coffee shop, and suddenly, things changed. I felt my control slipping. My schedule fragmenting. My environment shifting to include people and places and experiences that were new. And you," she said, the last two words quiet.

He had no clue where this was going. "Then clearly I should apologize for upending your perfect life."

He heard the sarcasm in his words. The bitterness. The anger.

"Jason…" She held out her hands.

"No," he said. "We're not doing this." He couldn't. She was destroying him bit by bit. "I get the message. I messed up your fine predictable life. Won't happen again. You've made your point."

His eyes burned. His chest was so tight, he wondered if a man his age could have a heart attack. For the second time in his life, he had made a wretched mistake. Apparently he had no clue what women wanted.

Gabby took two more steps. He backed away and bumped into a wall, or what would become a wall. "Leave," he said sharply. "I don't want you here."

She went white, but she didn't move. "I love you, Jason."

In an instant, the world stood still. His head echoed with weird noises. His hands tingled. "Don't say that," he muttered. "I don't need your pity."

"It's true." She wet her lips with her tongue. Her throat moved as she swallowed. "I love you. I've been so afraid to let myself *feel* things, but it's true. I love you. Quite desperately, in fact."

When he didn't speak—couldn't speak—she went on. "I know you're going to travel a lot. For your photography. I'm okay with that. Maybe I could tag along sometimes. And I know you have money. A *lot* of money. That was one reason I almost accepted the new job. So I could build a bigger bank account. But here's the thing, Jason. I'm tired of being that scared little girl who learned to hate peanut butter. She will always be part of me. I get that. Maybe I'll finally see a therapist one day soon. I've never wanted anyone peeking inside my brain. For years I couldn't afford it, and then when I could, I was arrogant enough to think I could handle all my problems on my own."

"A lot of people are that way," he said hoarsely. "Me included. We don't want to admit when we need help."

"Well, I'm trying," she said. "I want to be a better person."

He floundered mentally. She said she loved him. He wanted to believe her, but there were things she didn't know.

"I think you're a wonderful person, Gabby. Just the way you are."

Her smile was wistful and sweet. "Thanks for saying that."

"It's true."

He wanted to drag her close and kiss her until neither of them could breathe. But they weren't out of the woods yet.

Gabby's smile faded. "Where do we go from here? Oh shoot, scratch that," she said, seeming disgusted with herself. "The new Gabby is trying to live day to day. You'll have to forgive me when I screw up. I thought since I have more free time now, you could teach me how to renovate houses. This house, maybe."

Her words were shaky, vulnerable. But he had to get through this.

"I haven't been honest with you," he said bluntly. "In the last six weeks, I've gone behind your back. I've asked Leah to keep my secrets. Asked her not to tell you that she and I have been talking."

"Oh." Gabby bit her lip. "Well, I guess it wasn't a problem. I haven't been in contact with Leah *or* with Cate. I didn't want to talk about you. And me. To be honest, the only friend I've shared any of this with was my neighbor, Tanya."

"And what did she have to say?"

"Um…direct quote? *I don't understand why a woman as smart as you are could be so ignorant about love.*"

Jason lifted an eyebrow. "She's a straight shooter."

"You have no idea." Gabby stared at him, visibly troubled. "Are you going to tell me about these secrets?"

"Yes. First, I won't be doing much traveling. Not right now. But when I do, I'd love to have you go with me if you want to…"

"Okay."

He hunched his shoulders and muttered a curse. "You remember my trust funds from my grandparents?"

"Kind of hard to forget something like that," Gabby said. "Though I've tried, believe me."

"Well…" He inhaled sharply, still feeling incredulous that he had jumped into the deep end. "I gave away more than half of the total amount."

Gabby's eyes rounded. "Gave it away?"

"Yes. Not to make you more comfortable about us," he said hastily. "But if that's a side benefit, I'll be happy."

"Gave it to whom? To what? And why?"

Her frown bugged him. "I've spent a lot of time—since the debacle with Cate—trying to decide how my life should go. What I'll do. Where my passions are leading. It finally dawned on me that perhaps I needed to quit focusing on myself and do something for somebody else. Then hopefully, other areas of my life will fall into place."

"What prompted this revelation?" she asked, brow still creased.

He'd been hoping for an enthusiastic response. But her expression was more dubious than admiring.

He cleared his throat. Would this admission make her angry?

"It was you," he said quietly. "The more I learned about you and your mom, the more I realized that for years, you both were mostly invisible. And sadly, you aren't the only ones. There are so many families who are barely getting by...kids especially."

"I don't understand." Her intent gaze made him itchy, self-conscious.

"I've set up a foundation with the money," he said, trying to keep it simple, though the process had been anything but. "I'm going to fund a sizeable expansion at Leah's camp. And set up an endowment. Once all that is in place, I'll start looking for other organizations that need my help."

"Wow. Leah must be over the moon."

"She and Lucas are excited. I am, too. We're hoping you'll want to get involved."

"Of course I will," Gabby said.

He fell silent.

They looked at each other.

He ground his jaw. "If all you want from me is sex, I've decided that's okay. You don't have to say those words."

"You mean *I love you*?"

"Yes."

"But I do," she said, her eyes beginning to shine.

Tears? Happiness? Because he couldn't read her, he was mute.

Gabby kept talking, the words tumbling out in a rush. "I was hoping you still loved me. Even though I can be a pain in the ass."

"No, baby. You're not that at all," he said quickly. "You're prickly sometimes. And yes, you hide behind walls. But every time I kiss you, I know you're letting me see *all* of you. I fell in love with both women. The shy, reserved female and the wildcat in bed."

Her lips twitched. "Wildcat? Really?"

"I had the scratches to prove it," he said. "But it's been weeks. Everything healed." The muscles in his face finally loosened enough for him to smile. "Everything but my heart. You did a number on that."

He reached for her then, took her hand, pulled her close. Rested his chin on top of her head. His heart was in the attack range again. Pulse pounding. Oxygen evaporating.

In his arms, Gabby felt like all his dreams come true. "I love you," he said.

She tipped back her head so she could look at him. "I wasn't just saying what I thought you wanted to hear. I love you, too."

"Thank God." He kissed her then, feeling drunk with happiness. Their tongues tangled. Their breath mingled. He felt her heart beating in time with his.

She combed her fingers through his hair. "Will you make love to me? So I know this is real?"

He cupped her ass and pulled her hard against his pelvis. "It's real, Gabby. So real."

They removed their shoes, then knelt on the mattress and undressed each other. Her bra was pale lavender. It matched her sweater. The random thought bounced in his brain. But when he reached behind her to unfasten the clasp, they both sighed and groaned.

Her breasts nestled in his palms. Plump and soft and tipped with tiny, dark pink buds. He tasted her reverently.

Gabby squirmed. "Let me see you. I want you naked," she said, the words breathless.

"Okay." The word was barely audible. His throat closed up.

He had shrugged out of his jacket earlier. Now Gabby unbuttoned his shirt. She stroked her hands over his chest, then kissed his collarbone. "My bed has been *so* empty," she said. "January has been the longest month of my life."

"You don't have to tell me." He unzipped her jeans and

helped her slide out of them. Then they worked on his pants. When he was down to his boxers and Gabby wore nothing but bikini panties, he wrapped his arms around her and dragged the covers over them both. "I don't want you to get cold," he said, leaning on one elbow to look down at his lover.

Her dark silky hair looked good on his pillow. Her smile was radiant. "I'm not cold at all. Tell me we're going to be okay," she begged.

"We're going to be okay." He had never been surer of anything in his life. For Gabby to come here today and claim him was a huge step. He was humbled by her bravery. "Just so you know, I'll be buying you presents often. Maybe expensive ones."

She nodded soberly, but her eyes danced. "I'll learn to adjust."

He stared at her, memorizing every line of her face. "I have nothing at all unless I have you, Gabby," he said gruffly. "I wasn't sure you would ever believe in us...in me. I'll spend my whole life making you happy, I swear."

She cupped his cheek in one hand. "I want babies, Jason. *Your* babies. Our babies. And even though we'll teach them to be strong and independent, I won't ever let them feel hurt or abandoned. Not if it's in my power to protect them."

His jaw worked as a wave of emotion caught him and dug deep into his gut. "Agreed," he croaked.

Now she frowned. "Will you be okay if we have girls? I know families like yours do the whole lineage thing."

He lifted her hand to his lips and kissed it. "We can have half a dozen girls if you want. I love my parents. But *you're* going to be my family, Gabby. You and those babies. Do you believe me?"

A single tear found its way down her cheek, leaving a thin, shiny track on dewy soft skin. She licked it off her lip. "Yes, Jason. I do."

"Good. Now, can I have you?"

"Only if I can have you in return." Her cheeky grin was adorable.

He grabbed the protection he needed. It wasn't quite time for those babies. He wanted to keep this endlessly intriguing woman to himself. At least for now.

When he moved between her legs and pressed into her, their gazes held. The moment felt as sacred as any vow.

"I adore you, Gabriella Nolan," he said. "I won't ever let you go."

She caught her breath when he surged deep. "That's all I've ever wanted. You and me. It's like a dream."

"Better than a dream," he said. "It's a fantasy come to life. I've waited a long time to find you. To find us. Now close your eyes and let me show you a glimpse of our reward."

She gasped, her inner muscles squeezing him. "Reward?"

"For now and forever," he said. "You in my bed every night. A man couldn't ask for more."

# EPILOGUE

*March...*

"I'm sorry we didn't get married at Machu Picchu," Gabby said, resting her head on her husband's shoulder. His skin was warm, his collarbone solid. They were curled up in bed at the Brightmans' lake house near Blossom Branch.

Several hours earlier, they had stood in front of a judge in an Atlanta courthouse and promised to love each other always... for richer or poorer, in sickness and in health.

Jason yawned and stretched. "Too many complicated logistics. I didn't want to wait," he said, giving her a teasing glance. "You might have been a flight risk."

She laughed softly. "Nope. You're stuck with me." She kissed him just below his ear, grinning when he sucked in a sharp breath. "I do love you, Jason. So much it scares me."

His expression sobered as he turned on his side to face her. Carefully he tucked her hair behind her ear so he could see her face. "I think it's normal to be a little bit scared." He grimaced.

"I feel bad that your mother wasn't with us. I hope she doesn't get upset when she hears."

"She'll understand. After all, she and Dave did the same thing. It's *your* mom we should worry over. We deprived her of a society wedding. She's not going to be happy about that."

"True. But if we give Sheila and Dahlia those grandbabies they want, all our sins will be forgiven."

"Shall we start now?" she asked, giving him an innocent look as her hand trespassed beneath the sheet in dangerous territory.

He rolled onto his back, breaking the connection, his breathing ragged. "Not yet. I want you all to myself. At least for the first year. I guess that sounds selfish."

Gabby shifted on top of him but didn't join their bodies. "I want that, too." She stared at him, painfully aware that she was about to do a very un-Gabby thing. "Jason?" she said.

"Hmmm?"

"Open your eyes," she pleaded.

When he looked up at her, she sucked in a deep breath for courage. "How would you feel if I didn't look for another job?"

He sat up without warning, tumbling her onto the bed beside him. His gaze was sharp. "Is that what you want?"

She swallowed hard, still incredulous that she was being bold, taking what she needed. "I'd like to help you finish the house. And maybe tag along on some of your trips. Plus be part of the new charitable foundation. The work at Grimes & Hancock was never my dream. I only did it because I had to take care of my mom. But she's Dave's responsibility now. Or maybe her own…"

His gorgeous mouth curved in a wicked grin. "So I can keep you barefoot and pregnant? Feed you bonbons? Watch soaps with you in the afternoon? Have sex all day?"

Gabby reached up and traced his lips with her fingertip. "That's the general idea. Since my husband is loaded, I thought he might not mind."

Jason's smile was brilliant. Happiness radiated from his stunning eyes. "I think we might have been on the same wavelength."

Before she could protest, he slid out of bed and rummaged in his duffel. Moments later, he tossed a slim folio on the bed beside her. "These are open-ended. I was hoping I could convince you not to look for another position right away."

When Gabby saw what was inside, tears filled her eyes. The travel agency printout detailed four weeks in Europe. Eight countries. First-class accommodations. A honeymoon fit for a princess.

"Oh, Jason." She was overwhelmed suddenly by how much her life was going to change. "You can't spoil me like this all the time," she whispered.

He picked up her hand—the one with the gorgeous diamond solitaire—and kissed her fingers. "Wanna bet?"

Jason was drunk with relief...joy...humility. He'd put his worst mistake in the past. Now he had finally made the right choice.

Gabby was his perfect match, the complement to his personality. The yin to his yang. He would spend the rest of his life making her happy. Proving to her that they were the same in all the ways that mattered.

He slid his fingers through her hair. "I can't seem to get enough of you, Gabby." He moved on top of her and settled between her thighs. "Let me know if you get too much of a good thing."

When he entered her, his head spun, and his eyes stung. It felt like coming home, a home he'd been seeking for a very long time.

Gabby cupped his face in her hands and arched into his thrusts. "It's our wedding night," she whispered. "Never too much."

He didn't stop to point out that the sun was still up. That it was hours until this first day of their marriage was officially over.

Instead, he loved her well, giving them both a blissful release, and then starting all over again.

"I love you, my precious Gabriella," he said hoarsely.

She linked one arm around his neck and reached up to find his lips with hers. "And I love you, Jason. For now, and for always."

*Blossom Branch, Georgia*
*Three months later...*

Gabby was happy. The feeling was so light and extraordinary, she might possibly float away. She sat on a bench beneath a tree on the playground of Blossom Branch Elementary School.

Beside her sat Cate, with Leah on the other end of the bench.

Together, they watched three shirtless men hammer nails and saw wood. Jason had decided the students needed a new piece of play equipment. After checking with the local school board and getting the okay, he paid for the supplies, had them delivered, and convinced Harry and Lucas to join his building project.

Despite pretending to grouse about the heat and the bugs, it was clear Jason's two friends were in their element...as was he.

Cate sighed and laced her hands across her stomach. "I'm pregnant," she whispered. "But don't make a sound. I haven't told Harry. We're having a romantic dinner tonight."

Gabby and Leah screeched muted tones and hugged Cate tightly.

"Congratulations," Gabby said, feeling the tiniest bit of envy. "That's amazing."

Leah linked her fingers with Cate's. "I'm so happy for you, Cate. Who would have believed two years ago that we all would end up like this?"

"Like what?" Gabby asked.

"With our soulmates."

After a beat of silence, Gabby sighed. "It hasn't been an easy two years."

"No," Cate said, her expression contemplative. "But look what we found. Love. The real deal."

"Lucas has never lived in one place very long," Leah said. "But he told me yesterday that Blossom Branch feels like home."

"That's beautiful," Gabby said. "I'm so glad." She took a deep breath. "Y'all are going to have to help me. Jason's mom is still upset that we sneaked away to get married. She's throwing us a huge society reception at the end of the month. I may not survive."

Her friends chuckled in unison. Cate patted Gabby's knee. "We're here for you, darlin'. Don't worry about a thing."

Leah sighed. "I love happy endings."

Cate snickered. "I think this is only the beginning."

"Amen to that," Gabby said. "Look at how far we've come. You two will always be the sisters of my heart."

Amid tears and sniffles of joy, they went back to watching the men.

*Some things never get old…*

★ ★ ★ ★ ★

# NEVER LET ME GO

# Chapter 1

Jeff Grainger was having a bad day. His truck was in the shop, forcing him to fold his six-two body into his mother's tiny economy car. He'd lost a construction bid to a new guy in town who talked a big game but was a crooked scammer. And now he was about to face the only woman in the world who had ever made him question his sexual prowess.

Marisa Evans. Blonde. Beautiful. Girl-next-door looks.

And—until Jeff bungled a romantic interlude—a virgin.

Why the hell hadn't she told him?

They both lived in the slow-paced town of Blossom Branch, Georgia, but they'd barely spoken two words to each other in the intervening year and a half since the *incident*. As far as Jeff was concerned, the situation might have remained frozen indefinitely, each of them ignoring the other.

Unfortunately, the town council had asked Jeff and Marisa to coordinate a project together, and now Jeff was stuck. He couldn't say no without hurting his business reputation *and* making Marisa think he was avoiding her.

Which, of course, he was...

*Hell.*

He scrunched down in his seat as far as he could and scanned the area. No sign of her yet. They were supposed to meet at two o'clock beside the iconic Blossom Branch gazebo. The eight-sided structure located smack in the center of the town quad was impossible to miss. The beautiful park surrounding it was green and lush with large oak trees and plenty of room for picnic blankets, park benches and lovers' rendezvous.

Not that this appointment was anything like a lovers' rendezvous. He and Marisa had only been together in the biblical sense *one time.* That didn't make them lovers. Far from it.

They were just two people who had let a pheromone-fueled, romantic-as-hell Valentine's Day date spiral out of control. A blind date at that. Set up by his baby sister who thought he needed to socialize more.

Never again. Not a blind date, anyway.

He scanned the park a second time, and then he saw her. Immediately, his blood pressure shot up. She was tall and lean with precisely the right proportion of curves. Her skinny jeans and lemon yellow crop top revealed a section of her tanned midriff.

Barely two inches. Hardly worth mentioning. But even at this distance, she made him sweat.

*Get out of the car, Grainger.* He had to make his limbs move. It was five minutes before the appointed hour. Being late was unacceptable.

When he locked his vehicle and ambled across the quad, feigning calm, he saw she was wearing sexy gold sandals. Her long, wavy hair was pulled up in a ponytail. Since it was the end of August, her clothing choices were perfectly acceptable. It was hot today.

The problem was, he remembered kissing that sexy, flat belly and tickling those cute, feminine toes with the shell-pink nail polish.

*Get a grip. Get a grip.*

Marisa hadn't seen him yet. She was facing the opposite direction, looking at her phone...perhaps checking the time.

He sucked in a breath, closing the distance between them. He could swear her scent wafted on the air. Light, tantalizing. Intensely feminine.

A trio of teenagers crossed between them. Marisa still studied her phone. Maybe looking for a text from him?

He cleared his throat. "Marisa?"

She whirled around so suddenly, it made *him* dizzy.

"Jeff..."

The way she whispered his name made his sex twitch. Southern accents were a dime a dozen around here. But there was something about her low, slightly husky voice that made his scalp tingle and his body tighten.

Her blue-eyed gaze was wary.

"Hey," he said, trying to pretend their meeting was nothing special. "Thanks for coming."

Her brows narrowed. "I didn't have much choice. The town council sends a lot of business my way. Can't afford to get on their bad side."

That was exactly why Jeff was here as well, but it miffed him to hear the reluctance in her voice. "Same here," he said bluntly. "Might as well get this over with."

He hadn't meant the words to sound so curt.

A flicker of her eyelashes told him she felt the sting. "Of course," she said, her tone formal and frosty. "I've already sketched out notes. Subject to your approval—of course."

Was she mocking him?

The collar of his short-sleeved navy polo shirt felt unexpectedly hot. He'd dressed for a business meeting, which for him was still casual, even with neatly pressed khakis. His usual attire was a T-shirt and jeans. He spent his days overseeing his crew on various jobsites. No reason to get gussied up.

Today, though, he had made an effort. For her? Maybe.

Marisa didn't seem to notice.

"What if we sit in the gazebo?" he said. "At least we'll be out of the sun." Thunderheads built in the distance, and the wind had kicked up. The breeze did little to cool things off because of the oppressive humidity.

"Sounds good to me." She took off in that direction, her long legs eating up the distance and carrying her all the way up the gazebo steps, leaving him to follow in her wake. He tried not to notice the sexy motion of her hips or the way her jeans hugged a heart-shaped ass.

When they were seated—on opposite ends of a bench anchored to the gazebo wall—Jeff cleared his throat again. Unfortunately, that was becoming a nervous habit.

He *wasn't* nervous, he told himself. That was absurd.

"What did they tell you they wanted?" he asked.

She shrugged. "Probably the same thing they told you. The council has approved the construction of two temporary mini gazebos that will remain here on the quad, one on each side, from mid-September through mid-November. These refreshment stations will accommodate the tourists who show up for an ambitious series of events designed to bring visitor dollars to Blossom Branch. Craft festivals, outdoor concerts, motorcycle rallies..."

He nodded. Marisa had summed it up nicely. "Yep. Same spiel they gave me. But one thing I don't understand. Seems like this plan could adversely affect our local restaurants."

Marisa made a face. "Doesn't matter. Miss Ophelia wants it this way, and no one was willing to go toe-to-toe with her."

"That figures." He grimaced. Miss Ophelia's great-great-great grandfather had deeded a parcel of land to establish Blossom Branch back in the 1800s. The way she saw it, the town belonged to her—metaphorically speaking—and thus her opinion carried a heck of a lot of weight.

"It's not ideal," Marisa said, "but the snack stations will offer

just that. *Snacks*. Hopefully, the diner and other sit-down restaurants will still get foot traffic for meals."

"Maybe so."

One gold sandal tapped the floor. "You're the carpentry ex-
pert," she said. "It will be up to you to draw the actual plans.
But here's what they asked of me. The first two pages are a list
of items that will be offered for sale. Drinks in one mini gazebo,
food in the other. I've indicated how many electrical outlets we'll
need and how much counter space. Everything else is up to you."

He took the list and studied it, careful not to touch her. Already
his gut was in a knot. Her casual beauty messed with his head.

Because she rattled him, he made himself focus on the list
and read it very slowly. One of the mini gazebos would be
simpler than the other. It would offer a variety of coffees, also
hot chocolate with peppermint schnapps—or marshmallows—
and hot toddies.

He looked up at her. "Why does the customer have to get a drink
in one spot and then cross over to the other gazebo for snacks?"

When Marisa tucked a flyaway strand of hair behind her ear,
he told himself not to fixate on her suckable earlobe with the
tiny diamond stud. He started to sweat.

She studied him curiously. "Several council members had
the same question. It's part of Miss Ophelia's grand plan. She
thinks it will keep lines from getting too long. Plus the stream-
lined menu at each gazebo will make it easier for the servers
to move quickly."

"What kind of snacks?" he asked, reminding himself to pay
attention to the paper in his hand instead of trying to decipher
the unexpected vulnerability in Marisa's eyes.

"Cake. Lots of cake. Homemade granola. And fruit cups."

"Supplied by?"

"Me," she said, suddenly seeming self-conscious.

He frowned. "From what I remember, you work long hours.
How are you supposed to handle this, too?"

"I'm shifting my focus," she said, lifting her chin as if he had implied criticism. "Less corporate catering. More intimate, casual affairs. By the way, that second gazebo will need at least three small refrigerators."

No woman should expect to utter the words *intimate* and *affairs* in the same sentence and not have a man get antsy. Jeff nodded, trying not to notice the way her breasts filled out that yellow top. "Makes sense," he said gruffly.

He glanced at the sky, or at least the part he could see from under the gazebo's roof. "I'll get started on this, and we can meet again later to fine-tune the details. You should get home before the storm rolls in."

Marisa flinched when a crack of thunder followed a flash of lightning that hit close by. "You're right," she said. "That's enough for today. I don't want to get wet."

The thought of Marisa wet and available had him shuddering inwardly. God help him, he was still hung up on her. *Stupid, stupid, stupid.*

Before either of them could make a move to leave, an ominous but familiar sound filled the air. Tornado sirens.

His companion gasped. "I've got to go," she said. "Bye, Jeff."

He grabbed her wrist, feeling the delicate bones. "No time. My place is half a block from here."

She jerked away, her expression horrified. "I'm *not* going home with you."

Their one night of wild, wanton sexual excess had happened in his bed. The foreplay on his kitchen table. And halfway up the stairs.

The sirens screeched again. "Come on," he said. "We don't have time to argue." Three years ago, he had bought the abandoned First Georgia Bank on a side street off the town center and renovated it. The original safe in the cellar was now a completely outfitted storm shelter.

Marisa was still trying to argue with him when the sky turned an odd shade of green.

"Hell," he muttered. "This is bad."

There was no time to move cars or go anywhere except straight across the quad. All around them, people were running, faces filled with alarm.

The sirens continued their relentless shriek.

Jeff focused on a single goal. Keeping Marisa safe.

He had her wrist again, but she wasn't fighting him now. They ran in tandem, panting, sweating.

It took six and a half minutes. As they neared his front door, he dug in his pocket for keys. The wind howled now. Hail hit like bullets on the street around them.

"Hurry," Marisa said, her fingers twined with his.

Inside, they ran for the stairs.

He hit the light switch to the basement. "I have a generator," he said. "If the power goes out, we won't be in the dark." They scooted down the narrow flight of steps.

She balked momentarily at the door to the safe. "I might have a slight aversion to being buried alive," she said.

The attempt at humor failed miserably. Her face was dead white.

"It's not bad, I swear." He wrapped an arm around her waist, gently urging her forward. They were out of time.

From outside, a crash reverberated, and then they heard a sound no one wants to hear. The deafening roar of a freight train, soon to be right on top of them. The noise amplified second by second.

"Jeff!" Marisa cried out as he dragged the door shut and slammed the locking arm.

"We're safe," he said urgently. "We're safe."

His words sounded like the worst of lies, even to him. The town hadn't taken a direct hit from a tornado since 2011. Today, Blossom Branch's luck had run out. The shrieking moan of the wind was incredible.

He pulled her into his arms and held her tight. Suddenly, their silent animosity vanished, at least from where he was standing.

Marisa buried her face in his shoulder. Her arms wrapped around his waist. He felt the tremors in her body. Jeff was doing some shaking of his own. A man would be foolish not to be alarmed. Fear was a positive defense in a dangerous situation. This qualified.

Suddenly—when he thought things couldn't get any worse—the pressure in his ears increased, the unmistakable noise of breaking glass rained down like a horror movie, and a huge groaning boom exploded overhead.

"What was that?" Marisa burrowed closer.

He could barely hear her words until suddenly, everything was quiet.

In the distance, tornado sirens still wailed, but here in the basement the eerie absence of sound made the hair on his arms stand up in dread.

He tried to swallow the lump in his throat, stroking her hair and petting her as if comforting a child. But Marisa wasn't a child. She was a fascinating, talented, sexy woman. And at the moment, she was in his care.

"I think the building may have collapsed," he said.

Marisa pulled back, her expression aghast. "Your beautiful home? Oh, Jeff. Surely not. It's stood on this spot for a hundred years."

"We'll see," he said, not ready to release her. Not yet.

Despite their uneasy relationship, she made no move to step away from him. "How soon will it be safe to get out of here? It's gone, isn't it?"

"Well, this isn't the eye of a hurricane. Tornadoes don't last long," he said wryly. "You know that. The damage is done in seconds. And they don't come back for a second round. Unless we have a cluster of storms."

"Was that in the forecast?"

"I don't think so." In retrospect, he should have paid more attention to the day's conditions.

In this moment of postdisaster stress, he took the time to savor the way she felt pressed up against him. They fit together well. He'd noticed it the first time they slow-danced at the Peach Pit.

Blossom Branch's legendary bar and grill had been decked out in pink streamers and red tulle for the holiday. The first fifteen minutes of the blind date had been awkward, as blind dates usually were, but then he and Marisa had clicked.

They had the same taste in books and movies, the same sense of humor, and my God, the sexual attraction had been off the charts. It was as if he'd been struck by lightning.

Laughter had led to flirting. Flirting had led to kisses.

Then he had taken her home with him...

Marisa interrupted his trip down memory lane. She wriggled free of his embrace and looked around the storm cellar. "This is a great panic room—and I mean that literally—but can we please get out of here now?"

He exhaled, relieved they had survived. "Sure."

When he released the locking mechanism and pushed on the door, nothing happened. "Must be jammed," he said. "It gets damp down here in the summer." He checked to make sure he had unlocked the arm all the way and then pushed again.

His heart thudded hard in his chest. *Uh-oh...*

Marisa scooted up beside him, right at his shoulder. "What's wrong?" she said. "Why aren't you opening the door?"

The overhead light used an industrial, long-life bulb that cast a yellowish glow over everything. Marisa still looked beautiful.

Her eyes were wide. "Jeff?"

He rubbed the center of his forehead where a headache brewed. Probably triggered by the weather system. "Well..." He didn't want to upset her. But there wasn't a good way to spin this.

She grabbed his arm, her fingernails digging in and making him wince. "Jeff!"

He shrugged, meeting her wide-eyed gaze apologetically. "Obviously I can't tell for sure. But I think there's a possibility we may be trapped by some kind of debris."

Marisa stumbled backward, her hand over her mouth. Now, her skin had a green cast as if maybe she was trying not to throw up. "That's not funny, Jeff Grainger. Open the damn door. I don't have time for your jokes."

"Are you seriously claustrophobic?" he asked quietly.

She was a strong, capable woman, but right now he could see the faint trace of hysteria she was trying to hide.

"Yes." She wrinkled her nose. "Isn't everybody to some extent?"

"Not everybody, but this situation is out of the ordinary. There's no need to panic," he said. "The air supply is stable. We're not injured. Somebody will find us and get us out."

"Yippee, skippy," she said, turning to pace the small area.

He wanted to laugh, but he didn't think she would appreciate his response. Maybe fate had arranged this encounter. Maybe this was his chance to apologize. To bring resolution to an incident that had upset them both.

"We might as well get comfortable," he said. The inexpensive camp chairs would do for now. "I have plenty of bottled water and beef jerky."

"I don't want anything," she snapped. "I'm not going to be here that long. Maybe if we *both* push on the door, it will open."

Jeff realized they needed a diversion. "The door's not budging," he said flatly. "Come here and let me hold you."

She eyed him with an expression that made him feel like the lowest of snakes. "No, thanks," she said. "I'm fine."

He held out his hands. "We should talk about it, don't you think? The elephant in the room?"

# Chapter 2

Jeff watched, frustrated, as Marisa ignored him. She paced some more, pausing to pick up a bottle of water from a small shelf. "My parents will be frantic," she muttered. "But I'm guessing our phones won't work down here?"

"The walls are reinforced steel," he admitted. "But we can try."

It was a dead end. His phone had no bars at all. Hers only one.

"I'll try texting," she muttered. "Sometimes that goes through even when a call won't."

"Good idea."

Jeff didn't bother. His parents lived out of state now, and his sister was on a business trip. By the time any of them heard about the tornado, he and Marisa would probably be rescued.

His companion made a frustrated noise. "It says *not delivered*."

"I'm sorry. Surely they won't have to worry for long."

Marisa leaned against a wall and crossed her arms beneath her breasts. "I hope no one was hurt."

"Me, too. Sometimes these tornadoes touch down briefly and hop back up into the sky. Maybe this one wasn't so bad."

"It *sounded* bad," she said glumly.

He tried again. "Why didn't you tell me you were a virgin?" he asked quietly.

Her gaze darted away from his. Hot color flushed her cheeks. "I was embarrassed," she whispered. "It was our first date, so I didn't think sex was a possibility. And then when I realized that we..." She trailed off, the muscles in her throat working.

"That we couldn't keep out hands off each other?"

She nodded slowly. "It all happened so fast."

He winced. Not what a guy wanted to hear. "That was my fault. I hadn't been with a woman in six months. Work was hectic. I live in a small town. Not too many opportunities for sexual relationships without expending effort and energy I didn't have. So when I met you, I went a little wild."

"Because I was convenient and easy..." She scowled.

"No," he said forcefully. "No." He paused, trying to make her understand. That was a tall order since he didn't quite understand it himself. "Sexual attraction is unpredictable. Whatever buzzed between us that night was powerful and rare. I haven't done one-night stands since I was young and green. Taking a woman to bed on a first date isn't my style."

"But?" Her chin lifted again, and her gaze challenged him.

He rolled his shoulders and exhaled. "But I had to have you. I don't know how else to explain it. Though, if you had told me to stop, I would have, of course."

Chagrin painted her face. "You had no reason to stop. I was obviously right there with you. I'd like to blame my behavior on alcohol, but I only had one beer. You're right. We were at the mercy of our bodies, not our rational selves. Fortunately, that kind of impulsivity wears off in the light of day."

"Does it?" he asked, not at all kidding. He wanted her as much right now as he had that night.

She nodded firmly. "It does. I'm glad we had this talk. Closure is good. Now we can get on with our lives."

Her tidy summation of the situation pissed him off. "How does a woman get to be a twenty-four-year-old virgin? In the twenty-first century?"

Marisa glared at him. "First of all, that's an insulting question."

"I really want to know."

"It's not as unusual as you think. We're not unicorns. I've met several women like me."

"I don't care about *them*," he said. "I want to know about you."

She sighed. "My parents were very strict. I wasn't allowed to date until I was a senior in high school. By then, I had a reputation for being extremely shy, which was well deserved, by the way. I wasn't the kind of girl who talked easily to boys."

"And after you graduated? You told me you went to culinary school in Atlanta. Surely men noticed you. You're a stunning woman."

His flattery didn't appear to make a dent in her mood. "It's not a question of being noticed. Guys asked me out. But I was sharing an apartment with four other girls. Sexual intimacy wasn't an option there. Besides, I was living in a big, possibly dangerous city for the first time. I didn't feel safe going home with a guy to his place."

"You went home with me," Jeff pointed out.

Silence fell. Marisa's expression was a combination of shock and dismay. "I know. I'm not sure why. Especially since you bundled me up afterward and took me back to my place like an unwanted package. It was humiliating."

"I didn't know what else to do," he said quietly. "I felt like I had taken your innocence. And I didn't know why you had offered it."

She stared at him, lips parted, chest rising and falling with her rapid breathing. "You didn't *take* anything. And I didn't offer. It just happened. To be honest, I've done my best to forget about that night."

"Ouch." He rotated his neck.

"You should forget about it, too," she said firmly. "No reason for a guilty conscience. We both enjoyed a sexual encounter that was mutually satisfying. End of story."

He wanted to challenge her. Needed to challenge her. But until he understood what he wanted, perhaps it was best to leave things alone. "I still feel bad about how things played out," he said. "A woman's first time should be special, gentle. I'm really sorry, Marisa."

She was quiet for so long he started to think she was stonewalling him. But finally, she spoke. "I chose to be with you," she said. "Because I wanted you. And I have no complaints. It was very nice."

Nothing like damning with faint praise, he thought ruefully. He wasn't even entirely sure she had come. Likely not. The truth was, she had wound him up to a fever pitch and turned him into a desperate, ravenous mess.

He rubbed the back of his neck and took his own turn at pacing. The conversation had ground to a halt. Maybe he should concentrate on getting them out. If he could.

When he glanced at his phone a second time, he felt a jolt of relief. *He* had one bar now. Quickly, he dialed 9-1-1. A voice on the other end answered, but before Jeff could say a word, the call dropped. *Damn.*

Marisa straightened, downed half the bottle of water, and grimaced. "No luck?"

He shook his head slowly, hating the feeling of helplessness. He liked solving problems. "At least the call went through for a couple of seconds. Maybe they'll see the number and know where we are."

"Okay." She yawned and stretched. "We might as well sit

down now. I'm guessing we're gonna be here more than five minutes."

He watched her get settled and did the same. The fabric seat wasn't great, but it wasn't terrible. Soccer moms and dads all over the country sat in these things for hours. It only seemed uncomfortable because Jeff and Marisa had no idea how long they would be stranded.

For half an hour, neither of them spoke.

Finally, Marisa sighed. "Why did your sister set you up on a blind date, anyway? Jilly knows I have no social life. But what's your excuse?"

He stretched his legs out in front of him, flexing his feet. "Owning a business is hard. You know that as well as I do. I tend to bite off more than I can chew when it comes to projects and deadlines. I *had* to push hard and work hard when I was getting started. It became a habit. At night, I would fall into bed and then repeat the schedule the next day."

"I might know a little about that," she said.

"It's a vicious cycle. Before you know it, a week has passed. Then a month. And suddenly, you can't remember the last time you had a day off to go fishing or swim at the lake or head down to Florida for a long weekend."

Marisa nodded. "So how did she convince *you* to go on a blind date? Has she done that before?"

"She's always trying to set me up with someone. It's annoying mostly, but I know she loves me. Jilly wouldn't let this thing go. She said I was too old not to have a date for Valentine's Day..."

"Ah."

He frowned. "What does that mean?"

Marisa shot him a sideways glance. "Nothing."

"It didn't sound like nothing."

"I just think it's funny your sister thinks you're old."

"You don't?"

"No. From what I can tell, you're in your prime."

He blinked. "Are you flirting with me?" The blood in his veins began to pump harder.

She sniffed. "Don't let your ego run away with you. Why would I flirt with a man who's not my type?"

He felt his face burn. "Not your type? Holy hell, woman. We were all over each other that night. We could have set the bar on fire with the heat we generated. And you know it."

That gold-sandaled foot started tapping again. "Possibly. But then again, maybe we both just wanted to get laid. Any port in a storm and all that."

He rolled to his feet. "Get up," he said. "Right now."

Her face reflected alarm. "Why? Is the roof about to cave in?"

"Of course not. I'm going to kiss you again."

"Oh, no," she said. "We're not going to play that game."

He stared down at her, his hands in his pockets. "Why not?"

"Because I don't want you to kiss me."

"Liar."

Marisa didn't protest when Jeff reached down, took her wrists and pulled her to her feet. The adrenaline burst generated by the tornado's onslaught had faded, leaving her weak and shaky. She wanted and needed Jeff's comfort. Among other things.

His body was big and strong. When he drew her into his arms, he smelled good. Really good. Good enough to distract her from the current nightmarish situation.

"How hot is it going to get?" she asked, hating that her voice wobbled. She didn't want Jeff thinking she was a coward.

"Maybe not too bad," he said. "The generator will keep the AC going. Unless the unit was crushed. But I still feel air flowing, so I'm hopeful."

Finally, she asked the question that was bouncing around in her head. "How long do you think we'll be here?"

His body tensed. She could feel it.

"Don't lie to me," she said quickly. "I'd rather know the truth."

"Okay."

She felt his fingers brush the back of her neck as he played with her ponytail.

"Jeff?"

He sighed. "The answer is *I don't know*. But if the building did collapse, we could be stuck for some time. Rescue personnel will be looking for survivors. Often that means bringing in heavy equipment to move rubble. Several people know that I outfitted this walk-in safe as a storm cellar. Somebody will come for us. It's only a question of how long…"

Marisa told herself she wasn't going to whine. She was alive. She wasn't even hurt. Jeff had created this extremely effective safe room. They were lucky to be where they were.

"I understand." Being this close to him resurrected feelings she knew she should fight. She'd spent a year and a half getting over Jeff Grainger. One lousy tornado wasn't going to undo all that hard work. She wouldn't allow it. As a grown-ass woman, she could stand on her own two feet in an emergency.

And she would. In a few minutes.

She hadn't meant to flirt with him. Of course not. The words had come out wrong. That's all.

Jeff Grainger was nothing to her.

When she rested her cheek against his chest, she heard him sigh. "Maybe *you* should kiss *me*," he said. "So we're clear on the consent thing."

Her stomach flipped hard. "I don't think so," she whispered, already imagining it.

He nuzzled her nose with his. "Please," he cajoled.

"This is stupid." Something had happened to the air in her lungs. Maybe she and Jeff were slowly being deprived of oxygen. That could make people do impulsive things.

She put one hand behind his neck and pulled his head down

so her lips could find his. "So stupid," she whispered. And then she kissed him.

*Wow.* Eighteen long months had passed, and still she remembered how he tasted. Like Christmas and her birthday and cotton candy at the fair.

Her bones went liquid with pleasure, and her heart raced. His lips were warm but closed. His body was rigid.

"Kiss me back," she demanded. "This was your idea."

His thumb caressed her cheek as he exhaled jerkily. "We won't be able to put the genie back in the bottle. You know that, right?"

She pulled away a little and smiled wryly. "We've been through a traumatic, world altering event. Don't we need some kind of life-affirming action to make us feel alive?"

Jeff's deep brown eyes and wavy brown hair, coupled with a toned body, made him a very handsome man. He studied her face. "Maybe we do," he muttered. And then *he* took control.

Though he held her carefully, as if she was fragile and breakable, his kiss offered no quarter. He ravaged her mouth, taking and giving and taking until she was literally breathless.

"Jeff…" She whispered his name, falling into the madness that had caught them up on their first date.

His tongue stroked hers, tangling, caressing. "You make me so damn hot. Come here, sweet woman." He sat in a chair and pulled her across his lap. "Let me feel you."

Before she could do more than gasp, he had his hand under her shirt and her breast between his fingers plucking at the nipple.

Marisa moaned, lifting into his touch. "I didn't know how good it could be," she said. "If I had, I might have agreed to that blind date a lot sooner."

Jeff frowned. "What do you mean, *sooner*?"

"Jilly had been badgering me since Christmas to go out with you, but I thought you were too…um…"

"Too what?" he demanded, his scowl dark.

"Too overtly masculine. Too arrogant. I thought you would overpower me."

Now he looked appalled. "Is that what you think happened?"

He scooted her off his lap and lurched to his feet, putting the width of the safe between them, not watching as she straightened her clothes.

"Of course not," she said.

But he didn't respond. He stood, back stiff, facing away from her as he fiddled with his phone.

Marisa curled her legs beneath her in her own camp chair and tried to rest. She shouldn't have said anything. Now she had offended him or *something*. Which was exactly why she didn't date. She was bad at it.

She closed her eyes and tried to sleep, but it was the middle of the day. Even if the adrenaline surge had left her exhausted, her mind raced. Should she suggest a second chance for the two of them? Did she even want that?

Of course not. Jeff Grainger wasn't the man for her. She needed someone placid. Maybe a little boring. A guy who would love her but not swallow her up in his personality.

Sexual overwhelm was all well and good for one amazing night, but not for a steady diet.

The heartbreak she had experienced and later suppressed washed over her, leaving her wistful and depressed. She *did* want Jeff. But she didn't know how to make that happen.

Finally, he sat down with a sigh. Marisa kept her eyes closed.

In this small room, she could almost *feel* the invisible cord that drew them together. Was he fighting it as much as she was?

She might never have this time with him again. The two of them alone. This was her chance to rewrite the ending.

But she was petrified.

Jeff was a guy. A guy who'd had far more sex than Marisa

ever had. He was confident and kind and competent and sexy and a dozen other adjectives she could name.

Would it be worth it to be with him not knowing how their story might unfold?

She opened her eyes and found him watching her, his intense gaze guarded. "What are you thinking?" she asked.

"Were you afraid of me?" he asked. "That night?"

"No." She shook her head vehemently. "I might have been afraid I was doing the wrong thing, but I was never afraid of you. Never."

His body language relaxed. "I'm glad. When I found out you were a—"

She held out her hand, stopping him. "I *know* what you found out," she said impatiently. "You're making way too big a deal about that. My sexual state was situational, not some kind of declaration. I wasn't waiting for Mr. Right. You needn't have panicked."

"I didn't panic," he protested.

Marisa heard his words, but she didn't believe them. Why else would he have rushed her home so fast?

"I think maybe you did," she said slowly. "I had visions of spending the night with you. *All* night. But you couldn't get me out of your house fast enough. That was a crappy thing to do."

He stared at her, his jaw working. "You're right, Marisa. I handled the situation poorly. I'm sorry." He paused. "Would you consider giving me another chance?"

# Chapter 3

Jeff recognized the irony in their situation. They hadn't spoken in a year and a half. Now, amid a natural disaster, they were finally having a long overdue conversation.

Never mind that they might be here for hours or even days. All else paled beside the fact that the flame between them still burned.

Marisa was pale, her expression hunted. "That's a big ask," she said.

"I know. But I let you get away once, and I try not to repeat my mistakes. I wouldn't have chosen a century-old metal box for our heart-to-heart, but I'm not stupid enough to ignore this opportunity. You're worth it."

"Am I?" she asked. "To you, I mean? I'm completely useless when it comes to knowing what men like."

"I don't know about other men," he said. "But you know what *I* like. We've proven that already."

"It might have been a fluke."

"No." He smiled at her. "Not a fluke."

"Would there be ground rules?" she asked, her expression pensive.

He frowned. "Like what?"

"That while you're with me, you wouldn't be with other women?"

His temper flared, but he tamped it down. She really didn't understand at all. "Have you been with any other men in the last year and a half?" he asked, keeping his tone even.

Her eyes flared wide in shock. "Of course not."

"Why?"

She sputtered. "Well, because I...because we..."

"Exactly," he said. "Something extraordinary happened between us. I haven't been with another woman since that night."

"Oh?"

Her look of disbelief might have been insulting. But he didn't have time to be offended. "I'm serious, Marisa. Do you believe me?"

She chewed her bottom lip. "Why would you do that?" she asked. "Men your age like to have regular sex. It doesn't make sense."

He snorted. "Men *any* age like to have regular sex. That's not the point."

"Then what is the point? You're confusing me."

Again, he stood and pulled her from her chair. When he wrapped his arms around her, she didn't protest. But it was several moments before he felt the stiffness in her body language relax.

"The point is," he said softly, "there's something between us."

She picked at his shirt button with her fingernail. "Like what?"

Carefully, he tugged the rubber band from her ponytail and slid his fingers through her hair, spreading the strands until they fell smoothly around her shoulders.

"I may not be able to explain it well, but I know it's powerful enough to survive for eighteen long months and still give me insomnia."

"You've thought about me?"

He rested his chin on her head. "Every damn night."

"Oh." She unbuttoned the first two buttons on his shirt and slipped her hand inside, placing it right over his heart. "I've fantasized about you," she said quietly. "At night. In my bed. You're a hard man to forget."

He shuddered. His sex stiffened. "Please don't say things like that right now. I don't think I can handle it."

"How well did you outfit this tornado shelter?"

"What do you mean?"

"You mentioned water and beef jerky, but is there an air mattress?" When she leaned her head back to look at him, there was mischief on her face.

His mouth went dry, and his vision blurred. "An air mattress?"

"You know. So we can get out of these uncomfortable chairs. We could cuddle. And talk."

"Cuddle." His tongue felt paralyzed.

"Or whatever comes to mind." She tugged his shirt from his pants and slid both hands underneath, stroking from his pecs to his waist. "I love your chest. Did I mention that before?"

His knees nearly buckled. "There's an air mattress," he admitted. "But I don't have any protection."

"I saw my doctor and went on the pill a year ago," she said. The painful vulnerability was back. "It seemed like the grown-up thing to do."

He cupped her face in his hands, searching her beautiful eyes. "We're both hot and sweaty," he said. "I messed up the first time. I can't let the second be *this*." He waved a hand at their surroundings.

Marisa pulled away. "Fine," she said. "Forget I said any of that. Apparently, the fire has dimmed after all."

Beneath the sarcasm, he witnessed hurt. She was so unaware of what she did to him. Even now.

For a moment he considered reaching for her hand, putting it over his sex. Proving to her what he wanted. But if he really planned to get out of this room unscathed, that might make matters worse. He wouldn't take her like this. No matter how badly he wanted to sink inside her body and lose himself.

His forehead was clammy now. His heart thundered in his chest.

"Marisa, I…"

Before he could formulate a sentence, a faint voice sounded outside their crypt-like hiding place. "Helloooo. Anybody down there?"

He froze. Marisa did the same. They looked at each other.

"Yes!" Their cries rose in unison.

"Hang on…"

The voice sounded very far away. But that could be because the safe had thick walls. He glanced at his watch, marking the time. Who knew how long this would take?

Marisa paced again, clearly agitated. "I don't want anyone to get hurt," she said. "Saving us, I mean."

"They won't." His reply was automatic. He didn't truly know. Rescue guys and gals were trained, but anything could happen.

Five minutes passed. Then ten.

Jeff felt his impatience spiral out of control. "Anybody out there?" he called. "Anybody?"

"Still here. Hang on." The voice sounded farther away now.

Was his home a total disaster? Had he lost everything?

It didn't matter, he told himself. Marisa was safe. He was safe. All the rest of it could be rebuilt.

Thirty-two minutes passed before they heard a screeching and pounding close at hand.

"Stand back," someone shouted.

Jeff and Marisa moved to the rear of the safe. Without thinking, he put his arm around her waist, drawing her close.

Slowly, the door swung open. A helmet-clad fireman stood framed in the opening.

Jeff blinked. "Lucas? Shouldn't you be out saving the world?"

The tall blond man winked at Marisa. "Nothing's more important than rescuing my best bud."

Jeff didn't like the way Lucas grinned at Marisa. But then again, Lucas was newly married to Leah Marks, so maybe it was okay.

He made the introductions. "Marisa Evans—Lucas Carter."

"Nice to see you again, Marisa." He smiled at Jeff. "She sometimes brings food down to the station." Lucas scanned the confines of the safe and gave Jeff a thumbs-up. "You told me about this room, but I never got a chance to see it. Nicely done, man."

"Thanks." Jeff swallowed. "Before we get out of here, tell me. Is my whole building gone?"

Lucas shook his head, smiling. "Surprisingly, no. Tornadoes are unpredictable bitches. Today, that was a good thing."

Marisa spoke up. "How bad was it?"

"A strong F2. Maybe an F3. We'll let the experts make that call. It touched down on the north edge of town, bounced over the quad—then hit this street pretty hard. Blew a transformer. The empty warehouse in the block behind you is rubble. You've lost part of your roof, but as far as I can tell, that's the worst of it. One interior wall collapsed and took your stairs with it. The debris blocked the door. That's why you couldn't open the safe."

Jeff exhaled. "Could have been a lot worse."

Marisa was still tucked up against his side. "What about injuries?" she asked.

Lucas rolled his shoulders, for the first time betraying exhaustion. "Two who may not make it. They were in a mobile home that got tossed. Medics worked on them at the scene. They're both in the hospital now, undergoing surgery."

"I'm so sorry," she said.

"Yeah." He shook his head slowly. "Most of my guys and the rescue squad are on this street now going door-to-door. The 9-1-1 calls have slowed down. I think we've seen the worst of it."

Jeff stared at his friend. "Thanks for coming to get us out."

Marisa nodded feverishly. "Same here," she said. "Thanks a million times. It felt a little bit like being buried alive."

Lucas's smile beamed in their direction. "Happy to see you both intact. Let's get you up the ladder. I'm still on the clock, so I won't hang around if you two are okay."

"We're great," Jeff said.

A twelve-foot extension ladder had taken the place of the ruined steps. Jeff followed Marisa to the top, keeping her close in case she got woozy. But apparently, getting rescued had given her a burst of energy.

Lucas brought up the rear.

On the main floor once again, Jeff's heart sank. "Oh, man. Not my windows." He'd kept the original plate-glass ones from the bank. Now, they were shattered.

Rain had drenched almost everything. His furniture, his books, his vinyl collection.

Marisa slipped her hand in his. "It's just stuff," she whispered. "I can help you clean up."

"Me, too," Lucas said. "Leah and I have some time off."

"Thanks," Jeff said gruffly. He wasn't accustomed to *receiving help*. He looked at Lucas. "Is it safe to go upstairs?"

"Should be. The wall you lost wasn't load bearing. When the windows blew, the suction yanked it loose. And half your steps. But the other set of stairs in the back of the house wasn't affected."

"That's something, I guess." For a moment, Jeff was overwhelmed by the amount of work facing him. How was he supposed to keep up with his *real* job and repair his home, too?

Marisa had been texting her parents to check on them and let them know she was okay. But she picked up on his mood. "Let's go upstairs and see how bad it is. Knowing is better than not knowing."

Once he made sure the stairs were truly sturdy, he put Marisa behind him and climbed to the second floor. He'd refinished the beautiful wooden treads himself and preserved the original wood.

Upstairs, they wandered slowly and surveyed the damage. Here, the windows were untouched. But the large hole in the far-right corner of the ceiling had let water in. Fortunately, that was mostly over the bathroom. Not much to ruin there.

His mattress would have to be replaced. Everything was damp. When he first did the remodel, he had blocked off the back half of the second floor for storage. Ironically, nothing there was in bad shape.

He sighed. "Well, at least the building is still standing. I'm grateful for that."

Marisa grimaced. "I'm so sorry, Jeff. You did such an amazing job with the remodel. And you'll do it again. I suppose it will just take time."

"Yeah. Let's hope I can get roofing guys here quickly. That will be the first hurdle."

They were standing in his bedroom again. Despite the destruction, it was impossible not to remember this was the place where he and Marisa had first made love. Even now, he could see her on his bed, her face flushed with arousal and sleepy happiness.

Until afterward.

His stomach tightened. "We should probably get out of here. I'll get an inspector to do a full investigation. Insurance will require that anyway." He was talking too fast, not able to look at Marisa. What was she thinking?

Was he the only one having trouble reliving the past?

She slid her arms around his waist from behind and rested her cheek on his back. "I know it's depressing. It would be for anyone. But you'll get through this, Jeff."

Her quiet belief in him was balm to his uncertain mood. "Thanks," he said gruffly.

Marisa felt helpless to do anything for Jeff. Reclaiming his home would be a monumental task, and one that would take time.

Suddenly, she had an idea. It was dangerous. And open to misinterpretation. But it was the least she could do.

"Come live with me," she said impulsively. "I have a spare bedroom that's all yours for as long as you need it. Clearly, you can't sleep here."

He shrugged out of her embrace and turned to face her. His gaze was turbulent. "Not *your* bedroom?" The words were silky with challenge. The man was in a bad mood, and that made him dangerous.

She swallowed. "You're going to be in crisis mode for weeks. Maybe a couple of months. I don't know that it would be a good time to complicate your life."

"You're saying sex between you and me would be compli-cated?"

"I was speaking platonically," she said, the words prim.

His laugh held no humor. "You can't seriously believe that I'll move in with you, and we'll keep our hands to ourselves?"

"Maybe you're right. But my offer was sincere. You need a place to sleep, a place to relax at the end of the day. My house isn't as nice as this, but it's yours if you want it."

"You know what I want," he said.

The intensity in his words and the heat in his gaze made

her shiver. "I do," she said. "But maybe we could have a trial period first. We've been through a lot of stress. Let's give ourselves a week to recover. Then we'll talk."

"Talk?"

"Talk first," she said firmly. "After that, we'll see what happens."

She knew full well what would happen. Inviting the fox into the henhouse guaranteed turmoil. If eighteen months of living in opposite corners of the same town hadn't made their attraction fizzle, then cohabiting beneath the same roof was going to be incendiary.

Jeff rubbed his jaw. "I accept your kind offer," he said. "What if we seal our deal with a kiss?"

Heat flared in her midsection. "That's not necessary."

He smiled ruefully. "Maybe not necessary, but enjoyable. And besides, it's not like we could end up in bed."

She lifted her chin, grimacing at his sheets. "Certainly not." Though to be honest, something as simple as a wet bed might not be enough to put out the fire that smoldered between them.

"So you agree?" he asked, drawing her into his arms and sinking his teeth gently into the curve of her neck. "One kiss?"

It was madness. She knew that full well. But where Jeff Grainger was concerned, she was weak. "One kiss," she whispered.

He made a noise low in his chest. A sort of growling approval. And then he sank his fingers into her hair, anchored her head in his two big hands and settled his mouth over hers.

*Madness.*

It was as if the tornado still swirled around them. She felt wild and out of control. Everything inside her yearned for him.

Jeff was a master kisser. He knew exactly how to deepen her response and coax her farther into the dark, seductive passion that held them both in thrall. Her heart pounded so rapidly, it made her breathless and dizzy.

"I want you," he said, his voice low and hoarse. "I can't look at you without imagining you naked and sprawled on my bed. Beneath me. On top of me. Any way you can think of…"

She found the courage she needed to tell him the truth. Gently, she traced his cheekbone with her thumb. "I want you, too. I do. But I need to go into this with my eyes open. Not a fairy tale. Not a fantasy. An adult decision. Promise me a week. We've waited this long. Let's take a deep breath and a step back."

His expression was half sulky, half resigned. "You'll have your week," he promised. "But I want you to lock your door at night. I seem to have misplaced my willpower." He cupped her ass and pulled her closer. "You drive me out of my mind, Marisa. That was true when we were together and when we were apart. Now that I'm holding you again and tasting your soft, perfect lips, I think I might literally explode. Disappear in a puff of smoke. Return to the ether."

"Your hyperbole is duly noted," she said, laughing at him, but flattered by his intensity. "And honestly, I feel the same way. But I don't want to get hurt again," she said quietly.

"I don't want to hurt you," he said, his gaze troubled now. "I want to make you happy."

Marisa kissed him one last time, a gentle peck on the lips. "It's not your job to make me happy," she said. "That's up to me."

# Chapter 4

The morning after the tornado, Jeff felt like a poor slob on a medieval torture rack. Torn in different directions. And helpless.

Right now, he was at the mercy of half a dozen people. Getting professional help after a natural disaster was a humbling lesson in waiting. Waiting for roofing guys. Waiting for the inspector. Waiting for insurance approval.

Truth be told, he didn't mind dealing with decisions and forms and questions. It kept his mind off Marisa. And whether she was prepared to give him another chance.

He hadn't slept at her house last night. He couldn't. Instead, he had crashed on a friend's couch. The sofa was lumpy and too short, but it kept him away from temptation.

Tonight, though, Marisa was expecting him.

It was 6:00 p.m. when he made it to her place and parked at the curb. She had asked him to pick up pizza. The box resided in his back seat now, the smell making his mouth water. He'd known how to get here, of course. From the one time he had taken her home after their Valentine's Day date.

Back then, he had been in a hurry to go. Tonight, he studied her small house carefully. It was on a side street where the homes were modest and the lots small. Definitely a fixer-upper. He might have expected a woman in her midtwenties to choose an apartment, but maybe Marisa was renting this house.

His stomach flipped and flopped as he walked up the small path. Begonias and peonies bloomed in unrestrained profusion on either side of the front door. When he rang the bell, Marisa answered almost immediately.

Her face was flushed, her forehead damp. "Hey," she said. Her smile hit him deep in the gut.

"Hey, yourself." He kissed her casually, pretending not to notice when she became flustered.

She motioned him toward the kitchen. "I know it seems silly that I'm a caterer and I asked you to pick up pizza. But it was a busy day. I did make us homemade dessert, though."

He took a strand of her sunshiny hair and rubbed it between his fingers. "I don't expect you to cook for me," he said. "You're giving me a room. That's plenty."

Tonight, she was wearing shorts—neat khaki shorts that showed off her amazing legs. A pale pink T-shirt clung to her breasts in distracting fashion.

Marisa was uneasy. He could tell. She buzzed about her kitchen setting out napkins and silverware and small china plates.

"We can eat off paper," he protested.

She shook her head. "Food tastes better when the presentation is good."

"If you say so."

When they were seated at the table, she cocked her head and smiled. "You look frazzled. How did things go today?"

He leaned back in his chair and sighed. "Not as quickly as I had hoped. But reasonably well. The insurance is going to cover everything. If I'm lucky, they'll be able to do the roof soon. No rain in the forecast for the next week."

Marisa beamed. "That's wonderful."

Because he couldn't handle having her smile at him amid their platonic arrangement, he surveyed her kitchen. Now he understood why she had picked this house. The kitchen was spacious. Marisa had clearly done renovations in this room, even if the rest of the place still had a 1970s vibe.

Two high-end stoves were stacked in a wall unit. The dishwasher was a fancy model with plenty of cubic capacity. And her countertops offered ample room for food prep on a large scale.

He finished his first slice of pepperoni and started on a second. "I'm impressed with your setup," he said.

"Thanks. I've changed my focus these past few months. I'm doing more small events and individual family dinner parties. I think that's my sweet spot. By this time next year, I will have paid my parents back the money they gave me while I was in Atlanta."

"Was that part of the deal?"

"Oh, no," she said. "There were no strings attached to the cash. But I want to be free to make my own choices without feeling obligated. Mom and Dad are wonderful. But they thought I was going to do large-scale catering. That's how I started."

"So why the change?"

She shrugged. "I was already getting burned out. Cooking three hundred pieces of chicken all at once...or six pans of mashed potatoes. It's not easy without an industrial kitchen."

"Is that something you want? The bigger space?"

Her grin was wry. "Not really. And I'm as surprised as you are by that. But I suppose self-discovery is a bumpy road."

He poked at a burnt piece of cheese. "Am *I* one of those bumps in the road?" he asked, almost afraid to hear the answer.

Marisa's expression was solemn. "More like a ditch," she said. "A serious fender bender."

"You are hell on my ego, woman."

She patted his hand, her fingers lingering to trace his knuckles. "Your ego is just fine. I have it on good authority that you're one of this town's most eligible bachelors. Especially since Luscious Lucas is off the market."

"You know about that nickname?"

"Every unmarried woman in Blossom Branch knows that nickname. Too bad you don't have one."

"I'm just Jeff," he said. "What you see is what you get."

"Maybe."

While he finished his third slice, Marisa cut generous servings of something he didn't recognize. But it smelled amazing. She set a small plate in front of him. "I remember you said you were allergic to chocolate, but that you loved anything with lemon. So I dug out this recipe of my grandmother's. Lemon bars. Not a fancy name."

He took a bite and groaned. "These are incredible." The delicate crust was homemade, flaky perfection. The filling was addictive—much like the woman who baked it. He was touched that she remembered a throwaway comment from a year and a half ago.

She refilled his glass of cola and put the leftover pizza in aluminum foil. "Please make yourself at home," she said. The words were stiff. "Your room is down the hall, second door on the right. You have your own bathroom, though I warn you, it's very small."

"I'll manage," he said. "Sit down, Marisa. Let's talk."

"I can't. Prep work for tomorrow. You know." Her gaze landed everywhere but on him.

"Anything I can help with? I'm good with a potato peeler."

Her eyebrows shot up. Alarm flared in her eyes. "Oh, no.

Feel free to watch TV or check your email. I have everything under control."

"I'm glad somebody does," he muttered. He got to his feet reluctantly. She could barely wait for him to leave the room. Her unease was palpable. Perhaps it was best to give her what she wanted.

For the next half hour, he brought his suitcase inside, unpacked and explored her small house. His assigned room was spotlessly clean and tidy. Even the bedspread was pulled taut, nary a wrinkle in sight.

All the while, he could hear Marisa in the kitchen. Pots and pans banged. He noticed when the dishwasher clicked on. And then she was singing. *Singing.*

Here he was, fixated on what happened next between them, and Marisa was singing as if she hadn't a care in the world.

Glumly, he found himself on the sofa flipping channels on the television. Her cable package was limited. Finally, he landed on a ball game he wanted to watch.

One hour passed. Then two.

Slowly, it began to dawn on him that Marisa wasn't going to come out of the kitchen until he had gone to bed.

At nine, he sighed and shut off the TV. She had asked for a week. He'd been arrogant enough to believe he could change her mind. But he was clearly wrong. It looked like he'd better concentrate on repairing his home instead of fixating on a woman who might or might not want the same things he did.


The day after her pizza dinner with Jeff, Marisa searched for a sign from the universe. Shouldn't there be one? When a woman was on the verge of a major life decision?

Having Jeff in her house overnight was a bigger strain, a bigger test than she had imagined. Once, when she got up to use the bathroom, she found herself standing in front of his door, listening. She thought she could hear a gentle snore, but she wasn't sure.

The poor man had to be exhausted. Stress was draining. She had a hunch that he'd already started getting rid of his ruined belongings. Physical labor combined with the mental aftermath of a disaster would tax even the strongest of men.

Fortunately, her plate was full today. One of the clerks at the courthouse was going on maternity leave. Marisa was catering the baby shower.

It was a fun, completely feminine activity. Marisa found herself envious of the honoree, who was clearly fertile and happy. What was it like to be so sure of the future?

As the event wound down, the father-to-be showed up to carry gifts to the car. When he kissed his wife and they smiled at each other, Marisa felt as if she had witnessed something incredibly private and personal.

Would there ever be a man who looked at her like that? Jeff Grainger was in lust with her, but that would burn itself out eventually. Wouldn't it?

She had never once let herself consider the possibility that she might have fallen in love with him. How could a woman love a man on such short acquaintance?

Besides, after that first night they were together, he had eased her out of his life quickly and finally. The message was clear. He didn't want the responsibility of her innocence, and he didn't want her.

Yet here he was. Back in her life. And he seemed happy about it.

The week progressed slowly.

Oddly, after the first night they shared pizza, he started coming home very late. She had given him his own key. The second night, she heard the front door open and shut at midnight. The third night, eleven thirty.

It had now been four nights since the tornado. Which meant she had three more days to make up her mind.

What did she want from Jeff? A hookup? Something longer? Friends with benefits?

Or did she want a full-blown adult relationship with the possibility of marriage and babies and a future?

The trouble was—*her* wants were only a piece of the puzzle. She had to know what Jeff was thinking. What *he* wanted. Beyond sex. She knew where he stood on that point.

If she were a different woman, she might have met him at the front door wearing nothing but a smile to see where things ended up. But she didn't have that kind of sexual confidence. Not yet. Getting there, but not yet.

The fifth night came and went. Jeff never showed up. When she peeked into his room the next morning, the bed hadn't been slept in. No Jeff.

Was he avoiding her? Had he changed his mind?

Her heart shriveled in her chest. She had been so sure the flame was still alive, even after all this time. In Jeff's storm shelter, it had seemed that way. They'd been hungry for each other.

Or was the heat they generated simply heightened emotions from their precarious situation? Everyone knew that adrenaline produced from facing danger could make people do strange things.

On night six, she gave up hiding in her room. If her houseguest wasn't coming back until late, she might as well enjoy her favorite Netflix shows and pretend Jeff Grainger was no more to her than a passing acquaintance.

After taking a shower and feeling sorry for herself, she grabbed a bag of potato chips and curled up on the sofa wearing a ratty chenille robe that was blue with pink flowers. The familiar clothing was comforting in the same way it was when she had the flu or a cold or cramps. The robe was an old friend.

At nine thirty, she decided she'd had enough. Her heart

ached. Clearly, Jeff wasn't hung up on her. He was busy with his life.

In a painful burst of self-honesty, she admitted to herself she had offered him a room because she was hoping they might end up in bed together.

Picking at a loose thread on her robe, she sighed. Maybe she should try to be honest with herself about what she wanted.

She had just stood up to go to her room when the door swung open. Jeff sauntered in on a burst of damp wind and raindrops. His hair was wet. His eyes smiled, but his face revealed exhaustion.

"Look what the cat dragged in," she said, feeling the lump in her throat and the knot of uncertainty in her chest. "Are you okay?"

He closed the door and shrugged out of his rain jacket, hanging it on the hook by the door. "Yeah. I'm fine. They've been predicting this rain for seventy-two hours. Me and a couple of my guys finally got the front of my place covered and secured."

"New windows?"

"No, that will take some time. Those glass panes are huge specialty items. I have to get them delivered from Atlanta. We used heavy tarps and industrial grade tape to hold them in place."

"And the roof?"

"It's a work in progress. The company I've hired got everything covered in those blue plastic sheets you see after hurricanes. Hopefully, that will hold until the rain stops."

He sat down in an armchair and raked his hands through his hair. "Sorry I've been MIA. It's been a blur."

Marisa stood behind the sofa, gripping the back so tightly her knuckles turned white. She also deeply regretted her choice of wardrobe. "I was just heading to bed," she said, the words chirpy and overbright. "Help yourself to any of the leftovers in the fridge."

"Don't go," he said quietly. "Stay and talk to me. Please."

She bit her bottom lip hard enough to taste the tang of blood. It would be a mistake to misread the situation. Jeff was tired and probably dispirited. The job he faced was a huge one.

"Okay. But let me get dressed first."

His sexy smile was a fraction of its usual wattage, but sweet and potent, nevertheless. "Not on my account. You look cute, Marisa." He crooked a finger. "Keep me company."

She chose the end of the sofa farthest from his chair. When she sat down, she was careful to tuck her ancient robe beneath her so there were no embarrassing gaps. "Okay, I'm here. What do you want to talk about?"

His smile was mysterious. "I know you asked for a week, but I've been giving our situation some thought."

"Our *situation*? Should I be alarmed?" Her tart question was a cover for the butterflies in her stomach.

"I don't think so. I hope not." He shrugged. "I think you should move in with me."

There was a roaring in her ears, but it wasn't a tornado this time. *Move in with him?* "I don't understand. Why?"

For the first time, Jeff looked nervous. He leaned forward and rested his elbows on his knees. When he lifted his head to stare at her, his expression was part defiant determination and part unease. "We have something. I don't know that I believe in love at first sight, but whatever happened between us that Valentine's night hasn't gone away. We'd be foolish to ignore something so powerful."

Goose bumps bloomed across her skin. "You're not saying you love me." She made it a statement.

He grimaced. "I don't know. Maybe. But I don't want to lose you for another eighteen months. If you move in with me, we could gut this house and do a remodel for a larger food prep area and a bakery. You told me you had thought about doing that."

The bakery had been a passing comment during their first

date. "That's true," she said. She had dreamed more than once about baking cakes and pies and cookies with her own spin on them. Or maybe specializing in wedding cakes and special orders.

She sucked in a breath. "And what if I love you?"

He went white. "Do you?"

*Did she?* "I don't know. Maybe," she said, echoing his answer. "I guess it wouldn't be smart if I did. You haven't even told me your favorite color and whether you're a beach or a mountain guy."

"Blue," he said huskily. "Like your eyes. And both."

Something about his intense regard dried her mouth. "So this idea of yours is all about convenience and my future business plans?"

He stood to face her with only a large sofa between them. "No," he said evenly. "It's about having you in my bed. Every. Single. Night. It's all I can think about."

Tremors made her legs wobbly and her stomach shaky. "A breakup would be harder if we were living together. Blossom Branch is a small, gossipy town."

"Then we won't break up."

She wanted so badly to say yes. She wanted *him*. What he was suggesting was both exhilarating and terrifying.

There was just one problem.

She sucked in a breath. "I think I may have lied to you," she said.

# Chapter 5

Jeff groaned inwardly. For a moment there, he had been certain she was on the verge of saying yes. And besides, he could have sworn Marisa Evans was one of the least duplicitous women he had ever met.

"I don't care," he said recklessly.

"You should. It may scare you away again."

"I wasn't scared," he protested. But even that was a lie. He'd never been any woman's *first*. And he'd handled the situation poorly.

"If you say so."

Marisa wrung her hands, her expression agitated. "I told you my virginity wasn't a big deal. That it happened for a lot of reasons. That I hadn't been waiting for Mr. Right."

"I remember."

"What if that's not true?" she said. "What if—unconsciously—I was waiting all along for someone like you?"

The bottom fell out of his stomach. His heart pounded. Jubilation and relief flooded his chest followed by a wave of panic. Could he be the man she wanted and needed? What if he bobbled things again?

But then he looked at her brave sweet face and saw the uncertainty, the vulnerability. "If that's true," he said quietly, "then I'm the luckiest man alive. No other woman has ever made me feel the way you do. I've spent a year and a half feeling lost and unhappy and stupid, all because I let you get away. It won't happen again, my love. I swear."

A smile bloomed on her face. Her luminous beauty took his breath away.

"That's a pretty great promise," she said, the words soft.

"One question," he muttered, feeling himself lose his grip on common sense. "Are you wearing anything at all under that robe?"

Marisa ducked her head and grinned ruefully. "No."

He shuddered hard. His sex throbbed. "Is it too soon to kiss you?"

"Not at all." Her whisper was quiet, but he saw on her face that she was overwhelmed with the same feelings he was experiencing.

Instead of waiting for her to walk around the sofa, he took her in his arms and dragged her across the back. They tumbled onto the cushions, laughing. Touching. Feeling the moment of awe.

Against all odds, they had found each other.

He peeled back the lapels of her robe and sucked in a breath. She was naked as the day she was born. Her skin was soft and pale and smooth.

"You're the most beautiful thing I've ever seen," he said, stroking from her throat to her breasts to the slightly curved plane of her stomach.

"Make love to me, Jeff."

How could a man ever refuse such a request?

"I'm almost afraid to touch you," he joked. "I've been dreaming about this for months."

She cupped his face with her hand. "That makes two of us."

Her eyes sparkled up at him. His breathing got all jacked up, and he felt clumsy and uncoordinated.

"Should we take this to the bedroom?" he asked.

"What do *you* want?" she asked, her small grin mischievous.

"I'll show you," he whispered raggedly.

Having Marisa watch him as he undressed only made his erection harder and more painful. He felt like he'd been in a semipermanent state of arousal since the moment he met her at the gazebo.

When he was bare-ass naked, he put his hands on his hips, staring at her. While he was occupied, Marisa had sat up and was now clutching a light, furry throw blanket to her chest.

"Do you trust me?" he asked soberly.

"Yes."

Her instant answer soothed a few of his doubts. "Lie down and put your heel on the back of the sofa," he said.

Marisa's eyes widened, but she scooted down on her back and raised her leg.

*Holy hell.* The visual almost did him in. Perhaps he might last longer with the lights out. He tried to swallow, but a lump of emotion in his throat threatened to choke him.

Carefully, he settled himself between her legs, but kept his weight on his elbows and his erection to himself. "You okay, sweet thing?"

She nodded. "Yes." Her pupils were dilated. He was pretty sure she was holding her breath.

"Relax, love. It's just you and me. We'll do whatever you want."

"I want it all," she whispered.

She broke him then. Snapped his willpower right in two.

"Ah, sweetheart..." He surged deep, thrusting until he was all the way in, pressed against her womb. His scalp tightened, a sure warning sign that he was going to come.

*No, no, no...*

He pulled out, took one oxygen-deprived breath, and eased back in, watching her face to see what she liked.

Marisa's eyes were closed. A flush of pink covered her throat and chest.

"Look at me," he begged.

When her lashes fluttered and lifted, he found himself drowning in her eyes. Those beautiful blue eyes. Her golden hair was a mess, spread across the sofa pillow that cushioned her head.

"Does this feel good?" he asked.

She hooked her heels behind his back, her expression dreamy. "So good. Don't stop. Please."

His choked laugh was directed at himself. If he had his way, this would never end. But from the beginning, she had turned him inside out. Sent him to a place of wanting that was so dark and deep he might never find his way out.

For her, he would try to make it last.

He set up a gentle rhythm. Her body took him in, gripped him, made every cell in his body tingle with helpless need. It was as basic as the sun and moon and as irresistible as the tides.

Before he reached the edge of no return, he left her and moved onto his hip. Her face reflected alarm. "What are you doing?"

"Making up for all my sins." When he stroked her with a single finger, a feminine moan made every hair on his body stand up. She tried to clench her thighs, but he wouldn't allow it. "Don't hide from me, Marisa."

He pressed harder, finding the exact spot that made her writhe. She was beautiful in her journey, her body a living, breathing vessel of joy. When she hit the peak and cried out his name, he moved swiftly, entered her and found his own release in the final ripples of her climax.

Afterward, he lay on top of her, unable to feel his legs. He might have blacked out for a few seconds. He'd had good sex before, but this was next level. What did she do to him?

At last, he groaned and shifted, urging her onto her side so he could see her face.

Marisa met his gaze, but blushed. "That was fun," she said softly. When she ruffled his hair with her fingers, he was ready to go again.

"So you'll move in with me?" he asked, hoping he didn't sound as desperate as he felt.

Her smile dimmed but didn't disappear. "I do have one last question," she said. "You've been avoiding me for a year and a half. Now, suddenly, you want me under your roof. What changed, Jeff?"

It was a fair question.

But he had an answer.

He nuzzled her nose with his. "It was the storm," he said, shrugging. "When we were running across the quad and the sirens were blaring, a terrible thought flashed through my mind. If I survived and you didn't, I wouldn't be able to bear it. I knew the truth beyond any doubt. After that, *everything* changed. Maybe we're not ready to call it love, but it's powerful. And it's only getting stronger. Fate and my sister brought us together. I bungled it. Now, we have a second chance."

The quiet joy in her gaze wrapped him in satisfaction. "I'm glad I waited for you," she said, "even if I had no clue you were going to show up in my life one day. To an introvert like me, the thought of a blind date was horrifying, but your sister was very persuasive. Then I met you and *boom*, I was lost."

He stroked the curve from her rib cage to her hip. "My place won't be ready for at least a couple of weeks. How do you feel about entertaining a houseguest in your bed?"

She leaned forward to kiss him. Her lips were bold, her confidence sexy. "It's not a king-size bed. We'll have to snuggle."

"I think I can handle it," he croaked. Already, he wanted her again.

★ ★ ★

Marisa was giddy with happiness. The way Jeff looked at her made her breasts tighten and her body move restlessly. "Shall we adjourn to my room?" she asked. "I'm getting sleepy."

Disappointment clouded his gaze. "Sleepy?"

"Well, I'm not blasé enough yet to say that other word."

His lips twitched. "You mean the one that rhymes with *thorny*?" He stood and helped her up, pausing to kiss her lazily.

Marisa felt every inch of his body pressed against hers. "You are so bad," she whispered.

They walked arm in arm down the hall. In her tiny bathroom, they washed up and then tumbled into her bed.

Jeff leaned on one elbow, looking down at her. "We'll redo my place together," he said. "I want it to be *ours*. Or if you want, I'll sell it and we'll find somewhere else."

"No," she said firmly. "I love that bank building and the way you kept so many special features. Preserving the past makes sense to me. You've made it a showplace."

His grin was rueful. "Well, until a tornado knocked it around."

"We'll bring it back," she said. "I promise."

His gaze darkened. "I've never been part of a *we* before," he said. "I think I like it."

She snuggled closer. "Don't forget. We still have the gazebo project ahead of us. If you're not too busy. With all the repairs you have to do, maybe the town council will need to find another contactor. I'm sure they would understand. You have your other clients, too."

Jeff pretended to scowl. "No other contractors," he said firmly. "I don't want you *collaborating* with any guy but me."

"I'm sure I could find a female version of you," she said, laughing.

"That's still a *no*. I want to do this project *with* you."

"I'm glad," she said.

He stroked her hair, feeling the weight of everything that had happened catch up with him. He yawned. "Give me a couple of hours and I'll be ready to go again."

She rolled over in the bed, so he was spooning her. "Go to sleep," she said. "We've got all the time in the world."

"That's true," he murmured, already imagining it.

He'd seen his best buddy Lucas Carter find love. It hadn't been a smooth, easy path. Lucas and Leah had gone through a lot.

Maybe the best things in life required work.

Jeff was ready to face that with Marisa. He wasn't naive enough to think everything would be easy. They were two grown adults, likely set in their ways. Living together would require compromise. Understanding.

And if he eventually married her—*when* he eventually married her—the challenges would be greater still.

But, damn. She would be his. For always.

He closed his eyes, letting the peace of this bed, this room, this woman soothe his soul. Blossom Branch had always been his home. Now, it would be even more. It would be his future.

God willing, he and Marisa would grow old here.

He was a lucky man...

Maybe it had taken a tornado to knock some sense into him. But the picture was clear to him now. He'd found the woman meant for him.

And this time, he wasn't letting her get away...

★ ★ ★ ★ ★